A PLUME BOOK

GOING HOME

A. AMERICAN is the national bestselling author of the Survivalist series. He has been involved in prepping and survival communities since the early 1990s. An avid outdoorsman, he has spent considerable time learning edible and medicinal plants and their uses as well as primitive survival skills. He currently resides in Florida with his wife of more than twenty years and his three daughters. He is the author of *Surviving Home*, *Escaping Home*, *Forsaking Home*, and *Resurrecting Home.*

ALSO BY A. AMERICAN

Surviving Home
Escaping Home
Forsaking Home
Resurrecting Home

GOING HOME

Book 1 of the Survivalist Series

A. American

A PLUME BOOK

PLUME
Published by the Penguin Group
Penguin Group (USA) LLC
375 Hudson Street
New York, New York 10014

USA | Canada | UK | Ireland | Australia | New Zealand
India | South Africa | China
penguin.com
A Penguin Random House Company

Published by Plume, a member of Penguin Group (USA) LLC, 2015
Previously published in digital and print formats by the author.

ISBN 978-0-14-751695-4

Printed in the United States of America
10 9 8 7 6 5 4 3 2 1

GOING HOME

Chapter 1

This had been a good week. I worked from home all week until Wednesday, when I got a call and had to make a quick trip. The next day I had to run up to southern Georgia for a service call, but first I was going to finish polishing this stove. I picked up a little box woodstove at a yard sale. It looked rough, rusted all to hell. A little elbow grease and several wire wheels for the grinder, and she looked great. Now I was just finishing the stove polish.

I was hoping that I could get this thing put in over the weekend. Having this in my bedroom would be sweet. I already had all the pipe and fittings for the stack and plenty of "encouragement" from Mel to get it done. She never ceased to amaze me; in her mind, anything she could think up was *easy* to do. Like adding another bathroom to the addition—never mind the fact that it was lower than the rest of the house. I just couldn't seem to get it through her head that water flows downhill. I still love her, though.

Depending on where I was going and how far from home, I would adjust my gear. I had two different packs. One was a three-day assault style with a one-hundred-ounce water bladder, and the other was a rifleman's pack. This trip was taking me to Donalsonville, just north of Tallahassee. Since it was November and a little cold and far from home, I threw the rifleman's pack in the car. I went out to the shed and grabbed a half case of MREs and threw those onto the rear floorboard. The people I worked with would give me a lot of crap about the stuff I carried with me. It didn't bother me because I seldom saw any of them—that was the nice part about working from home.

I hate my alarm clock. The damn thing went off, and I, of course, snoozed it; fifteen minutes later, I snoozed it again. Finally, at six, I got up and hauled my ass to the shower. After taking care of my morning S's—shit, shower, and shave—I grabbed my bags and took them out to the car. Back in the house, I went in and kissed the girls, as well as Mel, good-bye.

"When will you be back?" Mel asked as she poured one of my stainless steel water bottles full of sweet tea.

"I should be home pretty early Friday. I don't think this will take that long," I replied.

"Good. Try and be home in time for dinner," she said.

"I'll try," I replied, kissing her and walking out the door.

Little Ash ran out to the porch as I was getting into the car. "I love you, Daddy!" she called out.

"I love you too!" I called back to her. She blew

me a kiss, and I acted as if I caught it and stuck it in my pocket. "I'll save it for later!" I said and waved good-bye.

The trip to the facility in Georgia went smoothly; finishing the job quickly, I headed home. Back on the road home, I was eager to start the weekend. I would be home in about four and a half hours and have an early start to my weekend. Coming down 27 into Tallahassee, I stopped in a Mickey D's to grab a burger and a large sweet tea, then jumped onto I-10, heading east. I was blissfully munching on a heart attack helper, listening to the radio, and cruising down the interstate, putting miles behind me; it couldn't get any better. I had almost 250 miles to be home, just a few hours.

The radio was pumping out a mix of country and alternative rock; I scanned the channels constantly. Crossing the Tallahassee city limits, the music stopped, and the abrasive emergency alert tone came onto the radio. The initial low and grating tone morphed into the high-pitched constant tone. "This is a test of the emergency alert system," I said out loud to myself. The tone stopped, and so did my car. I looked down at the dash, and all the gauges dropped; the engine was making an awkward noise, being forced to turn over by the momentum.

"Ah shit!" There went my early weekend. I pulled the shifter into neutral and turned the key—nothing. I coasted the car to the shoulder and stopped. Just outside of Tallahassee, I-10 got pretty rural real quick. It also went through a hilly area, up and down. I was in the bottom of a small valley created by two of these hills. There were no cars in the westbound lane, just me. I sat there for a minute, shaking my head.

"Damn you, Murphy!" I said.

Some people believe they have a guardian angel following them and looking over their shoulders. If anyone was following me around, looking over my shoulder, it was Murphy, and that prick had a horrible sense of humor. I often cursed him and "the gods" for messing with me. "The gods" refers back to when Greeks believed there were gods above that interfered with the lives of men for entertainment; sometimes it really felt that way. And this was one of those times.

I reached over onto the seat beside me and picked up my phone. The BlackBerry had a black screen—dead. It was plugged into the charger, so what the hell? I looked at the charger, and the little red LED that was always on wasn't there. Oh, this was just fucking great—the car died, there was no power, and the phone went at exactly the same moment. I sat there for a minute, and the calculator in my head started doing some math. First, no car had passed me since my car stopped; nothing was moving east or west on the interstate. Second, the emergency alert on the radio just stopped right when the car did. *One and two equal I'm screwed*, I thought.

I stepped out of the car and put on my light coat. People think it doesn't get cold in Florida, but this November was rather cold. Fortunately, the wind wasn't blowing, and it was clear and sunny. I looked both ways and didn't see anything moving. I walked around to the passenger side and opened the door. Lying on the passenger seat was my everyday carry, or EDC bag, a Maxpedition Devildog. I am a gear freak and love Maxpedition products. I unzipped it and pulled out my Springfield XD .45 and tucked it into my waistband on my right side and covered it with my shirt and coat.

I decided to walk back toward the west. Having just passed Tallahassee, it was the closest thing for help. I started walking west and crested the hill after about fifteen minutes. My knees got a little weak. There were cars all over the road—on the shoulder, in the travel lanes, and in the median. There were people milling about with no clear purpose. I looked back to the east, and it was the same sight over the next hill.

Walking back to my car, I carried on a rather lively conversation in my head.

Okay, there are only two things that could cause this: an electromagnetic pulse, EMP, or a coronal mass ejection, CME, I said to myself.

Does it matter? I replied.

Not really; the result is the same, I countered.

Getting back to the car, I sat down for a minute and started to think. *Okay, you have prepared for this very thing; you have everything you need in the back to walk home. Oh, shit, the girls, Mel. Where are they? Are they okay?* I was nauseous. I had to close my eyes and lay my head back. The bile was rising in my throat; throwing the door open, I vomited violently until I thought my throat would tear in half. I closed the door and sat back in my seat, leaning my head on the rest. Reaching over to the bag in the passenger seat, I pulled an OD green handkerchief out and wiped my mouth.

"Oh, God, the girls and Mel!" I groaned out loud. What were they going to do?

"I know what they are going to do. We've talked about this. There is a plan. You need to get your ass home!" I spoke out loud to myself. Living in a small town has benefits. Mel can walk to the school if she has to get the girls. But she has the Suburban, and its Cummins should start no matter what. I looked at my watch; it was almost five o'clock, too late to try to leave but still enough light to start getting ready. "I have to get home as fast as I can!" I said aloud. Time to get moving. My watch was an inexpensive Armitron automatic that my wife bought me. It didn't need a battery, and as long as I moved around or wound it every forty-eight hours, it worked.

With the sun heading toward the end of its arc on this side of the rock, the temp was dropping. I got out of the car and opened the rear door. I pulled the pack out and laid it on the hood. I took off my light coat and put on the mother-of-all coats, my Carhartt coat with arctic lining. This thing had been with me for years; it's worn, and I love it. Just putting it on reinforced my resolve. I thought of those days in Wyoming when the truck broke down out near Hell's Half Acre. The little shop was closed then. The area had a sign that said KEEP OUT, but Mel, the girls, and I all walked down into the alien hole in the ground and looked at the formations.

I decided to spend the night in the car just in case, by some weird coincidence, it was to be "fixed" in the morning. I pulled the MREs out of the back and opened them up. I went through and stripped them down. All the boxes and the outer bag were thrown onto the floorboard. I stuffed what I kept from the bags into the sustainment pouch on the right side of the pack with what was already there. With the car not working, I couldn't open the rear window or hatch; both used a solenoid for operation, and neither worked. I unlatched the rear seat and pulled the seat backs down to get to my tools. I grabbed my Klein linesman's pliers, a six-inch Crescent wrench, and a small pair of Channellocks. I looked at the wrench—"Anything you can do, the Channellocks can"—and threw the wrench back into the bag. I also pulled out a ten-in-one screwdriver. It was versatile enough to win a spot in the pack. I had to be careful, though. The pack was already heavy. I'm six feet tall and weigh about 260 pounds, not all muscle either. But I had carried this bag before, and I knew I could.

I decided to inventory the car. I looked under the seats and found a personal survival kit, or PSK, I had forgotten about. It was basic—water purification tabs, a small Uncle Henry folder, a coil of wire, a very small fire steel, and a short piece of a hacksaw blade. There were some first-aid items and other things in it; it was coming with me. Lying in the center console was a toenail clipper that went into the Devildog. In the compartment under the armrest was a cheap xenon flashlight that took CR123 batteries. I knew I had four spare batteries, so I put it in the Devildog too. In the door was a map of Florida; I took that and put it in the little bag. I pulled out of the back the suitcase that I always packed when traveling and went through its contents. There were about a dozen assorted bottles of hotel shampoo, body wash, and some mouthwash in the mesh compartment on the inside of the lid. There were also a couple changes of clothes. I pulled the skivvies and socks out and set them aside. I took my spare glasses out and set them aside. There was a small bottle of saline solution for my contacts; I set it out along with the spare contacts.

I knew the contacts would become an issue, but I would use them as long as practical. I set one pair of green Tru-Spec pants to the side as well. Another pair was in the pack, but if they would fit in the bag, they were going. I took the Q-tips out of the hygiene kit as well and set them aside. I opened the outside zipper pockets and found a Glo-Toob lithium light, an Energizer headlamp, and a two-liter Platypus bag. I thought about that for a minute and remembered putting them in there right before I left because I didn't feel like going out and getting my pack out to put them into it; I set them on the pile.

Lying beside the driver's seat by the door was my ESEE-5; I laid it on the pile. I put the Devildog on the pile as well. As my EDC, it had a number of things in it that I would need. There were two spare mags for the XD, an Otis tactical cleaning kit, a Silva compass, a Wilderness Outfitters SOS survival kit, a Swedish FireSteel, and other assorted items that I thought essential. I opened the pack and began trying to stuff all the items in. It was already pretty full. I could hear the guys on the board now screaming that any pack that weighed more than thirty pounds was stupid. When I was done, I estimated this thing weighed about sixty pounds. I do not subscribe to the "less is more" theory. I believe in having tools to provide for survival. If it turned out that I couldn't carry all this, then I'd start dumping it. But for now, it was all coming with me.

I put the pack into the backseat again and leaned against the hood. It was twilight; the orange glow to the west was beautiful, though fading fast. I looked to the east and saw a few people walking down the eastbound lane toward Tallahassee. No one was going east, everyone I saw was walking west. I went back and sat in the car; the windows were all up, and I couldn't put them down. I cracked the driver's door so it was open but latched and did the same to the passenger doors. I didn't want the inside to build up too much condensation and hoped this would help. The sun was dropping, and so was the temp. It was going to get cold tonight. I reached back and unzipped the lower pouch of the pack and fished around until I found the stuff sack with the poncho liner in it. I pulled it out, pulled the liner out of the sack, and wrapped myself up in my woobie.

No one that was heading toward the west came by the car; they all stayed in the eastbound lane. I reclined the seat back as far as it would go and kicked off my shoes. I wound my feet up in the liner and closed my eyes. All I could see was my wife and daughters; they were scared and far from one another. I hoped they would be back together soon. Their four faces were the last image in my mind. Sleep.

The sun's rays hitting me in the face woke me up. I had slept all night. I was *stiff*, though. The world outside was starting to lighten up; I looked at the inside of the car, and a light coat of condensation was on all the windows. Opening the driver's door, I stepped out. I had to piss, and bad, so I walked around to the passenger side and relieved myself by the front tire. No one was on the road in either direction.

"When the sun gets higher, there will be people heading west." I was talking out loud to myself. Just out of curiosity, I walked back around to the driver's side, leaned in, and tried the key. Nothing, not even a click. I reached in the back and pulled out my laptop bag. I set the laptop on the hood and opened it up and hit the power button. Dead as a doornail.

"Shit, this is bad. I mean, this is it. We're all fucked. At least most people are. I need to get home. I have to get home." I seemed to have started the odd habit of talking out loud to myself.

Okay, time to get a plan. I grabbed the map I set aside the day before and unfolded it on the hood. I was just to the east of Tallahassee. I had to decide whether to take I-10 to I-75 and turn south there or Highway 19 south. Nineteen was just a little way to the east of my current location. I knew for a fact that 19 would cut thirty-odd miles off my trip home. The GPS always showed that way as shorter but taking more time. It would take me through several small towns—Perry, Cross City, Chiefland, Bronson, and Williston—before getting me into Ocala. Once I was there, I had to cross the forest and would be home.

While I was weighing the options on the route home, I realized I was hungry. I pulled out the pack and opened the pouch with the chow. I had the stripped-down MREs as well as some other stuff—

foil packaged SPAM, tuna, and salmon, as well as a pouch full of condiments that I acquired from convenience stores over time, such as mayo, mustard, dill relish, and the like. In the sustainment pouch on the left side of the pack was my mess kit. It was a large single MSR pot. Inside it was a folding spoon/measuring cup for cooking, as well as a one-quart Ziploc bag full of rice. I had a smaller bag of quick-cook oats, a small bottle with a couple ounces of honey, a small bag of powdered milk, half a sponge/scrubby, a small bottle of cooking oil, and a small bottle of dish soap. A bag of bouillon cubes topped off its contents.

Looking at all this, it seemed like I had a lot of food. But when you stopped to think about the fact that I was over 250 miles from home, I didn't have nearly enough. I decided to make breakfast my big meal of the day. I would need the energy to get through the days ahead of me. Lunch would be light or not at all. Dinner would be light as well. I fished around and pulled out a single-serve SPAM pouch and an MRE Wheat Snack Bread, more like a Wheat Snack Heels. Nonetheless, I opened it up and sliced it open. I put the piece of SPAM in between and squeezed a packet of mayo onto the bread. This made a decent sandwich. I ate this while looking at the map and thinking about options. Opening the passenger door, I pulled out my stainless water bottle to wash down the SPAM.

I saw the first person heading west at about eight o'clock. A small group in the eastbound lane was heading west. I leaned against the hood and watched them come down the hill. There were five of them.

I could clearly see one of them carrying a laptop case. *Poor fool*, I thought. My laptop was back in the bag lying in the backseat, where it would remain, as far as I was concerned. I stood there watching these people go by. One of them broke off from the group and came across the interstate toward me. It was a young white guy wearing Dockers, a long-sleeved shirt, and a light coat.

"Hi, there," he said by way of greeting.

"How's it going?" I said.

"What's happened? You have any idea?"

"Well, there are only a couple of things that could cause this to happen. It doesn't really matter which it was. The result is the same," I told him. "Where's your car?"

He pointed back to the east. "Just over the hill there. It was so damn cold last night. We are looking for some help."

"Well, good luck," I said.

He looked at the ground kind of nervously and then looked up and asked, "You wouldn't happen to have any water, would you? My bottle is empty." He held up an empty Evian bottle and shook it back and forth to show it was empty.

"I have some water, but it's not Evian. I'll fill your bottle for you." I reached out, and he handed me the bottle. On the outside of the pack were one- and two-quart canteens clipped to the MOLLE. I pulled the two-quart out of the carrier and filled his bottle for him. As I handed it back, I noticed he was looking at the SPAM pouch lying on the hood.

"You, ah, wouldn't have any food, would you?" He was nervous when he asked the question.

"No, that was what was lying around. I have to go find some more food too." He accepted that answer.

"Yeah, sure, thanks anyhow for the water."

"Good luck to you too," I replied. I was glad they were close to Tallahassee, or they would have been screwed.

You would think that leaving would be easy; just grab your stuff and walk away. But I found myself procrastinating leaving. A few more people were heading west; now they were in both lanes. A few of them stopped to talk and ask the same question they all asked, "What happened?" My answer was always the same: "I have no idea either." I didn't want to appear any more prepared or aware than the rest of them. So far, everyone was polite and civil. No one was rude. No one was panicked. I knew that was going to change; the question was how long until it did.

Part of my EDC was an ESEE-4. I carried it recon style, horizontally. Only I carried it on my belt where my buckle would be. I would slide the buckle to the right and clip the Tek-Lok on the belt in the front where the buckle would be. I pulled the knife out of the Devildog and clipped it on the belt. I sat down in the driver's seat and changed into my Belleville boots. They were US issue, GORE-TEX with Vibram soles, and then strapped the Merrells onto the back of the pack. Then I strapped the Carhartt to the outside of the pack, using some paracord to keep it tight. The last thing to add was the foam sleep mat. I slid it under the two straps that held the top flap down. That was it; there was nothing left to do. I stood there for a minute, watching a couple walking in the eastbound lane. The girl was wearing flip-flops; she held a flannel shirt tight to herself. The man with her had on jeans and a T-shirt and a camo ball cap. His hands were shoved into his pockets, trying to resist the cold. I could only think of all the people that were waiting for help to come, help that might never come.

I grabbed the Devildog and pulled the waist strap out from the pouch in the back. I unclipped the shoulder strap and stowed it inside. Then I pulled the XD and its holster out of my pants and put it inside the pocket in the main compartment. After refilling the SS water bottle from the two-quart canteen, I dropped it into one of the mesh pockets on the outside. Then I strapped the belt around my waist with the bag in the front, kind of a reverse fanny pack. Standing the pack up on the hood, I slipped into the shoulder straps and took a step forward, taking the full weight of the pack.

"Ugh, holy shit, this thing is heavy!" I shouted, and then grabbed the waist belt for the pack, pulled it around me, hitched the pack up, clipped the belt together just above the other bag, adjusted the shoulder straps, and clipped in the chest strap. The load was pretty well balanced; it didn't feel as bad now. I hoped to make ten miles a day. I set the goal low on purpose; if I made better time, all the better. After adjusting the Tractor Supply cap on my head, I tucked my thumbs into the shoulder straps and started walking east.

The weight of the pack settled on my back and shoulders, but I knew that they would be sore tomorrow. Walking along on the side of the road, I passed several cars, some with people and some empty. Some of the people would try to talk; I just waved and said, "I gotta try and make it home." Most didn't try any further conversation.

I pulled the map out of my left cargo pocket and took it out of the Ziploc bag it was in. I was ten miles from Highway 19, give or take. Looking at the map though, I saw that 59 would take me to it in more of a straight line and get me off this damn interstate sooner. People were still civil, but I didn't want to be around them when they started not to be. I made it to the exit for 59 without too much trouble. Several people were walking on the interstate now. Many of them stopped to ask questions. It struck me as odd; with their normal routine interrupted, they just didn't know what to do. I knew there was a truck stop at this exit, on the south side, so I walked down the exit and turned to the south. This five or six miles had taken me over three hours, trying to get into the art of trekking with a pack.

The truck stop was pretty crowded. A number of trucks were in the lot, a few cars, and more people than there were cars. It had only been one day, so no one was totally crazy yet, although from some of the talk I heard, they were getting scared. I got a few looks from some of them; I was the only person there with a large pack. I went into the store; it was open, although there was no power. There was a little Indian guy behind the counter, dot not feather. When I came through the door, he looked at me and said, "Cash only."

"No problem. No power, no POS, huh?" I replied.

"I hope they get it back on soon. I can't sell fuel without it." He was totally clueless about the magnitude of what had happened. Who in the hell did he think he was going to sell fuel to? I walked around and grabbed a couple of bags of Jack Link's Beef Jerky; all I could think about was the Sasquatch commercials. Chuckling to myself, I went to the aisle with the little packs of meds and grabbed a few Excedrin packs, some Rolaids, and two packs of Imodium pills. Since the power had only been out overnight, the cooler was still pretty cold, so I grabbed two Cokes. I was trying to think of what else I would need. This was countered with the thought of how much more I could actually carry. Deciding that I couldn't carry much more, I took my shopping to the counter; he did the math on a calculator. "Nineteen dollars and seventy-five cents," he said.

I pulled some cash out of my pocket and handed him twenty dollars. "Keep the quarter," I said. I was scooping up the stuff when I had another thought. "Let me have a can of Copenhagen."

He reached back and pulled one down and laid it on the counter. "Six dollars." I handed him a ten, and he made the change.

I had quit chew last year; I loved the first dip of the day, and the one after a meal. I figured what the hell now. Not like I would be able to get any more anytime soon. He had put everything in a bag, so I carried it outside and walked around the building. I found what I was looking for on the far end, away from the interstate. I set the pack down and pulled the canteens out. Opening up the pack, I took the

Platypus bladder out. I topped off all of these from the hose bib on the wall; lastly, I filled the SS water bottle. The water pressure was still pretty good; I knew that wouldn't last either, and that gave me another idea.

While topping off the bottle, I heard a voice behind me. "Where ya headin'?" I looked over my shoulder and saw a large man in a red flannel shirt, jeans, and a Redman hat with what I was sure was a large chaw of the same in his left cheek. He was over six feet and barrel-chested.

I stood up and said, "Home, if I can make it."

"Whur's home?" He leaned to his left and spit a large brown puddle on the ground; it actually hit the ground before it broke from his lips.

"Down near Orlando," I replied as I stood up.

"That's a long walk. I need to get to Dothan."

"That's a pretty good hike too. You driving one of those rigs back there?"

He motioned with his shoulder. "I was drivin' that flatbed with the Cat on it." He spit a string again. "I shore don't want ta walk ta Dothan."

I looked past him and saw an old Cat front-end loader on the trailer. "Well, why don't you drop the chains on that loader and drive it till it gives out? Get some fuel out of your truck. If you find enough jugs, you might be able to carry enough fuel to make it."

"I was thinkin' the same thing," he said. "What' cha think happened?"

"Well, I would guess it was either an EMP or a CME. The radios are all out, and I guess no one knows for sure."

He looked at me for a minute and drawled out,

"I've heard of EMP. That's a nuke that causes that. What's a CME?"

"Coronal mass ejection, solar flare," I replied while putting some of the shopping into the pack.

"I heard about that on the news. They's been talkin' about it fer a week now. An' that would knock out the powar?"

"It could. I heard about it too. Didn't think it would do all this, though. I guess why doesn't really matter, though." I stood up and was looking at him.

"I don't much reckon it does. Well, good luck gettin' to Orlanda." He turned and walked toward his truck.

I lifted the pack onto one shoulder and walked back into the store. "You got a restroom I could use real quick?"

The little guy pointed to the back. "Back there. Don't piss on my floor, and flush it when you're done."

"Thanks." I figured I should take advantage of the chance to take a dump in comfort.

I walked out to the road and stopped for a minute. In the distance, you could hear chains being pulled through pad-eyes on a trailer. I slipped one of the Cokes out of my cargo pocket and took a long drink. Man, I was gonna miss this. After screwing the lid on and dropping it back in the pocket, I slipped the can of Cope out. I tapped the can in the palm of my hand for a minute while I thought about what was lying ahead. This damn pack was freakin' heavy. I needed a walking stick. I drew the ESEE-4 from its sheath and poked the blade through the paper on the lid of the can and ran it around it and sheathed the blade. Popping open the can, I grabbed a pinch and stuck it in my lip. Man, she would piss if she knew; I smiled to myself as I thought about how angry Mel would be if she knew what I was doing. Not that it really mattered at the moment.

I hitched up the pack and started walking south on 59. I needed to keep my eyes open for a walking stick. I knew what I wanted: a piece of wild myrtle. The wood was bone hard and light. It would be perfect. Several people were walking down the road, some coming and some going. At this point, no one appeared panicked; there wasn't any violence or trouble. It had only been one day, though, so it was certain to change. The walk down 59 was quiet. I encountered no one, only the occasional person who waved from a porch. Even that was rare, as there aren't that many houses on this stretch of road—lots of acreage. Smoke could be seen drifting from chimneys and smokestacks on some of the houses. About five and a half miles down the road, I came to Highway 19; this would be the road that would take me the farthest on my walk home. Turn south and keep on keeping on.

With my late start and the stop at the store, the day was getting late. I looked at my watch; it was almost four. I figured I would look for a place to sleep for the night. Since this was my first night out, I wanted time to sort out camp. On the southeast corner of 19 and 59 was a wooded lot. It looked like a good place to spend the night, so I walked into the tree line right beside a sign that said, PERRY 35 MILES. There was a field wire fence off the road behind the sign; I undid the straps on the pack and dropped it over. It felt like I would float away with the load off me. Crossing the fence, I walked out into the woods a little and found a camping spot. While there was still light, I took a minute to do a quick recon of the immediate area. All was quiet; no other sounds indicating people were in the air. The area I was in had no houses in the vicinity; this satisfied me that I should be alone tonight.

Back at my pack, it was time to decide what kind of shelter I wanted. In my pack were my Eagles Nest Outfitters hammock, Slap Straps, and bug net, as well as my seven-by-nine tarp and rigging. Since I was going to be moving every day, I wanted an expedient camp, something quick. For tonight, I decided on something real quick. I pulled out the sleeping bag and set it aside. Then I unrolled the sleeping mat, pulled the bag out of the compression bag, and unrolled it on top of the mat. Then I pulled out my GI poncho and threw it over the whole thing. The outer bag of the sleep system is GORE-TEX, but I didn't want dew all over it, as I planned to be off early in the morning. With my camp set, I decided to build a small fire. I didn't really need one, but since this was only the first day after . . . after what? *I guess I'll call it the Event.* I figured I could do this and not draw any undue attention. Later this would probably not be advisable.

I pulled my U-Dig-It trowel out and scraped a small fire pit after scraping the fallen pine needles away from a small spot on the ground. The combination of mostly pine and scattered oak provided plenty of firewood with very little effort. Using a butane lighter, I had a nice small fire in no time. I cut several palmetto fronds and made a break between the fire and the road, probably unnecessary but better to get into the habit now. I opened the chow pouch and fished around, pulling out everything in it. There were nine MRE entrées, six side dishes, six crackers, four pouches of MRE bread, six cheeses, five peanut butters, five packs of crackers, five accessory pouches, two pouches of MRE shake mixes, half a dozen drink mixes, and seven heaters. There were also four SPAM single-serving pouches and four foil packs each of tuna and salmon. Add this to the stuff in the mess kit pot and it was not a bad start.

I was hungry; that SPAM sandwich wore off hours ago. I wanted to eat something else but didn't want to because once I did, it would be gone—the only food I had was what I was carrying. Finally, I settled on a pouch of cheese squeezed onto some crackers. While munching on this, I went through the pack and pulled a couple of other things out—my Steiner Predator binos and the night vision, and a Pulsar Edge GS20. The bag for the Pulsar had four sets of batteries in it, plus the four spares in the Devildog bag. I should have plenty of batteries. There was also a Goal Zero Guide Plus kit; this would keep batteries charged for flashlights and whatnot. I wished I had found a way to charge the CR123 lithium batteries with it but hadn't got around to it. I started putting things away so that I could access them easily later. I pulled the mess kit out of the side pouch and took a bouillon cube out and then pulled the canteen and cup out of its pouch, poured in some water, dropped in the cube, and set it beside the fire.

I figured a hot cup of broth would be nice before going to sleep.

After finishing up my broth, I rinsed out the cup and stowed all the gear. I had the NVGs lying beside me and pulled the XD out of the Devildog. Climbing into the sleeping bag, I laid the XD on my chest and threw the poncho out to cover me and everything else up. I pulled out the NVGs and slipped them on. Looking up into the sky, the stars were magnified and washed out. I looked over to the side and could see into the woods. Happy the goggles were working, I put them in their pouch and set them down. I flipped the hood up on the sleeping bag and covered my face with the poncho.

As I lay there waiting for sleep, I started to think about my wife and girls. I missed them more than words could describe; that's partly why I tried not to think about them too much. My thoughts were interrupted by the report of several rapid shots drifting up into the night. They were far off, and there were no more, yet they were the first of many more to come. It was the earliest indication of the change that was already taking place in people.

Chapter 2

Opening my eyes, all I could see was the poncho; it was wet. I pulled it away from my face; drops of condensation fell into my eyes. Pulling the poncho away, the cold swirled around my face. "Damn!" It was cold; the temp had dropped overnight, and I did not want to get out of my sleeping bag. I finally crawled out and shoved my feet into those cold-ass boots, took the Carhartt from the pack, and put it on. My little fire was long gone; the ground was cold. A few steps away from my little camp, I took a leak. I was surprised how dark it was.

Cool weather can fool you; in hot weather, you drink because you have to. In colder weather, you have to make the conscious effort to hydrate. I pulled out some of the firewood I collected the night before and sparked up a little fire, making this one a little bigger. I needed to warm up. Taking the MSR pot from the pack, I pulled out the bag of oatmeal and the bottle of honey. The canteen and cup came out next, then the cup stove. I stuck the stove to the bottom of the cup, put about half a cup of oats in, and poured enough water to cover them. I took an accessory pack out, pulled out the little bag of salt, and dropped in a pinch, then added a couple of big spoons of powdered milk, and set the oatmeal by the fire to heat.

While breakfast was heating, I rolled up my sleeping bag and compressed it into its bag, rolled up the sleep mat, and got them ready to go. One of my two bandanas served as a towel to wipe the condensation off the poncho, and then it was rolled and packed. The NVGs went into their bag and back in the pack. I rooted around in the pack and found an inexpensive pair of leather work gloves from Harbor Freight, not the old rawhide-looking gray ones; these were actually pretty good for only seven dollars. With them was a pair of Poly-Pro liners; I pulled just those onto my hands. By now my oatmeal was ready. I kept a very thick piece of leather in my bag; it's about ten-by-ten inches and about one-fourth inch thick. I used it as a pot holder to pick up the canteen cup. I drizzled in some honey and stirred it all up. It was good and hot, and good. Did I say it was good? Too bad I only had a little more, maybe three servings if I stretched it. With breakfast done, my canteen cup was coated in glue. I poured it about half full of water and set it on the fire, adding a few more sticks to it. It boiled quickly; I stirred it with my spoon and scraped at anything I saw stuck to the side. After pitching the water, I set the cup and stove aside to cool and got ready to go. I drank all the water left in the water bottle and then pulled the Platypus bladder out, refilled it, stowed the bladder back in the pack, and then wiped out the cup with a bandana and stowed it too.

With everything stowed, I took off the Carhartt

and put on the lighter chore coat; that Carhartt would overheat me while hiking. I strapped it back on the pack, hung the binos around my neck, and hefted the pack up onto my shoulders. By now, the fire was all but gone; I stomped it out and kicked the dirt from digging the pit back onto it. There was barely any smoke, and I felt comfortable leaving it. I walked back out to the road; the sign was still there, PERRY 35. The sun was still low, but it was a clear and beautiful morning. I glassed the road as far as I could. There were a few cars on the road but no indication of people, so I started heading south. This is a beautiful part of north Florida, very rural and not that many people. The houses that were on 19 sit way off the road, and most were not visible from the road.

Plodding along, I came across, on the southbound side, a car with all the windows fogged up on the inside. I gave it a wide berth as I passed; I was just not in the mood to talk to anyone right now. I kept on walking. The sun was coming up, and I was getting a little warm. Undoing the chest strap, I unzipped my coat to cool down some. I was trying to keep my pace with some ranger beads; but, damn, you can't think of anything while doing that. I would be counting along, and then my mind would wander, and, "Crap, how many paces was that?" Oh, well.

I came up on a little abandoned-looking building on the right. Growing up on the side of it was a myrtle tree. I was going to get me a walking stick! I walked up to the building and looked in the windows. Nothing but someone's long-lost dreams of self-employment. Dropping my pack, I took the Leatherman Surge out of the little bag and opened the saw. A nice limb was coming out near the base; it was about one inch in diameter and good and straight for about five feet before it branched. I cut it close to the base; I wanted the little curve in it where it grew out and turned slightly to go up. With the limb in my hand, I pulled the ESEE-5 out of the sheath on the pack and trimmed all the limbs and then cut it off right below the branches. This would work great. I hefted the pack and struck back out with my new walking stick.

From time to time, as I was walking, I would glass the road ahead with the binos. There was never anything of concern. I made a concerted effort to count my pace and time my progress. I noted the time on my watch and began counting. I paced off two kilometers; it took about forty-eight minutes. Now I at least had an idea of how far I was going in an hour. The property on the side of the road was broken with wooded areas, clear fields, and a few planted ones. The planted ones were some sort of a green, too small yet to tell what they were, but I guessed collards or mustards.

About ten thirty, I heard an engine. It wasn't a car; it was a steady, low sound and had to be a diesel. I came up on a small planted field, and there was an older man on an old Massey Ferguson tractor. I walked toward the fence, and he came over.

"Howdy," I offered as a greeting.

"Mornin'."

"It's good to see something moving," I said, motioning to his tractor.

"It's the only damned thing thet runs 'round here. Powar's out, no phone. Whur you headed?"

"I'm trying to get home, down near Orlando," I answered.

He chuckled to himself. "Better you an' me! That's one hell of a stretch to try'n walk."

"Well, doesn't look like I got much choice. How's things going around here? Seen any trouble?" I asked.

Cocking his head to the side, he replied, "Naw, no trouble 'round here. We can handle trouble." He opened up his old weathered coat to reveal what looked like a Ruger Blackhawk in a nice leather holster.

"Yeah, that ought to handle any trouble. Nice piece. I thought field artillery was illegal in Florida," I said with a smile.

He laughed and slapped the top of the fence post he was leaning on. "Well, I don't think that much matters right now. I ain't seen any cars, 'cept a couple of old trucks and nothing that looked like a sheriff in the last two days." He tilted his head to the side and kind of squinted an eye. "You just headed down the highway here?"

"Yeah, toward Chiefland, then I'll cut over toward Ocala." I motioned with my chin in the general direction to the south.

"Down the road here a couple of miles is an intersection. Thar's two stores there. The first one you come to will probably have a bunch of fellas hangin' out in front of it. Watch them fellers—they're up to no good, they've been known to hurt folks. The store on the other side the intersection should be okay."

"I appreciate the info. Good luck to you. I'm gonna get on the road," I replied.

He pulled a glove off his hand and stuck it out. "Name's Frank Jessup."

I pulled off my glove, and we shook hands. "My name's Morgan Carter."

"If you have any trouble getting through the county by any of the deputies, you just tell 'em Frank said you is okay." He had a devilish grin on his face.

"I'll do it, Frank, but I sure hope to not see anyone, deputies or otherwise."

With a wave, I headed down the road. About an hour and a half later, I came around a small bend in the road. There on the right were the two stores. Just as Frank said, the first had about a dozen men standing around in front of it. They ranged in age from teens to some that I guessed were in their sixties. As I approached the first store, I unzipped the Devildog and laid one of the bandanas over the XD so it couldn't be seen at casual glance, just in case these guys were as dangerous as Frank said they were. I stayed on the road and paid no attention to those in front of the store. I heard some of them talking; I glanced over and saw four of them moving in my direction. Then one of them called, "Hey, white boy, where you goin'?"

I was just getting to the front of the store, not to it really yet. These guys were quick. Four of them were coming across the parking lot toward me; all of them were wearing hoodies. The hoodies they wore distinguished them so that I could give them nicknames in my head. One of them had gold dollar symbols on it; he was Gold Dollar. Another had silver dollars on his, so he was Silver Dollar. Of the other two, one had a Magic emblem, and one had a giant pot leaf. These two became Magic Man and Pothead.

They came trotting up in a group. "Hey, he look like a soldja boy!" yelled Magic Man.

"You a soldja, white boy?" asked Gold Dollar.

"Nope."

"Well, you gotta soldja pack. What'cha got in that soldja pack, boy?" Gold Dollar seemed proud of himself.

"That's none of your concern." With that, there was a series of oh-shits and daaammns.

"Well, look here, muthafucka. This here—this is my corner. Yo punk ass is in my muthafuckin' yard, and you sho' better start showin' some fuckin' respect!"

His underlings got a kick out of his show. "Tell his cracker-ass, Junior!"

My adrenaline was starting to run; this had the potential to go south real damn quick. There were three distinct groups in this little parking lot. There was the rabble I was currently confronted with, there were the kids, and then there was a group of older men under the awning of the store playing dominoes at a little table.

"Well, friend, respect is earned, not given. And from the look of you, you've never earned a damn thing in your life." It's often said the best defense is a good offense. Gold Dollar's crew laughed and hooted, and he did not like it. You might say he was pissed.

"You cracker-ass muthafucka, who in the fuck

you think you talkin' to? I own yo fuckin' ass. You got nowhere's to go; you fucked!" He was so mad that spittle was flying from his mouth. He was gesturing wildly with his arms and really working himself up. About this time, one of the old men started toward us. He had long arms and was bent at the waist slightly. In his youth, it was obvious he had been a big man.

"You boys let that man be!" He had one of his long arms out, pointing at the group. Gold Dollar looked back at him.

"Shut the fuck up, old man. I'll fuck yo ole ass up too. I know where yo ole ass stay at. Go play some damn dominos!" The old-timer stopped, resting his hands on his hips.

Gold Dollar turned to me. "Now, you gonna give me that fuckin' pack and everthin' else you gots, or I'm fixin' to bust yo ass and take it, bitch!" He turned to his crew. "Look, he so damn skeerd he don't know what to do."

Magic Man piped up, "He don't look too skeerd to me."

Gold Dollar turned on him in a flash. "Oh, you a bitch now, huh T? One muthafuckin' white boy, and you punk out!"

When Gold Dollar turned back toward me, he raised his hoodie and reached for a pistol. In pure reaction, I brought the XD out of the bag with a quick flip of my wrist. He wasn't ten feet from me; as soon as the muzzle cleared the bag, I squeezed the trigger three times in rapid succession. He immediately crumpled to the ground, letting out a terrifying wail. I quickly brought the weapon up and looked to see if any of his crew was going to retaliate, doing a quick 360 degrees. The three that were in front of me were nothing but assholes and elbows heading for the back of the store. The kids were likewise, only they were heading for the store across the street. The old men were all right where they had been. The one that tried to intervene was standing there, shaking his head.

"You don gotta worry 'bout me, son. He got what was cumin' to 'im. These punks gots no smarts dese days, talkin' 'bout respect. Day gots none fer no one en' nuthin'," he said.

I looked down at Gold Dollar; he was still wailing a high shriek. The iron smell of blood was heavy, as well as the overpowering stench of shit and piss. I pulled the weapon out of his hand and patted his pockets quickly. His right pocket had something in it; I turned it out and produced a roll of cash and four nickel bags of weed. Cash was soon to be useless, but I took two of the sacks; they may be useful later. He was starting to go into shock. A large blood clot slipped down his belly and onto the ground. A quick look showed one of the rounds hit his pelvis on his left side, and the other hit low in his abdomen, below his belt or where his belt should be worn. He was trying to talk. "Help me, h-h-help me."

I leaned down to him so he could hear me. "Just think, if you would have just left me alone, you wouldn't be lying here covered in your own blood, piss, an' shit, you stupid motherfucker."

The old man brought me back around. "Son, you bess go on now. Day goin' to be cummin' back with some more prolly." I stood up and looked at him; he pointed across the street to the other store. "Run on over there. Go on ta the back, pick up da trail an' get gone. I's goin' to tell 'em you went up da road here."

I reached down and picked up my stick and took off across the road. He may be setting me up, but I knew I had to go and right damn now. Running wasn't exactly an option; the pack was so damn heavy that anything resembling a run was out of the question. I was moving at a good double-time. I hit the trail; it fairly well paralleled 19. The path cut between houses and through yards; it looked like it was the neighborhood shortcut to the store. I kept going; the cleared areas gave way to a tree line. It was thin enough that I could see through it to the other side. I got through that little stretch, open field again. In front of me was another tree line; this one looked more substantial and looked like a planted pine. It was not an ideal place to hole up, but it was better than being out in the open.

I crossed the field without incident and got into the pines. I took a knee to catch my breath and to do a quick security check of my six. Looking into the pines, there was hardly any underbrush; it was wide open. About a hundred yards into the timber, it appeared to be thicker. I took off in that direction between the rows of pines. There was a bay head out there; I could clearly see the cypresses. Pausing at the edge of the swamp, I took a look around, searching for anywhere I could hole up. About forty yards into the swamp was a small island; it had two sable palms and a couple of large cypress trees growing on it. The remnants of a grape vine were clinging to the palms and creeping up the cypress. It would be a good place to hole up. I had decided to find somewhere and go to ground and wait for dark before trying to get out of the area. I didn't know what kind of friends ole Gol' Dolla' had.

The weather had been dry; there wasn't really any standing water, but a poke with my walking stick told me it was soft mud. I didn't want to walk straight to my hideout; a blind man would be able to follow my trail. I circled to the south a bit, looking for a way to get in, and finally managed to pick my way through to the island, stepping on downed logs, high clumps of pine-needle-covered earth, and the occasional properly placed cypress knee. Once on the island, I started to rearrange the vines a bit to provide better cover. Laying my sleeping mat on the damp ground, I sat down, and the weight of what had occurred landed on me. I didn't want to hurt anyone; all I wanted to do was get home. If things were this bad only two days in, we were in for a world of shit.

I pulled the can of Cope out of my pocket and took a dip; my hands were shaking so hard I could barely manage to get a pinch from the can. With the adrenaline wearing off I was suddenly not feeling so well. Holding the pinch of Cope up, my hand shook. After a moment I managed to get most of the dip into my mouth. *Damn, that's good.* I've carried a gun for many years and shot many a hole in paper, but until today never pulled the trigger on a person. I've read stories of men in combat and how they feel after their first engagement or the first time they know they've killed someone, now I can relate to it. After taking a long drink of water, it was obvious that the water situation needed some attention. The two-quart canteen was empty as well as the one quart. The Platypus bag was almost full, and the water bottle was half full. Tomorrow, I needed to keep an eye out for decent water.

It's about two thirty; it'll be dark in a few hours. I need to grab some sleep and get ready to move tonight. I laid the poncho liner out on the sleep pad. While rooting around in the pack, I found a little bag with my radio. It was a GP-L4 from County Comm. It was not the greatest radio, but it had AM, FM, and shortwave. It was in an antistatic foil bubble wrap bag, the same thing the NVGs were in. Since I worked for an electronics manufacturer, I had access to all sizes of these. I could only guess that this was what protected them.

I hoped the radio worked too. Taking it and the external reel antenna out of the bag, I put a set of AAs in and flipped the switch to the "light" position. There's an LED on the radio as well, and it came on. I took the earpiece and plugged it into the radio and turned it to FM. Scanning the entire band revealed nothing but static; AM was the same. The shortwave bands had something on them, but without putting up the antenna, the reception was weak. Even as weak as the signal was, I could tell it wasn't English.

After putting the radio away, I pulled the sleeping bag out to use as a pillow. I took the Taurus out; it was a stainless steel model PT92 9mm. Dropping the mag and pulling the slide back and locking it, the chambered round was ejected. It and the eight others in the mag were ball—nine rounds, that guy was going to take on the world with nine rounds.

Hell, I had three thirteen-round mags for the XD with Hydra Shocks, another box of fifty and a box of fifty Winchester White Box balls. Putting the loose round in the mag and pressing the slide release, I put the mag back in. I put the pistol in the sleeping bag compartment of the pack. I took the XD and dropped the mag and found the box of Hydra Shocks and replaced the three rounds and put the mag back in. I needed to get some sleep, so I wrapped up in the woobie and lay down on the pad with my boots still on and the XD in my hand. I hoped I didn't wake up too late.

I slept later than I intended; it was twenty after eight. Not that it really mattered; now was as good as any other time. Before setting out, I decided to get something to eat. Looked like it was going to be cheese tortellini. After adding water to the MRE heater and putting the pouch in, I set it aside to let the chemical reaction heat it up. My mouth tasted like crap; I dragged out my hygiene kit and took the toothbrush and paste out and brushed my teeth. I used a little of my water to wash my hands and wet a bandana to wipe my face and neck. I packed everything up and got ready to go. I took the NVGs out and stowed the bag. Using one of the MRE spoons, I ate my warm dinner.

With dinner done, it was time to head out. After stuffing my hat in a cargo pocket and shouldering the pack, I put the head gear for the NVGs on and turned them on. I gave them time to warm up and adjusted the intensity. I headed out of the swamp, trying to keep out of the muck. Back into the pines and moving toward the road, there was a screen of bush between the pines and road. Slipping into the line of brush, I took a look up and down the road, while keeping back in the brush line. I just stood there and watched and waited for a bit. Back toward the store, there was a little light coming from what I assumed were the houses on the opposite side of the road. It was dim like candles, but in the NVGs it looked like a damn flare. As I stood there looking, I saw a sudden flash and a glowing orb started to cross the street; that cigarette looked like a road flare stuck in his mouth. I couldn't see anyone else out and about, so I started walking south on 19 again, getting closer to home with each step.

Every ten or twelve steps, I did a security check on my back trail, just a short pause to look and listen. The road was light enough that I shut down the goggles and was walking by the moon and starlight. Without any man-made light, the stars really came through. The sky was beautiful; I paused for a moment, actually struck by the intensity of the stars. Every other security check, I would turn on the NVGs and check the road. With no one else on the road and nothing to stop me, I made really good time. After going about five miles, I came across a small pond. It was behind a field fence; I dropped the goggles down and did a security check. Everything looked okay, so I dropped my pack and took out all my canteens and water bottle. I found my SweetWater filter near the bottom of the pack and grabbed it.

Climbing the fence at a post, I was over quickly and checking the area again. Confident everything was okay, I walked over to the pond. In the NVGs, the water looked okay, but it was hard to tell. I dropped the intake tube in the pond and started filling everything up. It took about fifteen minutes. Climbing back over the fence, I stowed everything, hefted the pack, and started down the road after another security check.

Around three thirty in the morning, I was approaching Lamont, a small town, just a speck on the map. I was easing up the southbound lane shoulder when the first house came into sight. Kneeling down, I flipped the goggles down and watched the house. There was no sign of activity, but there were many signs of life. A little car was in the driveway and a swing set was in the front yard. The little house had a front porch with two lawn chairs on it.

Florida is full of little towns; actually "town" makes them sound bigger than they are. This was a typical backcountry burg. The little house was an old cracker house, all-wood construction with a tin roof. On my side of the road was an area of brush. I decided to head into it and find a place to camp for the rest of the evening. My intention was to get some sleep and start off in the daylight again; hopefully, this little speed bump on the road wouldn't be as bad as the first. I eased off into the brush, looking for another nest, something thick but that I could get into. There was little underbrush; tall pines blanketed the ground in pine needles. There wasn't anything that looked like a good place to hide. I kept looking and finally found a huge pine that had fallen over. It was long dead, all the bark having fallen off.

The crown of the big tree was in a heap. I set my pack down and started to work my way into it. The trunk was being supported by the large primary branches in the top. Toward the top, it was off the ground about two and a half feet. There were enough limbs scattered around it that I could lay under the log and not be seen. I didn't plan on being here all day anyway, just have a place to rest. I dragged the pack in behind me and pulled the woobie out and wrapped up in it once again. I had the NVGs lying at my side and the XD in my hand. My coat and boots on, this was sufficient to keep me warm to sleep. I drifted off pretty quickly.

My watch said it was eight thirty when I finally woke up. I had woken up once earlier but fell asleep again. This time, I crawled out from under the trunk and sat on the ground, leaning against it. I felt like crap. I wasn't real sure where exactly I was and didn't want to build a fire. In my little bag, I had an Esbit stove and six or seven trioxane tabs. I got it out and set up, took out my canteen cup, and poured some water into it. Seeing the water was clear was a relief. I put half a tab in the stove and lit it with a BIC and set the cup on. In the meantime, I fished out an accessory pack and pulled the coffee, sugar, and creamer out. While the water was heating, I opened a pack of the jerky. I sat there thinking Sasquatch would come out of the woods any minute. I got a chuckle thinking about those commercials.

While chewing on some jerky, I unfolded the map and took a look. Once I got through Lamont, I'd be crossing the Aucilla River. I hoped this little town was quiet. When the tab burned out, I mixed in all the coffee goodies. Instant MRE coffee tastes like shit, but it was good. After I finished my coffee and looked at the map, I packed everything away. I kept a piece of jerky in my mouth as I hefted the pack again, pulled my hat out of the pocket, and put it on. I checked the XD in the bag and covered it with a bandana and left the bag unzipped. I started out through the bush toward the road, stopping a little short, and took a look around. All was quiet, so I stepped out onto the shoulder of the road and headed into town.

Lamont isn't much of anything of a town; at the heart of it are three little stores clustered together and not much else. I saw a few people sitting on their porches, drinking coffee. You could smell wood smoke and charcoal in the air. I guess some folks had fired up the old barbie, using it to cook on. As I got close to the stores, I started to see more people; there were a number of folks around them. Two men were leaning against the wall on the side of one of the stores; as I approached, they nodded at me.

"Are any of these stores open?" I asked.

"This one here is, but it's cash only," one of them replied. "Where you comin' from?"

"I was up near Tallahassee, and I'm headed home. How are things around here?"

"No power or anything. There's a couple of old trucks that run, one car." He nodded toward an old rust bucket of a truck sitting in the parking lot.

"Good luck to you, fellas. I'm gonna check out the store." I gave the two a nod and headed for the door.

Walking into the store, it was like the millions of other independent little stores around the country. There was an Indian couple behind the counter, and a strong smell of spices filled the air.

"Cash only," he said as soon as I came through the door. "And leave your bag outside."

"Can I just set it by the counter? This is all I have, and I ain't about to leave it outside." As I said this, I was pulling cash out of my pocket so he could see it.

"Okay, sure, set it over here." He motioned to the front of the sales counter.

I gladly set the bag down and looked at what he had. I had almost a hundred dollars on me. I went over to the grocery section and started to grab cans. There were two cans of Dinty Moore beef stew, a can of corned beef hash, four cans of sardines in oil, and two cans of chili. I took all those. There were a few packs of ramen noodles; I took them. I went to the candy aisle and grabbed a couple of Snickers and a peanut butter cup. I piled all this on the counter. Thirty-eight bucks later, I was packing my bag. I was trying to cram the last of the cans into the pack when I heard an extremely loud engine. I looked and saw an old-ass truck coming into the parking lot of the store.

The truck, I assumed, was some variety of fifties-era pickup. There was no front bumper or glass in the rear window. There wasn't even a hint of paint remaining on the relic. The best part was the huge sow in the bed. Her rear legs were hobbled, and she was just enjoying the ride. I had to stop and marvel at this. Apparently, there wasn't even an exhaust pipe, as it sounded like the exhaust was coming right off the manifold; it was loud as hell. The truck lurched to a stop, and two guys that looked like characters out of some bad hillbilly movie climbed out. They were in their late twenties, or maybe early thirties.

The driver had on some sort of a felt hat, not a cowboy hat; but, well, I guess a hillbilly hat. There was a turkey feather sticking out of the band. He was wearing a pair of knee-high moccasins, black jeans, a Woodland BDU top, and a thin, sad attempt at a goatee. His partner was in a pair of jeans with logger boots and a Levi's jacket with faux wool lining. The two that were outside obviously knew this dynamic duo and walked over to them.

"Damn, Lonnie, where'd you get the truck?" one of them asked.

Lonnie's partner spoke up. "It was my granddaddy's. Lonnie got it runnin', so's now we gots wheels."

The other bystander spoke up. "Well, Thomas, why's Lonnie drivin' your truck?"

"Mind your own damn business, Walt. I fixed the damn thing, and it's my gas that's in it." He obviously was a little pissed.

"Thomas, go see if that damn Hodji wants this fuckin' pig." He was pointing at the store and instructing his underling. It was obvious who the brains was here.

One of the bystanders laughed out loud. "Lonnie, you dumb fuck, he's a damn Muslim." He stood there looking at Lonnie.

"So the fuck what?" Lonnie fired back.

"He don't eat pork, you fuckin' retard!" He was leaning over on his knees, laughing his ass off at Lonnie's stupidity. Lonnie didn't take well to that. He reached under his BDU top and pulled out a ten-inch Bowie knife from a sheath with an attempt at Indian beadwork on it.

"Fuck you, Walt! You need to watch how you talk to me, you dumb son of a bitch!" Lonnie was holding the knife horizontally at eye level, looking down the length of the blade with a squinted eye.

Walt just guffawed at him. "Whadda ya gonna do, Lonnie, scalp me?"

"I'm warnin' you, Walt, don't start with the Indian shit today. I ain't in no mood for it. You know damn well I'm part Indian."

This had all the earmarks of ending badly, really badly. I shouldered my pack and was making for the road. I didn't want to get into whatever shitstorm was about to break loose here. Some stupid-ass squabble between the local yokels was nothing I wanted any part of.

"Yeah, you're Indian all right, part of the Skin Flute tribe. Indian my fuckin' ass," Walt fired back.

Old Walt and his partner got a chuckle out of this last one; it must have been what they were waiting for. This must have been going on for years. Thomas was still standing by the door; after the Muslim comment he stopped, probably waiting for further instructions from Lonnie. Lonnie, however, had tunnel vision. He was on the warpath, pun intended.

"That's it, you motherfucker, you're gettin' yours today!" He started to move toward Walt, who just stood there and let him take about two steps, and then he reached into his jacket and pulled out a chrome 1911 and rocked the hammer back and leveled it at Lonnie's face. Lonnie stopped in his tracks and glared at Walt.

"Lonnie, you always have been a stupid motherfucker, and I'm about tired of your shit. Matter of fact, I'm about tired of seeing your fuckin' face. Take one more gawd damn step and I'm gonna shoot you in your ugly fuckin' head." He delivered this little diatribe in a calm and even voice. I didn't know these two men, but even I could tell Walt was ready to do just what he said.

Lonnie stood there for a minute, I assume weighing his options. Not wanting to be shown up in front of his underling, he said, "You ain't worth the fuckin' effort, Walt. You can kiss my ass. Thomas, let's take the hawg down to that ole nigger thet's got the still. He'll damn sure take it." Lonnie and Walt got into the truck and started it up. "You better not be here when I get back, Walt."

"Just when I thought you were startin' to smarten up, you go and say some dumb shit again. I'll be right here, Lonnie, and the next time I hear that piece of shit, I'm fillin' it full of holes." Walt let the hammer down on the pistol and dropped it to his side.

"Yeah, well at least this piece of shit runs, motherfucker!" And with that, he was tearing out of the driveway while letting out a really shameful attempt at a rebel yell.

While the dust was settling, I looked over to Walt. "Friend of yours?" I asked.

He just laughed. "Hardly. He's jist our village idiot. He been an asshole his whole life. No one likes him 'cept fer Thomas there, and that's only 'cause he's too damn dumb to know any better."

"Well, good luck dealing with him." With that, I turned and started toward the road.

Walking down the highway, I was gobbling

down a Snickers and drinking my other Coke. The air was about fifty degrees; it had warmed just a bit, and the Coke was just right. About one click out of Lamont, I crossed the Aucilla River. The weather was clear and beautiful; it made for a nice walk. I passed the occasional car on the side of the road; sometimes they were still in the travel lanes, but I never saw anyone. Plodding along, my mind started to wander a bit. I was thinking of home, Mel, and the girls. I really missed them but took comfort in the fact that every step took me closer to them. My muscles ached from the weight of the pack, and with my mind in neutral for a minute, I could really feel it. My mind changed directions, and I started to wonder why I wasn't seeing anyone. Nineteen was a substantial highway with four lanes but was kind of off the main route. Most people going north or south would use I-75.

I was jerked back to reality by the thundering sound of an engine, a really loud engine. I stopped and looked back. In the northbound lane was Lonnie's truck heading south. I guess he was doing that just because he could, with no authority and no rules. He let off the gas as he passed by. The median was between us, and Thomas threw a mason jar out the window; it shattered on the road. Looked like they managed to trade for some 'shine. That was all I needed, those two drunken idiots messing with me. But Lonnie got back on the gas and kept on down the highway. I walked for about another two hours; it was after two, and I stopped for a break. I slipped off the road into the woods a bit and dropped the pack and sat down.

I wasn't hungry, but I drank some water and just sat there stretched out in the sun. I took the opportunity to change my socks; I'd been wearing the same ones for three days, and they were getting crusty. I let my feet air out for a while; the sun felt good on the tops of my feet. While sitting there, not really thinking about anything or looking at anything in particular, I realized I was looking at a piece of survey ribbon, the kind a hunter would use to mark a trail. I looked back toward the road and realized I had actually walked down a very dim trail, unknowingly taking the path of least resistance as I entered the bush.

After putting the fresh socks on and my boots, I walked over to the ribbon and looked into the woods. From there, I could see another. I walked over to it and repeated the process. Eventually I came to a nice ladder stand chained to a tree. I climbed up into the stand and sat down. It was a great location; there was a nice group of oaks out front with acorns all over the ground. Those and the giant salt block guaranteed a kill. I was sitting there looking around when I noticed some dried palmetto fronds. They just looked out of place. I climbed down and went over to them; pulling them aside, I found a green Rubbermaid tub underneath. I popped the top on it; inside was an assortment of items.

On top of everything in the box was something I just had to have. I didn't really need it now, but I might later. It was a rather nice homemade gillie suit. It wasn't like the military ones made for crawling; this was a stalking suit. It had camo on the front as well. Going through the box didn't reveal anything else I thought I really needed. There were latex gloves—I already had some—and a bottle of water that might be water or a trucker bomb. There was a drag rope and a foam seat pad. Taking the suit, I headed back to my pack. This thing was too bulky to put in the pack. I cut some 550 cord and made some compression straps and compressed it as tight as I could and then tied it to the MOLLE webbing on the back of the pack.

Adding this weight was enough for me to reevaluate what I had that I could get rid of. Going through the pack, the only things I had that I couldn't justify were the lineman's pliers and the screwdriver. I took them out and set them aside. Strapping up the pack, I hefted it back on, hung the binos around my neck, and started out again. I had walked about an hour and a half when I heard the truck in the distance again. I stepped off the road, under the shade of the trees, and glassed the road. I could see the truck about a mile up; it turned off the road on the northbound side and disappeared. I really had to watch for those two idiots.

Approaching the area, I saw the truck turn. I went off the road; a screen of brush was growing along an old fence line. The fence was down, so I just went into the field behind it so as to have some cover between me and where the truck went. As I got closer, I could see it was a house. It was another little stick-built cracker house. It sat on old brick piers about three feet high. Getting closer, I heard some loud voices. Frick and Frack were standing out in front of the house. There was a woman on the porch with two children, one of whom was just a toddler, and an old man off to the side in the yard. I paused for a minute to observe what was going on.

I heard the woman telling them to leave; she obviously knew them and didn't want them around.

"Lonnie, you need to leave. Ryan wouldn't like you being here, and you know it." She was standing on the porch, leaning against a post, with her arms crossed.

"Ah, come on, Mandy, that's why I'm here, jus' ta check up on ya." Lonnie's speech was thick and slurred; he had obviously been into the 'shine pretty hard.

"I don't need you to check up on me. I'm fine. Mr. James is here, and Ryan will be back soon. You need to go," the woman replied.

"Mandy, I'm tryun' ta be nass, and yer treatin' me like shit. You ortta be nasser ta me. I kin hep ya till Ryan gits back." He was leaning over the hood of the truck as he spoke, a mason jar on the hood. Thomas had one foot up on the rear bumper and his hands hanging over the bed.

"Son, you're drunk, and she has asked you to leave. You need to go now." It was the old man. On the porch of the house next door, an old woman was watching what was unfolding.

Lonnie turned toward the old man, leaning against the truck and resting on an elbow propped on the hood. "Err, whut, ole man, you gonna make me? Whutcha gonna do, call the fuckin' law?" He laughed and reached over for the jar.

"Lonnie! I told you to git. I don't want you around here; now go!" Mandy was starting to get a little worried, and it showed in her voice.

Dammit, what the hell. I don't want to get involved in this shit, but this guy seems to attract it like a Muffin Monster. I dropped my pack and kept watching through the binos. With no man-made noise, and the fact they were all speaking in raised voices, I heard them clearly. Lonnie spun the lid off his jar and took a long pull; he drank the raw, hard liquor like only an alcoholic could, like it was water. He finished off by wiping his mouth with the back of his hand and spinning the lid back on.

"Mandy, I've tried to be nass, but yer jus' bein' a fuckin' bitch." He was looking at the old man when he said this. The old man took a step forward.

"All right now! You get—" He was cut off. Lonnie lunged from his rest on the truck with surprising coordination considering his level of intoxication. He caught the old man square in the nose with a hard right. His nose exploded, and he went down hard. Mandy screamed, as did the old woman next door; she was running toward her husband. Thomas came around the truck and was standing behind Lonnie.

"Ay, Thomas, throw 'iss piece a shit outta here." The old man was on the ground, and Thomas started for him.

Lonnie turned toward the porch. Mandy could see the crazy in his eyes. She ran into the house, herding the kids in front of her; they were already crying. Lonnie walked up onto the porch. Mandy had shut and locked the door. She was screaming through the door; you could hear the fear and the tears in her voice.

"Get outta here. Leave us alone!"

"I tried to be nass. Now wurr gonna do it my

way, bitch!" He reached behind his back and pulled out a stainless short-barreled revolver.

Mandy was still screaming, "Ryan's gonna kill you, Lonnie. You know he will!"

"Ryan is on a rig in the fuckin' gulf. He ain't cumin any tam soon en ewe know it. Now open this fuckin' door!" He was standing in front of the door, scratching at his head with the barrel of the revolver, his hillbilly hat rocking back and forth.

"He'll be here soon. Go away; please go away!" She was crying now.

From behind, in a taunting manner like that of a school yard bully, Thomas was pushing the old man back toward his house. He was saying something, but I couldn't hear him. What in the hell? What in the hell could I do? There were two of these window lickers and at least one gun.

"What's a matter, Mandy, you thank yer pussy's too good fer me? You always been a damn tease. Well, I got news for you, bitch; yer gettin' yers today!" With that, Lonnie kicked the door in.

The hard, dry pine of the old door frame splintered with a crack that sounded like a rifle shot. Mandy was immediately terrified, and this in turn terrified her kids. They were all screaming and crying, and Lonnie was screaming and cussing—all this served to bring the chaos unfolding in front of me to an overwhelming crescendo.

"Thomas! Get yer ass in 'ere!" Lonnie shouted.

From inside the house, the sounds of furniture slinging across the floor mixed with glass crashing and breaking. Adding this to all the existing chaos, it was more than the senses could take. My heart was pounding, and my adrenaline was pumping. Thomas turned and headed to the porch steps. When he did, suddenly everything slowed, and the sound was blocked out. It was as if I stepped outside the situation and was looking in. I dropped the Devildog from my waist and pulled the XD out and stuck it in my waistband. I pulled a spare mag out and put it in my left front pocket. I took my jacket off and dropped it on the pack. When I dropped the coat, I saw the hatchet. My Gerber hatchet was tucked between one of the sustainment pouches and the main pack; I pulled it out and removed its sheath.

Thomas was on the first step to the porch. I took off across the road in a crouch, double-time. I was moving at about thirty degrees away from the house toward the woods on the right side. I made it to the bush as Thomas entered the house. There were three windows on this side of the house. The one in the living room was blocked on the lower half by a fuel oil drum set on two concrete saddle stands. I used that as some cover and moved to the side of the house. Getting flat on the wall in front of the tank, I drew my pistol. Inside I heard Lonnie struggling with Mandy. She was definitely putting up a fight.

"Thomas, take 'ese two brats an' put 'em sumwhur!" Lonnie shouted.

"Leave my kids alone, you asshole!" Mandy screamed.

"Yew do whut yer told, and they won't git hurt!" Lonnie bellowed back.

"What'cha want me ta do with 'em, Lonnie?" Thomas was as dumb as I was told.

"Put 'em in the fuckin' closet!" Lonnie ordered.

Mandy was still struggling and cried out for her children. It sounded like she got away from him for a minute, but Lonnie had had enough. Mandy let out a cry. "That's it, bitch!" A loud slap came from the house, and it sounded like she hit the floor. I chanced a look into the window and could see Lonnie grab her by her hair and start to drag her down the hall.

"Git ur ass in the bedrum, dammit. I've waited a long tam fer this! Yew deal with 'em snot-nosed brats. Yew kin have a turn on 'er when I'm dun." With that Lonnie dragged her into the bedroom and partially closed the door. Thomas grabbed both of the wailing children by the arm and dragged them to the closet. He opened the door and threw them in. "Shut the fuck up, you damn brats!"

He slammed the door and started to pull the coffee table over to the door. While his back was to me, I crawled up onto the porch and got up beside the screen door. Taking off my hat, I threw it on the porch in front of the door by the steps and tried to get as flat as I could against the wall. The coffee table banged down on the floor.

"Gawd damn screamin' runts, fuck!" Thomas said as he walked toward the door. He stopped just inside the door, and I heard him digging around his pockets. The unmistakable sound of a Zippo lighter popping open came from no more than six inches from my face and then the strike. I could smell the tobacco catch and heard him close the lighter. In the back of the house, Mandy was still screaming, and the sound of tearing fabric filled the house.

"Now I'm gunna show yew whut yer good fer!" Lonnie yelled.

"Then I will," Thomas said as he pushed open the screen door and stepped out onto the porch, the door banging shut behind him. He stepped out to where my hat was lying on the porch. His right hand was in the pocket of his jeans, and I could see the grip of the revolver sticking out of his back pocket; Lonnie must have passed it to him, or he had his own. Thomas was looking down at the hat and stuck the toe of his boot out toward it. I took a step closer to him as I raised the hatchet. I brought it down with all my might on the crown of his head; the wet thunk sound was sickening. He immediately went limp and fell face first on the porch, his head hanging over the first step and the handle of the hatchet sticking straight up.

I opened the screen door and sidestepped inside. The bedroom door at the end of the short hall was open about four inches, and I could make out movement but not much else. I eased up to the door and brought my pistol up; my eyes were burning a hole through the front sight. Inside I heard Mandy gagging and Lonnie cursing.

"Open yer fuckin' mouth, bitch!"

I used my left elbow to push the door open. Mandy was sitting on the edge of the bed, naked. He was standing in front of her with his pants around his knees. He had two fists full of hair pulling her head toward him. "Hey, Lonnie," I said in a low voice. He turned his head over his left shoulder. I squeezed the trigger, and the round hit him just below the corner of his left eye, snapping his head back. That stupid-ass hillbilly hat flew from his head as his lifeless body fell to the floor. The explosion of the shot caused

Mandy to scream out; she flung herself back onto the bed and pulled her knees up into a fetal position. I looked down at the body. There was a terry cloth robe lying on the end of the bed. I picked it up and moved toward Mandy; my hands were shaking so badly that I thought I would drop it.

I tried to cover her, but she was fighting me, screaming like a banshee. "I'm not going to hurt you! Calm down!" She was obviously in shock. The last thing I wanted to do was hurt her. On the nightstand was a glass of water. I picked it up and threw the water on her. That stopped her, and she fell back on the bed, sobbing, not even trying to cover herself. I took the robe and covered her. "I'm not going to hurt you, and neither are they. Can you get up? I'm going to go get your kids. Can you get up?" I was trying to calm her down and get her head working again.

"My kids?" She sat up clutching the robe.

"Yeah, they're okay. I'll go get them. Get yourself together and come out. I don't want to bring them in here. She looked around the room and gasped, covering her mouth. Most of what little brains Lonnie had were on the wall and curtains, along with hair, meat, and bone. It was a horrible-looking damn mess. I pulled the comforter off the bed and threw it over his corpse. "Come out when you can, okay?"

I went out of the room. Pulling the table away from the door and opening it, I was greeted with the faces of two scared-shitless kids. Their eyes were red and puffy; the little one had snot all over her face.

"It's okay, guys. Mommy's okay. Come here." I picked the little one up; her diaper was full—I mean, we're talking load-test full. I reached out for the little guy's hand. "Come on, big brother, can you show me where mommy keeps the diaper bag so we can change sister's diaper?" He stood up, and I could see he had wet himself too. I can't blame them; I was surprised I didn't piss my pants. He took my hand and led me to the sofa, where he tried to pick up the bag from where it sat on the floor at the end of it.

I laid the little one out on the cushion. "Can you hand me a diaper, buddy?" He reached in and took one out. He had stopped crying, but the little one was still at it. He reached back into the bag and took a pacifier out and plugged it into her mouth, which did the trick. "Good job. Give me five!" I stuck my hand out, and he swatted it. In undoing the diaper, I was met with a horror. I would rather deal with Lonnie's brains, I thought. "Yikes!" I said, and little man chuckled. "Can you give me the wipies?" He went back into the bag and pulled out the tub of wipes, set them down, opened the lid, and handed me one. I went to work. By now he was relaxed, she wasn't crying, and it was quiet, except for the sound of Mandy retching down the hall. I finally got the little girl cleaned up and sat her up on the sofa. "You stay here and watch little sister. I'm gonna check on Mommy, okay?" He nodded.

I went to the kitchen and found the trash can. The bag in it had a little trash but not much. I pulled the bag out and dumped the contents into the can. I went to the bedroom; Mandy was in the bathroom with the door shut. I went over to the body; grabbing the bag by the bottom, I pulled it inside out up my arm. Reaching down, I grabbed a handful of

Lonnie's hair; it was thick and slimy and at the same time gritty. Lifting the head, I pulled the bag down over it with my other hand and dropped it back on the floor with a thud. "I don't guess that's going to help much," I said. The bedroom was a damn nightmare, and I leaned down to cover the body better with the comforter. In the living room, I heard Mandy talking to the kids; they were crying again, and so was she.

I walked out to the living room. "Miss, I'm gonna go over to your neighbors to check on them now. You gonna be okay for a minute?" She nodded, hugging her kids tight, with her face buried in their hair. I walked to the door. As I was pushing open the screen door, I heard, "Thank you."

I turned to look at her. With tears in her eyes, she said it again, "Thank you." After all the shit that just happened, this, this is what gets me kinda choked up. I felt a lump in my throat. All I could say was, "You're welcome." Then I turned and went out the door.

Walking out on the porch, I looked down at Thomas's body; I felt pity for him. If it wasn't for Lonnie, he wouldn't be here. He was probably a good guy, if a little dimwitted. *I'm sure he has a decent family that will miss him.* Grabbing the hatchet by the handle, I wrenched it from his skull. I was surprised at how little blood there was. The hatchet had effectively sealed the wound, which bled very little. Upon removing it, a small flow began. I grabbed his legs and flipped him off the porch.

"Hello, the house!" I shouted as I approached the neighbors, I didn't want to be shot.

The old man stepped out, this time with what looked like an old sixteen-gauge automatic shotgun cradled in his arms. He had cotton stuffed in both nostrils, and his eyes were already turning black. "Only one shot. Wur'd the uther'n go?"

"Neither of them are going anywhere. Could your wife come over and help her with the kids?" I motioned toward the house. As I did, an old woman came out of the house, holding her sweater closed across her stomach, and made for the house. She didn't even acknowledge me as she went by.

When she got to the porch, I saw her look down at the body of Thomas. She didn't even hesitate, going right up the stairs into the house. "Mandy!"

"Name's James. That's ma wife, Edith. You dun a good thang thur. He been comin' around the last two days. We always got him to leave, though. Never thought he'd do anythin' like is." He nodded toward the house. "It's good you was here. I don't know whut woulda happened if you wasn't." We started walking toward the house; he stopped at Thomas's body and looked down. "That's a hard thing you done, son. Be careful, or that sort of thing will consume ya. I outta know. I looked into the eyes of six men as I kilt 'em. It's somethin' that will be with you ferever." He looked at the hatchet in my hand, which I didn't realize I was still holding. "Hell ova thing, son, hell ova thing."

We went into the house. Mandy and Edith were sitting on the sofa. "Ladies," I said as I walked in.

Mandy looked up, "I can't thank you enough. I don't know what to say," she said.

"I didn't do anything anyone else wouldn't have.

I'm glad you an' the lil ones are safe. What are you going to do now?" I walked over and sat on the edge of the coffee table.

"I wanted to go to my mom an' dad's, but they live about fifteen miles from here an' I can't walk that far with the babies." She motioned to the two little ones, who had wandered over to James. Apparently he kept suckers in the pocket of his overalls, and they knew it.

"Why don't you load up what you and the kids need in that truck and get over there? It runs; you can make it." I pointed to the truck. Mandy and Edith just sat there for a minute.

"Well? There's no reason to stay here now. Go to your mom's," I said.

Edith jumped up. "Let's go, honey. I'll get the kids' stuff. You get what you need." And with that they were off.

While the ladies were packing up what they needed, James and I walked out to the truck. It was a rust bucket; James started it up, and it ran fine. It was without a doubt the loudest thing I had heard, though. It felt like being on the starting line at a damn funny car race. James shut the truck down. "Damn thing sounds like shit but runs strong," James said.

"Yeah, from the way I saw them two yahoos driving it, it should make it fifteen miles." I turned and went to the house.

The ladies had a pile of stuff by the front door. I started hauling it out to the truck and piled it in the back. They soon had everything they thought they needed. I went back into the house and poked around in the kitchen. There wasn't much there; actually there was nothing in there. Walking into the living room again, I asked, "Did you pack all your food up?"

"We didn't have any. If it wasn't for Edith and James, we wouldn't eat." She nodded toward the old couple.

"We couldn't let you and them babies go hungry." She tussled the little guy's hair as she said it. "We never had any grandkids, so these are as good as ours. We love 'em jus' the same." Mandy walked over and hugged the old woman, both of them tearing up.

Mandy stepped back wiping her eyes. "We should go. It's going to be dark soon."

"Mandy, do you have a gun?" I asked.

"No, Ryan had to take his to the pawnshop. He was out of work for six months before getting the job on the rig." You could tell she was afraid for him.

I walked out to the yard where Thomas's body was lying and flipped it over, pulling the revolver from his back pocket. I patted his pockets real quick and found the lighter, a pack of 305s, and a Buck 110. Going back into the house, I checked Lonnie's body. He had a BIC lighter and another pack of 305s. In his left front pocket were twelve .38-lead round-nose bullets. I flipped open the cylinder on the revolver, and it had the same thing. Pulling the knife from its sheath, I looked at the blade—it was cheap Pakistani steel—and dropped it on the floor. It wasn't worth its weight to me. On second thought, I pulled the sheath from the belt and stuffed the knife in it.

Back in the living room, I asked Mandy, "You know how to shoot a gun?"

"Yeah, Daddy taught me how. I learned on a .22 revolver."

I handed the revolver to her.

"Take this then. It's basically the same thing, just a little bigger." I held out the spare rounds and dropped them in her hand. She flipped open the cylinder and checked it and then, with a flip of her wrist, snapped it shut. *Oh yeah, she'll be just fine*, I thought.

We all walked out to the truck and helped her get the kids in and made sure she was ready to go. "Now don't stop for anyone or anything. If someone steps out in the road in front of you, just stomp on the gas. As loud as this thing is, if they're smart, they'll get out of the way. If not, then do what you gotta do." I kind of raised my eyebrows after that last part.

"After what happened today, ain't nobody getting in front of me again. Ever." You could tell she meant every word of it.

"Just don't let it burn you up. There's still good people out there. You just gotta look out for you n' your'n first," I said.

"Mandy, honey, you git to yer mom 'n' dad's. Tell yer daddy I said hi. We'll be here if ya need anything." James opened the door to the truck for her, and she got in. He shut the door behind her.

She looked out the window at me. "Ya know, I don't even know your name." She was looking me right in the eye.

"I'm Morgan." I stuck out my hand. She took it.

"I'm Mandy," she replied.

"I know, I heard your name many times this afternoon," I said with a smile.

"Well, Morgan, I can't thank you enough. I don't know what I would have done if you hadn't come by." Her look turned a little dark.

"Well, I did, and that's all that matters. You get going now, and remember, don't stop." With that she started the truck and backed out, leaving the three of us there, waving at her.

Once the truck was headed down the road, Edith looked at me and said, "Supper'll be ready in about an hour. An I ain't askin'!" She turned and headed for the house.

"You better be there, son. She got a willer tree out back. If ya ain't there, she'll come after ya with a switch." He grinned at me as he said it.

"Mr. James, I couldn't turn down home cookin'. But I don't want to put y'all out none," I replied.

"Don't worry, son, we got plenty. Come over an' get cleaned up fer supper," he said.

"If you don't mind, Mr. James, I'd like to do a couple of things in here first, but I'll be there in an hour." I nodded toward the house.

"Fine by me, son, jus' don't be late." He turned and walked to his house, and I went back inside.

I flopped down on the sofa and just sat there. So much had happened today, only four days after the . . . the what—what the hell did happen? In four days, I had killed three men and gone less than fifty miles. I was never gonna get home like this. I started thinking about some assholes breaking into my house, kicking in my front door—then a little smile spread across my lips—and being met with a hail of gunfire! Mel and the girls, the older two anyway, were trained to shoot. They aren't marksmen, but the shotty and the other XD left out for them were plenty enough for the women to take care of themselves. Not to mention where the house was and the neighbors. There were three deputies on our street, and Mike next door just got home a week ago from the Stan. They'd be fine.

I got up to take a look around. Walking into the bathroom, I saw myself in the mirror. "You look like shit," the reflection in the mirror told me, and I had to agree. I needed a bath and a shave. Bath was out of the question, but I could manage a whore's bath and shave if I could find some water. Searching the house, I found the hot water heater in the master bedroom closet. It was a small one set up on a stand off the floor. Opening the drain, my hand was filled with warm water; it wasn't hot, but it was sort of warm.

I hustled across the road and got my stuff and came back to the house. I took my hygiene kit out and laid it on the sink in the bathroom. I finally found a five-gallon bucket outside and brought it back to the hot water heater. Filling it about half full, I took it to the bathroom; after plugging the sink, I poured it full. On a shelf was a can of shaving cream, and I found a clean washcloth under the sink. I stripped down bare-assed. Using the bar of soap on the sink, I proceeded to wash my stinkin' ass. For washing in a sink, I thought I did a pretty good job; I certainly felt better. After draining the sink and refilling it, I soaked the cloth in the water and then wrapped it around my face. After letting it soak, I lathered my face and shaved. It was a little tough; the water wasn't really hot enough, but it was a damn sight better than a cold shave.

After dressing in a clean change of clothes, I went

through all the pockets of what I had been wearing for the last four days and dropped them into the bucket, even digging out the crusty socks from the day before. Lastly, I dropped the bandana I used for a sweat rag on top. Carrying the bucket and the bar of soap back to the water heater, I filled it till the clothes were covered and dropped the soap in on top. From a kitchen drawer, I took a potato masher and agitated the water and then removed the soap and let it set. I put on fresh socks and my Merrells—I needed a break from those boots—and walked next door.

Knocking on the door, I was told, "It's open. Come on in." I walked into a tidy little house. From the front door, I could see the kitchen and the table set for dinner. I walked into the kitchen and was surprised by the spread I saw on the table. With a rush, bygone days of my youth came back to me in a flash. For many years, I lived next door to my grandmother. She was the sweetest lady that ever lived, from the mountains of North Carolina, and solid as stone.

On the table was a cake of corn bread, real corn bread, not that yellow cake shit from a box. There was a water glass with green onions in it, a plate with sliced cucumbers and sliced tomatoes, a bowl full of green beans with large chunks of bacon throughout, and another bowl full of steaming stew beef. Edith was at the stove and turned to me. "Well, sit down. It ain't much but it'll do."

"Miss Edith, this looks wonderful. Reminds me of my granny." I took a seat at the table as James walked in.

"Good thing you's on time. That ole woman's

mean as a cottonmouth," he said while poking a thumb her direction.

"Knock it off, you old geezer!" she barked and threw a dish towel at him. He ducked like she was flinging a skillet at him.

"See what I gotta put up with?" You could tell these two old people were still in love. Actually it was more than that; they were two parts to one soul, inseparable. Edith walked over to the table and sat down, knocking James's elbows off the table when she did.

"Mind yer manners, ole man, an' say grace." They each folded their hands and bowed their heads. I'm not a religious man, but I followed suit.

"Lord, thank you for the bounty before us. May it nourish our bodies, an' thank you for Morgan showing up when he did. Lord, please keep Mandy and the youngins safe. An', Lord, watch over Morgan on his travels. Amen." And in true Baptist tradition, he continued, "Let's eat!"

Supper was awesome. Everything we had was grown on the land they owned. The beef was from a steer that Mr. James bought and butchered himself. He explained he bought one every year from a fella down the road and processed it himself. Some of it they canned; some they froze. This was from what had been in the freezer; Miss Edith went to canning everything as soon as the power went out. They had a propane stove, but as Mr. James explained, they had a wood cookstove that belonged to his grandmother out in the barn that he would put in when the gas ran out. The talk was light and enjoyable, like eating with a couple of old friends. The hard veneer Miss Edith put out was a true front. She was a sweet woman; she stuffed more food in me than I knew I could hold.

"There's a spare bed in the sewin' room. You can sleep in there." She was clearing the table and piling dishes in the sink.

I stood with a couple of dishes in my hand and headed for the sink. "I appreciate it, ma'am, but I'll stay next door. There's a few things I need to do over there. But thank you."

She turned to look at me. "Give me those! I'll take care of this; you git. No guest in my house is cleanin' up supper!" She took the dishes out of my hands and shooed me out of the kitchen.

"Don't worry, son, she don't let me help out in there. I get even though. I don't let her in my shop!" He chuckled.

"Breakfast'll be ready about six. I 'spect you'll be here," he said over his shoulder.

"Mr. James, I appreciate it. Supper was terrific, but I really don't want to impose." I felt kinda bad, these good folks giving me food they can't replace.

"Son, I weren't askin'. We're fine. If you ain't here, I'll send Edith over fer ya. Your choice." He was looking at me sideways with a squint.

"I have a feelin' I'd rather sandpaper a wildcat's ass than tangle with her." That got him to laughing.

"You're a pretty smart kid. I'll see you in the morning. By the way, there's a jug of kerosene on the back porch for that heater." He stuck out his hand, and I took it. "Thank you for what you done today, son. I mean that." He held onto my hand while he said it and then continued, "You're a good man, an' I hope you git where yer goin'." With that, we shook hands.

"Thank you, Mr. James. I appreciate it. But I'm just a regular guy."

"Good night, son. See you in the morning," he said as he turned to go into the house.

"Good night, Mr. James, and tell Miss Edith thank you for supper. She's a real hoot." With that, I headed back to the house.

"Oh, by the way, if ya need any water, there's a pitcher pump out back of my place. Jus' help yourself."

"Thanks, that'll be great," I replied.

The house was dark when I went inside. Taking my flashlight from the right cargo pocket, I lit my way inside. From my pack, I took out the Glo-Toob and turned it on and the flashlight off. Using this, I went back to where the bucket of laundry was and carried it into the living room. I found my headlamp in the pack and put it on. Carrying the laundry, I went over to the back of James's house. After pouring off the soapy water, I pumped the handle on the old pump, covering the clothes again. I agitated the water until it was soapy again, repeating this process until the water was clearish. I wrung out the clothes, getting as much as I could out of them. Laying them over my arm, I headed back to the house.

After laying the wet laundry on the kitchen counter, I went back to the living room and pulled the fuel tank from the heater. It was an old catalytic style heater; I had two of them in the shop back at the house. On the back porch, I filled the tank and returned to the heater and dropped it back in. Going through the start-up procedure, I got the heater lit. As it was warming up, I looked around the living room for a place to make a clothesline. By the door were a couple of coat hooks. The only other thing I could find was one of the latches on a window. Taking a roll of 550 cord from my pack, I tied one end to the latch and stretched it across the room. About a foot from the coat hook, I tied a loop in the line and then wrapped it around the coat hook. Running the loose end through the loop, I pulled it back using the added leverage to get it tight and secured it with a couple of half hitches. With the line in place, I moved the heater so it was close but not under the line, and hung my clothes up. It took a couple of adjustments to get the line tight enough to hold them off the floor.

The sofa was going to be my bed for the night. There were a couple of throw pillows on it; they would do fine. I laid the poncho liner on the sofa and sat down. Between the orange glow of the heater and the light from the Glo-Toob, the room was sufficiently lit. I dragged the pack over to the sofa and fished out my radio and set the alarm for five thirty. I didn't want to get woken up with a willer switch in the morning. This thought brought a smile to my face. Not that Edith would do it; I don't think so, but it was kinda funny.

I walked back to the bedroom, lighting the way with my LED flashlight, and pushed open the door. Lonnie's mocs were sticking out from under the comforter. The light glinting off the spent shell casing caught my eye. Kneeling down, I picked it up and rolled it around in my hand. Tomorrow we had to do something with these bodies. Walking out, I tossed the casing back on the floor and closed the door. In the bathroom, I opened the medicine cabinet again. There wasn't really anything there—makeup, a bottle of glycerin, and some odds 'n' ends. I thought about taking the makeup, but none of it was my shade. This made me chuckle and started an interesting conversation with myself.

He-he, now you're slipping. My mind spoke out.

Maybe, but imagine the look on the zombie's face if you were walking around in full makeup and a gillie suit! Think Eddie Izzard! This actually caused me to laugh out loud, thinking of his bit about infantry in drag.

Back in the living room, I flopped onto the sofa and turned off the little lamp. Lying there, I started to think of home and my girls. I hoped they were okay. We did everything we could with what we had. I know we were miles ahead of most folks but nowhere near where I wanted to be. Danny and Bobbie were down the road, and I knew they would be there to help; after all, the girls lived at their house half the time as it was. Danny always wanted kids, but Bobbie wouldn't. Since Bobbie is Mel's aunt and only a couple years older than her, the kids have grown up with them, and they treated them like their own. The orange glow of the heater was the last thing I saw before drifting off.

After brushing my teeth and putting my boots on, I headed for the door, using my flashlight to get around with. I picked up the XD from the coffee table and tucked the holster in my waistband and clipped the knife onto my belt. I stepped out on the porch; it was cold, and I could see my breath. I slipped the Carhartt on. Looking over at James's house, the windows were full of a warm orange glow. Smoke was coming from a stack, and James was standing on the porch holding a coffee cup. He raised the cup to me. "Mornin', neighbor."

"Mornin', Mr. James," I replied and walked over to him.

"You hungry?" he asked as he took a sip of steaming brew.

"I could eat." I patted my stomach.

"Good, Edith has a big spread laid out. An' you better fill yerself up," he said, jutting the cup out toward me.

"I will; if it's half as good as supper was, it ain't gonna be hard. Mr. James, after breakfast, can I borrow a shovel?" I asked.

"Sure, but whut fer?" he replied with raised brows.

"Well, I need to dig a couple of graves, I guess. Can't really leave 'em like this." I nodded toward the corpse lying in the yard next door.

"Well, I been thinkin' on that. My tractor has a bucket on the front. We'll use that to carry 'em out to the woods. Then I'll scoop out as much as I can. We shouldn't have to hand dig much. Let's go en eat. We'll worry about that later." He grabbed my shoulder, and we headed into the house.

Inside, Miss Edith truly did have a spread laid out. As I came through the door, she called out to me without even turning around from the stove, "How do you like your hen apples?"

"Over medium if it isn't any trouble, Miss Edith," I answered.

"Ain't no trouble. You take a seat, and they'll be there in a minute." She was busy cracking eggs on the edge of a coal black cast-iron skillet.

I took a seat, and Mr. James sat down beside me. "Coffee?" I held up my cup, and he filled it. "We got powdered creamer, if ya want it, an' sugar." He reached behind his back to a little set of triangular shelves built into the corner of the kitchen and set them out.

I doctored my coffee, and Miss Edith set a plate of three perfectly cooked eggs in front of me.

"Help yerself."

On the table was a bowl of grits, a plate of perfectly browned biscuits, and another bowl of what I assumed was sausage gravy. And to top it off was a plate of thick, fat bacon lying on paper towels. Mmmm, bacon. I loaded my plate, putting the grits 'n' gravy right on top of the eggs and chopped it all up together. A generous dashing of black pepper, and my mouth was watering.

Miss Edith came to the table and sat down. While we ate, we talked about family. Miss Edith told me they had a nephew that was "plain white trash," as she put it, and didn't claim him. They didn't have any other family in the area. I talked of my family and where I was going. They both expressed their hope for me to make it.

We talked of what happened only five days ago and what had happened since and some "what may come." Even with talking about some of the more sinister aspects of what was going on, we had a great breakfast. These two people were very comfortable to be around. Mr. James and Miss Edith cut up a little, and after a few minutes of back and forth, we were all giggling at the table with mouthfuls of biscuit, eggs, 'n' gravy. I was mopping my plate with the last bite of my second biscuit; there was one left on the plate. Miss Edith picked it up and dropped it on my plate, went to the pantry, and came back with a jar of strawberry preserves. Now, I love Smucker's preserves. She spun the lid off the jar. "I made these myself."

"They taste like soap." James fired off as he was taking a sip of coffee. He obviously wasn't thinking clearly. Edith reached over and tipped his elbow, and he spilled coffee down his shirt.

"Dang it, old woman!" he hollered as he pulled his shirt up to get the hot coffee off his chest.

"Serves you right, old man. Tastes like soap. I guess that's why you done 'n' ate two jars of 'em!" she barked at him.

I got a chuckle out of that one. She threw him her ever-present dish towel, and he mopped at his chest as I dug a spoon into the jar and piled preserves onto my biscuit. Putting the two halves back together, red gooey goodness mashed out all around it. I took a bite. Soap my ass!

"Mmm, ah, Miss Edith, this is great. Like sunshine in a jar." I licked jam off my fingers and from around the edge of the biscuit. "What kinda soap do you use, and where do you get it?" She started to cackle, and James choked on a sip of coffee.

With breakfast done and my belly tighter'n a drum, Miss Edith went about cleaning up. James stood up. "Let's go 'n' get the tractor started. It's an old 'n' cold-natured beast." He headed toward the door.

"Jus' like you." Edith popped over her shoulder. He stopped in the door, looked at me, and shook his head.

I had never seen the back of the house in the light. There was a nice barn; off to the left side was a huge woodpile. The old tractor sat beside it in the barn, a workbench running along the length of the barn on the other side. There was a large garden plot. Collards were coming up along with other cold weather crops. These folks would do just fine.

James took a can of starting fluid off the workbench; turning to the tractor, he sprayed a quick shot into the air cleaner on the old tractor. He set the can down and adjusted the choke and hit the starter. It rumbled for a couple of turns and then caught and started, banging hard with the ether in the cylinders. Thick white smoke belched from the exhaust stack with every chug of the engine. While the tractor was warming up, James went into a door on the barn and came back with a couple of shovels and tossed 'em into the bucket with a clang.

"I'll meet you 'round front. We'll load him up, then take the other'n out the back door." I nodded to him and headed over to the house.

Walking between the houses, I heard the tractor throttle up and then go into gear, and with a moan, it was moving. I was standing there, looking at the body when he came around from the far side of his house and pulled up, dropping the bucket down and tilting it back slightly. Climbing down off the tractor, he looked down. "Hell of a thing. A dead man layin' in the front yard all night an' no one comes 'round. Let's get this business over with," he said as he reached down.

I stepped up to Thomas's shoulders; reaching down I grabbed the coat. James grabbed the cold, stiff legs. Rigor had set in; with the cold, he was stiff as a board. We hefted him up and tossed the body in the bucket. It lay in the bucket at an awkward angle; it didn't look real. James climbed up on the tractor, and I went into the house and opened the back door. While he was pulling around back, I rolled Lonnie up in the blanket. Grabbing the ends of it, I pulled him across the old knotty pine floors to the back door. James already had the bucket raised; I slid the bundle across the porch and dropped the end I had in the bucket then grabbed the other end and flipped the stiff body on top of the other.

"Foller me," James called out as he backed the tractor up, turned it around, and headed off into the woods behind the houses. He drove down a trail that was obviously well traveled. Pulling off the trail into the pines, he stopped at a little clearing with a small depression in it. It was about eighteen inches lower than the surrounding area. He unceremoniously dumped the load off to the side of the depression. Lonnie rolled out of the blanket, the bag still around his head.

Using the bucket, he scooped out as much earth as he could get. When he was done, the hole was another three and a half feet deeper. Above the rumble of the tractor, "I think this'll be deep enough. I'll pile some hunks of concrete from a pile over yonder on top of it." He jutted his thumb over his shoulder.

After climbing off the tractor, James and I heaved the bodies into the hole. Afterward, we stood there for several long seconds looking down, the tractor idling in the background. He climbed back on the tractor and slowly pushed the cold earth on top of the bodies, completely covering them, and removing them from the light. At this moment, what I had done hit me. I killed these two men. Could I have done something differently? I didn't even warn them; I ambushed both of 'em. I took their lives without warning and, even more bothersome, at the time without remorse. I thought of Gol' Dolla'; I killed him too. Although that was different; he was a clear danger to me, personally. Then the image of Lonnie in front of Mandy's naked body and what he was doing flashed into my mind. No, he wasn't a danger to me, but he damn sure was to her. Anyone would have to agree with that. No, it was right. What I did was right.

James drove the tractor back to the barn, and I walked slowly back to the house, my fists shoved into the pockets of the coat. I started to think about the road, the long road I had to take. I hoped, I prayed, it got easier. But in my mind's eye, I could see the road stretching out in front of me off to the horizon—a horizon consumed with black, angry clouds; lightning flashed in them. Not thunderbolts, just flashes followed by low rumbling thunder. I could feel it in my chest now, just thinking about it. The clouds blocked everything but the road that disappeared into it.

I met James back at the barn. He shut down the tractor and climbed off. He looked at me, his lips were pressed hard together, and he just gave his head a slight nod. I nodded back, dropping my head as I did. "Don't worry, son, you did what you had to. It don't make it any easier; just know you did right, and there's some people safe 'cause of it." He put his arm around my shoulders, and we walked in the house.

Miss Edith was still in the kitchen. I wondered if she ever left it. "I packed you some sammiches and a moon pie for lunch." She leaned against the sink and crossed her arms. "You be careful, Morgan. Them girls are countin' on you. You gotta get home to 'em no matter what."

"Yes, ma'am. I aim to. I cannot thank you enough for all you done for me. Your cookin' has ruined me. Canned beef stew just can't match it." I gave her a smile.

"It was nothin'. We was glad to have you. It's what yer s'pose to do, help folks. Jes like you did," she replied.

"You need anything? Is there anything we can help you with?" James offered.

"No, sir, I think I got everything I need. I couldn't carry too much more anyhow. That pack is heavy enough already."

"Well, if you think of anything, jus' let me know. When you gonna head out?" he asked.

"Pretty quick. It's early, and I want to get some miles behind me if I can." I turned toward the front door. "I'll come by before I go."

"That'll be fine. We'll be here," James replied.

I walked out, crossed the yard and went into the house. I started to gather my gear, packed my clean and surprisingly dry clothes, and took down the line. I changed coats and strapped the Carhartt to the back of the pack. I put one pack of smokes and the lighter in my left cargo pocket and the rest of the stuff from the bodies in the pouch with my mess kit. Strapping the shoes to my pack, I was ready. I took the pistol out of my waistband and put it inside the Devildog, strapped it around my waist, and turned the heater off. Grabbing the pack by the top carry handle, I lugged it out the door and went over to James's. He and Edith saw me coming and met me on the porch.

"Thanks again for all you did. You guys take care of yourself. Mr. James, you should keep that smoke pole of yours handy. I think there's a storm a brewin'." I looked out toward the road.

"We'll be fine. You watch out fer yerself out there." He stuck out his hand; I took it. We stood there for a minute; he was looking into my eyes—a look can convey a lot. I liked him. We shook, and Miss Edith spoke up.

"You be careful an' keep yerself warm an' dry. Rain's comin' soon." She handed me the lunch, and I tucked it under the top flap of the pack.

"Thank you, Miss Edith. Keep this ole codger in line." I tilted my head toward James; he chuckled. She reached out and gave me a hug; she was a short woman and had to stand on her toes to do it. She hugged my neck tight, and I wrapped my free arm around her. With a tear in her eye, she said, "Times a waste'n; you git goin'." She turned and went in the house.

"Take care, Mr. James." With that I hefted my pack and strapped it up. I turned and walked out to the road, stopping just shy of the asphalt.

"Be careful, son." I looked back over my shoulder and gave him a nod, then stepped onto the road.

Chapter 3

This stretch of 19 is very rural; very few houses are along here. I suddenly realized that I forgot my walking stick. "Dammit!" I shouted. Oh well, I was not going back. I hadn't gone real far, maybe half a mile, but going back would add a mile to my trip, and I'd rather be a mile closer to home. It was a beautiful crisp morning. The sky was clear, and I guessed the temp to be in the midforties. The sun was getting up in the sky, and it would warm up nicely. I used the binos to glass the road ahead. Stopping, I took a better look. It looked like there were a couple of people ahead of me; they were headed toward Perry, same way I was going. Dropping the binos, I started off again.

I was actually making good time. Looking at my watch, it was about eleven. I started thinking about the lunch Miss Edith made for me. *One more hour, then you can stop for lunch*, I thought. It felt like I was making good time. The road was passing quickly and smoothly. In the few houses I passed, I saw the occasional person; they never noticed me or at least didn't indicate they did. I noticed what looked like a couple of people approaching. Bringing up the binos, I glassed the road. It was a couple, a man and a woman. They were on the same side of the road as I was, headed right for me.

I checked the waist bag to ensure the XD was within easy reach. I covered it with the bandana and kept plodding along. As they got closer and I could see them better, I could tell they didn't have any packs with them; they were carrying some stuff in their hands, but it appeared they didn't have much. As we approached each other, I was watching them carefully. The man gave a wave as we got close enough to talk.

"Hi," he offered.

"Mornin'," I replied. "Where you guys headed?"

"Trying to get to Bonnifay," the man replied.

"Do you have any water?" It was the woman. She was holding an empty Evian bottle.

I had checked out these two as they approached. There wasn't anything remarkable about them. They looked like normal folks, unprepared as hell for what they were in for. The clothes they had on were not suited to being on the road. She had a little fleece blanket over her shoulders; both had on light coats. He was wearing some sort of running shoes, not bad, but she had on some sort of fashionable flats. She was in trouble.

"Is that the only bottle you have?" I asked as I pulled the water bottle from the waist bag.

"Yeah, it doesn't last long, either," the man replied.

"Here, let me see your bottle." I stuck my hand out for the bottle. She handed it over, and I refilled her bottle. "Go ahead and drink as much as you can. Then I'll refill it," I said, handing it back. They took turns gulping the water. I was a little leery of these two, but they seemed harmless, so I dropped my pack and pulled out the two-quart canteen. I refilled the bottle again and again; they gulped at it in turns. This time, though, they only managed to down about half of it. I topped it off again and handed it back; then refilled my own water bottle and put it back in the waist bag.

"Thanks for the water. We really needed that." He was spinning the top back on the bottle.

"No problem. You guys have a long walk ahead of you. You should keep your eyes out for another bottle or two and fill 'em every chance you get," I said.

"You mean, pick them up off the side of the road?" The girl had a look of disgust on her face.

"Yeah. You got a better idea?" I gave her a what-the-fuck look.

"That's gross. I'm not drinking from a trash bottle." She was shaking her head.

"Suit yerself," I said as I started to lift my pack. "Did you guys come through Perry?"

"Yeah, we were there last night. They have a shelter set up and some food. That's where we got the bottle. We had two, but one of them must have fallen out of the blanket, and we lost it," the guy replied.

"Did they have security, police, or anything—any trouble?" I was trying to get as much intel as I could out of 'em.

"The police are around. They have some trucks, a bunch of ATVs an' stuff like that. There wasn't any trouble. They were actually really nice. It was nice to sleep on a cot for the night and have something to eat. You would think there would be more help. The authorities are doing a shit job taking care of people. There's a bunch of people there wanting to go to Tallahassee and places farther. We all asked if they could use one of the trucks to take us, and they wouldn't. Said they needed it for their town," he said.

Just from what little these two had said, I had a pretty good feel for them. Sheeple, no idea how to take care of themselves. But what they said made me feel better about going through Perry. I wanted to get through quick.

"Is there a curfew in town?" I was trying to seem casual.

"Yeah, the police have a roadblock set up on both sides of town. During the day, you can walk in, but from seven p.m. to seven a.m., you can't be on the street. They don't arrest you, but they do take you to a holding area and keep you there till morning. That's what happened to us when we first got there. But they gave us food and water, and the fire department had a tent set up for medical stuff," he said. The girl looked like she was getting impatient.

"They should do that for people. They actually should do more. There are a couple of hotels there, and they wouldn't let us stay in one. We had to sleep in a tent in the Walmart parking lot. It was awful." She had that look of disgust on her face again.

"It wasn't that bad; at least we had something to sleep on," he countered her.

"Well, good luck to you guys. I'm going to try

and get into town as soon as I can." I gave them a nod and started to walk off.

Over my shoulder, I heard the woman say, "Ask him."

In a hesitant voice he said, "Hey, uh, could you give us one of your water bottles? I mean, there's two of us, and we don't have enough." I could tell he was uncomfortable asking and was only doing it because the girl made him. I had a feeling she was going to bring some hell down on the two of them. I decided to take this little issue head-on and squash it.

Turning to them, I said, "No, I can't. I have a long way to go and need everything I have. Sorry."

"But you have three different ones, and God only knows what else is in that big-ass bag. We don't have anything. You need to help us!" She was practically screaming at me.

"Let me share a piece of advice with you; things are different now. The only person you can rely on is yourself. You need to take care of you. No one is going to do it for you. And you're going to come across some people that aren't as nice as I am. You need to be careful and watch out for your safety. As for helping you, I did. I gave you water to drink and asked nothing in return. Be grateful for what you got." I tried not to sound threatening, but she made me sick.

"Danny, take it from him. Just take it!" I could not believe this chick. He looked at me. I stared right back at him.

"I really, really suggest you think about that." He never moved.

"Come on, Kim. Let's go. Hey, man, thanks for the water." He stepped over and took her by the arm. "Come on."

"You're a pussy," she said in disgust to him.

"A word of advice, friend, that chick is going to get you killed. Lady, you need to calm down or some seriously bad shit is in store for you." I turned and started back down the road.

"Fuck you, asshole!" she shouted at me as she turned to walk away.

I didn't even bother turning around; I just kept walking. I heard her giving that poor bastard hell. I wonder how long till he left her ass on the side of the road.

Walking on, I passed a few others in the opposite lanes heading north. There was no attempt by either party to communicate. Most of them looked pretty haggard. You could tell the whole situation was starting to wear some folks down. That got me thinking about how people would react to this, this sudden plunge into a more primitive lifestyle. Hell, I knew what it was doing to me. I worked in the tech sector, I had a laptop with me at all times, and I am a CrackBerry addict. However, I also enjoy getting away from it all, just not this damn far away!

When things first went dark, I imagined most folks did what I did—just sat down and waited; some probably took right off looking for help. So the first real wave of people moving would be on the second or maybe the third day postevent. Most would find some place to provide support, in a town somewhere. That would last a couple of days until they figured out that the only way they were getting anywhere was to walk. I was sure this thought wouldn't occur to them until they had exhausted every possible resource that might be even remotely available to them, or pissed off the locals/host where they were.

That sets them to walking again. Let's say that part lasted two to three days. So that puts a bunch of folks getting out on the road today and tomorrow, and the numbers only increasing from there. The locals where all these people were would be glad to see them leave, saving valuable resources for the community and probably bringing the tension down a bit. Now in another day or two, and every day after that, others were going to start streaming in, looking for resources. They were going to expect whatever authority was in control to take care of them. After all, when you're in trouble, all you have to do is call 911, and all the help in the world comes to your aid. I figure in about another five to six days, people on both sides of this equation were going to hit a wall. The locals were going to be fed up with people coming in, looking for a handout, and those on the road were going to start to resent the treatment they get from them. Not that it was either side's fault. It was not like you could go into Walmart or Winn-Dixie and buy a sack of grub now. What you had was all you were going to have until something changed. Who knew, maybe the gov was already rolling the FEMA cavalry on its way to the rescue. Although I imagined that that cavalry looked more like the First Cav rolling into Iraq than the Red Cross.

After a quick security check to make sure no one was around, I dipped off the road into the bush. There was a screen of trees off the road, then a break about six feet wide, and then a fence and planted pines. I dropped my pack against the fence and walked back out to the road. Staying inside the brush, I checked the road with the binos to make sure no one was around. All clear in both directions. Returning to my pack, I pulled out the lunch from under the top flap, sat down, and leaned back against the pack, which rested against the fence. The sun was warm and bright. I opened the brown paper bag and found two sandwiches wrapped in wax paper, a pack of peanut butter cheese crackers, and a moon pie. That moon pie brought a smile to my face—thanks, Miss Edith.

Unwrapping the first sandwich, I discovered it was ham and cheese with lettuce, tomato, mayo, and mustard. The ham wasn't prepackaged lunch meat either. It was carved-off-the-bone ham. "Oh, good Lord, that looks good," I said out loud. "Good" being half muffled as I stuffed that Dagwood sammich in my mouth. After two of those and half a bottle of water, I was done. I let out a belch that Miss Edith would surely have admonished me for, stretched out my legs, pulled my hat down over my eyes, tucked my hands behind my head, and snoozed. I didn't sleep; this was different. I was awake and aware, just kinda like when your computer goes into sleep mode. You touch the mouse or tap a key and it wakes right up. It was like that—I was full, comfortable, and relaxed.

I was roused by the sound of a truck engine. I

couldn't see the road from where I was but clearly heard a truck. Standing up, I moved toward the road and just caught sight of an old deuce and a half headed south on the road. It didn't have a cover on the back, and I saw several people in the rear. A couple of them were standing and looking out over the top of the cab. "Huh, look at that." Going back to the pack, I pulled the two-quart canteen out to refill the water bottle; it was almost empty. I pulled the Platypus bag out and topped off the bottle, leaving the bag a little under half full. *Hmm, I'm gonna need to find water. Maybe there is something set up in Perry; those two said they had water. It wasn't critical yet; the one quart was still full, the water bottle was full, and the bag was almost half full. I was all right.*

From where I stopped for my lunch, I was less than a mile from a rest area. I didn't realize it when I stopped there, though, but I was glad I had lunch before I got here. This place was a bit of a zoo. People were all over the damn place. The little pavilions had been taken over by various groups and had all manners of "siding" added to them, everything from sheets and pieces of plastic and blue tarps to one very nicely done with palm fronds. Approaching it on the access road, I decided quickly that I didn't want to venture in. There was what looked like an area where folks were trying to barter for stuff as well as a couple of very animated arguments going on. The one that caught my ear was over the accused theft of a coat. One guy had it, and another was claiming it as his. I didn't see any weapons or anyone trying to intervene.

Think I'll just bypass this lil patch of heaven, I

thought. That was when a woman started walking out toward me from the side of the big rock. There was this big-ass rock sitting near the restrooms at this rest area; even before this, the rock was perpetually coated in graffiti. Her approach was a little too determined for my comfort, though. As she got closer, she spoke up. "Where ya headed?"

"Home," was all I replied.

She kind of rolled her eyes. "Well, duh, we're all trying to get home." She closed that with a big smile. "Where's home?"

"Down south." I just jutted my head in a southerly direction.

"I'm trying to get to Gainesville." She was now walking along with me. "My name's Jessica." *Ah, shit, this is getting way more involved than I want to be.* I stopped and looked at her. She was at least twenty years younger than me, not a bombshell but attractive.

"Look, I don't want to be rude, but I'm not looking for any company. As a matter of fact, I'm looking for the opposite. All I want to do is get home to my wife and kids." I was trying to put her off, but I think I screwed that up.

"Look, mister, all I want is to get home too. My mom and dad are just outside of Gainesville. I've been here since everything went out, and it's starting to get pretty rough. They were bringing food and water from town out here to us, I guess to keep us from walking in there, but this morning they said it was the last trip. They also said if we came to town all they would do was let us pass through; we can't stay there." The look in her eyes showed the very real desperation she felt. "A single girl on the road doesn't have a chance. I'd never make it, just like a single man can't always watch his back." This was her deal closer.

"I'm sorry; I just don't have the stuff to take care of you. I'm sorry." I was starting to feel bad, but what the hell could I do?

"I have everything I need. I go to FSU. Dad hates it, being from Gainesville and all. But I was going home on a break, so I have all my stuff with me—clothes, backpack, blankets, everything. I don't really have any food, but who does? You said you're married with kids, and you aren't ogling me, and you're like what, thirty-five? Please just let me walk with you. Please?"

Well, fuck me runnin'! I did not need this crap. But she was right about not being able to watch my back; one man cannot provide sufficient security for himself. But since when was thirty-five old? And I had a few more years than that too.

"How did you end up here?" I was still looking for an out.

"I was at the rest area taking a pee break. When I came out, the car wouldn't start." That answered my next question about where her stuff was. I guess I was resigned to my fate here.

"Look, Jessica, it's a free country, and I can't stop you from walking down the road, but I'm also not going to let you hold me up. I have a long walk ahead of me and people depending on me on the other end." I was definitely resigned to my fate at this point.

Like a teenage girl, a huge smile spread across her

face. She clasped her hands together in front of her chest and let out a little squeal. "Let me get my stuff. I'll be right back!" She took off at a run toward her car.

Oh, this is just fuckin' great. What in the hell are you going to do with a twenty-two-year-old girl? I was thinking when the other side of my brain piped up, *I can think of a few—*

Don't even think about it.

Can't blame me for tryin'. I was really starting to get a little worried about these intracranial discussions.

I was watching her as she was heading back toward me. A guy called out to her, "Hey, where you goin'?"

"I'm gonna walk home. Can't wait any longer." She turned quickly away and started walking. The dude was standing there with his arms half raised and palms out.

"Aww, come on."

I was standing there shaking my head when she came back up. She had a large black JanSport backpack on. There was some sort of a blanket rolled up and strapped to the bottom of it. She was in jeans and running shoes and had a North Face jacket on.

"Friend of yours?" I asked.

"He wishes," she said with a sour look. "He's part of the reason I want out of here. Acts like he's the great white hunter and is taking care of me. I know what he's up to. I'm not going to hold you up, and I'm not some weak little girl, either. I'll do what I have to do to get home. What's your name, anyway?"

"Name's Morgan. You know what you're in for here, right?" I wanted to see how aware she was.

"I can shit in the woods, Morgan." That made me laugh; she smiled.

"Okay, then, let's go."

We headed down the road, walking for a while without talking much. More people were on the road—not many but certainly more than I had seen in the last few days. Most were loping along. They weren't interested in talking. They looked—resigned, I guess would be the way they looked. Reality was setting in. You could see it on their faces and by the way they carried themselves. I was surprised that Jessica wasn't talking her head off. I really expected her to be yakking at me to the point of insanity.

I was the one that actually spoke first. "What made you ask to walk with me?"

"You were the only person that came by that didn't come into the rest area. You have that pack and just look like you have your shit together." She was very matter-of-fact.

"So all the people there have been drifting in?" I asked.

"Some of them were there from the beginning. Like that guy that was talking to me, Luke. He was there from the start, him and his dad. They had the pavilion with all the blue tarps on it. They kind of took over. They act like they run the place." She was shaking her head as she spoke. "Luke acted like I was his woman. Oh, he was real nice, but I could tell where it was going. He wasn't going to keep taking no for an answer much longer, if ya know what I mean." She raised her eyebrows as she said that last line. She had stepped up beside me now.

"Any violence there, or did everyone just kinda get along?" I was curious to see how people were reacting. I hadn't been around too many people. At least not too many I hadn't killed. This thought brought me down; it's kinda like a weight that will settle on you if you let it. I brushed it aside.

"Not really. Luke's dad has a big-ass revolver. He appointed himself the de facto law. It was actually kind of a good thing. He kept a bunch of fights from getting out of hand. But at the same time, whatever he wanted, he got. No one argued with him because no one else there had a gun."

"Well, that's the new reality. We used to say it was the golden rule—he who has the gold makes the rules. Now it's going to be the law of lead—he who has the most lead makes the rules." She just looked over at me and didn't say anything.

We had been walking for a couple of hours and were coming up to a wood mill on the south side of the road. I knew this was only a couple of miles outside of Perry. We would be there in the early afternoon, plenty of time to get in and get out.

"Is there anything you need to try and get when we get in town?" I was hoping the answer would be no.

"Well, if they are giving anything out, I'm gonna get whatever I can, especially food. I don't have any. And water, I only have one little water bottle." She held up a Zephyrhills water bottle that was about half full. I thought about what she said. At least she was smart enough to know what the priorities were.

"Well, I don't want to be there long. I want to get in and out as fast as we can. There isn't anything I really need. I want to put some distance between us and town before it gets too dark to find a place to sleep."

"Yeah, they won't let us stay in town anyway, and there will probably be a bunch of people hitting the road when they start telling them to leave." She made a point I hadn't considered.

"When did they tell you guys that they wouldn't let you stay in town?" I asked.

"This morning, Luke's dad started saying they should march on the town. He's a freakin' idiot."

We walked along for a few more hours, not really saying much. The terrain had changed little since we passed the mill, except there were more houses and more people. The closer we got, the more there was. I wouldn't call it urban, far from it, but compared to what we had walked through, it was like the big city. I glassed the road ahead.

"Looks like we should be in town soon. I think I can see the roadblock up ahead." I nodded up the road.

"Yeah, it'll be interesting to see what happens when we get there," Jessica said.

After another fifteen or twenty minutes, we approached the roadblock. It was located at Main Street and Highway 19 and was exactly what you would expect. They had a bunch of cars pushed out into the road. They had them set up so you had to walk through a kind of gauntlet; it wasn't a straight shot through. At each of the places that made a ninety-degree turn, the barricade was two cars deep. You weren't just going to crash through here even if you could find a vehicle to try it with.

The roadblock was manned by an assortment of police and what would come to be known as militia. The weapons were as assorted as you might think, everything from deer rifles and shotguns to the occasional battle rifle. Whoever set these guys up, though, had some tactical experience. Those with shotguns were along the edge of the gauntlet. They had defined fields of fire and were staggered throughout the maze. There was one guy with a scoped rifle and another with a battle rifle at the entrance. There were others with scoped rifles on the backside of the barricade, along with a couple of battle rifles. To the rear of the barricade was an old Chevron station; it was closed down, but the garage doors had been opened up. A couple of old trucks and a few ATVs were parked under the gas pump awning. Milling about was what appeared to be the reaction force—about ten men just hanging out, all armed.

As we approached the roadblock, I got a surprise. "Hey, Dale," Jessica called out.

"Hey, Jess." It was one of the Perry cops. "You decided to try and get home?"

"Yeah, I had to get the hell out of there. Dale, this is Morgan." She did a quick introduction.

I stuck out my hand, and the officer shook it. "Morgan Carter," I said.

"Dale Chattam," he replied. "I know where Jess is going. Where you headed, Morgan?" He was casual and at ease, but I didn't want to give out too much info.

"Down near Orlando, long ways," I said with a smile.

"Yeah, that's a hell of a walk. Jess, you guys need anything?" He had turned his attention back to her.

"We could use some food, and I need a water bottle—something that will get me home." She was holding the bottle by the cap, swishing it back and forth.

"I think I can help you out with that." Dale reached in his pocket and took out a little pad. He made some notes on it and handed it to Jessica. "This'll get you to Walmart; everything has been stockpiled there. Go to the registration tent and give 'em this; they'll give you what you need." He smiled as he handed her the slip of paper. She took it and looked at it and gave him a little smile.

"Could I ask for something else I just thought of, maybe a sleeping bag and tarp?" She was giving him a look that only a girl can, and I knew it was gonna work. His reaching out and taking the slip back as he clicked his pen proved me right.

"Yer pushin' yer luck, girl." He smiled as he scribbled on the paper and handed it back with a smile. "Morgan, you take care of her and get her home, okay?" I nodded at him. He gave a word to the men behind him, and they let us through. *This little girl is pretty sharp*, I thought.

After we cleared the barricade, I had to ask, "What's that all about?" gesturing over my shoulder.

"Dale was one of the cops that came out to the rest area on the run. He was sweet on me. He always brought me something extra. He's nice." She smiled and looked at me with a squint.

"Whatever works. Got you a sleeping bag and canteen of some sort," I said.

"And some food," she added.

Walmart was off Jefferson Street in Perry. It took us a little over an hour to walk down there. Along the way, there was a lot of activity; a lot was going on in this little town. These folks seemed to have their shit together already. When we got to Walmart, I was shocked at what I saw. A number of tents were set up, and stuff was stacked everywhere. The fire department had a station set up; a couple of churches had tents, and there was even a vet. The vet made sense, as there were a number of people on horses. We found the registration tent, and Jessica walked up and handed the slip of paper to a young woman sitting there at a folding table.

She greeted us with, "How y'all doin'?"

"Good, thanks. Dale gave me this and told me to bring it here," Jessica replied.

The lady looked the slip over. "Okay, give me a second here, and we'll get you guys fixed up." She turned to a young man and started giving him instructions. He took off on an ATV. "You guys need something to eat?"

"We could use a little something if it isn't a problem," Jessica replied.

The woman pointed down the line of tents. "There is a large white tent down there on the left. They are feeding everyone there. Just go on in and get'cha some lunch. When you get back, your stuff'll be here." With that, she smiled and turned to talk to some people behind her.

"Ma'am, is there a place to fill our water bottles?" I asked.

"Oh, sure, over toward the entrance to the store

is a water tank. Go over there, and you can fill up." She just seemed too damn cheery, considering all that was going on.

"Thanks, I appreciate it." She smiled again, and we walked off.

"Let's go get some food, if they're willing to feed us, let's take advantage of it." I motioned down the row of tents.

"Sounds good to me. I'm starving." Jessica patted her stomach.

We found the mess tent by following our noses! It smelled wonderful. I hadn't exactly gone hungry yet, but even I can't resist good barbecue. The tent had a huge smoker out back and a large stack of wood, oak from the looks of it. The smell was truly incredible; inside the tent a series of long tables with trays of food was set up. They actually had people serving the food! We loaded our plates with barbecued pork, beans, corn on the cob, coleslaw, and a couple of slices of bread. At the end of the line, several five-gallon water kegs were set out. Some were water, or punches of some kind, but two had sweet tea—God bless these people. *I love sweet tea! It's like crack to me.* I filled my cup with tea, and we looked for an open spot to sit among the knots of people.

Three men and two women were at the table we chose. One was a cop; one was a fireman, or should I say firewoman; and another was in camo with a yellow bandana tied around his left bicep.

"How y'all doin'?" asked the cop with a mouthful of beans.

"We're good. Food looks great," Jessica replied.

"Yeah, Cooper, out there on that grill, does a damn fine job," the female firefighter interjected.

"You know, always leave the cookin' to a fat man," the cop replied. The firefighter nudged him.

"Where you guys headed?" This was the guy with the armband.

"I'm trying to get to Gainesville," Jessica answered. "He's going south." She nodded her head toward me.

"Well, be careful. I hear parts of Gville are pure T hell right now," the cop managed to say while stuffing a slice of bread soaked in barbecue sauce into his mouth. "You should be okay in Chiefland. It's a little rough, from what I hear, but they're getting a handle on it."

"How about Ocala?" I was curious how the larger spots on my route were looking.

"The west side is pretty bad. They're holdin' the cops off. At least that's what a guy told us that came through this morning." It was camo guy again.

"Thanks for the info. What's with the armband?" I asked with a nod of my head.

"Means I'm in the militia. We're part of the law now."

"Looks like you guys are doing a hell of a job. Had any real trouble?" I was probing now.

The cop spoke up this time. "We had some on the second day. You'll see 'em on your way out of town. After that, everyone just fell into line pretty well. All we're doin' is tryin' to work together to get through this."

"Who's in charge of this operation?" I asked, stuffing a fork full of pork into my mouth.

"The mayor and the emergency operations staff. The police chief has the final say on all security issues, but the mayor handles the humanitarian stuff. Ya know, food, water—that kind of thing." This time, it was the firefighter.

"Where did they get all this stuff? I mean, there's shit everywhere." I gestured around.

"They declared a state of emergency real quick an' seized all the stores, everything—grocery stores, hardware, gas stations, you name it," the cop replied.

"Did they confiscate stuff from the folks in town?" If he was willing to talk, I was gonna get all I could.

"Hell, no! What's yers, is yers. But if ya need something ya come down here, and we do what we can." With that, the cop dropped a crumbled napkin on his paper plate.

"I hear you guys are going to put out anyone who doesn't live here today." *Pushing your luck*, I thought as I said it.

"Well, it ain't really like that. We just can't take in every Tom, Dick, 'n' Harry that comes along. So we got to get folks movin'. We're gonna help 'em out, but they got to get movin' on." With that, he stood up. "Good luck to you folks," he said as he stepped over the bench we were sitting on and walked off; the others followed suit pretty quickly.

"Looks like things are going to get interesting," Jessica piped up.

"Yeah, we should get out of here so we can find a place for the night. You done? I mean, eat all you can now. I'm gonna get some more tea. Damn, it's good." I stood up and picked up my plate.

"I'm good. Let's go see what they got for us and hit the road. I just want to make one stop if you don't mind." She was standing too.

"Sure, where?" I asked.

"I saw a line of Porta-Potties. It might be a while, so I want the chance to pee like a lady, if you know what I mean." She gave me a goofy look.

"That sounds good. I think I will too, but what I'm gonna do ain't gonna be real ladylike." I gave her a big cheesy grin.

"Ewwww, you're gross." She was shaking her head.

"Oh, an' I suppose your shit smells like rose petals?" I laughed out loud.

"You're sick, and for your info, yes." With that, she twirled away from me and walked off.

We hit the Porta-Potties and went back to the tent where they had a little pile of stuff waiting on us. The lady behind the table saw us coming and picked up a canvas tote bag and sleeping bag in a stuff sack.

"Here ya go. Good luck to you guys," she said with a smile, a smile that just didn't fit the reality of the situation.

Jessica took the bag. "Thank you so much."

"Let's head over to the water tank and fill up our canteens." I motioned toward the front of Walmart.

We walked over, and there was a short line. Jessica took the canteen they gave her out of the box; it was one of those big round ones with the fake felt on the outside. We waited in the line. It was short, and we got our chance to fill up. I filled everything I had that held water.

As we were walking off, I said, "Let's get out of here, and we'll sort your gear."

"Okay."

Once we made it back to the highway, we stopped on the sidewalk and sorted through what was in the bag. There were several cans of ravioli and different varieties of the same kind of thing—several pouches of tuna, one of salmon, a bunch of ramen noodles, and a few of the Cup O' Noodles. They had also tossed in a box of granola bars and about six pouches of instant oatmeal. There was also a six-by-eight green nylon tarp, a pack of Wally World grade cordage, and an Ozark Trail sleeping bag—at least it was black—and the canteen.

After getting her new gear sorted out and spreading the extra food between the two packs, we headed south. It was getting late, and there was no way we could make it far before dark. Closing in on the edge of town, we found the "problem" people old Dale told us about. There was a truck stop on the way out with a huge-ass flagpole. The flag was still there, and below the flag hung the bodies of four people—one woman and three men. There was a huge poorly painted sign underneath them, leaning against the pole; it read: "Looters will not be shot, they will be HUNG!!!!!!!!" I guess that kinda got the point across.

I spotted the corpses from way off. I just assumed Jessica saw them too; apparently I was wrong.

"What the fuck!" she screamed, jumping back and covering her mouth.

"Sign pretty much sums it up," I said.

"What? The death penalty for looting? What the

hell's wrong with these fucking people?" She was quite animated, not hysterical but highly pissed.

"Chill out there, chica. It's not you hangin' up there. As the old saying goes, times, they are a-changing," I replied.

"But that is insane! I mean, what are people doing?" She was still staring at the bodies.

I pulled her by her arm. "Come on; let's go. We need to find a place to camp for the night. You remember me asking you if you were ready for this?" I had us moving again and was trying to keep her focused on walking.

"Yeah, I'm ready to walk home, to shit in the woods, and to pee behind a tree. I'm not ready for Mad Max!" She sounded confused.

"Well, you remember when I asked you why you wanted to walk with me?" I didn't even look up, just stared at the road.

"Yeah, why?"

"Do I look like Mad Max to you?" I wasn't sure if this was the right way to do this or not, but we were about to find out.

She looked at me for a second. "What?"

"Since this thing started, I've killed three men." I looked over at her; she stopped in her tracks, looking at me.

"I told you things were different. People are going to behave differently. There is no law. You can't call 911 anymore, and some people are going to take advantage of the situation. If you want to live through this, you have to be willing to do things that you would not normally do. Understand?" She was still standing there, looking at me. I snapped my fingers. "Hey, do you understand?"

"Uh, yeah. But—"

"Come on, let's keep moving." I wanted to try and get her moving again.

We walked along for a while, neither of us speaking. I could imagine what was coming and was trying to form the answer the best way I could.

"Who, I mean, why? What caused it?" She was staring at the road, her eyes wide and her mouth hanging open.

"If someone was trying to hurt you, would you fight back? Or would you just give up and let them do whatever they wanted to you?"

"I'd fight, of course. Who wouldn't?" she replied.

"What if it meant you had to kill someone?" I asked.

She thought about that for a minute. "I don't want to have to kill anyone. I don't know if I could."

"Well, you need to figure that out for yourself and soon. It's a different world out here now."

"What happened?" she asked; she was keeping up on her own now, so I gave her a quick rundown of what happened.

"So you had to. I guess you could have walked by the girl's house, but you didn't. You helped her." She was still running it all through her head.

"I hope I don't have to make the choice ever again. I don't know if I would make the same choice," I said, shaking my head.

"Yeah, you would. I think you would."

We kept walking for a while. In a bit, we came to a bridge over a small creek, something or another "Holloway." The brush on either side of the road was thicker, and I started looking for a place to camp. I decided to head off into the bush to find a place.

"Let's head off into the woods here and see if we can find a place to stay tonight." I checked down the road to make sure no one was within sight. Jessica followed me into the woods. Walking off into the scrub, I decided this wasn't an ideal place. It was only a couple of hundred yards wide; a planted field was on the other side. Turning back, I moved toward the creek. There was a spot of thicker brush there, and I found a place big enough to set up camp.

"I'm going to put up my tarp here between these two trees," I said, pointing at a couple of young live oaks.

"Where am I going to put my tarp?" she asked.

"We only need one." I didn't really expect the look I got from her. It was kind of a split between shock and terror.

"No, no, no, not like that. We are going to sleep in turns so one of us can stand watch, see?" I had my hands out in front of me, palms up. I can only imagine what this poor chick thought. I could see the look of relief wash over her.

"You'll sleep first. I'll take the first watch." I was pulling stuff out of the pack and had our camp set up quickly. I unrolled the sleeping pad under the tarp and then her sleeping bag on top of it. "You're not hungry, are you?" She hadn't said much while I put up camp.

"No, I'm still full. You gonna be okay to stay up by yourself?" she asked as she was arranging her sleeping bag and some of her stuff.

"I'll be fine. Get some rest. I'll wake you up when I need a break. Do you have a flashlight?" I pulled my headlamp and the LED light out of my cargo pocket.

"Yeah." She started digging in her pack. "I have one of those little Maglites." She pulled out a Mini Mag.

With that, she climbed into the bag. "Night, Morgan," she said.

"Good night, Jessica."

"Call me Jess, Morgan."

"Okay, Jess. Good night."

After Jess was in the shelter and bedding down, I pulled out the NVGs and turned them on to check the settings. They looked good. There wasn't much of a moon; but without much cloud cover, the stars provided plenty of light. Securing the NVGs to my head, I decided to take a little walk out toward the road, just to see what there was to see.

"Hey, Jess, I'm gonna be walking around a bit but won't be far from you, okay?"

"Okay. Don't go far, an' don't get lost," came the muffled reply from inside of her sleeping bag.

Now that's something I didn't really think about. I guess I could get lost out here in the dark. Before leaving, I took out the Glo-Toob and turned it on. The lithium version of this device is programmable. By clicking the power switch on and off, you can select any number of various modes. Setting it to strobe, I covered it with a pile of pine needles, so just a little light was coming out. I started walking toward the road. After about ten or twelve steps, I turned and, through the NVGs, could clearly see the pulsating glow from the little light. Turning, I kept going toward the road. I figured that in the next couple of days, things were going to get really rough.

The road was clearly visible through the trees. With no overhead cover, it stood out brilliantly in the goggles. Looking back toward camp, I could still see the light pulsing on and off. I found a large oak tree and took a knee under it, surveying the road up and down its length. What I saw surprised me a bit. I counted three distinct sources of light that were obviously three campfires, two on the far side and one on my side, farther south. Far to the south was a substantial glow in the sky. It was hard to tell its actual distance, but it was certainly there. I raised the goggles and just stared out into the dark. Without much to do, my mind began to drift.

We had been prepping for a couple of years. Mel really came on board in the last year. We had a bit of a fight over a pistol I purchased; she was mad about another "toy" coming into the house. I didn't help my case any when she asked me, "How many guns do you need?" and I replied, "One more." Bad idea. I thought it was funny; she did not. I hoped she remembered the combo to the safe. I wondered if the solar panels still worked. I wondered if she set up the Butterfly stove and found the lamp oil. These were just some of the unanswered questions flooding my head.

I started to picture the girls from that morning before I left. My youngest one asked why I took all that "stuff," as she put it, with me when I left home. "So I can always get home to you, gorgeous," I replied.

"Oh, Daddy, you'll always come home." Her seven-year-old face lit up with a smile.

I tussled her hair and said, "You know it. I promise." My oldest was in the bathroom, getting ready for school. At sixteen, everything had to be right, yet she wouldn't go to sleep at night until I tucked her in. My middle daughter was still in bed; she got to sleep a little later than the others, being in middle school. I went into her room and told her good-bye. She told me she loved me and asked when I would be home. "Tomorrow afternoon," I told her. I sure wish I had been able to keep that promise.

I hoped they were all right. There was plenty of food and stored water. The backup water pump was connected to the solar system and was DC; so even if the inverter was shot, I hoped the pump still ran. I had a spare pump and spare inverter in a Job Box in my shop. I kept it on two pieces of four-by-fours, insulating it from the ground, not to mention that the shop itself is a metal building on a wood floor supported by concrete posts. The whole thing should make a pretty good Faraday cage, if that helps.

The sky was full of stars. A couple of days without man-made light and no exhaust polluting the air made a difference that I wouldn't have believed possible. I couldn't imagine being able to count all those stars; it was truly beautiful. I wondered how long the sky would stay like this. Dropping the goggles back down, I looked back north up the road. Another campfire was burning up that way; it looked like it was right on the side of the road. Looking south, I saw what I thought were a couple of new fires burning in that direction, one of which was definitely on the edge of the road. *More people on the move*, I thought.

Wandering back to our camp, everything was just as I left it. I picked up the little pulsating light, turned it off, and put it back in my bag. I sat down under one of the little oaks and got comfortable, took the NVGs off my head, and turned them off. Sitting there in the dark, listening to the sounds of the night, I waited. It wasn't too hard to stay awake. I had always been a night owl anyway, staying up as late as three and then going to bed and getting up around eight, one of the perks of working from home. About two, I went over and woke Jess up. She got right up, almost cheery. I gave her a demonstration on the NVGs and told her to hang around the camp and not go anywhere. I gave her a quick lesson on light discipline and told her about the fires that I saw and that it meant others were in the area and that it was important not to go shining her light at every noise in the night. She said she understood and sat down where I had been.

I pulled my bag out of the pack and unrolled it on the mat, took off my boots and coat, and climbed in. Jess was sitting there with her little Maglite, yawning. "Stay awake now," I said.

"Don't worry about me. Get some sleep. I can't believe you stayed up so late." She had her hands shoved into the pockets of her coat.

The light coming out of the east and bringing the woods back to life brought me out of my sleep. That and what sounded like a drunk staggering through the woods. I looked out, and Jess was not there. I got out of my bag as fast as I could, pistol in hand, and jumped up. "Morning, sunshine." I spun around and saw Jess standing there with an armload of wood.

Rubbing the sleep from my eyes, I said, "You scared the shit outta me. Sounded like a bum with bad feet stumbling through here."

"I'm getting some firewood so we can make some breakfast." She dumped her load of wood on the ground.

"That's great, but no fires," I said.

"What? How are we going to fix something to eat?" I could tell she was hungry.

"I'll take care of it. Dig the oatmeal out of your bag." Going to my pack, I pulled out my Primus multifuel stove. I had one bottle of compressed gas and one bottle of white gas with me. I took the compressed gas out with the stove and set them aside. I took out the one-quart canteen along with the cup from its cover and set them beside the stove. Using my foot I kicked all the leaf litter, pine needles, and other forest debris out of the way to form a circle about two feet in diameter.

"Hand me that green bag, would ya?" I pointed at the Devildog.

She picked it up. "Holy shit! What in the hell is in here? This thing weighs a ton!" She swung it over to me with a grunt.

"Just the necessities of life. Here, put three of those packs of oatmeal in this cup." I handed her the canteen cup. She started tearing open the bags and dumping the contents in the cup.

I set up the stove and connected the bottle to the fuel hose. From the bag, I took out my fire steel. Turning the valve on the stove, the hiss of fuel came to my ears. I quickly struck the steel at the stove, and it fired up immediately. Jess handed me the cup. I poured in some water from the canteen and set it on the stove. I know they call it "instant" oatmeal, but I still like to cook it.

"You seem to know what you're doing." Jess was sitting there, looking at the blue flame licking around the edge of the cup.

"Well, I've done this kind of thing before. I like to camp."

"There is no way I could have managed this on my own. I mean, they gave me the oatmeal, but I didn't have anything to cook it in."

"You would have found an old can or something. You need to think outside the box. Everything you see you need to think how it could help you." I took two spoons from the outside pouch of the pack. "I hope you don't mind, but we're going to share the cup, but ya get your own spoon." I held up the spoon and gave her a little grin.

She took the spoon from me. "A spoon. I don't have a spoon."

"Or a can opener," I said. She dropped her head to her chest.

"This is going to be way harder than I thought."

We sat close together to share the cup of oatmeal. I took the chance to ask her a few questions. I was starting to get a feel for her attitude and had a couple of ideas to help bolster it.

"Do you have a knife or a way to make a fire?" I asked as I passed the cup to her and shoved a spoon of gooey oatmeal in my mouth.

"No, I don't smoke or anything and never needed a knife before." She passed the cup back. I took a quick bite and handed it back and then reached over to my pack and pulled out the Buck 110 folder I took off Thomas.

"Here, take this"—I offered and then reached into my pocket and took out the BIC—"and this too. Put them in your pockets, not your pack. That way they are always on your body. If you lose your pack, you'll still have these." I handed the two to her. She opened the knife and looked at it.

"It's big." I had to show her how to close it. She tucked both of them into her pants pocket.

"Do you know how to shoot?" I was very curious about this one.

"Yeah, Dad was big into the Boy Scouts with my brothers, so some of that rubbed off on me. I like a rifle, but I can shoot a pistol too. Dad had a Beretta that we got to shoot." *Perfect*, I thought.

Taking the Taurus out of the bottom pouch, I dropped the mag and cleared the weapon and handed it to her.

"Then you should know how to use this." She took the pistol and pulled the slide back, looking into the chamber. I handed her the mag; she inserted it, racked the slide, and pressed the decocking lever, leaving the weapon on safe.

"It's a lot like the Beretta, just the safety is on the frame and not on the slide." She laid it down in front of her.

"There are only nine rounds in it. I don't have any ammo for it. That's all you got. Keep it on you at all times; never go anywhere without it, and I do mean anywhere. Never leave it." She picked it back up and cradled it on her lap, looking at it.

"You really think it's going to be that bad?" she asked without looking up.

"It already is, and it's going to get worse. Desperate people will do desperate things. These packs will look like a Walmart to some folks who have nothing. That brings up another thing—we can't trust anyone, not anyone. It's going to be hard. There will be times we want to, but we have to look out for ourselves first. Everyone else is second. Got it?" I said, trying to get the point across to her.

"Yeah, I got it. Sounds horrible though." She was still looking at the pistol.

"Let's strike camp and get on the road. It's early, and most folks will hopefully wait for it to warm up a bit." With that, we went about breaking camp, washing the cup and spoons, packing the stove and tarp, and packing up our sleeping bags. When everything was ready, we hefted our packs and started toward the road in silence.

Pausing just inside the tree line, I glassed the road. No people. I could see smoke from a couple of the fires, but no one was visible on the road yet.

"All right, let's head out, but remember what I said about others. We'll be nice and polite, but we gotta keep moving. No stopping by any campfires to chat."

"All right; whatever you say. I just want to get home." She was rubbing her hands together against the morning cold, her every breath fogging in the cold air.

"Me too." And with that we stepped out of the trees and onto the road. The sun was getting higher in the morning sky. A light fog was on the ground, and the air was still and cold. The crunch of gravel under our feet was the only sound. After walking out onto the road, I moved over to the far lane, against the center median. I knew others were ahead, and I wanted a little distance between us. Granted, moving out like that put us in the open with no cover, but I was hoping we weren't to the point of open combat yet.

Chapter 4

As we walked along, we passed one of the campsites. Two men and two women were huddled around a smoky fire. They looked miserable, disheveled, and cold. They looked up at us; I concentrated on not making eye contact with them but watched through my peripheral vision. They never moved. I never saw them attempt to speak to one another. We simply kept going on down the road. After about a mile, we came to a little store. It's the last thing on the way out of Perry for quite a ways. There were a couple of burn barrels, and several people were milling about out front.

"You want to stop by there?" Jess asked, looking over at the store.

"Hell, no; look at that rabble. I'm not going anywhere near them. Stay close and let's try and not get involved in any deep philosophical debates with them." Fortunately, the store was on the other side of the road. I slowly drifted us back to the right shoulder, putting as much distance between us and them as I could. Keeping an eye on the store, I clearly saw a couple of weapons. I know I saw two long guns and what I thought was a holster and pistol barrel sticking out from under a coat on one of the guys.

As we drew near, they took notice. I just kept my head down and kept right on walking. I could tell they were talking among themselves and gesturing in our direction. That was when it sunk in that they were all men. As we drew abreast of the store, one of them called out, "Hey, come on over by the fire and warm up!" We simply kept walking. "Hey, man, bring that pretty girl over here, and let her warm up!" They started to snicker.

"Morgan, I'm scared. What do we do if they come over here?" She had moved, so I was between her and the store.

"You have your pistol, right?"

"Yeah, but there's more of them than us."

"Most predators do not expect any resistance from those they prey upon. If this goes south, just follow me. Drop your pack, and engage the closest one to you. We will move toward them, quickly firing as we go. We have to shock them with violence of action. Understand?" I was dreading this; I prayed these idiots stayed where they were.

"Are you out of your freaking mind? Move toward them? You're fuckin' nuts!" She was incredulous at the thought.

"Look, it's the only chance we'll have. We have to shock them, put them off balance. Believe me, it's our only chance against superior numbers."

"You're crazy and are gonna get us killed. I picked a madman to walk with." She was shaking her head.

During this little exchange, we managed to pass

the store without too much more from the crew milling about. I glanced over my shoulder, and my stomach sank. Three of them had started walking down the road, not behind us; they kept to their side of the road. They were certainly trailing us and not trying to hide the fact. On our side of the road was another camp. This one had two men, young guys. They looked like skater kids and were as miserable as the last one we passed; we kept moving. After a bit, I looked over my shoulder; our new groupies were now on our side of the road.

As we approached another roadside camp, I saw it was occupied by a single black man sitting beside a small fire. He was wearing a camo M65 field coat and gray watch cap. He was looking at us with a little too much interest. As we came closer, he stood up. *Oh shit, just what I need. More fuckin' trouble. Holy shit!* I thought. After he stood up, I saw just how big a guy he was; he was fuckin' huge. He was unarmed, though, and was walking toward us casually. I'd have to shoot this big bastard; if he got ahold of me, he would pull my head right off my shoulders, and yank out my arms like the wings of a fly.

"How y'all doin'?" he asked as he approached.

Stopping a little short of him, I replied, "As good as can be." Jess stepped behind me.

"Where ya headed?" he asked.

"Tryin' to get home down south," I said. I was suddenly aware that I was totally at ease talking to this guy. That little voice in my head was quiet, and I was comfortable.

He nodded his head down the road over my shoulder. "Looks like you got some company."

I looked back and noticed that the three following us had stopped and were milling around on the road. "Yeah. They called out to us as we passed the store. I think we offended them by not coming over to their fire."

"They're creepy," Jess said. The big man let out a laugh.

"You call them creepy, but stand here talkin' to me? Now that's funny!" He laughed again.

Sticking out a hand the size of a country ham, he said, "My name's Thadius. Call me Thad."

I took the big hand best as I could and shook. "I'm Morgan. This is Jess," I said, nodding my head toward her.

"Hi, Jess." He nodded his head toward her. "I'm headed to Tampa. Y'all said you was going south, so maybe we walk together. Seems safer in a group to me."

"We are headed south, but I don't want to seem like an asshole. I don't know you, and you don't know me," I said matter-of-factly.

"You got a point, Morgan. Sometimes you just gotta take a chance, and trust your gut. Do I look like the kind of guy that people are drawn to?"

"Ah, to put it lightly, nope," I replied. He chuckled again.

"Everyone who sees me is gonna be afraid, or want to try me, just because I'm big. And black. See, either one of those is enough reason for folks to look to fight or flight, but add 'em together and it jus' gets worse. What'cha think?" He crossed his arms and waited for an answer.

"Thad, I got to say you just expressed exactly

what I was thinking. And the fact you got the stones and the brains to acknowledge it says a lot about you. I'll take a chance."

Thad walked back over to his camp under some trees on the edge of the road to collect his gear. Jess was fidgeting, and I asked her what was wrong.

"You said not to trust anyone, and here you are taking on the black Incredible Hulk. What the hell?" She had her hands on her hips and her head cocked to one side. I imagined this was the stance she used when chewing out some boyfriend.

"You're right, I did, but like he said, sometimes you gotta go with your gut. He said everything I was thinking; laid it out for us all to see. He came out unarmed and was smart enough to see what was going on behind us. I think he will be a help." I was doing my best to convince her; I really had a feeling that Thad would be a benefit to us.

"We don't have enough food to feed him. I imagine he would eat everything we have in one sitting." She was looking at him. He was kicking out the small fire he had burning. There was a large Alice pack hanging from one shoulder, and he held a double-barrel shotgun in the other hand. "He still scares me."

"Well, give it a little while. If he still creeps you out, we'll part ways." That seemed to make her a little more comfortable.

Thad came up with his gear; he had a sleeping bag strapped to the bottom of the pack, and the bag was stuffed full. In the outside pockets were a couple of Nalgene bottles. He slipped his other arm into the pack straps, which were not the original Alice straps but more along the lines of the "modified or advanced" packs you saw online. He took the weight of the pack with ease.

"That's an interesting choice." I pointed to the shotty.

"Yeah, it was my granddaddy's. I had it cut down by a gunsmith. I drive a truck on a route between Tampa and Tallahassee, hauling mail. I keep this stuff in the truck just in case. Looks like I was right about it." He held the weapon out with one hand, looking at it.

The three that had been following us decided to go back toward the store. I guess the appearance of "The Hulk," as Jess called him, was enough to make it not worth the effort. I looked back and saw them walking away. Looking back at Thad, he had a big smile on his face. "See what I mean?"

Without saying anything, we all started to walk down the road. As we walked, we talked about how we each got to where we were now. Thad told of his wife and son in Tampa. He was sure they were all right; his mother lived with them, and they were out in the country a bit—didn't have any of the "hood trash" near his place, as he put it. His mother grew up on a tobacco farm in Virginia and knew what hard times were. As a result, she kept a full larder just in case. After Jess gave her story, Thad looked at us. "Y'all ain't a couple?"

"Oh, no, no, no!" Jess answered quickly. I looked at her with a WTF look on my face.

"Gee, thanks," I said. Thad started to laugh.

Through his laughter, he managed to say, "Oh, man, you should have seen your face. That was priceless."

Jess was embarrassed; her cheeks flushed a little. "I didn't mean it like that. I mean, ya know, we're . . ." She wasn't sure how to finish that statement.

"Don't worry, Jess; it takes a hell of a lot more than that to hurt my feelings." I had to let her off the hook; she felt bad, and it showed. "You're not my type anyway." I kind of raised my eyebrows and looked down my nose at her.

"What?" She looked up with surprise, and Thad erupted into laughter again, bending over and holding his stomach. This made me start to laugh, and then, finally, Jess caught on and laughed.

"You two is somethin' else," Thad choked out.

We walked along for some time without talking much more. There were others on the road; most of them passed us by without a word. It was not like it was crowded or anything, but we did encounter them in ones and twos. Once, on the opposite side of the road, there was a group of five or six adults along with a couple of kids. They shuffled along, never acknowledging our presence. It was when we paused for a little break in the early afternoon that a couple approached us.

We were sitting under an oak where a small dirt road took off into a stand of planted pine. Jess had to pee, so Thad and I sat down in the sun for a minute. Jess came out and sat with us; we were just enjoying the feeling of the sun on our face, relaxing, when a couple walking north came over to us. They looked pretty rough. The woman, who on any normal day would have been pretty, looked like hell. Her long blonde hair was tangled and matted-looking. The guy hadn't shaved in what looked like four or five days. He was carrying a plastic shopping bag with a couple of things in it. Both were wearing light coats, nothing near warm enough for the nights we'd been having.

The guy raised his hand in a weak wave. "Hi."

Thad and I, almost in unison, responded, "Howdy." I looked at Thad, and he had a big smile spread across his face. "Jinx."

Looking back to the couple, I asked, "Where you guys headed?"

"We're trying to get to Panama City," the man replied.

Thad let out a low whistle. "That's a long ways."

"Yeah, it's tough too. I mean, there's nothing—no help, no cars. I don't know how we're going to do it." The woman was just standing there; she had what could be called the "thousand-yard stare." It looked like she had checked out.

"You guys couldn't spare any food or water, could you?" You could tell this was a guy that wasn't used to asking for anything; if he wanted something, he got it. You could tell from the expensive shoes he was wearing, plus the little alligator on his coat, that he had money. And money didn't mean shit now. I looked at him; he just raised his eyebrows and shrugged his shoulders.

"Do you have anything to carry water in?" I asked.

"Yeah." Opening the plastic bag, he took out two Fiji water bottles. "We have these. It's all we could find in the Jag when it quit. He held out the empty bottles. I took his bottles and filled them from the two-quart canteen from my pack and handed them back.

"Thank you. We haven't had anything to eat in

almost three days. Could you spare something, anything? I'm worried about Gloria, my wife." He reached over and put an arm around her; she didn't indicate she noticed.

I looked at Jess. Our eyes met, and she gave me a little nod. She opened her pack and took out three of the granola bars and handed them to me. I passed them to the man; he immediately tore one open, giving one of the two bars inside to his wife. She took it indifferently. He raised her hand to her mouth, and it finally seemed to register with her. She took a bite and then seemed to come around a bit. The man was eating the other bar between sips of water.

"Thank you," the woman said. "No one seems to want to help us."

"I'm sorry we can't do more for you. But we don't have much either." I felt bad for them, but it was obvious they were never going to see Panama City.

"Thank you for this. I really appreciate it. God bless you and good luck." With that he took his wife's hand and started down the road again.

We sat there for a minute in silence, and then Thad spoke. "They don't stand a chance in hell of ever seeing Panama City."

"Nope," I replied.

"It's sad. We should have given them more," Jess lamented.

"Anything we give them would be a waste. Sounds harsh but that's just the way it is," I said.

"Sad but true," Thad said as he stood up. "Let's get moving. There's a little town up ahead, not really a town but a wide spot in the road."

We all stood, shouldering our respective packs, and then started out again.

We arrived in Salem in late afternoon. Just as Thad had said, it was nothing more than a wide spot in the road. There was nothing left here anymore, not that there had been to begin with. Just the remains of an old motel in the process of falling in on itself and a small store; both had obviously been long defunct. The motel seemed to be the center of activity for stranded travelers. It had been turned into a camp of sorts with an odd collection of people inhabiting the windowless, mold-filled rooms. The little store had been broken into and looted, not that it looked like there was really anything in there to begin with.

A number of people were in this little hamlet. I wondered how all these new residents sat with the locals. Our little group drew a few looks as we passed through, but there were enough people around; many of them were passing through, and we didn't get as many looks as one would think. That or the sight of Thad and his old coach gun kept 'em from staring long.

"Gettin' late. We need to find a place for the night." Thad was looking around.

"I'm tired too," Jess said.

"You want to try and stay around here or keep going?" I was looking the area over as well.

"Too many folks 'round here for my comfort," the big man replied.

"I agree. Let's keep going and see what we can find," I said.

Continuing through town, we came to the post

office, the only thing that really put this berg on the map. Just past the post office was a little dirt spur off the paved road, running nearly parallel to it. Thad was in the lead and started down it. Not long after getting on it, we came up to a small pond surrounded by a swampy area.

"I need water," said Thad, dropping his pack.

"Me too; I'm out." Jess dropped her pack and sat down beside it.

"Yeah, I guess we should fill up while we can." Thad pulled his Nalgene bottles out along with a bottle of purification tabs.

"Give me your canteen, Jess." He stuck out a hand for it.

I dropped my pack as well. "Don't use those, Thad." I opened my pack and pulled out the SweetWater filter. "Use this. Save those for later." My filter had the viral guard on it as well as the silt stopper; it was a great filter. I handed the little bag over to him. "Know how to use that?"

"Oh, I always wanted one of these, but I never had the money. I was looking at the Katadyn." He was pulling the filter out of the bag and attaching the handle.

"What is that, a filter?" Jess was looking over at Thad as he worked.

"Yeah, it's pretty good. Keeps all the nastiness out of the water," I replied.

"Is it safe to drink? I mean, will it get everything out of the water?" She looked a little skeptical.

"Oh yeah; between the filter element and the other attachments there, it'll get rid of anything in the water." I pulled my canteens out and set them down beside Thad. “You mind filling these too? I’ll scout out a campsite.” Jess had pulled out the little bag we got from the Walmart parking lot back in Perry and piled all the bottles in it. Thad dropped the filter in the bag and picked up his shotgun.

“Good idea, Morgan. Jess, you goin’ with him or stayin’ here?”

“If you guys don’t mind I’ll stay here,” she said.

“Fine by me, just watch the road while I go fill these up.” Thad walked to the water’s edge.

“I’ll see what I can find,” I said as I started down the little dirt road.

“Be careful,” Jess called out.

I didn’t have to look far to find a decent place to camp. There was a nice open area under some pines. I figured tonight, since there were so many people around anyway, we would make a fire. With three of us in the watch rotation, we could each get some sleep and still keep an eye out. I was just starting to head back when I heard the thunderous explosion of what could only be Thad’s scatter gun, followed immediately by a scream from Jess. I took off at a run, drawing my pistol. Coming back to the pond, I heard Thad cussing. Jess was on her feet, but I didn’t see anyone else.

“I fuckin’ hate snakes!” Thad yelled out.

“What?” Jess yelled out.

“What the hell happened?” I yelled out as I approached.

“Damn snake in the pond. He was coming right at me! I got his ass, though!” The shotgun was swinging from his right hand, the filter in his left.

“You shot a damn snake?” I couldn’t believe this.

"You damn right I shot a snake; only good snake is a dead snake." He was indignant.

"What kind of snake was it? That's a waste of a shell, don't ya think?" I said.

"It was the snake kinda snake. They all the same to me! I . . . don't . . . like . . . snakes!" I had to laugh at him now; he was almost shrieking as he yelled that last one out.

"Damn you, Thad. You scared the shit outta me!" Jess yelled at him. "I think I peed a little."

This made Thad and me both start to laugh. Jess didn't see the humor in it.

We made our way to the spot I picked for a camp. It was just a little piece down the dirt road to the south of Highway 19. The area was under some large pines at the edge of a little bay head. Under the pines was open with no underbrush. I figured we would make our camp at the edge of the bay head to provide cover but still have a good view of the area under the pines. By the time we got to camp, Thad had calmed down. That guy is truly afraid of snakes.

"Hey, Thad, what do you think about a fire tonight?" I asked.

"I'd love a fire. It's been so cold. Sitting around a fire would be nice," Jess piped up before he could answer.

"Sounds like Jess made up my mind for me. I like a fire at night anyway." Thad leaned his shotty against a tree, dropped his pack, and looked around.

"I'm gonna get some wood. Do you have anything for a shelter, Morgan?" He picked up his shotgun and started to move out into the pines.

"Yeah, I got a tarp, an' Jess has one too." I set my pack down and began opening it up.

"You got anything, Thad?"

"Not really. I've got a poncho, but that's it."

"Well, you get some wood, and Jess and me'll set up a camp. Since someone has to be on watch all the time, it only has to be big enough for two of us. My tarp should cover that." I pulled the bag containing the tarp and the Figure 9s out.

"I'll help you, Thad." Jess set her pack beside mine and turned to follow him.

"I thought you didn't like him, Jess?" I teased her.

"Sometimes you just gotta trust your gut, Morgan." She turned and followed Thad out into the pines. "Can I build the fire? I haven't done that in a long time. I want to see if I still can."

"Sure, Jess. You can cook dinner too," Thad ribbed her.

"Speaking of dinner, you have any food, Thad?" Now Jess was going to get her ribbin' in.

"I have a little, mostly instant stuff, and not much of that."

Jess called out to me, "Hey, Morgan, you feel like beef stew for dinner tonight?" I looked up to see her stick her tongue out at Thad.

"Sure, sounds good to me." I could tell she was having fun messing with him.

"That ain't right y'all; that just ain't right." He stood there shaking his head.

Jess was skipping around, "Mmmm, beef stew."

"Don't worry, Thad, we have enough for you too." He gave me one of his huge smiles.

"I appreciate that, Morgan. It's nice to have friends." Looking at Jess, he dropped the smile and glared at her.

"Oh, come on, Thad, you know I was gonna share," she pleaded.

"Careful, Jess, you probably shouldn't make something that big mad." Now was my turn.

"Mess with the bull, get the horns." Thad couldn't keep it up, though, and smiled at her. She smiled back, and they went back to piling up wood.

It didn't take them long to have a nice pile of wood laid up. We weren't going to have a big fire anyway. By the time they were done with the wood, I had the tarp up in a lean-to configuration. It was large enough that we could all sit under it. I had the open side facing out to the pines, with the back to the bay head. Thad kicked all the pine needles out of a circle and used his heel to kick out a hole. Jess went about building a fire in the hole while Thad helped break up some wood.

I pulled out the two cans of stew from my pack as well as the Grilliput. This little thing was heavy, but I loved it. I set the cans down near the fire and dropped down beside it to start assembling the grill.

Thad looked over at me. "What the hell is that, Morgan, a damn Erector Set?"

"Naw, it's a grill. You'll like this."

"No way. Really?" He came up and sat down beside me, watching as I worked.

"That thing is cool." Thad was really impressed with the little grill. Jess got a small fire going and promptly smothered it with too much wood. Thad went over and helped her coax the fire to life.

"We'll let that fire burn down a little, get some good coals, then heat up the stew." I set the completed grill down.

"That's pretty neat, Morgan, but couldn't we just set the cans by the fire?" Jess was holding the grill, looking at it.

"Yes, we could, but I wanted to use my grill." I gave her a snooty look.

"Why do you have this thing? You have that stove. Why this? I'm just curious," she asked.

"Well, I bought that thing for when I go kayak camping. I like to cook fish over it. I threw it in the pack after thinking about the fuel for the stove. It will only last so long. With this, I can cook over a fire easier and grill meat if I need to."

"I like it. I'd like to have one." Thad had picked it up, turning it over in his hands, looking at it.

"I guess that makes sense. But you can only carry so much stuff. Seems kinda heavy." Jess had her arms wrapped around her knees with her chin resting on them.

"Well, right now, what you got is all you got. And who knows, this might make a valuable trade, or cook our dinner," I replied with a smile.

We piled on a decent amount of wood to ensure a good bed of coals. While it was burning, we enjoyed the fire and made small talk. I would never have guessed that Thad was a college grad, and for accounting no less. Hell, I never went to college.

"You don't look like an accountant," Jess said with a laugh.

"An' that's why I ain't behind no desk now. No one would hire me. I always had a thing for numbers. I was always really good at it. Momma wanted me to go to school. She worked hard and paid for it, so I went. Never really thought about not being able to get a job." Thad's big hands were folded in his lap. He was staring into the fire; obviously his mind was elsewhere at the moment.

Leaving him to his thoughts, I opened the two cans and used a stick to knock the coals around, moving most of the good coals to one side and larger fuel to the other. I set the grill over the fire and placed the cans on it with their lids poking up. While the stew heated, we sat in silence, each to our own thoughts. The sun was just down past the horizon; the light from the fire cast shadows all around our little camp.

With the sun dropping, so did the temp; the warmth from the fire was really nice. It's funny how you can learn to appreciate things like a fire so quickly. The stew was bubbling on the grill, and the aroma was mouthwatering. We hadn't had lunch today, so we were all hungry.

"Man, does that smell good." Thad rubbed his hands together.

"I'm starving. It smells so good." Jess dug her spoon out of her pack.

"Why don't we just pass the cans around, each taking a bite? That way we don't have any dishes to wash." I figured this would be the easiest way. I reached into my pack and pulled out the piece of leather I keep in it. It's a thick piece of cowhide to use for a potholder.

"Sounds good to me. Let's eat!" Thad pulled a metal spoon from the top pocket of his field coat. I picked up one of the cans by the lid and set it on the leather and held it by the bottom with the leather resting on my palm. I took a nice big bite; it was freakin' hot!

"Careful, guys, it's hotter'n shit." I passed the can to Thad, who learned quickly I was telling the truth.

We were all sitting around the fire; my back was to the lean-to, passing around the second can when I saw movement over Thad's shoulder. Jess was about to hand me the can when I jumped up, drawing my pistol. Thad didn't miss a beat; he was on his feet almost as fast. Jess was sitting there, looking at us, oblivious to the four people walking up on us. Thad had his scatter gun leveled in their direction. I pulled out the LED light from my cargo pocket and lit 'em up. This little light was bright; it was brighter than a Surefire G2, and more economical on batteries.

Thad lowered his gun when the light revealed a man, a woman, and two children. The man had his hands up; there was a little boy hiding behind his leg. The woman was holding another child on her shoulder. "Don't shoot," the man said. "We're not armed."

I lowered my pistol but kept the light on them. Jess had stood up by now.

"We smelled the food. We haven't eaten in days. Please, the kids are hungry. I'm worried about them. Can you spare something for them? The man was pleading; the look on his face conveyed his sincerity. For a moment, no one moved, we were all just standing there. I heard the woman say, "I told you this was a bad idea," quietly to the man.

Thad was the first to move and speak. He set the shotgun down against a tree and stepped toward them. They took a step back in fright.

"Y'all bring them babies over here, get 'em warm, and we'll get 'em something to eat." He was holding his arms out, trying to usher them toward the fire. He looked over his shoulder at us. "Them kids can have whatever I was gonna eat." His jaw was set; there was no discussion on this issue.

"Don't worry, man, we're with you," I told him. "Come on over here by the fire. We can certainly spare some for the kids."

The couple came up a little hesitantly, but they did walk up, stopping a little short of the fire. "I'm Robert; this my wife, Brenda. This here is Nathan, and that is Zach." He pointed to the little one his wife was holding.

"My name's Thad; that's Morgan, and this is Jess." He held out his hand as he made the introductions. "Come on, y'all, sit down."

The family took a seat around our fire. Little Zack was in his mother's lap, with Nathan leaning against his father's shoulder. Thad went into his pack and pulled out a quart Ziploc bag full of rice.

"Morgan, you got a pot we can cook this up in? All I have is a small stainless cup." He held out the bag of rice.

"Yeah, sure, I have a good pot." I pulled the pot out of the outside pocket and dumped out the contents after unstrapping the lid. Using my measuring cup/spoon, I measured out two cups of rice and added the water and then dropped in three bouillon cubes and set it on the fire.

"Let's cook this rice, and then we'll dump the stew in with it. Make it go a little further," I said as I put the lid on the pot.

Thad was digging around in his pack and pulled out an item. "Ma'am, would your little ones like a cookie?"

The couple looked at one another and then at the kids. "Uh, sure. Thank you," Brenda replied.

"Well, I only got chocolate. You guys don't like chocolate, do you?" He was looking at Nathan. From the looks on the boy's face, he did indeed like chocolate.

Thad tore open an MRE package containing a big chocolate mint cookie and broke it in half. He handed one half to Nathan and the other to Brenda, who gave it to Zack. "Thank you," she said.

"Thanks for doing this for us," Robert said. "We haven't had much to eat. It's been hard. I mean, what the hell happened? Do you guys know?"

"No one does for sure, but it sure has put us in one hell of a spot," I replied.

"Where are you guys going?" Jess asked.

"We live just the other side of Perry. We were in Chiefland when everything went out. We hung around there for a couple of days till things got out of hand, and we left." Robert was staring into the fire.

"What happened there?" I had to ask, as we were heading that way.

"It was okay at first. Things were kinda normal. You could get food an' all if you had cash. But we ran out of money pretty quickly, and then people started thinking this may be some big deal and started to get weird. Then the looting started. The Walmart was trashed. The police tried to stop it. It was stupid; people were taking TVs and Blu-ray players; it was just stupid. I mean, they were taking everything, but seeing someone running out with a flat-screen under the circumstances was stupid. The cops tried to stop it, and then someone started shooting. Only like three cops were there, but when the shooting started, it was bad. There were people piled up at the front door. They were just gunned down."

"The cops just shot 'em?" Jess asked.

"Once the shooting started, it was nuts. We saw a cop get hit, so someone was shooting at them. It was bad. After that, people went ape shit. They declared martial law in town. You couldn't be on the streets. We didn't have a place to stay, so it was leave, or they would put you in the high school gym. I just wanted to get home, so we left. We got lucky and got a ride in an old army truck. This old guy was driving it down the road and picked us up and took us to the turnoff to Steinhatchee. That's where he was headed. We started walking after that," Robert said.

The rice was done cooking, so I dumped the stew into it and stirred it up. Using the pot clamp, I set it down in front of them and put two spoons in. "You guys eat your fill. Don't worry about us; y'all eat."

They were a little embarrassed to eat in front of us; the boys, though, were not. We let them eat; it was obvious they were hungry. The two boys ate more than I thought a kid could.

Thad stood up. "If you folks will excuse me, I need to tend to nature real quick." He caught my eye and gave me a nod that said, "Come with me."

I stood up, "Me too, Thad." We walked over out of earshot and out of the light of the fire.

"Morgan, I don't know about you, but I think we should let them stay here tonight. I feel bad for their kids." He had his hands on his hips.

"I feel for 'em too, Thad, but we can't save everyone. You do know that, right?"

He gave me a look that screamed, "No shit!" "I know that, but they are here. And I can't send 'em away. The little one reminds me of my boy, an' if it was my wife and boy out there, I would hope someone would help them. Look at it as a deposit in the Karma bank, Morgan."

He had me there. I would hope someone would help my wife and girls too. And after what had happened in the last few days, I could use a deposit in that bank for damn sure.

"Okay, Thad, they can stay. But look, we gotta be careful. They were almost on top of us before I saw them. We need to do better at OPSEC. If they were some kind of zombies, they would have had our ass." I was laying it out to him now.

"I understand. We need to be more careful, but what the hell is OPSEC?" He had a quizzical look on his face.

"Operational security. Keeping our asses alive," I replied.

"OPSEC, zombies, that pack full of crazy shit, is there anything you don't have in there?" He was smiling again.

"Yeah, a ride home," I said with a grin.

"You one weird dude, Morgan," Thad said, shaking his head.

"I'll take that as a compliment." We walked back over to the fire. Jess and Brenda were talking, and Robert was adding wood to the fire. They had eaten all they wanted; there was little left, so we let Jess finish that. For a chick with a pretty good figure, she had an appetite. We offered the family the use of our shelter for the night.

"That's very nice, but you've already done a lot for us. We couldn't impose." Brenda spoke up quickly.

"Come on now, Brenda, let's not be impolite. These nice folks have offered us a safe place to sleep. Think of the boys," Robert replied.

"Well, they have already given us so much, more than anyone else has. I think they have done more than enough for us. We should go back," Brenda came back.

Until now, I had been perfectly at ease with these folks. Suddenly my stomach was falling. I did not like the tone of the conversation between these two. "Back to where, Brenda? I thought you guys were walking when you came across us?"

"We were, but we had found a place for the night before coming across you guys. When we smelled the food, we came in." Robert looked like he meant what he said, but I still didn't feel good about it.

I looked over at Thad and raised my eyebrows, kind of a "What now?" look. He was sitting on the ground with his knees up and his folded hands resting on them; he opened his palms and kind of shrugged. "You folks understand we are naturally a little cautious," Thad said.

"Of course; we all are. I tell you what; I'll sit watch. I don't have a weapon, but if I hear anything, I'll wake you guys up. It's the least we can do for all you've done," Robert said.

"I appreciate the offer, Robert, but we'll keep watch. You guys sleep." I wasn't about to let this guy stand watch over me while I slept.

"No, no, I insist. I'll stand watch. You folks have been kind to us, and I want to repay the debt somehow." Robert stood up to make his point.

"I don't mind if he stands watch, Morgan. Him and Brenda are real nice. I think we can trust them," Jess injected into the conversation.

"Thanks all the same, Robert, but you're not standing any watch. And that's final." I stood up and looked across the fire at him.

"Easy, Morgan; you're being an ass," Jess came back at me; she was sitting beside Brenda, who was looking at the ground between her feet and saying nothing. Brenda's lack of action only reinforced how I felt; this cheese had turned.

"You act like you don't trust me, Morgan. Your friends are okay. I'm starting to get a little offended," Robert said, making his play now.

"I don't give a damn if you're offended. You're welcome to stay here, but you'll sleep, and I'll stand watch."

"I agree with ya, Morgan. Brenda, you folks are welcome, but we take care of our own security." Thad had stood up beside me. Jess, however, was not on board.

"You guys are being rude. They haven't done anything to us. I can see why he's offended." Now Jess was on her feet. The only person not in this conversation was Brenda; she was still staring at the ground.

"Brenda, what do you think you should do?" I was looking down at her. She didn't look up, didn't react. "Brenda?"

She looked up and looked at all of us. "I think it's

a hard life, an' we have to make hard decisions. Robert, I think we should move on. They done enough for us." Wearily she stood, and took the boys by the hand. "Come on, boys, these nice folks have done enough for us. Thank you for everything." With that she turned and started to walk off into the darkness.

"You gonna send my wife an' kids out into the cold of night?" The light from the fire dancing off his face gave Robert a sinister appearance.

"Time you move on, Robert. Best catch up with your family." Thad reached down and hefted the shotgun from the tree it was leaning against.

"All right; after all, I ain't got a gun." He looked at Jess. "You want to come with us? These two seem like assholes." Jess looked at him and then at us. Thad met her eyes and slightly shook his head from side to side. She looked afraid, confused, maybe uncertain.

Stepping forward I told Robert, "You need to go now. I'm not askin'; I'm tellin'." Robert started to back away from the fire, the light fading down his face as he did.

After Robert was out of sight, we stood in silence for a moment around the fire. After giving it a couple of minutes, it was time to act. I told Thad and Jess to break camp; we needed to move quickly.

"What? Why do we need to move, and where are we going?" Jess was surprised.

"I don't think they are alone, and I think they will be back with others," I said quickly. "We need to hurry."

"I think you're right, Morgan. I think we were wrong about them. Let's get moving," Thad spoke up.

Jess reluctantly went along. We quickly took down the tarp. I stuffed it in my pack without folding it, along with the support lines. I asked Jess to wash the pot real quick. "Just give it a quick wash. In that pile of stuff I dumped out is a half sponge and a small bottle of dish soap. Wash it real quick, then set it by the fire to dry. Hurry up."

Jess didn't say anything; she started to do it. Thad grabbed the grill and set it by his pack. While I was closing my bag, I spotted my ditty bag full of "trap" supplies; it gave me an idea. I threw my big canteen to Jess. "Here, rinse out those two stew cans, just rinse the leftovers out of them, and then throw 'em on the fire to dry." She looked up but didn't say anything, just picked up the cans and set to it.

"Where we gonna go, Morgan? We need to get away from here, but it's dark. I don't think the road is the way to go." Thad was looking out into the darkness toward the road, cradling the shotgun in his arms.

"Me neither, man. What we'll do is go along the bay, out that way." I pointed to the east into the woods. "We'll follow along the edge of it but stay out under the pines. If we're careful and pick up our feet and don't stumble around, we won't leave any tracks. They would have a hard time following us in the dark anyway."

"These cans are dry, Morgan." Jess looked dejected; it was obvious she wasn't used to thinking about people as a threat.

"You okay there, Jess?" I asked as I pulled the ditty bag out of my pack.

"Yeah, it's just, if you can't trust a family with a couple of kids, who can you trust? How am I going to get home if everyone out there is out to get me?" She was staring into the fire.

"You can't trust anyone, Jess; that's why we're together. That's why we got to stay together," Thad answered her.

"But that's just it, we trust each other. We are helping each other. We can't be the only ones like that," she replied, still staring into the flames.

"We're not. The world is still full of good people. The problem is we can't tell who's who." I turned to Thad. "Give me a hand real quick. I want to do something to slow them down a little." I stood and Thad followed me into the pines.

From the bag, I took out a roll of military trip wire. Finding a suitable sapling, I wrapped the end around the base about eight inches off the ground and stretched it out nearly twenty feet to another one. Using my knife, I jabbed a hole in the lid of the can and ran the wire through it and then wrapped it around the base of the second tree and tied it off tight.

"Oh, I see what you're doing. Something to trip 'em up, make 'em think we know they're coming." Thad was standing over me, holding the shotty.

"Yeah, just so they'll know we know what they're up to."

"Would work better if we had some rocks to put in the cans though." Thad was right, but where the hell are we gonna get rocks?

"You gotta a pocket full of rocks? I damn sure don't," I said as I was cutting the wire. Then I thought about my pockets.

"Hey, you got any change?" I asked him as I stuffed my hand down into my own pocket.

"Yeah, I do. Good idea." He pulled out a handful of change as I did the same. As quietly as I could, I placed the coins into the can. We repeated the process with the other can, covering an area about thirty or so yards from the front of our camp. We ran back over to the fire, where Jess was still sitting; she hadn't moved.

"Should we put out the fire?" Thad asked.

I thought about it for a minute. "No, stoke it up with all the wood we have, an' let's go." While Thad and Jess piled the remaining wood on the fire, I pulled the NVGs out of the pack. I worked quickly to close it up and then shouldered the pack and put the NVGs on. Thad and Jess both picked up their packs.

"What the hell is that?" Thad looked surprised at the rig on my head.

"Night vision. Follow me and remember, pick up your feet." We started out in a line, with Thad bringing up the rear and me on point.

The bay continued to the east for a while and then started to curve south. We followed it until it started back to the west. This little bay was shaped like a big, fat thumb stuck out into the pines. Once we were on the other side, I could see the fire from our campsite without the goggles. I dropped to my knees, and the others did likewise. "Let's stay here. We'll crawl into the brush here and wait for first light. They aren't about to come through there in the dark, and if they try, we'll know about it long before they get here."

It was incredibly dark out; the moon had been waning the last few nights and was now gone. We were close enough that I could see them nodding their heads in the dark. The ground on the edge of the swamp was damp, so I pulled my poncho out and spread it on the ground. Thad, seeing what I was doing, did the same.

"Jess, put your bag on here. We'll take turns on watch tonight but from our bags right here. I don't want to be moving around making any noise at all. Anyone need to use the head?" They just looked at me.

"The toilet, or rather, bush?" That they understood.

"I do, but I'm out of TP. Do you have any, Morgan?" Jess was unrolling her bag. I reached into the top of my pack and took out the Ziploc bag containing my roll. I had removed the tube to make it pack tighter.

"Here." I tossed it onto her bag. "But go easy on it. It's all I got."

"Yeah, yeah." Jess started to move off into the bush for a little privacy.

"This ground's wet. What'r you gonna put your bag on?" Thad was unrolling his.

"Mine's got a GORE-TEX bivy. I'll be okay."

Jess came out of the darkness. She was surprisingly quiet. We all settled into our bags and established the watch order. Jess wanted to go first, and I would go last. We agreed to two-hour watches; that would leave my watch ending about five.

It was about three thirty in the morning when I heard coins beat against the inside of a can. The sky was clear and cold, and the sound carried easily through the swamp. I was startled by how loud it actually was. A muffled "Shit!" immediately followed, and then silence again. These guys were playing it right—give us enough time to wear ourselves out trying to stay awake waiting for them. Somehow I don't think this was the first time they had pulled this little stunt. I made a mental note of that; our security was going to have to get a lot better.

Thad sat up; Jess was awake but lying very still in her bag. After a few moments of quiet, the sound of low voices came across the swamp. We couldn't really tell what they were saying, but there were three or maybe four distinct voices. After a lively back-and-forth between them, one of them shouted out, "I know you're out there! This ain't over!"

Thad leaned over and in a low whisper said, "You think they're gonna leave?"

"I hope so. If they stay, things are going to get complicated." We lay in our bags in silence. Looking back across the swamp, we could still see our campfire; they must have stoked it up. I spent the rest of the early-morning hours watching the flames dance through the tangle of the swamp and listening to the sounds of low voices. The entire time, I was hoping they would just leave. We didn't do anything to them; we helped them. *What in the hell is wrong with people?*

"Guys, I'm scared. What are we going to do if they don't leave?" Jess's voice came out of the early-morning dark, putting into words the very thing we were all thinking.

"I don't know. We'll have to see what they do when it gets light," I whispered back.

The eastern sky was beginning to lighten up, going from the blue black of night to the dark gray of morning. The coming of the morning has often brought relief to those caught out in the dark of night. This morning, however, brought no relief. In fact, it was quite the opposite. With the dawn, I feared, came the hunt. And we would be the prey.

As dawn came fully on, we started to make preparations to bug out. We quietly stored our sleep gear and prepped the bags. Jess pulled out some more granola bars. We sat and ate them in silence for a bit, and then she spoke up.

"You guys think we should try and sneak away?" she asked, following it with a drink from her water bottle.

"I don't know. We don't know for sure how many there are or how, an' if, they're armed. We don't have weapons to make a stand. There's just too much unknown," I replied while looking through the swamp.

"I think we should just stay right here and wait 'em out. They don't know where we are, which way we went. They ain't gonna spend all day looking for us." Thad voiced his opinion.

It was then we heard an engine on the road to the west of us; it was rough, but it was running. The sound passed us and then began to get louder again.

"It's on the dirt road," Thad said. The sound grew steadily louder, drawing closer to us. Now it was abreast of us on the little dirt track. The engine kept going, slowly, the sound fading as it went.

"They're looking for us. Remember, Robert said that this dirt road came off 19 farther south and rejoins it behind us back there?" Now I was really getting worried.

"Yeah, Brenda said they walked down there. That's where they smelled the food from." It was Jess.

The guys on the other side of the swamp started making a little noise; it was obvious they were starting to look for us. I listened to them as they worked their way east along the swamp, the same way we came. They were shouting back and forth; others were on the western edge, along the road, from the sounds of it. If they kept coming east, they would round the bay and realize what was on the other side and might decide to take a look. To me, it would be obvious; there wasn't anywhere else to go. To the east was just a huge stand of pines planted in rows with almost no underbrush. You could stand on one end and see almost all the way to the other. I started to come up with an idea.

"Thad, if they come around the end of the swamp down there, we're going to have to ambush them here, if they make it this far."

"I was thinking the same thing." He was nodding back to me. "If they come down here, I'll cut loose with this gauge. You'll have to be ready to pick up whoever is left standing."

"How many shells do you have for that thing?" I motioned to the shotty.

"I got twenty buckshot shells and six slugs. And this." He reached under his coat and drew out a Glock 19.

I had an obvious look of surprise on my face. "I didn't know you had that!" I never noticed it before; but then, on his frame, he could carry a Colt army revolver, and it wouldn't show. "How much ammo do you have for it?"

"I have two full mags and a box of fifty," he replied.

"Can you give some to Jess? She has a Taurus but only nine rounds." This would make a difference, knowing she had a full mag.

"Yeah, of course." He reached into his pack and pulled out a box of Remington FMJ, handing it to Jess. She dropped the mag from her pistol and started to top it off.

"You guys really think we'll have to shoot our way out of here? I mean, shoot at people?" She was steadily stuffing rounds into the mag.

"I hope the hell not, but it may come to it. We didn't do anything to them. Hell, we helped them, and this is how they thank us. Remember I said we can't trust anyone?" I answered.

"Listen guys, here's what I'm thinking. If they round the end of the swamp and come up here, we ambush whoever it is. Then you two jump and run to the south, to the other tree line. If there is anyone else, they will come to the sound of the shots and try and follow. I'll be behind them. We can try and get them in a cross fire." This was really off the cuff; I was thinking out loud more than anything else.

"I don't like it, Morgan. I agree with the first part, but then you need to come with us. We all go. We stay together." Thad really didn't like the idea of us getting separated.

"I'm with Thad. We stay together, no matter what." Jess sealed the deal.

"You're right, I agree. Make sure you got all your stuff and be ready to move. Do you guys see that little palm right there?" I was pointing out to our front; it was about fifteen yards away. "From there to the little cherry tree is the kill zone. When they enter there, Thad you fire first. I'll follow up. Jess, you wait. You're the reserve." With that we sat in silence, listening to the men hunting for us.

It was about seven thirty when I caught movement out to the east, first one and then two; Robert was the second one. They were working their way toward us, checking the pines to our front and the edge of the swamp we were lying in. They worked their way along the edge, getting closer to us with every step. They stopped just shy of the palm tree marking the eastern edge of the kill zone. We clearly heard them talking.

"Come on, man, let's go back. They're gone, dude." It was the other man.

"Where in the hell could they have gone? We were on the road last night. They didn't come out that way. All they could have done was come out here," Robert replied.

"We ain't seen no tracks. If they went out here, they're pretty damn good. I don't think I want to fuck with 'em." He was practically looking at me. "They'll be more people. We'll get what we need," the other man said.

Robert was holding a lever-action .30-30. The other man didn't have any visible weapon. They stood there for another couple of minutes, looking around.

"Come on, man, let's get the hell out of here; go that way. I ain't walking back around this swamp. When we get out to the dirt road, we'll wait on the truck." Robert turned and started to walk to the west; in less than a dozen paces, he passed the palm tree.

Thad looked over at me; I shook my head slowly. They were leaving; they gave up. Once they were gone, we could sneak away. But that was when Murphy made his appearance. In the center of the kill zone, directly in front of us, Robert put his arm out across the chest of the second man, stopping him in his tracks.

"Is that a boot print?" Robert still had his arm across the other man's chest when Thad's shotgun coughed fire and thunder.

The two barrels seemed to fire almost simultaneously but were separated by a fraction of a second—the shot tearing through the brush, kicking up a cloud of debris: leaves, dirt, and twigs went flying into the air. Both of the figures in front of us collapsed, one of them letting out a painful scream. Jess dropped her head and covered it with her hands. *Boom!*

It felt like I was hit in the back of the head with a hammer. Fire, something was on fire and smelled awful. Dull thuds landed on my head, causing pain to shoot through my skull. Thad was gone. I couldn't hear. I saw Jess's face; she was screaming. There was a monster; it had to be a monster. No man could make the sound that fought through the fog in my head to my ears. Popping, lots of popping; the monster was bellowing, thunder, screams, more thunder. Time seemed to have slowed; it was surreal.

I couldn't see well. Reaching up to my face, my glasses were gone. I struggled to my feet. Someone was pulling on me. I saw Jess's face. She was still screaming.

She had me by my left arm, and the poncho was wadded up in the other; she was dragging me along. I had the XD in my right hand and was dragging my pack with the other while Jess pulled me along. Coming out of the swamp, two bodies were lying on the pine needles, covered in blood and gore.

From the dirt track in front of us, a truck crashed into the pines, heading right for us. I raised my pistol and fired. I had no kind of sight picture; the shot went wild. Jess slapped my arm down as the truck skidded to a stop in front of us. The windshield had several bullet holes. Thad stepped from the truck; his mouth was moving, but all I heard was a muffled bellow. This was the monster, I thought fuzzily. He ran up and grabbed my pack. Jess pushed me around to the passenger side. Opening the door, she shoved me in and slammed the door behind her as she scrambled in. The truck slammed into reverse and tore through the trees, bouncing out onto the little dirt road, then swung around to the left and bounced hard over the bodies lying on the road. Thad slammed on the brakes, shifted into gear, and took off, slinging dirt as it lurched away, leaving two bodies in its wake behind us.

Jess was still screaming. Thad was yelling back.

"He's bleeding . . . shot . . . put pressure on his . . . around his head." I couldn't tell who said what. At the moment I didn't care. My head was pounding, and the vague realization that I had been shot in the head came to me. I wasn't afraid; I wasn't anything.

I was jerked from sleep when little Ashley landed on my chest. "Wake up, Daddy, wake up!" I only wish I had that kind of energy! At seven years old, she was a ball of energy. She was bouncing up and down on my bed.

Mel rolled over. "You're being summoned. Go." She planted her palm on the center of my back and pushed. I planted my feet on the floor.

Ashley landed on my back. "Piggyback! Go, Daddy, go!"

The truck jerking roused me again. I couldn't see out of my right eye now. My head still throbbed; my right ear was on fire. It only lasted a minute, though.

I walked out into the kitchen, Ashley still on my back. "Pancakes, Daddy, I want pancakes!" Saturday mornings at my house usually worked a couple of ways; this was one of my favorites. "Can I crack the egg, Daddy? I want to stir it. Let me stir it!" I set a ten-inch skillet on the stove and turned the knob. With a whoosh, the blue flame jumped from around the edge of the pan.

Thad had his big hands around my head. We were stopped. Jess was crying. "I'm so sorry. I'm so sorry."

"Open his pack. Get his first-aid kit. Come on. Look, shit happens, get it? Hurry now, we can't be here long." Thad was moving my head from side to side.

"Morgan, can you hear me?" He lifted my face up. "Can you hear me?"

"Unnghh." I tried to nod.

"Take it easy, man. I'm gonna wrap your head up, gonna have to cover your right eye, okay? It's just a bandage, okay?" He was tearing open an Israeli bandage.

"Mkpph." I tried to answer; it still sounded like I was at the bottom of a well. I caught sight of Jess. Her eyes were red and puffy, tears staining her face. My right eye got fuzzy and then dark. My head was laid back on the seat. We started to move again.

The sizzle of pancake mix hitting the skillet and the sound of the other girls moving around in the kitchen filled the house. Taylor was juicing some oranges; she loved orange juice. Lee Ann was making coffee. Sixteen years old, and she drank coffee like a crewman on a sub. "Who wants pancakes?" Little Ash was flipping pancakes; she loved to help cook.

Chapter 5

Someone was pawing at my head again, moving it around. I tried to open my eyes.

"He's lucky . . . came out here . . . stitches . . . clean and dry." A thin white face was in front of me. A hat with a 101st Airborne Division patch sat on the head; it was perfectly pressed, as was the collared work shirt under it. "Lie down, son, take . . ."

I finally came around, surprised to be in an actual bed. Thad was sitting in a chair beside the bed I was in. Opening my left eye—the right one was still in the dark—I saw I was lying on a neat little bed in an equally sparse but neat room. The curtains were open on the windows, light filling the small room. Several framed documents were on the wall—but I couldn't focus enough to tell what they were. My ears were still ringing, but there was a strange noise in the background, like someone talking, but it was obscured by static.

Thad's face was covered with that big smile of his. "Hey, man, how you feelin'?"

In a hoarse voice, I replied, "Like shit; my fuckin' head is pounding. Water, I need some water."

Thad handed me a glass of cool water. I took a sip. "Take it easy. You been out for a couple of days."

This statement made me cough on the water. "What, how long, what the hell happened? Last thing I really remember was your gun going off. What the hell happened?"

"They saw a footprint. They were gonna find us. So I fired and took both of them out. Then I heard the truck on the road, so I ran out to it. They tried to get out, but I had the drop on 'em and got 'em both," Thad said.

"What happened to me? Did they hit me?" I put a hand up to my head.

"It was an accident. Jess has cried the entire time. I finally got her to go to bed earlier today. She sat up with you for two days, wouldn't leave your side. She feels real bad." He lowered his head. "When I fired, it scared her. She covered her head with her hands, but she had the pistol in it. When she did it went off and hit you."

"Jess shot me in the damn head?" I was starting to put some of the pieces together.

"Man, she feels bad. It was an accident. You're lucky, though. Linus said if it was a hollow point that hit you, you'd be dead, but it was one of the ball rounds I gave her. It went in behind your right ear and came out the back of your head. It just went under the skin, didn't crack your skull or anything. Just two little holes, in and out."

"I remember something burning. What was burning?" I was trying to remember.

"Your hair. The pistol wasn't a foot from your head. It set your hair on fire from the muzzle blast. Jess slapped on your head to put it out." He sat back in the chair and crossed his arms. Another man walked into the room. "How's he doin', Thad?" It was the man I saw earlier. Standing in front of me now, I saw that even his pants were pressed and his shirt was tucked in with a perfect military line. He was probably in his late fifties.

"He's awake, but his head hurts. Morgan, this is Linus Mitchell. We're at his place." Thad nodded toward him.

"First Sergeant Mitchell. Hell, it oughtta hurt. He took a round point-blank. You're lucky, son," he offered as an introduction.

I spent the next day in bed. Sarge wouldn't have it any other way, and he was one persuasive dude. While I was "confined," as Sarge termed it, I got the rundown on how and why we were here. Thad, being a truck driver doing a rather long and boring route, would sometimes detour from I-75 over to Highway 19. Sarge was retired and spent his days on the 'net, monitoring his radios. He was a serious ham and CB ratchet jaw. It was how he spent his retirement, talking up folks from all around the world.

He and Thad had started talking on Thad's frequent passes and developed a friendship. They finally met in person when Thad dropped by Linus's place on a return trip from Tallahassee. Hitting it off right away, they became true friends. Thad had that kind of personality; he made friends with anybody, and I was truly thankful he and I had.

Thad came into the room carrying a tray. "You hungry? I hope so 'cause Sarge said you gotta eat, an' if you ain't gonna, you gotta tell him so." He set the tray down on the chair beside my bed. I looked over at it; there was a bowl of chicken noodle soup and a cut-up apple accompanied by what looked like a glass of tea.

"Is that tea?" I had my eyes locked on the glass.

"Yeah, why?" Thad looked a little confused.

"Sweet tea?"

"Is there another kind?" Linus walked into the room. "What, you one of them damn Yankees that don't like sweet tea? You know what a damn Yankee is, don't ya?"

"Yeah, one like you that came here and didn't leave," I replied. He was standing in the doorway with his hands on his hips; our eyes were locked, waiting to see who blinked first. Knowing he was retired army, there was no way I could stare him down. Instead, I stared at him for a minute and then started to make my right eye and the right side of mouth start to twitch. After I blinked, I shouted, "I didn't blink; not my fault! It's the head wound, dammit!" Then a big smile broke out across my face.

Linus held his stare a minute longer and then burst out laughing. "You're right, Thad. He's all right."

Thad was still standing beside the bed, laughing as well. The only person I didn't see around was Jess. I'd have to see how she was doing.

"And for your info, son, I'm no damn Yankee. I'm purebred Florida cracker," Sarge replied.

"Well, Sarge, we have something in common then—so am I." I picked up the tea and took a long drink. "Damn, that's good. You don't boil the bags, do you?"

"Hell, no. Who the hell does that?" Sarge barked back.

"Damn Yankees," I replied as I took another sip. He and Thad both broke out into laughter again.

"You eat your lunch. I'm gonna go check on the radios." Linus turned and started out the door.

"Radios, what radios? How the hell do you have radios, and who the hell are you talking to?" This shocked the shit out of me. How can he have radios?

"You get some rest, Morgan. There's plenty of time for me to show you my setup." He walked out.

"You know, I said you was weird. Sarge is one of them super survivalists." Thad's eyebrows were raised, which made him look surprised. "He's got more shit stacked up around here than you would believe. And the radio thing, that's just weird on a whole 'nuther level. He's got a whole room of them, and the closet is full of batteries and stuff." Thad reached over and turned on the lamp on the bedside table. "See, his whole house is wired up to it."

"He must have a solar system. I wonder how he protected all of it. I have one at my house. It can't run the whole place, but it runs a lot of it. If his are working, then mine might too." I hoped mine was working. It would make Mel's life so much easier.

"Hey, man, where's Jess?" She had been on my mind. I'm sure she was pretty upset.

"She's outside doing laundry. She is trying to clean up your clothes."

I hadn't thought of that. I lifted the covers on the bed and looked down and then back up at Thad. "Ah, who undressed me?"

That big smile spread across his face again. "I did, why?" I guess my face betrayed me and showed my embarrassment. "Don't worry; you ain't got nuthin'

I ain't never seen before. Just smaller and paler." With that he let out a bellowing laugh.

"Oh, thanks a lot. Kick a guy when he's down, classy. Get your ass outta here." I threw a pillow at him.

"Soon as you feel up to it, Sarge is gonna give you the grand tour. You'll be impressed." He turned to walk out of the room.

"Hey, where are we anyway?" I asked, catching him before he left.

"Outside of Old Town."

"Ah, thanks. And thanks for getting my ass out of there. I mean it." I nodded my head at him.

"Don't worry about it. You'd a done it for me. Let's just hope you don't have to repay that debt."

"Amen, my friend, amen." Thad walked out, and I ate my lunch, finally enjoying the soft bed I was in.

Jess came in after Thad left. As soon as she saw me, she started to cry again. I have a wife and three daughters and see more than my fair share of crying.

"Oh, knock it off," I said as she came in. She looked up with surprise. "I know what happened. It was an accident. Just learn from it 'cause if you ever shoot me again, I'm shootin' back." I gave her a little smile.

"I'm really sorry. I had no idea it would be like that. I've never seen anything like that before." She sat on the edge of the bed.

"Like I told you several times already, it's a different world now. You gotta meet the challenge or you're going to die. Do you want to die?" She had her head down; she wouldn't look at me.

"No. But I don't want to kill someone by accident either." She looked up at me and started to cry again.

"Look, I don't blame you. I gave you the gun. It's my fault really. I should have spent time training you to make sure you were comfortable. Don't blame yourself anymore. It's done and over." She wiped her eyes.

"Okay."

"One thing, though. You gotta do me a favor," I was going to try to make her feel a little better.

"Sure, what?"

"Keep your finger off the trigger, okay?" I smiled at her, and she finally cracked a smile.

"I promise." She gave me a hug and left my room.

My dinner was brought to me in bed. I still wasn't allowed up yet. I was surprised by the fried fish, I mean, like fresh filleted fish. There was also corn bread and pinto beans. It was like being back at James and Edith's house. The fish was great and, of course, so was the sweet tea that came with it. After dinner, Sarge came in, and we talked a little about things—what had happened, and what may come. This seemed to be the number one conversation these days. I told him what I had done to get here, at least all I remembered.

"You haven't heard any outside news?" Linus was sitting in the chair beside the bed, leaning back with his palms on his knees.

"No, nothing. I have a small shortwave. I tried it once but never heard anything; never tried it again." I was sitting up in the bed.

"Well, I've heard lots of news. And from what

I can gather, this wasn't an accident"—he paused for a minute—"and may not be an outside event."

"Huh, what do you mean?" I was perplexed. How could this be an inside job?

"Well, first, there hasn't been the first hint of information coming out of the government, nothing. And when one side isn't talking, they're acting. They're up to something. I've been in their employ long enough to know that." He folded his arms.

"Well, then, what do you think happened?" The wheels were turning in my head, but they weren't really grabbing any traction.

"I have a theory, but I'm gonna keep that to myself for a while. You get some sleep tonight. I'll see you tomorrow." He got up and walked out. I turned out the lamp and tried to go to sleep, without much success.

The next day, I was approved for limited duty, according to the first sergeant. On the dresser across the room was a change of my clothes, freshly laundered and folded. I got up and got dressed. I felt a little stiff, and it hurt to turn my head. Thankfully my shirt was a Columbia PFG button-up fishing shirt, another part of my "uniform," as Mel called it. My Merrell shoes were there, so I slipped into them; they seemed so light after wearing the boots for so long. I walked out of the room and down a small hallway that led into the living room. The entire length of the hall was lined with framed documents denoting various achievements during Sarge's long military career. There were also several other documents. I wasn't sure what they were. They were all different; some had what looked like old nose art from the World War II aircraft. All of them had what I assume was a call sign in bold print, along with a time and date designation.

Coming out into the living room, it was empty. *Wonder where everyone is?* I walked through into the kitchen; no one there. Off the kitchen was a door. There was the sound of people talking, some of whom were obviously over the radios. I also heard Thad's husky voice coming through the door. I rapped my knuckles on the door and opened it. I could not believe what I saw.

This was Sarge's "Comm Cave" as he called it. The walls were covered in more of the same documents I saw in the hallway, as well as more military documents in frames. There were also a number of framed photos that had been taken all around the world, from the look of the people in them. Common to all these photos was what had to be a younger First Sergeant Mitchell. In all of them, he was with a small band of various warriors, and also common to all of them was a radio antenna jutting up over his right shoulder.

"Watch your step," Sarge called out over his shoulder before I entered the room. I looked down, and the room had a raised floor.

"What's this?" I asked as I kicked the edge of the floor.

"Protective measures. You don't think this stuff survived through sheer luck, do you?" He was removing his headphones as he spun in the office chair he was seated in.

"No, I figured you had some sort of Faraday cage," I answered in reply.

"I do; step into my Faraday cage." He cracked a smile.

"You mean the whole room?" My eyes were wide as I looked around.

"Yep, the whole damn thing; instead of trying to protect some of my gear, I decided to protect all of it. Inside the walls is a copper mesh. It's also under this raised floor and in the ceiling. It ties into a 4/0 bare copper ground grid that circles the entire house. There are ground rods that I had driven thirty feet into the ground. That really confused the electrical contractor; he stopped asking me questions when I told him it stopped the radio waves from getting into my head." He crossed his arms and rocked back in the chair, awaiting the forthcoming admiration.

"Damn!" I replied in a long exhale. "That's impressive. I wish I had this setup."

"You and everyone else right now. See, I left the army 'cause I didn't like the smell coming from upstairs. As soon as I got out, I built this house and took, ah, how shall we say, the necessary precautions." He stood up. "Let me show you around. This is the radio bank. This here is a Yaesu FT-817ND. It's little five-watt AM radio. This one is an FT-857D. It puts out a solid hundred watts. This is the one I use for DX, or long range." He was pointing out the radios.

The radios were sitting on a table that had a shelf mounted to the wall over it. All sorts of power and signal strength gauges were mounted on it, as well as power supplies and other gadgets.

"How in the hell do you power all this, especially

that hundred-watt monster?" I was pointing to the larger, only slightly, of the two radios.

"Ah, that's the best part." He walked over to a small door and opened it; he pulled the cord on a keyless fixture in the ceiling, and the fluorescent lamp in it started to warm up and fill the closet with the pale bluish light.

"This is a five-thousand-watt pure sine wave inverter." He was pointing to a big black box mounted to a shelf about eye level. "These are eight-volt, eight-hundred-twenty-amp hour batteries wired series parallel." He was kicking at six huge red batteries on the floor. "This is the charge controller that charges them from the panels outside. I have more panels than I need, but I want plenty of capacity. This system runs parts of the house, basically everything except the AC," Sarge answered in obvious delight.

"What about your hot water heater?" I asked out of reflex. I have hooked up many standby systems for generators and knew this was one of the real killers for those systems.

"Don't have one. I use the tankless type. This system carries it just fine. I don't shower every day, though, to conserve power," he replied.

"You mean we can take a shower?" I couldn't believe this.

"You mean you haven't yet? Everyone else has." He almost looked surprised, at least for him.

"No, some old grumpy fucker has kept me in bed for the last couple of days, making me piss in a damn jar." I thought that would get his dander up.

"Who in the hell are you callin' grumpy?" He had his fists balled up at his waist.

"If the shoe fits," I started to laugh; Thad and Jess joined in. I really liked this guy; he was my type of person. One of those that if they weren't insulting you, or you them, then they weren't happy. It was definitely a military thing.

"You ungrateful little shit! Get your stinkin' ass into the shower right now! And don't make me do a hygiene inspection! And that's an order." He was pumping his fists up and down as he bellowed. I could only imagine what it would be like to be on the receiving end of an ass chewing from him.

"You better get going, Morgan. He already made us take one." Thad was sitting in the office chair in front of the radios.

Just to really get him fired up, I responded, "Sir, yes, sir!" and snapped into a salute.

"Dammit, I work for a living. You don't salute me! Get out of my sight!" I thought his eyes would pop out of his head. He reminded me for all the world of Gunny Ermey. I performed an about-face and started out the door.

In a much softer voice, he said, "Take your time, and wash the wounds on your head real good too. Towels are in the closet in the hall."

I looked back over my shoulder, and he was smiling at me. "You know, if I didn't know any better, I'd think you enjoyed that," he added.

"As much as you do," I replied. He smiled at me, and I walked out to find a bathroom with hot water. Hot water!

I took my time, just soaking up the heat from the hot water. A week is a long time to go without a hot shower, or any shower, as far as that goes. I also shaved in the shower, using bar soap in lieu of shaving cream. It is amazing how much better a hot shower can make you feel. After drying off and re-dressing, I went back to the room where I had been staying and fished around my pack for my contacts. I had been wearing my glasses since the second day; but since I was here, I thought I would go ahead and wear the lenses again. *My glasses, where are they?* I thought. Looking in the mirror, I was horrified at what I saw. I hadn't looked into one since taking a round to the grape. The hair on the right side of my head was seriously fucked up. My ear had what looked like a black stain on it that wouldn't come off. *Powder burn*, I thought. I was in serious need of a haircut.

After putting my eyeballs in, I went back out and found everyone in the kitchen. They were discussing dinner options when I walked in. Sarge was the first to speak up. "Feel better?"

"Yes, I do! That was almost as good as sex," I replied. "Hey, Sarge, you got a pair of clippers? I need a haircut."

"You betcha; I do my own." He removed his hat to show me a neat set of whitewalls with a flat top.

I pointed at his head and said, "I'll take that."

"Grab one of those chairs and take it out on the back deck. I'll get the clippers." He pointed to the kitchen chairs and left the room.

"Oh, I gotta see this," Thad said as I walked out of the kitchen.

"Me too!" Jess piped up.

Stepping out onto the deck, I was met with a beautiful view of the Suwannee River. Linus's house sat on a bluff overlooking the river. A boardwalk that cut through it led down to the river proper. It was a stunning view; standing there in the afternoon sun, you could forget about everything for a minute. Sarge walked out with a set of clippers in one hand and an actual barber's cape draped over the other.

"Take a seat," he ordered and then plugged the clippers into a receptacle beside the door into the house. I set the chair close enough for him to work and plopped my ass into it. He swung the cape around my shoulders and secured it behind my neck, taking care not to hit the wounds.

"Just take a little off the top, clean up the sides, and then a nice shampoo and blow-dry, please." I just couldn't leave well enough alone. Thad and Jess both laughed. I thought at me, but I would find out later they were laughing at him and the expression on his face.

"Oh, no problem. Would you like a massage and a facial too?" Sarge had bent over at the waist with his face right in mine; he had this huge, freakin' scary-ass smile on his face. That smile just wasn't right.

"Uh, I'll pass on the facial. I don't think I want you doing anything to my face." Anything to make that smile go away.

"Smart choice, cupcake!" He flipped the clippers on as he shouted that. I felt the clippers bump into the top of my head. "Oops!" he called out. Thad and Jess started cracking up again. I just sat there, wondering why in the hell I asked this madman to cut my hair.

The clippers finally clicked off, and he stepped back and looked at me. "There you go. I did the best

I could, but I ain't never sheared a basketball before. Your head is fuckin' huge."

"Thanks so much. Let me go see the damage." I walked into the house and to the bathroom. Looking in the mirror, I was surprised to see a perfectly executed military regulation haircut. I walked back out to the deck. Jess was sweeping the hair off. "Looks like someone sheared a Sasquatch out here," she said.

"Go ahead, yuk it up. How 'bout you, Thad, what do you got to say?" I looked over at him, expecting him to have some sort of wisecrack.

"I ain't got no room to talk." He pulled the ever-present watch cap off his head to reveal a polished dome. "See?"

"Well, you got me there," I replied.

"Holy shit, can I touch it?" Jess cried out. Thad leaned over, and Jess rubbed her hands over his big head.

Looking at Sarge, I said, "You said I had a big head. Look at the size of that freakin' punkin'!" Everyone except Thad broke out into laughter.

"Yeah, yeah, ain't nuthin' I haven't heard before." We were interrupted by a sound from the river. Rounding a bend was a small skiff with an outboard on it, heading upriver. On board were two men and what appeared to be a woman. We were all looking down at the little boat. Sarge raised a hand to wave to the crew. They didn't respond.

"Friendly folks around here, huh?" I said.

"I don't know. I've seen a couple of boats the last couple of days. I figured folks would start to get around soon. We'll see." Sarge watched the boat disappear down the river.

We went back into the house and started making preparations for dinner. Linus had some serious preps. He had a large pantry full of canned and freeze-dried foods as well as a rather large chest freezer I was shocked to learn was 24vac, much more efficient than trying to run on 110vac on the setup he had. I'd only seen a little bit of the place so far, but I was already impressed. Sarge decided to treat everyone to steaks that he had pulled from the freezer earlier in the day, accompanied by stewed okra and tomatoes, along with a pot of rice. Thad and Jess took over the side dishes, as Thad said he had a thing for okra in any form. Sarge and I went out on the deck and fired up the gas grill for the steaks.

Sarge dropped the steaks on the grill with a hiss and dusted them with salt and pepper and looked over at me.

"You know anything about ham?"

"Not really; it was always something I wanted to get into, but with everything else I was doing, I never had the money." I was watching the fat bubble on the rib eyes.

"I don't understand how anyone who considers themselves a prepper doesn't have one. It is truly the only form of uncontrolled communication left to us." He jabbed a big fork into a steak and turned it, then the others.

"True, but you know, when you're worried about food, water, sanitation, power, hygiene, and all the other stuff, it can be seen as less important than those things. I wish now I had one. I wish my wife had one. There is an old guy in the neighborhood that is into it pretty big," I replied.

"That's true, but relying on the mass media is a huge mistake. Now there is no other way to get any news. With those rigs, you can talk around the world depending on the antenna, atmosphere, and a couple of things. Where's home?" Sarge asked.

"Altoona, down near Eustis in Lake County," I answered.

"Oh yeah, I know it, just outside the Ocala Forest," Sarge replied, kind of looking off into space.

"Yep, that's it," I quipped.

"So what's the plan? Thad's headed to Tampa. Jess lives outside of Gainesville. You're south of her. What are you guys going to do?" Sarge moved the steaks off the flame to a cooler part of the grill.

"There really wasn't a plan. Jess asked for help to get home. We came across Thad on the road, and we all agreed to walk together for mutual support. I guess I need to help Jess get home. Thad is going to have to finish his trip without me, though. I'm not detouring to Tampa, no way in hell," I said.

"I agree with you. I damn sure wouldn't want to go anywhere near there. He's got a hell of a trip ahead of him. I cleaned your pistol up for you. You don't have a long gun?" Sarge said. I think Sarge was leading up to something.

"No. I mean I do, just not with me. Carrying a weapon in my car to the places I work is touchy enough; a rifle is out of the question," I replied.

"How do you like your steak?" He was poking at the steaks with the fork. The smell was almost too much.

"Medium."

"Good man," he replied with a smile. Sarge took

the steaks off, piled them on a plate, and we went back inside. Jess and Thad were setting the other dishes on the table when we came in—perfect timing. We sat and ate dinner with light conversation, nothing too deep. It was another nice meal with good friends. I knew I for one was thinking about the incredible circumstances that brought us all together. I wondered how much longer this sort of thing was going to be possible, to sit around like things were normal.

The conversation died down as dinner was finished. Thad stood up. "Jess an' me'll clean up. I'm sure Morgan would like to see more of the radios. Hey, Sarge, what do I do with the scraps?"

"Throw the bones into the river. Put the other stuff in the compost pile out there." He pointed out to the rear of the house. "Come on, Morgan. I'll show you a couple of things."

Back in the cave, I was looking at all the documents on the wall. "What are these?" I asked, pointing to one of them.

"Those are QSL cards. Hams exchange these after we make contact with one another." He walked over to one of the more colorful ones pinned to the wall. "See, this here is his call sign, the date, time, and frequency we communicated on. The time is always in Zulu."

"Looks like you have a bunch of them." I was looking all around the room. On the opposite side of the room from the radio bench he showed me earlier sat another, much larger radio. Sarge sat down in front of it, tuning some dials and going through the frequencies. I walked up and looked over his shoulder; he was slowly moving through them like he was looking for something.

"So what's happened since this all went down?" I asked.

"The balloon went up all over the world. The rag heads in the Middle East took the chance to go at the Israelis. They naturally unleashed nukes on 'em all; then Iran tossed one back, but, of course, they don't have any. Then China went after Taiwan. It sounds like the Russians are trying to consolidate their base again and bring some lost sheep back into the fold. They was backing Iran when they got nuked. Russia turned some birds loose too." He sat back in the chair and put his hands behind his head. "But you know what the funniest thing to all this is?"

"No, what?"

"We haven't been hit with anything. That means we didn't use our arsenal on anyone either. Remember I said I had a theory about this?" He was rocking back and forth in the chair.

"Yeah, so you think we gave someone the green light?" I gathered.

"We obviously gave someone some assurances that the US would not interfere, and then this happened to us here. So that's why I said I don't think this was an accident. Add to that the fact that there has been zero info out of our own government since this all started, and it stinks like three-day-old fish." He swiveled back around in his chair and turned up the volume on the big radio.

"Why do you have all these on in here?" I motioned to all the radios scattered around.

"Oh, this is my baby. This is an FT DX 5000. It's the latest and greatest thing out there. I've only had it about two weeks. It's a damn work of art." He laid his hand on top of the huge radio.

"I didn't think those were what you used; I mean, you aren't going to get far on a hundred amps and that five-watt; you might as well be talking through two cans and a piece of string." I motioned to the two radios he'd already showed me.

"Don't underestimate those radios. With the right antenna, you can really reach out there. Don't worry; they'll do everything you need," he replied with a smile.

"I'll need—what the hell does that mean?" That statement confused me.

"Go hit the rack, Morgan. We have a lot to do tomorrow. You and Thad have a lot to learn and only a little time. You guys need to get on the road headed home as soon as you can." He gave me a dismissive smile and turned back to the big radio.

I walked out of the room and found Thad in the living room. He was sitting in a chair, reading the Bible. I took a seat across from him and sat there for a minute, thinking about what Sarge had said. *What the hell is that grumpy ole bastard planning?* I thought. I started thinking about getting home. Old Town was due west of Gainesville. With the truck, we could get Jess home in a couple of hours with no problems. But then Thad needed to get to Tampa. We were going in entirely different directions; we were going to have to part ways soon enough. That thought really saddened me. I had come to really like him, but I really wanted to get home, bad.

"What's that ole coot up to?" I asked.

"We been working on a plan. You know we are going to have to split up soon, right?" He closed the Bible.

"Of course; you're headed west, and I'm heading south. We got to figure out what we're gonna do," I replied.

"The way we figure it, if you agree, we'll use the truck to get Jess home, and then split up. Since I have so far to go, I want to take the truck." He was looking a little concerned.

I thought about that for a minute. He was right. He did have a whole hell of a lot farther to go than I did. Plus, from Jess's house to mine was mostly through the forest. There shouldn't be that many people out there. I know the area real well and can get through there without too much trouble. "That's cool. My trip from her place to mine shouldn't be too bad—shouldn't take more than a couple of days."

"I was hoping you'd say that. I was worried. I know you want to get home too." He looked a little relieved.

"When do you think we'll head out? I'm ready to—" I was cut off by a beeping noise that sounded from the kitchen. Thad and I looked at each other with a WTF look. Sarge busted out of the comm shack with an AR in his hands.

"That's my gate alarm. Someone is coming up the driveway. Come in here and get a weapon." He ducked back into the cave. Thad and I followed him inside. He had opened a gun safe that I hadn't noticed before. He pulled out an M1 carbine and handed it to me. "You know how to use that?" He quickly handed me two thirty-round magazines. "Yeah, I used to have one, great little rifle—" He cut me off, rushing past me out of the door. We met Thad back in the living room. He had left to get his shotty.

"I ain't expecting any visitors, and you'd have to either cut the chain or climb over the fence to get in here. Someone is sneaking around." He was amped up. You could see the anticipation on his face. He had slung on a tac vest with AR mags and his 1911 in a cross-draw holster. "You good with that?" He pointed to Thad's shotgun. Thad nodded affirmative.

Sarge handed us each a GMRS radio with a headset. "Put these on. The channel is already set. This is the PTT button." He held a little switch on the cable about chest height. "You guys go out the back. To your right is a trail. It parallels the driveway. You'll be able to see it through the brush. I'm going to ease up the driveway. Let's just keep in mind where each other are so we don't shoot one another." It was dark out, and the risk of friendly fire was a real possibility. Then I remembered the NVGs.

"Sarge, I have a set of NVGs. Let me get them," I said.

"You mean like these?" He pulled a set of third-gen goggles from a pouch on the vest he was wearing. They were nice.

"No, not like that, but they work," I said, heading to my room to get them.

Jess came into the room. Sarge looked at her. "No offense, but I want you to stay in here. Get your pistol. Keep your finger off the damn trigger. We will call you by Annie Oakley when we come back. If it isn't us, shoot whoever is there." She left and came back with her pistol, checked the action, and turned the safety on. The three of us headed out the door to the deck and went down the stairs where Sarge pointed out the trail; he continued around to the front of the house, while Thad and I headed down the trail with him in the lead. Sarge's driveway was long as hell and switched back and forth. Thad was in the lead. "How long is this freakin' driveway?" I whispered.

"It's long. You see anything?" he asked.

"Let's hold up and listen for a minute," I whispered again. From where we stopped, I had a view of about twenty yards of the driveway that went straight away from us and started to curve back to the left at the far end. There was no sound, no noise whatsoever. I was watching the far end of the driveway when I caught a glimpse of movement. Watching the spot for a minute, there was no other movement. I was reaching for Thad's shoulder to tap him and move on when I saw movement again. A lone figure came into view; he was close to the brush on the left side of the trail and was using as much stealth as he could. He took about five steps and stopped again. I clearly saw him now; he was in a uniform of some kind, carrying an M4 or a clone thereof and a large pack. That's when I realized he was wearing NVGs as well. I put my hand on Thad's shoulder and pressed down. He looked at me, and I nodded to get down. "Very slowly," I whispered so low that it was almost inaudible.

After about a minute, he took another few steps and stopped again. This time, he slowly went down on one knee. He knelt there for a minute, surveying the road ahead of him, and then he raised his left hand and gave a wave forward with just his fingers.

I keyed the mic. "We have multiple armed individuals in uniform, with NVGs, coming up the driveway," I whispered into the boom on my jaw.

"How many?" came the whispered reply.

"Two, no, three." Two more men came into view. They were all three in a low crouch, and one was covering their rear. These were not your average looters.

In my earpiece came the low, breathy voice of Sarge. "I'm coming down the drive. You guys hold tight. If they do anything hinky, open fire."

"10-4," I replied.

The men on the trail had just risen and were about to start forward again when I heard Sarge call out, "POTUS!" The three instantly froze; they were scanning 360 around them. Again, Sarge's voice rang out, "POTUS!"

The men paused a moment longer, and then one of them called out, "SNAFU!"

Sarge's voice came into my ear again. "I think I know these guys. I wasn't expecting them, but if they're here, then something must be bad wrong. You guys hold your position; if anything happens, open up on 'em." Looking down the trail, I saw Sarge come into view. He stepped out into the center of the trail, weapon at the ready, and called out, "Patriots," this time in a lower voice.

"Sucks," came the quick reply.

"Mike, is that you?" Linus lowered his weapon.

"Yeah, you scared the shit outta us. I didn't think

you'd see us coming." The three men were walking toward him.

"Shit, you know you can't sneak up on me. Hell, I trained your ass." Mike walked up, and the two men shook hands.

"Yeah, well, three to one, you wouldn't have stood a chance," Mike replied with a smile.

"You sure about that?" Linus stood there for a minute. "Come on out, guys." Thad and I walked out of the brush not ten yards from where the four men stood.

"I guess you had the drop on us, huh?" One of the other men replied.

"Damn right, Teddy," Linus snapped back. "Who's this?" Sarge pointed to the third man.

"This is Ronnie. He's with us. You can trust him. Ronnie, this is First Sergeant Linus Mitchell." Ted performed the introduction. "Who you got here, Sarge?"

"Fellas, this is Thad and Morgan. They have been staying here for a bit. Let's go up to the house." With that, we all headed up to the house. Stepping up on the porch, Linus called out, "We're coming in, Annie." The deadbolt clicked open. Stepping inside, Jess was introduced to the new crew.

The guys stowed all their gear in the comm cave; they were carrying one hell of a load. These guys all looked like active-duty operators. They were all in their late twenties or early thirties, and the gear they were carrying didn't come from any surplus store, either. We were all sitting around in the living room when Linus came in carrying a case of Bass Ale. This old shit had everything! To a chorus of cheers, he passed out the bottles. Mike looked over at me and asked about my head.

"Oh, just a little friendly-fire incident," I replied. Jess looked down at the floor.

"Doc, take a look at it, will ya? Ronnie's a medic. We all call him Doc." Mike took a sip of his beer.

Doc went over my head and concluded that I was one lucky SOB and that it was healing nicely and shouldn't have any complications. We sat around drinking and talking; these guys were all active duty but wouldn't say what they were up to or why they were here. The secrecy was a little unnerving. I wasn't sure what was going on. The talk was pretty light. The woodstove in the living room was warm; the brew made me feel even warmer.

"Hey, Sarge, what's with the challenges you guys used? I mean, I understand the POTUS/SNAFU—that makes sense. But the Patriots one confuses me. What's that about?" I drained my bottle.

Mike spoke up real quick. "Oh, he's a huge Patriots fan." He finished with a laugh.

"Fuck you, Mike. You know I hate New England. And then there's that stupid-ass book," Sarge fired back.

"So, Mike, you guys don't look like you were out deer hunting. What were y'all up to?" I was going to see what kind of info I could get out of them. The three MultiCam-clad soldiers looked at one another, and then Ted answered.

"We were inserted by a helicopter down southwest of here," he started, but Thad cut him off quick.

"You were what!" he barked out quick, sitting up in his seat.

"Just what I said; not everything is down, guys. The military, at least from what we know of, is fully operational." Ted looked around the room at all of us.

"Then why aren't they out here helping us?" Jess took the chance to get into the conversation.

Mike answered that one, "We don't know. But the secretary of DHS is now in charge."

"What was your objective, and why did it bring you here?" I leaned forward, resting my elbows on my knees.

Once again, the three looked at one another. This time it was Mike who spoke up. "Our mission didn't bring us here, an' I'm not going to tell you what our mission was. It doesn't matter now anyway. We're off the reservation." He looked up at Sarge. Linus's expression didn't change.

"I know, son. When you showed up here, I knew it must be bad," he replied to Mike's glance. "How bad is it?"

Mike looked over at Thad, Jess, and me. "You guys need to get to wherever you're going in a hurry. That's all I'm gonna say right now. There is probably another week before the hammer falls."

We all sat there for a minute; each of us was lost in our thoughts. What in the hell did that mean? These guys obviously knew something they weren't sharing. We sat around for a while longer, finishing the case of Bass. Apparently Jess was a lightweight. After about three brews, she was half in the bag and making a fool of herself. She was coming on to everyone in the room. To their credit, though, none of the guys came on to her. She was helped to her room and put into her bed, fully clothed. It was also politely recommended that Thad and I turn in as well. Because I was tired and feeling the effects of a few brews, I agreed.

I don't know how late the rest of them stayed up, but they were all up before we were. I woke to the smell of frying bacon—mmm, bacon. I dressed quickly and headed out for the kitchen. Doc was there frying bacon and eggs. The others were all in the cave. I grabbed a cup from the cabinet and poured myself a cup of coffee from the percolator on the stove.

"Mornin', Doc," I said, taking a drink of the black elixir, savoring the smell of the coffee. I'm not a big coffee drinker, but I love it on a cold morning.

"Howdy, Morgan, how's the head?" he replied while cracking an egg into a skillet of bacon grease. He looked funny standing there at the stove with a dish towel over his camo'd shoulder and a pistol in a drop leg holster.

"Not bad, just a little tender around the extra holes," I replied. Doc gave that a little chuckle.

"Extra holes." He looked over his shoulder. "You're one lucky bastard. I'll give you that. How do you take your eggs?"

"I prefer them at home, but since that's out of the question, over medium is fine, thanks." I gave him a slap on the back and headed for the cave, leaving him to cook.

I found everyone but Jess in the cave. All of our gear was laid out on the floor. "What're y'all up to?" I asked, coming through the door. I didn't really like people sniffing around my stuff. I was greeted with a chorus of "Morning, Morgan."

Sarge had an armload of canned food from my pack. "We're tuning your gear up for you. I'm taking all this canned stuff and replacing it with stripped down MREs. They'll lighten your load a little. The rest of your stuff is pretty good. I like that little grill." I had forgotten all about that thing. The last time I saw it, Thad was carrying it as we ran from the camp in the dark of night.

"That thing is neat. Wish I had one," Thad spoke up. He reached over and picked up Lonnie's knife. It had been in the bottom of my pack, and I had completely forgotten about it.

"Where'd you get this thing?" he asked, pulling the big blade out of the sheath. "It's big."

"Ah, long story. You can have it if you want it." I nodded toward him.

He looked up at me with raised eyebrows. "You sure?"

"Hell, yeah, it's the least I could do for you, and don't let it ever be said I didn't do the least I could." I got a laugh out of Mike and Ted.

"You look pretty well set up to get home, no farther than you have to go. We're going to add a few things to your load, though." Mike was taking some boxes out of Sarge's safe.

"Morgan, I want you to take that carbine with you. There's four thirty-round mags. They're fully loaded, and there is another two hundred rounds here for it. If you need more than that you really fucked up somewhere." Sarge laid the carbine against my pack. "Now get down here and pack your shit up." He stood up, and I knelt down and went to work organizing my gear.

"Dump your shit, Thad." Ted handed the big man his pack.

"This ain't gonna be pretty, boys." Thad took the pack and, opening the top, upended it onto the floor.

"Is that all that you got?" Ted was eyeing the contents.

"Yep, the only reason I have this is 'cause of Sarge. He stayed on my ass about keeping some stuff with me." Thad was looking down at the little pile of gear on the floor.

"We gotta fix that," Sarge said and then quickly left the room. Mike started going through the stuff. He threw all the ramen noodles out to the side and then pawed around at the rest of it. A few minutes later, Sarge was back with a duffel bag full of stuff and promptly dumped it on the floor. There was a GI cold-weather sleeping bag and carrying straps, a first-aid kit, a canteen cup, and a spoon. There was also a magnesium fire steel, a GI compass, and a couple of pairs of socks. He went over to his gun safe and took out a couple boxes of 00 buck, a box of slugs, and two boxes of 9mm ball and threw it onto the pile. Lastly, he dropped a poncho and a hank of 550 cord.

"There, that oughta help." He stood over the pile, examining his work. Mike walked over and set nine MREs down. "Strip all the boxes and extra crap outta these and pack them too."

Next, they went through Jess's pack, doing the same thing. They changed all her canned food for MREs and added a first-aid kit, canteen cup, and fire steel. She had clothes, a tarp, and a sleeping bag, and, hopefully, she was going to be home tonight.

Ronnie poked his head through the door. "Breakfast's ready, and I'll wait on you like one hungry dog does another." He flipped his dish towel back on his shoulder and headed back to the kitchen with all of us in tow. It is amazing how you come across people in life that you blend with so well. These guys, all of us, got along like we had known each other our entire lives. Sarge and the trio had known each other for years, apparently. Thad, Jess, and I had only known each other a few days, and the others only one. But as we were heading to the kitchen to sit together and eat, it was like a high-school football team coming out of the locker room.

Mike and Ted were pushing and shoving each other to try to be first in. Sarge grabbed Mike by the scruff of his neck and kicked his left leg out from under, throwing him off balance. As Mike fell, he reached out and grabbed Ted. Sarge kicked the back of Ted's heel as he took a step, throwing his leg way out, and, with Mike hanging on him, they both went to the floor. Sarge stepped over their sprawled bodies. "Age and deceit will overcome youth and vigor every time!" he shouted as he landed in a chair in the kitchen.

Jess was already there as everyone took a seat. "I feel like shit," she said with her hands over her face.

"Funny, it really shows," Ted responded, with Mike shoving him on the shoulder. Thad and I just sat there looking at these clowns. These are the kind of people that will walk into a firefight with a smile on their face, but here they are, acting like a bunch of damn kids, maybe worse.

"Gee, thanks," she replied, the embarrassment obvious in her voice. We sat and ate; the cutting up continued throughout. I gotta hand it to Ronnie, though. That guy could cook. There was a plate of eggs and sausage patties and bacon, a bowl of grits, and a plate full of cathead biscuits. Man, I was going to miss eating like that. When breakfast was done, everyone pitched in to clean up, which, with so many people, made it take twice as long. Somehow we got through it without breaking anything.

With breakfast done, Sarge announced that there was work to do. He laid out the day he and his crew had planned out to get us ready for our trip home. They had established waypoints for the trip and a schedule for us to call and check in. The two radios shown to us earlier were going with us. Ted was going to mount one in the truck; the other was going into my pack. With that, we started the preparations to get on the road.

We were each given a call sign. These guys had a little fun with that. I was to be Walker because I was walking. Thad was Driver, as he was driving, and poor Jess was stuck with Annie. We were each shown how to operate the radios and given a quick course in how to string the wire antennas and their various configurations. I was surprised at how simple it was. I always thought this was far more complicated. They also provided us maps of our route, clearly marked out. While we were going over the radios, I had an idea.

"Hey, Sarge, one of my neighbors is a ham. We never really talked much about it. I just know he is. You think we could try and call him?" I asked.

"You know his call sign?" He was already headed to his big radio.

"No, just his name. What if we try using the name of the road I live on and his name?" I didn't have any other idea how to try to contact him, or if his radio was even working.

"We can try, but this will probably take awhile, since I don't know what frequency he would be on, if his radio even works, and if he'll answer to it. But I'll give it a try. What's his name?" He was tuning his radio and putting on his headset.

"His name is Howard," I replied.

"Okay, so Howard on John Long Road in Altoona, right?"

"Yeah, let's try, I guess." It was worth a try.

"I'll work on this. You go out with the boys. They're going to show you guys a few things." With that, Linus went to work on the radio.

Thad, Jess, and I were led outside by the guys, where they put us through an intense crash course on vehicle security. They had us performing ambush drills, driving through them, backing out of them, firing from the vehicle, providing security during stops, dealing with a disabled vehicle, and, finally, a course on combat first aid. These guys were intense, to say the least. This training took the rest of the morning and into the early afternoon. It was during instruction on applying tourniquets that Sarge came out of the house.

"Morgan! Get in here, on the double!" he shouted from the porch.

I rushed into the cave, where Sarge was at the radio. He was talking into the mic as I came in.

"Here he is. Hold on." He stood up so that I could sit down at the radio. "I think this is your guy; just be careful and make sure." I put the headset on and picked up the mic.

Keying the mic, I asked, "Howard, is that you?"

The reply came back clear. "Roger that."

"Howard, this is Morgan. How many dogs do I have?" This had been a running joke between the two of us for years.

"Two and half. It's good to hear from you. Your wife and girls are worried sick about you," he came back.

"I'm sure worried about them too. How are things over there?"

"As good as can be. No real trouble," he replied.

"Is there any way you could get Mel over to your place so I could talk to her?" I was hoping he could.

"It'll take a while, but I'll get her. It's fourteen hundred local now. Come back at sixteen hundred, and I'll have her here."

"Will do. Thanks a lot, Howard," I said.

"No problem. She's been helping out around here. I charge my batteries at your place and get water." Howard came back.

"My power is up?" That was some damn good news.

"Yeah, the whole system works. It's made a huge difference around here. Let me go find her." With that, he signed off. I'd have to wait another couple of hours to talk to her.

"Sounds like you have a pretty good setup, and your family is all right," Sarge said over my shoulder.

"Yeah, I hope so. Thanks a lot, man. I really appreciate it. You have no idea what this does for me, not to mention everything else you have already done. I don't know how to repay you." I swiveled around in the chair; he sat down in one across from me.

"I don't expect anything from you. If I thought you weren't worth the trouble, I wouldn't have helped you. But there is something you can do; me and the guys have been talking, and we may need your help." He crossed his arms and sat back in the chair.

"You name it," I replied.

"You better hear me out before you sign up." He went on to tell me some of what the guys talked about last night. It boiled down to what had occurred was not an act of nature or an outside event. While they didn't know the full extent of what happened, it was clear that this was some sort of false flag event, the object of which was yet unknown. What they wanted from me was to keep my eyes and ears open in my area and provide situational intelligence on what was going on in my area. If the need arose, they also wanted me to provide material support for anyone coming into my area that may need it. From the sound of it, he acted as though we were going to war with the government.

"You really think this is what it's coming to? You really think we can take on the military?" I thought he was out of his mind. This wasn't some fantasy survival fiction where the good guys had a fairy godmother following them around and always came out on top.

Very calmly, he replied, "Yes, I do think this is

what it's coming to. Can we take on the military alone? No, but we aren't going to be alone. The rank and file are not all going to fall in line with this. Don't get me wrong, the upper ranks have been filled with bootlickers that will do what they're told, but there are many who won't. The NCOs, who really run the military, are not going to go for this, especially since the armed forces are now under the control of the DHS—and martial law has been declared. The average Joe just don't know it yet, and when they do let y'all know, it's going to be too late to do anything about it."

We spent the next couple of hours stowing our gear in the truck and getting ready to leave. Mike, Ted, and Doc traveled here by only moving at night, so we decided to follow their lead. They never encountered anyone, and we hoped to repeat their success, but then those guys were pros. We were all a little anxious. I know I was on edge, not to mention I was waiting to talk to Mel. About fifteen minutes before it was time to make the call, I went to the cave. Sarge was already there; he had the radio tuned up and ready to go. At sixteen hundred, Howard's voice came over the radio. "Morgan, you there?"

"Yeah, I'm here, Howard." I had a pit in my stomach.

"Hang on a sec; got some folks here that want to talk to you." There was a pause on the other end.

"Morgan?" It was Mel.

"Hey, babe, how are you guys doing?" I was starting to get a little choked up.

"We're okay. Where are you? Are you all right? Are you going to be able to get home?"

She sounded like she was about to cry. She had stopped talking but still had the mic keyed until I heard Howard in the background tell her to let off the PTT button. When the station cleared, I responded, "One at a time. I'm a little over a hundred miles from home. I'm okay, and yes, I will be home, promise. It's gonna take a week or so, but I'll be there. How are the girls?" I heard them in the background when she was speaking.

"They are good. They want to talk to you." I spent a few minutes talking to them, each one getting a turn. They were all upset but happy to talk to me. Not nearly as happy as I was to hear their voices, though. I was starting to tear up thinking about them. I talked to Mel a little more. I told her we shouldn't talk too much over the radio, but I told her that I would be able to call every day and that Howard and I would work out a schedule for when we would talk.

"Hey, Danny's here. He wants to talk to you too." That kind of surprised me. In a minute, I heard his voice come over the headset.

"Hey, man, how's it goin'?"

"As good as it can. How are you guys?" I replied.

"We're good. Hey, Mel can't remember the combo to your safe. Can you give it to her?"

There was no way I was going to call that over the air, but I had a plan for this very thing. "Go into my shop. There is a piece of paper stapled to the backside of the front two-by-four of the workbench that has it. Use it and then burn it for me."

"Will do. I'm gonna pull some ammo. We have had a couple of little problems, nothing major, but I want more at my house," Danny replied.

"No problem, but do not hand any of it out to anyone else around there, not till I get home." I needed to see how things were around there before I went passing out ammo, not that I had that much to pass out.

"Oh, hell no. I'm not giving any of that away. You gonna be able to call in tomorrow?" he asked.

"I'm gonna try. I have a radio, and if things work out, I should be able to call. I'll work it out with Howard. You guys take care and be safe. I should be home in a little over a week, maybe sooner," I said.

"Be careful, man; things are getting nasty out there. People are getting desperate. We're starting to see some people trying to walk into the forest." That kind of concerned me. I often read on the forums of people thinking they were going to head for the Ocala National Forest when the shit hit the fan, and we were right at the front door.

"Tell me about it; you have no idea. Really," I replied. Danny left, and Howard and I worked out a schedule for him to be monitoring the radio and what frequencies. He told me to use the call sign of Long Howard, mixing the road name and his. He didn't have a tactical call sign. I gave him my call sign of Walker. I signed off and told him I would call tomorrow.

After talking to my family and friends back home, I was ready to get home—more than ready. After getting off the radio, we started making final preps to leave around dark. Sarge took the time to talk to Jess and Thad while I was on the radio, bringing them up to speed on what he and I talked about. With that news, Thad was just as eager as I was to get home. Jess was just plain old ready. Life on the road, living out of a backpack was getting old to her. She was "done with the camping thing," as she put it.

"There are enough heaters for those MREs that you guys shouldn't need to make any fires. You all have a sleeping bag rated for the weather now so you should be okay. Move only at night if you can, and be careful." We found Mike back in the cave. "Here are the maps and some more batteries for the NVGs. They're not rechargeable like your others, so save them for last. We also put two five-gallon gas cans that Sarge provided from his supply in the bed of the truck."

Ronnie walked in with a small bag. "Here are some goodies for your aid kit. Keep your head clean and dry, and you should be all right." He handed me a small pouch of stuff.

"Be careful driving with those goggles of yours. They are decent, but depth perception is a bitch. Take it slow at first until you get accustomed to it." Ted stuck out his hand. I took it, and we shook.

We spent the next few minutes saying our goodbyes. Jess gave all the guys a hug and got a little teary-eyed. Linus gave her a big hug and whispered something in her ear, causing her to laugh as she wiped away tears from her face. When he turned her loose, he looked at Thad and me.

"You guys get her home, and then get your asses home. I expect to hear from you on schedule. You give us a SITREP based on the codes we discussed along with your location based on the closest waypoint."

Thad spoke up. "Hey, Sarge, you haven't given us your call sign yet. You got one, don't ya?" I hadn't even thought of that. They gave us all call signs, but never gave us theirs. Mike spoke up real quick.

"Oh, yeah, he's got a great call sign." Linus snapped around to face him, poking a finger to his face.

"I dare ya; I fucking dare ya to say it!" He was squinting one eye and jabbing that finger at him.

Mike put his hands up and started to back up. "Roger that, Sarge. I was just having a little fun." He was trying not to laugh.

"Keep it up, and you'll be having a little recovery from a grade A ass whoppin'!" He wasn't backing down. Mike was still trying not to laugh. Ted was looking at the floor, not daring to make eye contact with Sarge, who was giving him the stink eye.

Thad cocked his head to one side and crossed his huge arms across his chest. "Now I gotta hear this. I ain't leaving until I do." He puffed out his chest a little more.

"These snot-nosed little shits are just trying to get a rise outta me," he barked back.

"Looks like it worked," I said. He shot me one of those looks that if it could kill, I would've turned into dust where I stood.

"Ah, come on, Sarge, just tell 'em; they can use something else, but you gotta admit it's pretty damn funny." Mike was pushing his luck, from the look on Sarge's face.

His expression stiffened; he crossed his arms like Thad had and rocked back on his heels. "All right, I'll tell y'all what smart-ass over there is referring to.

But I'll warn you all now that your pay grade isn't high enough to use it. And if any of you so much as giggle, I'll throttle you to death." He looked at all of us. Jess looked scared; she just didn't understand this kind of thing. I knew this had to be good.

Sarge took a deep breath. "Blanket. Some people call me Blanket." I immediately got it and had to turn around so he couldn't see my face. Jess was standing there looking confused. "Blanket? I don't get it. What's wrong with that?" she asked.

Thad had a huge smile on his face. It looked like it was about to split in half. "Linus's blanket, from *Peanuts*," he blurted out; he couldn't hold it anymore and broke out in a deep rumbling laugh that caused the rest of us to follow suit, much to Mike's relief. He was about to explode but wasn't about to be the first.

Sarge was turning every shade of red known to Sherwin-Williams. Hell, he had shades they never thought of. "Fuck you, asshole, the whole lot of you!" With that he shoved Ted across the room and made for the door.

The time to get back on the road had come. I made a little gift, not really a gift, but I left the gillie suit and the hand tools I had in my pack with Sarge and the guys. The added weight of the radio and its batteries meant I had to lighten the load. Ted wired two twelve-volt seven-amp-hour dry cells in parallel to run the radio. These batteries wouldn't run it long, but they would give me the ability to transmit on the run.

"One more thing; we will not be transmitting from here anymore. The same goes for you. After you make contact, you need to displace at least five miles before the next transmission if at all possible. And you will use Foxtrot Sierra Mike for my call sign, and that better be the only one I hear." Sarge gave Ted and Mike a cross look.

"All right. Why exactly are we keeping in touch for this trip? I mean, it isn't like you can come help us if anything goes wrong." I had wondered about this for a little while.

"Do not underestimate what we're capable of. What you have seen in your stay here is all I let you see. We will be seeing each other again. I promise," Sarge replied.

"Well, fellas, I for one can't thank you enough for all you've done for us. Linus, thank you. You were right all along, and I should have listened better," Thad spoke up.

"Well, better late than never. Some lessons just need to be learned the hard way. You're smarter now though, ain't ya?" Linus replied to him.

"Yeah, I shore am smarter now." Thad dropped his head with a little laugh.

"You keep these meatheads in line, Jess. Make sure they call me when you get there." Linus smiled at her.

"I will; thanks. You've been so nice to us, and that isn't common right now. I hope to make it up to you someday." Jess smiled back at him.

"You just get home safe," Sarge replied.

We were loaded up and on the road just as the sun dipped below the horizon. There was still enough light to see, so I wasn't wearing the NVGs. We weren't using the headlights and had removed the bulbs from the taillights and blinkers, just to be safe. The first leg of our route would take us east on 26 toward Trenton. It was a small town and shouldn't be a problem. By the time we were out of Old Town, it was dark enough that I needed the NVGs. Ted was right about the depth perception thing; it really sucked.

The road was open and deserted; there aren't any houses on this section of the road, so we made good time. I was only running about forty-five, just in case. It only took about twenty minutes to make the outskirts of Trenton. I slowed as we approached town. There were houses now, some of which had dim light coming from the windows. I slowed the truck as we got closer to town; there weren't any people around that I could see, but there were signs of life in the form of lights and smoke from fires.

It was fully dark now, and the goggles were doing great. They really lit up when I looked at a house that had candles, lanterns, or some other forms of light in them. It was the glow of a cigarette that caught my attention—actually it was two. They were on the left side of the road ahead. I stopped the truck and turned on the IR source on the goggles. With the additional source, I saw the roadblock and the men manning it. They obviously heard the truck, but since we were running blacked out, they couldn't see us.

"What's up?" Thad asked as he shifted the shotgun in his hands.

"Roadblock," I replied.

"What's it look like?"

"There are a couple of guys I can see, but there

may be more. I don't like the look of it, though. I think we should find another way. Showing up in the dark blacked out like this isn't going to win us any points with 'em for sure. The guys said not to make contact with anyone if we could." I was watching the men at the roadblock. Every time one of them took a drag from his smoke, I could see their faces. They were looking down the road for the source of the engine. "Besides, any town with a PD is probably going to take the truck."

"My ass. This is my ride home. Let's see if we can find a route around it. Jess, you know anything about this area?" Thad asked.

"I've been through here before, but I don't know the area at all," she replied.

I tried to back the truck up, but that just wasn't happening. Trying to look in the mirror through the goggles was a no-go. I did a three-point turn in the road and headed back out of town. There was a road on the left, heading south, and I took it. It was a residential street with houses on both sides. Fortunately, it was still kinda cool out, and no one was hanging around outside. As we passed by, I saw the occasional door open and a curious head poke out, but no one ever came out to investigate.

It took what seemed like hours, but we eventually came out on the east side of Trenton on 26 again. I knew that Newberry was up ahead and would probably have the same thing going. We came out far enough east that I didn't see the roadblock on this side, but I was certain there was one. We drove on without talking; everyone was on edge. It was quite the change from how we all felt at Sarge's house. Out on the road, we all felt vulnerable.

We passed a large timber operation on the left. I knew from personal experience that Newberry wasn't far ahead. Slowing down, I started to look for a turnoff. I found a paved road heading south and took it. There weren't any roads leading back to the east, so we kept heading south. The road took a sweeping turn to the west, but there was a spur that continued south. It was a lime rock road and looked well-traveled, so I took the spur. Shortly after getting on it, there was another road of the same type that headed east, so we turned off.

This stretch of road was mostly farmland, with hardly any houses. As we passed one of the few that were there, I heard a shot. Everyone instinctively ducked their heads. We didn't know if it was aimed at us or not, but I stomped on the gas a little harder. After a mile or so, we came to another lime rock intersection and took the north side. This brought us back to 26 east of Newberry. We took off down a paved road again. We were getting close to the west side of Gainesville and really needed to get off the highway. Our goal was Wacahoota Road. It's a small road that would keep us away from Gainesville proper and would tie into US 441. Our map, though, didn't show all the roads in this area, which was full of little roads and dirt paths. I needed a break from the goggles, plus it was time to look at the map and see what we could find for a route.

It was going on ten o'clock. In four hours, we had gone only thirty miles. It was a hell of a lot faster than walking but still seemed to take forever. I was looking for a place to stop when we came across a mud pit. It was an honest to goodness mud boggin' hole. There were a few tent-type carports scattered around, and a few trucks were sitting here and there. I turned off onto the road and came to a stop at the entrance. As I was checking the area for any signs of life, Thad asked, "What'cha got?"

"Looks like a muddin' hole. Doesn't look like there is anyone around. I need to take a break from these goggles and to look over the map," I answered.

"I don't like it out here. Place has got to be full of rednecks," Jess said.

"Well, I don't see any necks, red or otherwise, and we need to stop," I replied to her.

"I need to pee." Jess was squirming in her seat.

"Yeah, me too," I answered absentmindedly.

"And that makes three. Let's stop here for a minute and take a break," Thad said. He was looking out the window into the night.

After pulling in and parking the truck, we all climbed out. I took the XD from my bag and tucked it and its holster into my pants and slung the carbine over my shoulder. Thad extricated himself from the truck and tilted the barrel of his shotty over his shoulder, looking around. Jess came out and made for a clump of palmettos not far from the truck with a roll of TP in her hand. I went to the tailgate of the truck and dropped it. It fell almost straight down. Thad reached in and pulled out a loop of rope that was tied off to an eye on the top of the bed, lifted the gate, and hooked the loop around the pin of the gate. "We put this on today after Ted did the same thing you just did." I just stood there shaking my head.

"At least this thing didn't have a bumper back here, or it would have made one hell of a noise," I said. Thad just grunted his agreement. "Keep your eyes open, man. It's blacker'n a well digger's ass out here," I said over my shoulder as I stepped off to take a leak.

Thad let out a combination chuckle and grunt. "That's not what I thought you was gonna say. You had me there for a minute."

I turned right to him; he wasn't four feet from me, and I stuck my hand out, feeling around. "Who said that? Who's there?" Thad let out a laugh again and stepped off himself.

After getting some relief, we were at the back of the truck. Jess's head was on a swivel; she was way nervous. I laid out the map and started to look it over. "Thad, grab a poncho, would ya?"

"Sure, what for?" he asked as he was pulling one out of his pack.

"We're going to use it as a cover so I can turn on a light and look at this map. I don't want a light shining all over the place out here." I unrolled the poncho and threw it over my head and leaned over the map.

"I'll keep an eye out." I heard Thad's big feet crunching the dirt as he moved around.

Looking at the map, it looked like SW143 ST was the closest thing to us that would go far enough south to be worth taking. The problem was it petered out on the map. There just wasn't anything else that would keep us west of Gainesville and out of residential areas. Hell, even this road would probably be residential. After taking a little break with sandwiches—Sarge was probably the only guy around with a couple dozen loaves of bread in the freezer—and some coffee, it was time to get back on the road. I told Jess and Thad what I had planned and kind of where we were headed. I admitted to them that I didn't exactly know how we were going to get there, but we'd figure it out.

"Anywhere is better than here. This place gives me the creeps," Jess complained.

"Well, saddle up then." We all piled into the truck and got back on the road without a hint of Jess's zombie rednecks. We hit 143 about two miles after leaving. We were getting dangerously close to Gville, in my opinion, but I hoped it was worth the risk. It turned out to be a decent road with only a couple of houses; but instead of running out like the map showed, it made a hard right. There was a gravel lane that kept on straight with a very prominent PRIVATE ROAD sign on it. I stopped the truck at the edge of the gravel, looking ahead for any sign that someone might be out there.

"What is it?" Thad asked.

"Sign says private road. But I think we should keep going; there is a lot of forest ahead, and if we can stay in it, we would be better off." I continued to scan the area ahead as I spoke.

"Then go. I don't want to sit here any longer than I have to." Thad was looking out the window.

I started down the drive. We didn't see hide nor hair of anyone. The lane led to what looked like a barn. I swung the truck toward the east, and there was a path into the trees. I eased the truck into it, and we were headed east again. The little path opened up into a trail through the woods. The old truck bumped along for a ways until the trail opened up further onto a power line right-of-way. It was clear sailing to the east, no houses and no worries. Bumping along with the useless power lines overhead, I was thinking about people or what seemed like the lack of them. We hadn't had direct contact with a single person since we left and very little sign of any. I checked my watch; it was almost midnight. We were supposed to check in with Sarge so I figured out here would be as good a place as any. At least we could see anyone who might sneak up on us before they got too close.

I stopped the truck, and Thad strung the antenna while I kept watch. He was going to make the first call. I just wanted to stand still for a minute in the quiet. We discussed where we roughly were, and then I walked away from the truck a little. I was thinking of how much closer to home I was when I heard Thad start talking into the radio. He kept it short, just as we were supposed to. I didn't hear the reply, as he was wearing a headset. He signed off and started to take the antenna down. I went over and helped him, and then we all loaded into the truck again.

Things were going fine until we started to pass what looked like a school, or possibly a day care. We had the windows cracked when the sounds of shouting voices came through the thin row of trees separating us from the building. The beams of several flashlights cut through the darkness and really lit up my goggles. I was forced to take them off when the bright headlights from a Jeep came to life at about my two o'clock, followed by the screaming whine of a couple of quads. These weren't like utility machines; these where high-wheeled racers, like the old Quadzilla.

All this was happening on Thad's side of the truck. "Go, go! Get us the fuck outta here!" he yelled.

I floored the gas, and the truck lurched forward. The ATVs were coming on fast, cutting through the trees. The Jeep was racing parallel to us on the drive to the building. I had no idea what these guys wanted, but they were certainly coming on awful strong. That question was answered when one of the ATVs came alongside, and a rider jumped into the bed of the truck. Jess let out a scream. Thad pulled his Glock and fired through the back glass, point-blank into the man's chest. He dropped into the bed of the truck.

The sight of one of their company getting shot didn't deter them at all. The second ATV came up on my side. The passenger pointed a large revolver at my face; he was so close that it was like looking down a sewer pipe. Tapping the brake, I jerked the front end of the truck into the ATV. The jolt rattled the gunman, and he fired a wild shot over the roof of the truck; the muzzle blast was so big it looked for all the world like it was going to set the truck on fire. The fender caught both riders in their right legs, having come in between the wheels. The front wheel of the ATV was being pushed sideways down the road as the nose of the four-wheeler came slowly around the front of the truck. It was the large root of a pine tree that caught the tire and allowed the wheel of the truck to catch it. The tire stopped moving, but the body of the machine was being pushed by the fender, causing it and its two riders to cartwheel. I jerked the wheel to the right, and the whole rolling mess passed by in a blur.

This all happened in a matter of seconds. It seemed like it was in slow motion. I will never forget the look on their faces, or the TapouT shirt the driver was wearing. The first ATV wheeled around to check on his partners. The Jeep was still coming, though. At some point during all of this, I had turned on the headlights. I saw a paved road coming into view ahead. The headlights of the Jeep were flashing strobe-like through the trees in a flashing blur. As we were almost to the paved road, Thad yelled out, "Stop!" I slammed on the brakes and heard his side-by-side roar, and flame filled the truck with a brief flash. He fired both barrels at the same time, filling the Jeep's driver's door and window with holes.

The Jeep passed in front of us and went off the far side of the paved road. There was no sign of brake lights. The truck was filled with the smell of cordite, and I slowly became aware of the high-pitched shrieks of Jess. Thad was reloading the shotty; I tried to calm Jess down.

"Hey, hey, shut the fuck up!" I yelled. I was just a little stressed at the moment, and her caterwauling wasn't helping any. She slapped her hands over her mouth and looked at me with wide eyes. I heard her breath being forced through her fingers.

"What the hell was that about?" Thad's eyes were huge; sweat was pouring down his face.

"I have no idea. I guess it's the new norm," I replied.

I made a quick right onto the paved road and floored it again, trying to put some distance between us and whoever was back there. The wind coming over the top of the windows was the only sound in the cab, the cool air putting a chill on us as we cooled down from the adrenaline rush. Thad looked over his shoulder into the bed of the truck and gasped. "Pull over, Morgan, pull over!"

"Fuck, what now!" I was looking into the rearview mirror. "I don't see anything!"

"In the bed; that guy is in the bed, an' he's movin'!" Thad was looking back through the spiderwebbed glass. Jess was squirming around to look out as well. I quickly stopped the truck, right in the middle of the road—not like anyone was coming. We jumped out and ran around to the bed. There was a young guy lying in there. He was clutching his chest and gasping for breath. Pink frothy blood was around his mouth, running down his cheek.

Thad and I dropped the tailgate, letting it fall this time, and pulled him out onto the ground. We laid him on the pavement; he offered no resistance. Jess came around and looked down. Her hands went to her mouth again, her all too common "oh shit" face. Lying on the road in front of us was what looked like a sixteen- or seventeen-year-old kid. His Dixie Cotton Company T-shirt was covered in blood; the cuff of his Wranglers was slit up the seam to go down over his Justin Ropers. He looked like every kid I saw back around the house.

With a feeble voice, the young man begged for

our help. "Help me; *(gag)* help me." He tried to spit blood out of his mouth, but he simply didn't have enough air in his lungs to do it. A wad of pink frothy blood spilled out onto his chin.

"Oh, shit, he's just a kid. I shot a fucking kid!" Thad had his hands on the top of his head, eyes wide and starting to panic.

"Jess, grab the trauma kit out of my pack." She didn't move. "Jess!" She jumped and moved closer to the bed. Reaching in, she had to throw Thad's pack out of the way to get to mine. Her face went white as she brought her palm up to see it covered in thick, viscous blood.

"Hurry!" I yelled.

She opened my pack. "What's it look like?" She was obviously in shock. Come to think of it, so was this kid.

"It's the bag with the big red fuckin' cross. Now hurry!" She dug down and came out with the pouch, using only her clean hand, the other held out in front of her as if it wasn't hers. I ran around and grabbed my headlamp out of the bag on the floorboard of the truck and put it on as I came back around.

Kneeling down, I cut his shirt off with the EMT sheers from the kit. There was one hole, just low and left of center in his chest. I'm no medic, but the location of the hole and foam on his mouth told me he was hit in the lung. I pulled a Vaseline-coated gauze pad from the kit and some tape. Using the sheers, I cut one side of the gauze package open, slipped it out, and set it on top of the package. Then I tore open a large abdominal pad and used that to wipe the blood away from the wound; then I laid the gauze over the hole and the package on top of that. I tapped down the top, bottom, and inside edge of the dressing to his chest. I pulled a Mylar blanket out of the kit and threw it to Thad. "Here, open this up and cover him. Jess, help him."

Thad was still standing there wide-eyed. Jess was crying. Thad caught the tightly wrapped blanket when I tossed it to him, but he didn't move. He stood there staring down. "Come on, man, open that thing up!" I yelled. Thad finally unfolded it and knelt down beside the kid.

"You stupid ass, why'd you come after us? We weren't bothering you!" Thad was laying the blanket out over him.

The kid was still having a hard time breathing, but he tried to talk. "That's my aunt's day care you robbed." His eyes were wide, and he kept swallowing hard.

"We didn't rob anything!" Thad shouted back. "You think we robbed that damn place. Is that why you came after us?"

"You . . . you didn't break in?" He was not looking good.

"No, we didn't. Can you feel this?" I was rubbing his hands.

"We thought . . . thought you broke in, so we was . . ." he trailed off.

"You just came out after the first people that came along and went after the wrong ones," I said. He rolled his head to the side, looking at me. "Thad, take his feet. We're going to roll him onto his side."

"Oh my god, oh my god, it was all a mistake,

and we shot him!" Jess was starting to freak out again.

Thad was shaking his head. "I can't believe this. He's gonna die, and it was a damned mistake!"

"We have to take him to get some help!" Jess yelled. She seemed frantic and couldn't stand still.

"Where in the hell do you think we're going to take him?" I was holding the kid's head off the pavement. His gold rope chain was hanging out of what was left of his shirt.

Thad stood and looked down the road. "We'll take him to Newberry. It's just back there. Let's pick him up!" He knelt and grabbed the kid's feet and looked up, expecting me to stand and raise his head.

"And do what, Thad? Drive into a town where he's the local and tell them he got shot? How are you going to explain it to them? Look at him. You really think his buddies are going to let *you* ride out of town?" There was no way in hell I was driving this kid back into town.

"What the hell you want to do then? You just gonna leave him here to die? This was an accident. It wasn't our fault!" Thad shouted.

Jess joined in. "We can't do this. We can't leave him here on the side of the road." She was still crying, snot running down her face.

"Look, I don't want to leave him here, but this is his fault, not ours. We were simply the first people to come by, so in their mind we were guilty of a crime we didn't commit." I cannot believe these two. *This is not the time to completely fall the fuck apart.*

"They was just looking for justice for what was

done to them. They made a mistake." Thad just wasn't getting this.

"No, they weren't looking for justice. They were looking for vengeance," I replied.

It looked like I was starting to piss Thad off. He locked eyes with me, and his face was expressionless. "Same thing, Morgan; you're splitting hairs. What we did was wrong, and he's dying. We need to get moving."

"All right, you guys can take him." I stood and pulled my gear from the truck. "But look at it like this. If someone robbed your house, are you going to go outside and beat the first person you catch? Or do you want the guy that robbed your house caught and punished?" I was trying to keep a level voice in the hope he would come around.

"I'd want the guy that did it punished, but what does that have to do with this?" He was getting impatient.

"Because punishing the guy that robbed you is justice. Beating the shit outta the first person you find after it is vengeance. These guys were looking for vengeance, not justice. They made a mistake, not me, and I'm not putting my neck out on the line for his." It looked like he was coming around. Jess, however, was another story.

"You are one coldhearted bastard! How can you be so callous?" she screamed at me. "He's just a kid!"

"You think I'm callous? Maybe I am. Since all this started, I have had to kill three men I know of, maybe more, and been shot in the fuckin' head, and all I want to do is go home! If that makes me callous, then so be it. I am one callous motherfucker. I haven't taken anything from anyone." Well, that wasn't technically true, but then they were dead when I took it. Her whole attitude changed when I mentioned the shot-in-the-head thing. Suddenly, she just didn't have the heart to keep up the argument.

I don't know how much longer we would have gone around about this, but our little circle jerk was interrupted by headlights coming down the road. "Look, here comes someone. If you guys want to wait and explain all this, fine. I'm outta here."

I grabbed my pack and hefted it and was headed to the cab to get the rest of my stuff when I heard Thad yell, "Get in; let's go!" He was headed around the other side. I threw my pack over the side of the bed and climbed in. Jess was still standing there. "You coming or not?" She finally broke out of her trance and made her way around to the passenger side and climbed in. I shut off the headlights, pulled my goggles on, and stomped on the gas as the four-wheeler gained ground. Thad watched out the back window as the ATV came to a stop where the kid was lying on the road.

"They stopped," he said.

"Good," I replied. Both of them were looking solemn. "Hey." They looked over at me. I saw their green faces in the goggles. "He was alive when we left him. We did what we could." In the glowing green gloom of the NVGs, it didn't appear that either of them took any solace in that fact.

We rolled along in silence for a little while. No one was talking. Glancing over at my two companions, it was clear they were distraught. I felt bad for them that they were so upset by what just happened. It was just a different world now. I damn sure didn't want to leave some kid to die on the side of the road, but he and his partners instigated the whole situation, and, fortunately, they had to suffer the consequences, not us. *I'm willing to work with these guys to get us all home, but if they get crazy, I'll leave them in the blink of an eye because, after all, I'm a callous asshole.*

Passing a sign, I saw we were on Parker Road. I remembered that from our map, so I hazarded a stop to check it. As I suspected, this thing ran into US 24 after changing names a couple of times. It was getting late. I just didn't think we would reach Jess's tonight. We were going to have to find a place to stay for what was left of the night.

"Guys, we're going to have to spend the night out. We're not going to make it to your house before it gets light out, and I just don't want to travel in the daylight if we don't have to." I was looking at Jess. Neither of them acknowledged my comment; they both just sat there. I took that as they didn't care either way.

We crossed over 24 without issue. It was so late that the odds of seeing anyone were slim. I kept heading south on what was once Parker Road. I gave up trying to look at the street signs. The road made a little jog ahead; a sand track went off to the east. Stopping there, I pondered the options and decided to take the little track. Easing onto it, I let the truck idle along, watching for any sign of life, and saw nothing. After about a quarter mile, the little track got pretty rough, but I pushed ahead. Trees were on both sides of us, but we entered a field that was open on the left, with a tree line on our right side. Passing the field, we came back into the trees again. Crossing a little road, we entered another stand of planted pine. In the middle was a small clearing with a strip of trees running down the center.

Stopping the truck under those trees and killing the engine, we sat and listened for any sound. There was nothing on the air. "We'll stay here tonight. Let's get out and take a look around." I hopped out and stretched. The other two finally made their way out and just milled about on the passenger side. "Look, you two need to snap out of this shit. What's done is done, and we didn't start that fight."

"It don't change nothing," Thad said as he walked off to look around.

"I'll stay here and watch the truck," Jess said as she let the tailgate down, looping the rope around the pin and sitting down.

"Suit yourself," I said as I walked away, slinging the carbine over my shoulder to have a look around. This little clearing was shaped sort of like a kidney bean, with that strip of trees running down the length of it. There didn't appear to be any houses nearby or any other roads. This would work just fine.

Heading back to the truck, I pulled out the antenna and slick line. Throwing the slick line up through one of the tall pines in the center of the clearing, I pulled the antenna up and connected it to the radio. I sat in the truck and scanned the frequencies for any traffic. I heard some stuff, a lot of foreign languages, but very little in the way of English. Thad and Jess were rummaging around in their packs. I assumed they were hungry; they weren't saying much.

We had a couple more hours before we needed to check in with Sarge. So I decided to set my tarp up off the side of the truck, tying one side to the bed and staking out the other with the tent stakes. I unrolled my sleeping pad and laid my bag out on it. With home set for the night, I wasn't really hungry but decided to make a cup of coffee using one of the heaters and the "Hot Beverage Bag." This made a nice, warm cup of water, and that just wasn't going to cut it. I pulled out my stove and set it up on the tailgate and used a canteen cup to make a real cup of coffee, as real as MRE instant coffee can be anyway.

Seeing how those two were acting, I told them I would take the first watch and for them to try to get some sleep. They set their shelters up on the other side of the truck from mine. Guess they were pissed at me, but we were all still alive and had a set of wheels. If we had gone back to Newberry, we would have certainly lost one or both of those. I sat on the tailgate with the carbine across my lap and enjoyed my coffee. It was quiet and cool out. There were no clouds in the sky, and stars shone with an intensity seldom seen prior to the event. I had plenty of time to sit and think about home and what might happen next.

Sarge's words about martial law came back to mind—how it had already been declared, but we just didn't know yet. If that was true, it made for a really ominous thought. Why isn't the government around to help folks? What was their intent? And what was their endgame? It was around five in the morning while I was lost in thoughts of home when a strange sound came out of the night. It took me a minute to realize I was actually hearing something. I stood up and looked around, scanning the sky all around. The low wump, wump, wump was getting a little louder; it had to be a helicopter. Somewhere up there was a helicopter. Grabbing the goggles, I pulled them on and scanned the visible sky, nothing. But there was no doubt it was out there.

That disembodied sound gave me the creeps. Mike and his guys said they were inserted by helo for a recon that they wouldn't talk about. Thinking about that bothered me too. If those guys were "off the reservation" as they said, why wouldn't they spill the beans about what they knew? If they were truly on our side, it seems to me they would be willing to give any intel they had. So helicopters used to insert troops. Helicopter heard overhead. Are troops being inserted around here? Now that was just paranoia. No time for that. I guess if they have a FLIR on board, they might see the truck, but no one was actively looking for us. I hoped.

Six o'clock rolled around, and it was time to make a call. I powered up the radio and tuned to the preset freq for the day. "Walker calling Foxtrot Sierra Mike." I repeated the call.

"Walker, this is Foxtrot Sierra Mike. I have you five-by-five," came the reply through the headset.

"Foxtrot Sierra Mike, authenticate blue," I referenced my code sheet.

"Walker, I authenticate Lima," came the voice again.

I started into the SITREP. "SITREP to follow, SNAFU, ten miles east-southeast of Delta."

What this told them was that nothing had changed and gave them an idea of where we were. This code wasn't very sophisticated, but we weren't dealing with anything really important.

"Roger Walker, I copy SNAFU, ten miles east-southeast of Delta. Use caution; there are unfriendly ears on the air now. Foxtrot Sierra Mike out."

"Roger, Walker out," I replied.

I wondered what the hell that meant, "unfriendly ears"? Who else was listening, the government? And if so, why in the hell was that a bad thing? We couldn't use the radio as we drove because all we had was the wire antenna; the ability to listen to it as we drove, getting more intel as to what was going on, sure would be nice.

I sat up until after sunrise, letting the others sleep. The sound of the helo last night disappeared not long after I heard it, almost as fast as it showed up. I went around to the other side of the truck and woke up Thad. "Hey, man, your watch." I kicked the bottom of his sleeping bag. He climbed out and stretched.

"Sorry about the way I acted, Morg," he said by way of a morning greeting.

"No sweat, man. It's a hard thing to do. I didn't like it any better than you guys, but I want to get home," I replied.

"Well, I want to get home too. It's just a lot to get used to," he said as he went around to the back of the truck.

"Yes, it is. My stove is back there if you want to

make some coffee or anything," I said as I crawled into my bag.

"Thanks, man, get some sleep." I heard him digging around in his pack.

"Oh, by the way, I heard a helicopter last night," I said as I took off my coat.

He quickly came over to where he could see into my shelter, "A helicopter, really?"

"Yeah, never saw it though. Just be careful, and don't draw any attention if you see one," I said.

"Yeah, probably not a good idea," he said and walked back to the tailgate of the truck. I went to sleep quickly and didn't dream.

I slept until about five in the afternoon. I guess last night's events took a lot out of me. When I woke up, I was seriously hungry. Jess and Thad both seemed to be in a better mood. We were all gathered around the tailgate, eating our MRE dinner. I made a canteen cup of "grape drank." It was a nice change from just water but would probably give me the shits.

"You guys feeling better?" I asked as I stuffed some meatloaf into my mouth. Thad nodded and grunted as he chewed on some enchilada.

Jess was picking through her something and macaroni. "Yeah, I had time to think about what happened, and you're right. If we had taken him into Newberry, we would have had some trouble. No matter how right we were, they probably wouldn't have wanted to hear what we had to say. I remember a picture I saw in school of an Asian soldier shooting a guy in the head with a little pistol. That could have happened to us. Just thinking about it scared the shit out of me. I just want to go home."

"It could have, or they may have understood. We could have all said our apologies and gone on our way, but it's a gamble that's just not worth it. I want to get home too," I replied. "Did you guys hear or see anything today?"

Thad was licking his spoon clean. "I heard a motorcycle or an ATV earlier, but it was far off and never came close." He stuck his spoon in the pocket of the coat. "Let's start to pack up so we can get on the road as soon as it's dark. How long do you think till we get to Jess's?"

"It shouldn't take too long. We can't be more than ten or fifteen miles at the outside," I answered as I finished the last bite of loaf. We took down all our shelters and packed our gear back in our packs. They started to just throw their stuff in the bed of the truck, but I told them we needed to be packed in case we had to bail from the truck. It was about six o'clock, and time to make our call. I went to the cab of the truck and turned the radio on. Consulting my code sheet, I tuned to today's frequency. "Walker calling Foxtrot Sierra Mike." Again, I repeated the call.

"Foxtrot Sierra Mike, I have you five by nine. Go ahead, Walker."

"Authenticate yellow," I gave our simple challenge.

"Authenticate Delta," came the correct answer.

"SITREP to follow, SNAFU, same location as last." We had agreed to keep things as brief as possible and to the point.

"Roger that, Walker. I copy SNAFU, same location as previous. Foxtrot Sierra Mike out." Sarge, or one of the other guys, from the sound of the voice, signed off.

Before I could sign off, another transmission came over the radio. "Foxtrot Sierra Mike, this is Army Blackhawk Yankee Whisky five-niner. Please identify yourself." I clearly heard the wump, wump, wump in the background. We had discussed this sort of thing, although the guys didn't think it was likely. In the event we were called by anyone else on the radio, we were to immediately "go dark" and displace. We were to cease all transmissions for twenty-four hours.

Jumping out of the truck, I started to pull down the disconnected antenna. "We gotta move, guys, quick! Let's get moving."

"What's up? Did you get ahold of them?" Thad was closing the tailgate.

"Yeah, I got them, but an Army Blackhawk came over the radio, calling them. They said if anything like this happened, we were to move right away. So let's go." I threw the antenna onto the floor of the truck and jumped into the driver's seat, my carbine lying by the door.

"What's a Blackhawk, what's that?" Jess asked.

"It's an Army helicopter, and prolly ain't no good for us," Thad said as he climbed into the passenger side and slammed the door.

"But it isn't dark yet. We aren't supposed to leave until it's dark," she countered.

"Yeah, but we need to move. We were supposed to move after making our call last night. I just didn't feel like it. Won't do that again," I said as I started the truck and headed across the clearing. "Keep your ears open for any helicopters," I said. Thad and I both rolled down our windows.

We finally found our way out of the trees, coming out behind a small neighborhood of houses. It was twilight and not quite dark out yet. Showing up behind these houses got us some looks from a couple of people. One house had some folks in their backyard cooking on a Weber Grill. When we came out of the trees, they just stood there frozen, staring at the truck. I sped up to get us away from the houses as fast as possible. As we passed the last house, a young woman came out from the side, waving her arms and yelling. We didn't give her any notice beyond making sure she wasn't armed.

Just past the last house was a paved road—a small rural road with houses off either side; however, they were set pretty far back from the road. This road ran east, and that was just the way I wanted to go. I was running pretty fast down the road; it was now dark enough that I needed the goggles. "Jess, hold the wheel." I pulled out the goggles, pulled them onto my head and powered 'em up. In less than a mile, the road dead-ended into another paved road. There was a sign just before the intersection that said SR 121. That was good news because the road we wanted was off that. The only problem was I didn't know if we were north or south of it.

"All right, guys, which way? North or south?" We had a fifty-fifty chance on this.

"Left," Thad and Jess both said about the same time.

"Good, that's what I thought too," I replied as I turned out onto the road.

Thank the Lord for rural, sparsely inhabited roads. There isn't much on SW Williston Road, the other name for SR 121. We rolled along without incident for quite a while. Another road intersected with 121 on the right side, but it came in at about a thirty-degree angle, or less. I actually passed it and had to back up to see the street sign, Wacahoota Road. This was the one we were looking for. I made a hard right turn onto the road and started down it. This was the home stretch for us. I was speeding up without noticing it; I just wanted to get to her house. At about eight o'clock, we came around a corner, and I saw the light from a small fire in the distance.

"There's something up ahead," I said.

"Yeah, I can see the light," Thad said, squinting his eyes against the dark. "What is it?"

"Looks like a little fire. But I can't really tell." We were sitting in the road, the truck was idling. I started to creep forward, giving the truck just enough gas to move. As we slowly got closer, I started to realize what it was. There was an overpass ahead.

"It's an overpass over 75, but it looks like there is a roadblock on it," I said, keeping my eyes on the light of the dancing flame. It looked like it was a burn barrel, and I saw two men on this side. Who knew how many were on the other side?

"I know where we are now. On the other side is 441. We make a left, and our house isn't far," Jess said.

"That's great, but there's a highway, and this overpass, between us and it. How the hell are we going to get around these guys?" Thad asked.

"I don't know," I said absentmindedly.

If we were this close to Jess's house, we really needed to get across this bridge. I started to come up with an idea. "Let's try this," I said.

"Jess, you get out and walk up there. I'm going to follow you off to the side with the goggles. I'll be close. Try and talk to them, and see if we can get through. If anything hinky happens, I'll be right there."

"I'm not going out there in the dark—no freakin' way, man," she protested.

"Look, we're close to your house. There could be someone you know up there. If anything happens, I'll be right there. We have to get across this. It's our last barrier." I was trying to reason with her.

"What about me?" Thad asked.

"You stay with the truck. If it's clear I'll flash my light at you three times, then you can bring the truck up." This could work, depending on what happened on the bridge.

"I don't want to, and I'm telling you now this isn't going to go well," Jess complained.

"Fine; let me out," Jess said, so Thad opened his door and got out. Jess followed him. I got out of my side and took the carbine with me. Thad got in the driver's side, and Jess and I started down the road.

"You better be right behind me," Jess said with an edge to her voice.

"I'll be right behind you, just don't be looking back, and call out to them as you get close. You don't want them to think you're sneaking up on them. If there is any shooting, hit the ground." I moved farther off the edge of the road, trying to stay in shadows as best as I could. Trying to move with some stealth, Jess got out ahead of me, not far, but there was now enough distance that it offered me a little protection from being sighted.

When Jess was about thirty or forty yards from the roadblock, she called out to them. I immediately took a knee behind a clump of wild grapevines.

"Hello!"

The three men at the roadblock instantly jumped, grabbing up their rifles. I don't know where that third one had been, but we were pretty far away when I first saw them. What I hadn't expected was the damn spotlight they turned on. It instantly caused the goggles to shut down. Moving very slowly, I took them off and laid them at my feet and readied my rifle, turning the safety off.

"Who's there?" a voice called out.

"It's just me. Can I come closer?" Jess was shading her eyes with her hand from the intense light.

"Are you alone? Who are you?" The voice from behind the light came again.

"Yes, I'm alone. Can I come up?"

"Come on up," the spotlight said again. I heard the three men talking but couldn't really understand them. From my position I saw one of them run down the embankment of the overpass to the left, opposite my side of the road. Jess was walking up with her hand still over her eyes.

"That's far enough. Raise your jacket and turn around," the spotlight said. Jess lifted her jacket and did a little circle.

"Is that a gun?" the voice called out.

"Of course it is. Who in the hell would be out

without one?" she answered. They saw her pistol that she had stuck in her back pocket.

"You just keep your hands where we can see 'em and stay there. Mark, go out there and check her out. See what she wants." The man that had run down the embankment came out from the brush at the side of the road. He held a shotgun at waist level and walked out to her. As he got closer, he lowered his weapon and rushed forward. Jess turned toward him and wrapped her arms around him, and he, his free arm around her. They stood there for a moment in an embrace before they released one another and began to ask rapid questions of each other. After a moment of animated talk, Jess turned and called out, "Morgan, come over here!" I walked out from behind the clump of vines I was hiding behind, slung my rifle, and walked over to them.

"Morgan, this is my brother, Mark!" she said in an animated tone. "Mark, this is Morgan. He helped me get home." The young man stuck out his hand, and I shook it.

"Nice to meet you. You guys had us worried," I said.

"Well, to be honest, you scared the shit out of me. I didn't even see you," he replied.

I pulled the flashlight from my cargo pocket, pointed it down the road and flashed it three times. The headlights on the truck came on, and it started to move forward. Mark looked down the road. "There's more of you?"

"Yeah, that's Thad. He helped too," Jess said. She was holding her older brother's hand and bouncing on the balls of her feet. Thad pulled up and climbed out of the truck. Mark's eyes got wide. "Damn, you're a big dude!"

"So I've been told. Thad." He stuck his huge hand out, and Mark's hand disappeared into it as they shook.

"Looks like you had plenty of help to get back," Mark said to his sister. "I hope she wasn't too much trouble for you guys."

Thad looked at me and started to laugh. "You have no idea," I slowly replied.

Chapter 6

We were escorted across the bridge over I-75. There was a roadblock on the other side with a couple more guys there. This was a real ad hoc affair with no clear picture of what they were actually up to. I hopped into the back of the truck and let Mark and Jess ride up front, with Thad driving. We turned north off the little road not far from the overpass. Apparently, though, this wasn't Jess's house. We pulled off into a nice little hammock of oaks. There were a couple of houses under here and what looked like a damn campground. The truck pulling in brought some people running up and others fleeing in the opposite direction.

Jess and her brother got out. He was talking to a few people in the crowd. Jess looked a little confused. "What are we doing here?" she asked as she climbed out.

"We had to move here. It wasn't safe at our house. There are some bad dudes running around," Mark replied. About that time, an older man came running up, and Jess threw her arms around him. He grabbed her in his and lifted her off the ground, spinning her around. They hugged for a moment until an older woman came up; he released her, and she and the woman embraced. A small crowd was around them. I assumed they were her mom and dad.

While they were saying their hellos, I looked around the area. What looked like family campsites were scattered around under the trees, with a few houses spaced around the little area. From the looks of things, a number of these folks were accidental residents. Some of the shelters were like shanties from the slums of Rio or some other third world hellhole. Several small fires were burning, some with pots over them, and some with children and adults sitting around the flames. There appeared to be an attempt at order to all this, but it was weak.

The old man I took to be Jess's dad walked up to me and stuck out his hand. "I want to thank you for getting my daughter home to me. We were so worried about her. We didn't know what to do. We were scared we'd never see her again. Thanks." We shook hands. He had tears in his eyes, and it was obvious his words were heartfelt.

"No problem. It was quite a journey, but we made it. I'm Morgan."

"Name's Jim," he replied. "Nice to meet you."

"Likewise. Looks like you have quite a few folks here," I said, looking around the area.

"Yeah. It's been hell. We had to leave our house. There's a band of brigands running around, taking what they want, raping, killing. A bunch of us came here to kinda help each other out. That house there belongs to my friend Bill Higgins." He pointed to a nice little house sitting in a patch of trees. A smokestack jutted out from the side of it before turning up above the roof.

"So all these folks are from the area?" I asked.

"No, not all of them. Some of them came off the interstate. They didn't have anywhere to go, so we took them in. Most of them are in the camps. We just had to make do with what we had." He nodded toward some of the shanties. "There's a bunch of kids here too; they're having a hard time with all this. There isn't enough food, water, clothes, or anything, for that matter. We can't really go look for anything because none of the cars around here run, but now that you're here with that truck, we can." He was looking at our truck expectantly.

"Well, Jim, we aren't going to be around here long. Thad and I want to get home as soon as we can." I looked over at Thad.

"What? You guys can't leave. Those animals out there will kill ya. You should stay here with us. We could use the help, and you need a safe place to stay—just makes sense." He had an earnest look on his face. He believed in what he was saying, but it just wasn't going to happen. I didn't want to try to get into this discussion right now, so I just dismissed it.

"How are you guys fixed for security?" I was curious about this, as I didn't see anyone armed in the camp.

"We have the roadblocks at both ends of the overpass you saw. Then at the end of the road, down here at 441, there is another. It has more men because that's where most of the trouble comes from. We have enough guns at those places that no one has tried anything yet. There's been one of them big, older army trucks that cruises by every now and then with a bunch of guys in it." He was cut off by Jess's mom walking up.

She came up to me with tears in her eyes and wrapped her arms around my neck, squeezing me tight. Thad was behind her with that big grin on his face. She finally let me go. "Morgan, I can't thank you enough for bringing Jessica home to me. I have been worried to death; I couldn't sleep. But she's here now. The Lord provided you two to bring her back safe and sound."

"You're welcome. We all helped each other. I'm just glad we made it here. There were a couple of times we were really worried." I gave her a smile.

"Well, you're safe now. You're here with us. You made it," she said in return.

"We are here, ma'am, but Thad and I will be on our way soon. We both want to get home also." The look on her face was the same one Jim had given me.

"You know what it's like out there; you need to stay here with us. It's just too dangerous," she countered.

"Yes, ma'am, I know what it's like out there, but I have a family that I need to get home to." I gave her another smile.

She just looked at me and smiled. "We'll talk about it tomorrow after you've had some rest. By the way, I'm Beth. Thank you again," she said.

With that she walked away and headed toward the truck. Thad came up beside me. "They seem awful set on us staying here with 'em."

"Not nearly as set as I am about getting home. How about you?" I cocked my head toward him.

"I'm with ya. I'm ready to leave right now. But they keep talking about the bandits out there. They shore are scared of 'em. Must be a bad bunch," he replied to me.

"Maybe. Let's check things out and get a feel for this place. Maybe we can refill our water. I say tomorrow night we head out."

"Sounds good to me," Thad replied.

We walked over to the truck, where a small group gathered around it. We made our way through it to find people pulling our packs out of the bed. "Hold on there; I'll take that." I grabbed my pack from a guy in his twenties. Thad had to grab his from another.

"Hey, man, we were just going to go put this with all the other stuff. We have to share everything so we all have enough." He reluctantly released his grip on my bag.

"That's fine and dandy, but this is mine, and we don't plan on staying here. We'll be on our way tomorrow," I said to him. He obviously didn't like what I had to say.

Cutting his eyes toward the cab of the truck, he said, "Yeah, well, you'll have to leave your guns in the house. No one carries guns around here. It keeps people from fighting and getting out of hand."

"So who sees to that?" I asked.

"We have security. They carry guns." He gave a sideways glance to the man that had been holding Thad's pack.

"That's all fine and good, but we are keeping our guns," Thad said. I nodded in agreement.

"We'll see what Bill has to say about that," the guy said over his shoulder as he walked off.

"I'm gonna grab the key to the truck and keep it with me. I don't trust these folks." I walked around to the driver's side and pulled the key out and pocketed it.

Jess came walking up. "Hey, guys, y'all come with me. You're going to stay with us tonight. Mom's making dinner, and there is a spare room you two can sleep in."

"Sounds good to me. I'm hungry," Thad said, patting his belly.

"You're always hungry. I bet you ate like a horse when you were a kid," I said as I shouldered one strap of my pack and picked up the carbine with my other hand.

"Yeah, Momma said she felt like she was feeding the entire football team," he said with a smile.

We followed Jess into the house; it was another typical little Florida house built of cypress board siding, with a wraparound porch on two sides and a metal roof. It was a nice little house. Inside, the walls looked like the same cypress paneling, only these were sealed. The floors were heart pine boards. A fireplace occupied a corner of the small living room, a nice fire of oak logs burning in it. Beyond the living room was the kitchen; a plump older woman was in there at work on a propane stove. Jess's mom was there as well. Another man came out from a door off the living room. He walked up and offered his hand.

"Bill Higgins, nice to meet cha," he said in a thick southern drawl. "That's ma wife, Mary, thur in the kitchen." The round-faced woman looked up and gave us a smile with her lips pressed hard together. Thad and I introduced ourselves, and we all shook hands. "Come on in and have a seat. You can set yer gear by the door thur." He motioned to the kitchen; a nice butcher-block style table with side chairs took up a prominent place.

Thad and I set our packs down and took off our coats. I took off the small pack on my waist and laid it down but pulled the XD out and placed it in my waistband. Thad had his pistol in a nylon Uncle Mike's holster on his waist. Jim came in behind us with an armload of wood. He set the wood down by the fireplace and came into the kitchen. We all took a seat around the table. Mary and Beth were still at work in the kitchen. Mary came over and set a coffee percolator on the table along with several mugs. She went back to the counter and returned with a can of powdered creamer, a jar of sugar, and a spoon, and laid it on the table without saying a word.

"Thank you, ma'am," Thad said. She looked back with another tight-lipped smile, and I raised my mug to her and tipped my head. She turned and went back to the counter with Beth.

Bill passed the pot around. We all poured a cup except Jess. After everyone had their cups filled, Bill looked at Thad and me. "How was the trip?"

"About what you'd expect. Things are getting worse," Thad said as he took a drink of black coffee from his cup.

"They sure are. That's why we're all here," Jim said, looking at Bill and nodding his head. I was getting the distinct feeling that Bill was the man around here.

"Y'all run inta any bandits or have trouble with anyone?" Bill asked.

Thad and I took turns giving a rather vanilla version of our trip. We gave them the basic facts but didn't elaborate. When Thad shared the part about my head wound, Jess dropped her head and stared at the table. Bill and her dad both looked at her. As we were winding down, Mary carried a large pot over to the table and sat it on a pot holder. Beth carried over a stack of bowls and, using a large ladle, poured a scoop into each bowl and passed them around. Mary returned with a cake of corn bread, the bright yellow kind from the mix sold in small boxes. Mary and Beth disappeared from the kitchen. Bill put his hands out to Jim and Thad, "Let's say grace." We all joined hands around the table. Bill closed his eyes and began to pray.

"Lord, thank you for the food we are about to receive. Thank you for the blessings you have bestowed upon us, and thank you for bringing little Jessica home to us. We thank you for these two men, Morgan and Thad, who didn't abandon her in her time of need. We pray that you will watch over us and give us your blessing. In Jesus's name, amen." There were a few amens from around the table, and everyone took up their spoons.

The stew, soup, or whatever it was, was rather tasty if a little watery. It was obvious these folks were trying to stretch everything. Bill was chewing a spoonful of stew when he looked over at me. "From what ya've told me, y'all ran into some hard times. Did you have to kill?" He was looking at the pistol on Thad's side.

"Yes, sir, we did. I took no joy from it. I pray I never have to again," I said directly to him.

"That's a hard thing," he said. He was looking through a spot on the table. "We have taken in a lot of people here. Some of them are far from home and have no hope of ever seeing it again. We gotta do what we have to to survive. You boys are welcome here. You'll be a big help to us. With that truck we can go out and find more food and be able to bring back more water at a time." He took another bite of the stew.

"Mr. Higgins, we appreciate your hospitality, we truly do. But I got a wife and a boy I need to get home to. Morgan has a family too. We'll be on the road tomorrow." Thad laid his spoon down, ready for the argument he knew was coming.

Nothing more was said about the issue. We finished eating, and the ladies came and took the bowls. Those that wanted it had another cup of coffee. We talked of such things as getting water and rationing food. Lake Wauberg was at the end of the road, on the other side of 441. They were using a garden cart and any container they could find to collect water from the lake and bring it back. Water for drinking was boiled in a huge stockpot. They were eating whatever they could find. Those that came here from their homes nearby brought whatever food they had. They fished in the lake and tried to hunt, unsuccessfully so far.

There were seventeen people here now, and every day more came out of Gainesville down 411 and others from I-75. They were turning people away now, not letting them into the small area they occupied, sandwiched between the interstate and 441. It was far from an ideal position. Bill stood up. "I'm gonna turn in. You boys is welcome to sleep in the spare room. They's two beds in there." He left the kitchen, and we heard a door shut. I never saw Mary, but I assume she was already in there.

Jim looked at Thad. "You'll have to leave your pistol here. We lock 'em so no one tries anything. This many people around it can get dangerous." He sat with his hands folded on the table and said it as if it was a matter of fact.

"Mr. Jim, I am sorry, but ain't no one takin' my guns from me, period. We'll be leaving tomorrow. We'll just hang onto them until then." Thad stood up. "I'll sleep in the truck tonight." Thad headed for the door, picked up his gear, and walked out.

Jim looked at me sorta wide-eyed. "But we had to do this. There has been some trouble. We can't let folks walk around with guns. Bill set the rules. This is his place."

"I can appreciate that, but we aren't staying. We'll be gone tomorrow, and I agree with Thad, I will not give my guns up." I stood up and turned for the door.

"We need that truck. There's so many people here. We need to be able to go out and find things, food an' such." Jim stood up.

"That truck is ours, and we're leaving tomorrow. Thank you for the dinner." I headed for the door and grabbed my gear, slinging the rifle African style over my left shoulder.

"Where you goin'? The room's right there." Jim was walking out of the kitchen.

"I'm gonna sleep in the truck too." I walked out the door.

I closed the door without waiting for his protest. Back outside, things appeared to be winding down. Many were sitting around their fires; some were already in their shanties. I found Thad at the truck talking with another man. He was one of the ones that had gathered around the truck earlier. Thad gave me a sideways look as I came up. The other man noticed me and stuck out his hand. "Hey, name's Dave." I shook his hand and introduced myself.

"I hear you guys say you're leaving tomorrow." He leaned an elbow on the bed.

"Yes, we are, soon as we can," I replied matter-of-factly.

"I heard you're headed south." He was fishing. I knew what he was up to.

"I am; he isn't, and we aren't taking on any passengers. We stopped by to drop her off. This isn't the city bus," Thad said. Dave didn't take that well. His entire demeanor changed, a furrow deepening in his brow.

"I want to get home too. Who the hell are you to tell me I can't?" He stood upright and straightened his back. For all the world he looked as if he was ready to fight. "This isn't even your truck. Jess told us how you got it—you stole it!"

"Look, this isn't the fucking debate club, and we aren't going to debate this with you. I didn't say you couldn't go home. You're free to do what you want, except ride in this truck. You can walk to wherever you're going just as I'm going to do. As for stealing the truck, we didn't steal it. The previous occupants attacked us, and they came out on the short end of the stick on that deal. This is our truck." I had had about all of these freakin' people that I could stand.

"Yeah, I heard about that. If it wasn't for Jess, you'd be dead," he threw his impotent taunt out. Thad started to laugh; the man faced him. "What're you laughin' at?"

"That's funny, 'if it wasn't for Jess.' You know she is the one that shot him in the head, right?" Thad hung his head, shaking it back and forth, laughing.

"But if she didn't drag him out, he'd be dead." He was trying to make a point that didn't exist.

Thad looked up at him. "No, he wouldn't be either. I'd have got him." His face was expressionless.

Dave decided to take the offensive since his fucked-up logic wasn't working. "Who the hell do you guys think you are to decide who's gonna do what?"

"We're not; like I already said, you're free to go as you will. Now, I'm done talking to you." I expected him to leave, but he just stood there. "Now."

"You can't tell me to do anything!" he yelled back. I raised my face to the sky. *What the hell is wrong with people?*

Thad reached into the cab of the truck and pulled his thunder stick out. "Now I've had enough. Get the hell away from us." He was holding the shotty with one hand, down his leg. Apparently this guy wasn't a complete paste-eating fool. He got that message and stomped off muttering to himself.

"I knew that was coming. He was asking all

kinds of questions. He wanted us to take him and his wife down toward Polk City," Thad said.

"It's amazing how everyone turns into a good little collectivist when they don't have anything," I replied, shaking my head. I was standing there, leaning against the bed, when I noticed the gas cans were not there. "Hey, man, where are the gas cans?"

Thad looked over the side. "Don't know."

"Those rotten sons of bitches. You stay here. I'm gonna find them. I have an idea where they are," I said as I picked the carbine back up.

"Oh yeah, where?" Thad asked.

"Well, the lights were on in ole Bill's house. There has to be a generator somewhere," I replied. I started off toward Bill's house. I couldn't hear a generator, but I was sure it was there somewhere. Jim came out of the dark as I got closer to the house.

"What'cha doing there, Morgan?" he asked in a friendly enough voice.

"I'm looking for my gas cans. Know where they are?" I was equally polite and nonthreatening.

"Yeah, we took 'em to use on the generators. We needed the gas. We're almost out," he replied.

"Did you ever consider asking for it? Or did your folks just take it?" I was still nice and polite.

"Oh, well, one of the guys brought it over. We just thought you would be sharing it. Here we share everything, equally." He seemed a little surprised by my question.

"Well, I need them back. It's my gas, not yours. I already told you we weren't staying here. Where's my cans?" I said with a slight edge to my voice.

"They're back there." He pointed to a small shed

off to the side of the house. "But like I said, if any of us are gonna make it, we gotta work together. We have to share equally."

I walked past him toward the shed; he was immediately on my heels. The shed had a padlock on the door. I turned to him. "Open it."

"I don't have the key," he said, shaking his head.

"Equal, huh? Go get the key, or I'll take the lock off permanently." I shifted the carbine in my hands so the muzzle was pointing at the lock.

"Hold on now, just hold on. I'll go get it." He turned to the house and disappeared in the dark. Standing there in the dark, I heard him go into the house. In the clear, cold air of night, I heard him shuffling around on the wood floors. A moment later, I heard the door open again, and he came out talking with another person. I wasn't surprised to see Bill with him.

"What can I do fer ya?" Bill said as he walked up. Jim stayed behind him.

"You can open this shed and give me my gas cans back. My full gas cans. We are about ready to be on our way," I said.

"Well, now, we figured since y'all was here, you'd be willing to help ever'one out. I mean, after all, we helped you." He stuck his thumbs through his suspenders, rather proud of the spot he thought he had us in.

"And how exactly have you helped us?" I looked past Bill to Jim. "We're only here because we brought your daughter home. I don't owe you shit. If anything you owe me. But I'm not asking for anything other than to have what is mine returned to me."

"Well, you set at my table tonight and ate my food. Now you owe me. Jess is his daughter, not mine." Bill was definitely the chief over this rabble.

"Oh, for fuck sake, you invited us in. I'm done with this discussion. You going to open the damn door or not? If not I'll open it." I raised the rifle.

"Now hold on there, son. Come on out, boys." Three men walked out of the darkness, all armed, and formed a line behind Bill. "The way I see it, we'll just call us even, the gas for the meal."

"I certainly don't see it that way. Last chance," I said.

"If you pull that trigger, these men will shoot you. It's a fair deal. You can be on your way." Bill was stacking the deck, and three armed men made it less than favorable odds for me.

I stood there for a minute; Bill never blinked. It was obvious he was quite happy with his new position of having everyone around beholden to him. "You ready to die too, Bill, 'cause I guarantee you one thing, I will kill you."

"I guess I'm as ready as you are," he said. I thought about the situation and came up with another idea.

"I tell you what, Bill, you can keep it. But if anyone comes out near our truck, I'll shoot 'em on sight. We'll be on our way soon." I turned and walked away.

"We ain't gonna bother ya none. Good luck to ya," he said as I walked away. I heard him talking to the little group gathered around him. "See, little simple logic works ever' time." They all got a little chuckle out of it.

Thad was still at the truck when I got back. "Where's the gas?" he asked.

"They have it locked up. Bill brought his boys with him to make a point. He claims it's an even trade for the wonderful dinner we had."

"That's bullshit. We need that gas. It ain't enough for me to get home, but it will get me a long way. How are we going to get more gas? Why don't we just take it? It's ours." Thad was pissed, and so was I.

"Is ten gallons of gas worth killing over? I mean, I want it as bad as you do, but are you ready to kill people for it? In their fucked-up logic, they are doing what they think is right; right or wrong, they are looking out for themselves." I didn't know what to do.

"I don't want to kill anyone, man. All I want to do is go home, but they are doing the same thing to us as those raiders they keep talking about. They're no better than them. How much gas is left in the truck?" I threw him the key, and he leaned into the driver's door and turned the key on. "Just over a quarter of a tank, if it's right," he said as he came out of the cab.

"Well, we got two choices: we leave with what we got, or we try and take it back," I said.

"How do we try and get it back?" Thad pulled the key and put it in his pocket.

"Wait till everyone is asleep and break into the shed. The hasp on it is on wrong—the screws are exposed on one side. I can take them out with my Leatherman tool. Then we try and get the hell out of here without getting shot." I noticed the hasp configuration when I had the muzzle of the carbine pointed at it. I hadn't seen anyone around here with guns other than the crew that came out with Bill; with the guys at the two roadblocks, that didn't leave too many more here, but I was sure there had to be someone around. I was looking around the area but didn't see anyone.

Thad and I spent the next few hours sitting around in the back of the truck. I had the NGVs out and would look around every now and then. No one was about; the little camp was quiet, and the houses were dark. We weren't talking much, trying to keep quiet. What little talking we did was in low whispers. At about a quarter to three in the morning, I heard a door shut on one of the houses; it didn't slam, but I definitely heard the hinge squeak and the latch catch. Looking through the goggles, I scanned the area, looking for whoever was out. The glow of a flashlight behind a house caught my attention. It was illuminating the trees above and was obviously moving. I tapped Thad on the shoulder and pointed in the direction of the light. He let out a low "Uh-huh."

The light came out from behind the house, and I took off the goggles. The light went to the shed. Whoever was holding it fumbled around for a minute, and the distinct rattle of a padlock being opened drifted through the night.

I leaned over to Thad and in a low whisper, said, "It's one guy; now's our chance. If we want to take it, we have to go now. What do you want to do?"

"Let's go get it. It's ours, and I need it." He stood up and grabbed his shotty. "If we sneak up on him, we can get him without any noise. I can put him to sleep," he said and then started toward the shed in a low crouch. Thankfully, the area was sandy, and there were few leaves on the ground. I flipped the goggles down and moved in a low crouch toward the shed. The man who opened it went in and closed the door, light from his flashlight leaking around the door.

For a big man, Thad was quite stealthy. He moved in near silence. The only sound I heard was my heart trying to beat its way out of my chest. We came up to the shed on the hinge side of the door; Thad was in front of me. He stuck his coach gun out, and I took it. We heard the man in there—cans thumping together, the sound of boxes being opened. We stood there for what seemed like forever. Finally, the door swung open, and the man came out with a box under one arm. He stepped out and turned to close the door. Thad instantly grabbed him in a sleeper hold and lifted him off his feet. The box hit the ground with a dull thud. He was grabbing at Thad's huge forearm, trying to break free. With Thad's python of a forearm wrapped around his neck, he wasn't able to call out. Thad had him locked up. In a few seconds, he went limp. The big man gently laid him on the ground. "We need to hurry."

Stepping in front of the door, I clicked on my flashlight. All we could do was stand there. We were shocked at what we saw.

Sitting on a mattress on the floor were two young girls in their teens. They were chained to the floor; their clothes were filthy, and they were terrified. When the beam from my light fell on them, they turned their faces and tried to move to the walls, hiding their faces with their hands. Stacked in a corner was flat after flat of various canned goods. Boxes of dry goods filled shelves in the back of the shed. "What the fuck?" Thad said in a low voice. The guy on the ground started to groan; he was coming around. Thad reached down with one hand and pulled him to his feet. "What the fuck is this?" he said in a hoarse whisper into his face.

When the girls heard Thad's voice, they looked over as he pulled the man up. Almost in unison they cried out, "Help us! Please help us!" They tried to stand, but the chains tied their hands to their feet, and they were unable to.

I looked at the girls, my index finger over my lips. "Shh, shh."

"It's, it's not me. Bill keeps 'em here. He makes us do it," he stammered out.

I looked over at him. "You bunch of sick fucks, what is he doing with them?" We were trying to keep our voices low, but it was getting loud.

"He calls them his concubines, says he has the right since everyone needs him."

Thad had him against the wall. I looked down at the floor. Empty dog food cans were on the floor. In one corner was a stack of porn magazines and various sex toys. I kicked the cans. "What the hell is that about?"

One of the girls began to talk rapidly; her eyes were growing wider with every word. "He makes us eat the dog food. It's all they give us. That fat bastard calls us his bitches and says bitches eat Alpo." Her voice was getting louder.

I knelt down beside her, looking at the two of them. I said, "Shh, we're going to get you two out of here, but you gotta be quiet."

"Why the fuck didn't you people do anything about this?" I asked the man that Thad had now lifted off the ground.

"He's the only one with guns, him and his people. Everyone here isn't here 'cause they want to be. If you try and leave, they come after you with that big truck. He has his group of men. They take women around here when they want to, no matter if they are married or young or anything; they've killed people an' made us watch." Thad dropped him to the ground; the girls flinched.

One of the girls began to cry. "Please get us out of here. I can't take it anymore, please." She started to sob harder, her shoulders bouncing up and down. "Don't leave me here."

"Unlock the damn chains," Thad said in a low stern voice. "Now." He kicked the man's boot.

"I, I don't have the key. Bill's the only one that's got it. I only have the key to this lock," he cried out. He sat on the floor, convulsing in sobs.

"How many of the men around here are in on this?" I asked.

"There's five of 'em. One of 'em is at the roadblock at all times. The other's off," he blubbered.

"Where do they stay when they're off?" I asked.

With a shaky hand, he pointed to a house just past Bill's. "So three of them are in there now?" I asked. "Yes. Please don't kill me. I'm just trying to keep them away from my own daughter. She's only twelve."

"Well, I got a key for them chains," Thad said as he pointed the shotty at the eyebolt in the floor that held one end of the chain. I put my hand out. "Don't do that. They'll just come running. I have an idea that will take care of them in a fitting manner. Stay here and watch him. I'll be back in a few."

"What're you gonna do?" he asked.

"Get ready for a barbecue," I said.

Taking one of the cans of gas from the back of the shed and a roll of duct tape, I ran over to the truck. Rummaging around in the pack, I found one of the MRE accessory packs and took the book of matches from it, along with a hank of paracord. Taking the matchbook, I pulled it apart, taking one of the two pieces of matches and folded it back on itself in thirds. Then I took the cover and laid the striking surface on the stem of the matches, folded it around them, and taped it down. I pulled out a piece of paracord from the hank about eight feet long and cut it off and then pulled all the inner strands out; two of these went with me. I pulled four pieces of duct tape about six inches long off the roll and stuck them on my sleeve. I headed to the building that pathetic sack of shit had pointed to. The house was small, cypress sided like the others, with a wrap-around porch.

Slipping up on the porch, I eased up to the front door; a screen door hung from squeaky hinges. Kneeling down, I poked a hole in the screen at the bottom right corner. Gently opening the door a crack, I stuck one piece of the inner strand through it and tied it off. Cutting it off about eighteen inches, I tied the other end to the match stems sticking out of the book. Feeling my way along the bottom board of cypress siding, I found a crack. Tying a knot in the second strand, I slipped it behind the crack and pulled it tight, tugging on it to make sure it wouldn't come out. Stretching the strand back out, I cut it off, leaving enough to tie the free end to the match cover, folded it over the string, and wrapped it with duct tape.

Making sure everything was set, I opened the can and started pouring the gas on the plywood floor of the porch, quietly going all the way around and coming back to the front door, where I laid the can on its side, gas still running out of it. Stepping off the porch, I ran back to the shed. Thad was still there. The man lying on the ground was weeping. Thad had opened some cans of ravioli and gave them to the girls, who were eating it with their bare hands, bottles of water at their feet.

"Okay, I'm going to go out behind that tree in front of Bill's house. When I give you the signal, fire a couple of rounds into the air. When Bill comes out, I'll drop him. Anyone you see with a gun, drop them. There are two of his culprits at the roadblock. They may or may not come up here." I was looking around; this felt like it was all taking way too long.

"Sounds good to me. I'm ready. What about him?" Thad nudged the man with his boot, who flinched at the touch.

"Leave him, unless he gets involved. He's got to live with what he's done. Maybe he'll think about it every time he looks at his daughter," I replied. The man was looking up at us, completely impotent.

I ran over to the tree and got prone. I looked over at Thad and gave him a little wave. He drew his Glock and fired two rounds and then three more. Just as I suspected, a light came on in both Bill's house and the one next to his. Bill's cronies were a little faster than he was. I heard the front door open, and then the screen door flew open. The matchbook initiator was pulled rapidly apart, igniting the matches, in turn igniting the pool of gas on the floor. The gas went up with a whoosh; the poor bastard standing in it went up with it. The flames ran around the house, and the dry, oiled cypress caught easily. The screams of the flaming body writhing in front of the house were horrible. The other two men inside were screaming, trying to find a way out.

Bill came out on his porch, shotgun in one hand, the other thumbing a suspender over his naked shoulder. He looked over at the flaming house and stopped in his tracks. I centered the peep on his temple, dropped the front sight into view, and squeezed the trigger. The little rifle barked, and he collapsed in a heap. A scream ripped through the night, and glass crashed with a shrill sound. One of the two guys in the second house had jumped out through a window. I quickly put two rounds in him from the little carbine. Standing up, I walked toward the burning house, a now-motionless smoking corpse lying in front of it; small flames still flickered from pieces of the clothes. Another shriek tore through the night. I spun to my right and saw a short, fat woman, Mary, in a long nightgown standing on the porch beside Bill's body. She raised a huge revolver at me. *Boom! Boom!* She tumbled back into the house. I looked over, and the barrels of Thad's thunder stick were smoking.

Again, everything seemed to slow down. Thad was there, slight tendrils of smoke drifting from the barrels of the coach gun still held to his shoulder. Light from the flames danced off the trees, and screams from the man still inside the house echoed under the canopy of oaks. Then in a surreal moment, Johnny Cash's voice came into my head. It started low and grew louder until I realized what he was singing: *"I fell into a burning ring of fire; I went down, down, down, and the flames went higher."*

The poor bastard in the house finally crashed through what was left of the front door; his clothes were a flaming mess. He fell down the steps into the yard, writhing in pain. Three rapid pops ended his misery. I looked to my right and saw Jim standing there, with trembling hands holding the pistol I had given to Jess, orange light from the flames reflecting off the slide. He dropped the pistol and fell to his knees; Beth and Jess ran out to him. Others were coming out of the darkness.

I walked over to where they were huddled around him; he was convulsing in sobs. "How could you allow this to happen?" I asked.

With red, swollen eyes he looked up at me and said, "You just don't understand; you couldn't understand." Thad walked up as Jim began to tell of their quick slide into the innermost circle of Dante's Inferno.

He told us Bill was a pedophile, a registered sex offender. He knew of Bill's past but always treated him with detached respect, neither condemning nor approving of what he had done. Jim was a Christian man and believed it was up to God to pass judgment. In his dealings, Bill was a trustworthy individual that would offer a hand to fell a tree or carry you to town for that forgotten part at NAPA.

When things changed, so did Bill. He had always struggled with his inner demons. When the yoke of civilization was lifted from him, he reverted to what he really was. In the past, he had been a master at what he did; he easily gained the trust of his intended victim's family. But this was different; they were coming to him. All he had to do was show them a little kindness. He offered them food, water, shelter, and safety.

In the beginning, that was all he had to do to get what he was looking for. But, as with every addict, over time it takes more to achieve the same high. Before long simply molesting the kids wasn't enough. He turned to humiliation. This worked for a while as well, and then that wasn't enough. Then he went to pure brutality. That was what we found in the shed.

Others had come around us; all listened in silence as Jim laid the despicable acts out for all. "Why didn't you stop him? Why didn't any of you stop him?" I asked.

"How could we? Him and his men had the guns. No one here has any guns. Plus, if you interfered, he would withhold food," Jim said.

"Or threaten *our* kids," a voice from somewhere in the dark crowd said.

Thad looked over at Mark. "You had a gun when we got here. Why didn't you do anything?"

"One of Bill's boys was there. My gun and anyone else's that wasn't part of their little group wasn't chambered. The guns were kept at the roadblock. We never carried them around. They made us keep the chamber empty so they would have a chance at us if we tried anything," Mark replied.

"I know it sounds unbelievable, but we all had to come to terms with this in our own way. Some were protecting their kids. Some of us did it to stay warm, safe, and dry. It's cowardly, I know, and I will have to live with that for the rest of my days." Jim lowered his head and began to cry again.

Beth looked over at me. "If it wasn't for Jim, Bill and his gang of monsters would have done far worse. They did some horrible things to people around here that knew about him and had mistreated him. Bill held real resentment against some of those folks. And when he got the chance, he loosed his malice upon them in truly horrible ways." She wrapped her arms around her husband.

"Where are the families of those girls?" I asked.

"They are the daughters of one of the locals that truly despised Bill for what he had done. Bill had his men go and get him. They killed him here under these trees; only they did it really slowly. Then they took his wife. I will hear the screams from the two of them for the rest of my life. He had owned a liquor store and wouldn't sell to Bill. When they took him, his house was full of liquor. They all got real drunk and then did what they did. Bill said the girls were his; the others weren't allowed to touch them. He said he was owed," Jim said, his face in his palms.

Thad walked up onto the porch where Bill lay; he found the keys to the locks holding the girls. Coming back down, he reached out and took Beth's hand and placed the keys into it. "Go make it right," he said as he pushed the keys into her palm. She and the other women went to the shed, where they set to the task of freeing the girls, doing their best to comfort them.

I walked away from all the others. I needed a minute to think; this was simply overwhelming. The rancid smell of burnt hair, cotton, and flesh hung in the air like a putrid cloak. You simply could not escape it. *"I went down, down, down, and the flames went higher."*

A diesel engine cranking and coughing to life brought me around. I turned toward Jim, still in the arms of his wife. "What the hell is that?" The engine began to growl, getting louder.

"It's that big truck, back there." He pointed into the woods behind the houses. I walked toward the back of the house. Thad came up alongside me. He had the barrels open and was dropping two fresh shells in. It sounded as if the truck was coming right at us, crashing and crushing its way through the brush.

Jim picked up the pistol and stood up. Everyone was staring off into the dark bush, marking the location of the thundering truck with their eyes. The old deuce and a half smashed out of the brush to the left of the houses. Whoever was driving it was running blacked out. The huge old truck strained to gain speed. Jim raised the pistol and began shooting. The pop, pop, pop from the 9mm barked in rapid succession. Thad and I both just stood there as the truck hit the paved road in front of the houses, turned west, and headed for the overpass. Jim stood there holding the now empty pistol, its slide locked to the rear. "That was the other two. Why didn't you guys shoot?" he asked.

I looked over at him. "I'm getting a little weary of all the killing," I said.

Thad followed with, "Amen."

Now that the last of their oppressors were gone, the folks in the little hammock began to relax a little. The girls had been released from their restraints; others were distributing the food that was stored in there as well. A couple of the men went into Bill's house, looking for weapons. "We ain't gonna let this happen to us again," they said as they came out with a couple of rifles, one of them stuffing the pistol Mary had been holding into his pants.

I noticed that the man that picked up the pistol was the one wanting a ride. He looked over at me. I stared back at him; he knelt down and continued rifling through Bill's pockets. I sure hoped he didn't try anything stupid.

Jess came over to where Thad and I were standing. "Hey, I'm so sorry for all this. My dad wanted to tell you guys about it, but he was afraid; that's why we haven't been around. He is so ashamed. But they were all so scared. You guys brought me home, and then you did this. I don't know what to say. I wanted to get home so bad—this isn't home; this is hell, or it was. If it wasn't for you two, who knows what would have happened after you left?"

"We did what had to be done, nothing more.

I really don't feel for anyone here but those girls. Everyone else just stood by and let it happen," Thad said.

"They were all so afraid, and those guys had all the guns. What do you think they could have done?" Jess replied.

"There's an old quote; I don't remember it exactly, but it's something like, 'All it takes for evil to succeed is for good men to do nothing.' There is always an option. I just hope the girls will be all right someday," I said as I walked toward the truck. Jess stood there, Thad followed along.

We both sat on the tailgate of the truck. The fire had died down somewhat; it was still a big fire, just not the inferno it had been. Both of us sat there for a bit, neither of us talking. After a little while, Thad said, "What now? I want to get home an' soon, and I damn sure don't want to stay around here."

"Me neither, you should just take the truck and get on the interstate. It's right there. I need to go south and east from here; you need to go southwest, and you have a hell of a lot farther to go than I do." At the moment, I didn't really care what happened. I felt deflated; I just didn't give a shit. Two weeks and people were already doing this, only two weeks! What was it going to be like in two months?

"You sure?" Thad tilted his head toward me as he asked.

"Yeah, man, it's been the plan the whole time. I'm not real far from home now. Once I get around Ocala, I'll be in the forest the rest of the way and shouldn't have any trouble at all," I answered. "When are you gonna head out?"

He sat there for a minute in silence. "I feel like I'm running out on you."

"Dude, don't worry about it. You have a long way to go. To be honest, I'm glad it's not me. You're gonna have a hard time, so be careful, and take care of yourself." I slapped him on the back as I said it.

"Well, then, I'm leaving now, if you don't care," he said.

I hopped off the tailgate. "Good, get your big ass outta here. I don't even like you anyway," I said, finishing with a big, cheesy grin.

He stood up. "Feeling's mutual; now get your shit outta my truck." We both laughed, and he helped me gather my stuff from the bed. I went through the cab to make sure I didn't leave anything behind.

Once all my gear was stacked and accounted for, we said good-bye. "Be careful; check the notebook and call in. I'll be on too, so we will know where each other is. You have my address; in the weird-ass event you ever get over my way, stop by."

"Yeah, I'll ride my horse over to your house," Thad chuckled as he said it. "You be careful too. You're on foot, so take your time and stay outta sight."

"Oh, I will. Now that Jess isn't there, maybe I won't get shot again." I started to laugh, and he joined in. "Don't get on the radio until about six tonight. Sarge and the boys won't be on till then," I said.

"All right." He walked around to the driver's door and opened it. We shook hands; he climbed in and started the old truck up. As he put it in gear, he looked out the window at me and gave a nod with that huge head of his; then he pulled out onto the road, turned toward the overpass, and drove off. I gave a wave to the back of the truck as it moved away. I sure hoped I'd see him again.

It was almost five thirty by my watch. The sun would be up soon, and I didn't particularly want to stay around here. I just wanted to go someplace and sleep. I was so damn tired. As it was still dark, and no one was around for the moment, I stowed all my loose gear in my pack and shouldered it. I secured the NVGs on my head and slung the carbine over my shoulder and headed toward the road. The sound of rapid footsteps behind me caused me to turn, unslinging the carbine and bringing it up at the same time. Jess stopped short and raised her hands. "Don't shoot," she said.

I lowered the carbine and looked around behind her. "What's up?" I asked.

"You leaving? Were you at least going to say good-bye? I saw the truck leave and figured it was Thad. I didn't expect you to just walk away without a good-bye." She looked hurt. I'm sure she also wished that Thad had given her a minute.

"Yeah, I was heading out. Sorry, I wasn't really thinking. I just wanted to get the hell out of here," I replied, looking over her shoulder at the flames still jumping in the ruins of the house.

"Why don't you stay here tonight, get some rest, and leave tomorrow? We were really hoping you would stick around a couple of days and help to get things in order around here," she said.

"I know, an' I'm sorry. But I really want to get on

the road." I set my pack down, fished around in the Devildog for the notebook I had, and scribbled out my address. Tearing out the sheet, I handed it to her. "Look, if anything happens, and you guys end up down my way, drop in. You're always welcome." I gave her a little smile.

She immediately started to tear up. With the folded piece of waterproof paper in her hand, she took a small step toward me, looking at the ground. I stepped toward her and wrapped my arms around her. "I'm just glad we got you home. I'm glad you're safe now." I gave her shoulders a hard squeeze.

With her head buried in my shoulder, she sniffled. "Thank you, Morgan." She stepped back and looked at me. "I would never, ever, have made that trip on my own." She looked down at the ground for a moment. "I mean, I was totally unprepared for it. Remember you asked me if I knew what I was getting into?"

I thought back for a moment and chuckled. "Yeah, all I wanted was rid of your ass," I said with a smile.

She let out a little laugh. "Yeah, but you took me anyway."

"No, I didn't. I told you it was still a free world, and I couldn't stop you from walking down the road, as I remember." I gave a little smile, and she seemed to warm to it a bit, laughing.

"Yeah, well, thanks anyway. If anything happens, and you need to come back, you are always welcome here," she said with a smile.

We stood there for another minute, and then she came up and gave me another hug. "You be careful, Morgan Carter. Get home to your wife and kids."

"I will, Jess; take care of your mom and dad. They need it right now," I replied to her.

I stood there for another moment before I shouldered my pack and slung the carbine again. Jess stood there and watched as I got myself together. I took one more look at her; she had tears running down her cheeks.

Chapter 7

I took one more look at the little hammock; people were still moving around, evidenced by lights moving around the camp. I gave Jess a last wave; she returned it. Turning around, I headed off into the woods. I finally found a place that suited me; these were some of the tallest palmettos I had ever seen. The stalks were a good four feet tall, the fans blooming out of the top. Looking back, I couldn't see any sign of lights. I guess I was at least 150 or 200 yards into the woods.

I set up a ridgeline for the tarp between two large stalks, about three feet off the ground, then stretched the tarp out and staked it out. After putting the pad and sleeping bag in, I dragged the pack in under the tarp with me. I quickly shucked my coat and boots and got into the bag. I laid the carbine down just under the edge of the bag and had the XD inside it with me. I was asleep before the sun ever breached the horizon.

Inside the bag, I was as warm as I could want. I slept well, although I woke up a few times, each time falling back into a restful sleep. The sun rose over a cloudy sky; it was very overcast, with a stiff breeze blowing, the sound of the tarp popping in the occasional gust that found its way through the trees. I stuck my head out of the bag and looked out the end of the shelter. *Hmm, it's gonna get cold.* Checking my watch, it was three thirty in the afternoon.

Before the rain that I felt was inevitable started, I climbed out and stuck my feet in the boots, taking the antenna and slick line with me to get it put up. I knew I was supposed to move, but the weather was going to be shit, and I wasn't moving; I just didn't give a damn. It took several tries to get the slick line through the top of a large pine, but I finally got the wire pulled up and strung back to the shelter. Once inside, I pulled the radio out of the bag and turned it on. Putting the headset on, I started to scan the frequencies, just to see what I could find.

The traffic on the radio was picking up, or maybe I just had a better set for the antenna—I don't know. I heard a transmission from a guy near Dallas. He was talking with another ham in Phoenix. They were comparing their situations. From the sounds of it, both cities were absolute hellholes.

The operator in Phoenix said the Mexican gangs were running wild. The local authorities tried to maintain order for a while, but they finally gave up. A group of MS13 attacked a food distribution site with automatic weapons. There were many deaths on both sides. Civilians caught in the cross fire died from rounds fired by both the gang members and LEOs on site.

In Dallas, some parts of the city were burning. There were areas where no one could go without being attacked and robbed of everything they had, including their clothes and shoes—left unconscious in the street, many times, or dead. Every store that had anything of any value, including absolutely useless electronics, was looted. In the beginning, it was just that sort of useless shit that people took—jewelry, trendy clothes, and shoes. He said he saw a group of guys pushing a new Cadillac CTS down the road, even though it would never run again.

Changing frequencies, I found a ham in the Bitterroot Mountains of Montana talking with a ham in San Francisco. From what I gathered, the guy in Montana was weathering things nicely. He had an old International Scout that still ran; he was so far off in the mountains that his house was off the grid. He had enough hay and grain for his livestock, and his tractor still ran. He was set for the winter and would take a look in the spring.

The guy in San Fran was in an entirely different situation. For the first few days, everyone dealt with it. The little farmers' markets still operated, with folks bringing things in on handcarts and bikes. One guy near him was doing a booming business building trailers from parts he scavenged from his mountain of scrapped bikes. Water was their biggest problem; that and the junkies. Water could be dealt with, but the drug addicts were accustomed to a city that handed out free needles and acted as a codependent spouse; the city was now no longer supporting them. With no way to transport the drugs into the city, fighting soon broke out for what was left. When the drug wars started, others joined in for their own reasons, fighting over food, fuel, and clean water.

All the talk of food and water made me hungry

and thirsty. I pulled a "chicken with noodles" MRE out and stuck it in a heater with some water. Setting it down to heat, I switched the radio to Howard's frequency. I was calling home. I needed to talk to them.

I keyed the mic, "Long Howard, you out there Long Howard?" After about a minute without a reply, I made the call again. This time, after a couple of minutes, he came back over the radio.

"That you, Morgan?"

"Hey, Howard, it's me. How's things there?" I asked.

"They're fine. We thought you were gonna call yesterday."

"Yeah, things got a little hectic. Is there any way you can get Mel over so I can talk to her?" I asked.

"Sure, give me a bit to go find her. Hang on."

"I'll be right here," I replied.

While I waited, I had some water and opened a pack of crackers and pouch of cheese spread, my favorite part of an MRE. I was spreading cheese on the second cracker when the radio crackled.

"You there, Morgan?"

Keying up the mic, I replied, "Yeah, I'm here."

Mel's voice came through the headset, "Hey, babe, how are you?"

"I'm good. How are you guys?" I was really starting to feel the strain of being away, what with everything that had happened.

"We're okay. The girls are down at Danny's. I was at home putting some beans in to soak," she said.

"Gonna soak the farts out of 'em." That brought a smile to my face.

She came back with a little laugh. "Yeah, how much longer till you get home? Where are you?"

"I'm closer, near Gainesville. I don't know how much longer. I just wanted to talk to you. I miss you guys a lot," I said.

"We miss you too. The girls ask me a hundred times a day if I talked to you," she replied into the radio.

"Well, now you can tell them you have. If you are at Howard's around seven every evening, we can talk for a minute. I need to go. The batteries for this thing don't last long, so let's try and talk tomorrow. I love you. Give the girls a kiss for me." I released the PTT button, feeling worse than I did before I called her. It was nice to talk to her, but it really brought her and the kids into the forefront of my mind. I had managed to keep them in that special place that I can lock away, but speaking with Mel unlocked that door, and now they filled my head.

"Okay, be safe. We all love you. You have to get home; you promised. I'll be here tomorrow." With that, we were done. I pulled the headset off and dropped them beside the radio. Turning the radio off, I lay back on the bag with my hands behind my head, staring up at the tarp.

Knowing it was close to the end of the twenty-four-hour break in comms with Sarge, I went ahead and finished my cracker and cheese, and then my chicken and noodles. While spooning noodles in my mouth, the rain started. It was light rain that became a steady hard drizzle, the sort of thing that you just knew was going to be here for a while. I finished my food without much enthusiasm. I still had about an hour to wait, so I lay back on the bag and listened to the rain.

At twenty minutes after six, I turned the radio back on; checking my little code sheet, I found today's frequency and tuned the radio. At twenty-five after I keyed the mic; I started, "Walker calling Foxtrot Sierra Mike." Repeating the call, I waited for the reply. After a five-minute wait, I made the call again. A few seconds after this attempt, Sarge's gravelly voice came back over the radio.

"Foxtrot Sierra Mike, Walker, we are Bingo, repeat we are Bingo. Switch to Romeo in one four. SITREP." The station cleared, and I proceeded with my quick report.

"Copy, you are Bingo, execute Romeo in one four. My count is one. Annie's on the farm and Driver is in motion. Currently half click south of Delta, proceeding to Hotel."

"Copy, Foxtrot Sierra Mike out." Sarge signed off, and I picked up my code sheet to see what he was telling me. Sarge and his boys had put an amazing effort into this thing; it was written on a Rite in the Rain four-by-six notebook. At the time, I thought they were going overboard, but now I was starting to think it was a good idea.

On a page with a header labeled "Situation" was the code Bingo. I was surprised by what it said. Bingo was the code for "Breaking contact with OPFOR and relocating to alternate hide, location TBD." Breaking contact? With whom? Someone was actively after them to the point that they had to bug out of Sarge's place.

I found Romeo on a page labeled "Actions." And

I did not like what it said. Romeo indicated I needed to move immediately from my current location, ninety degrees from my original direction of travel, no less than ten miles. One four indicated I was to make contact again in twenty-one hours, as we added half of the number back to achieve the count. So I had twenty-one hours to move ten miles, or as far as I could, and call him back. Laying the pad down, I looked out the end of the shelter; it was still raining. Five minutes in this rain, and I would be soaked.

I pulled the poncho out of my pack and started packing everything up. I keep two of the big black drum liner–type bags in my pack. Using one of them, I wrapped up the radio and batteries and stowed them away. Very reluctantly, I pulled the poncho over my head and climbed out of the hooch. I took the shelter down along with the ridgeline and packed it all away. With everything ready, I hefted the pack again and got everything comfortable and started out due east.

I was able to cross 441 without being seen as far as I know. I was sure the rain helped. My map showed this area as mostly forest. There were very few marked roads; this would keep me from running into anyone but could also put me into some serious trouble as far as terrain. I had to stop to get my NVGs out shortly after crossing the road and also hung my compass around my neck. It was getting too dark to see under the trees; what with the cloud cover and rain, it was very dark. There was so little ambient light that the goggles could hardly magnify it; I had to switch the IR light on to be able to see. With that, it was like looking around with a flashlight. Wherever I turned my head, it was lit up. The raindrops slashed through my view, illuminated by the IR source.

Walking was pretty easy; the underbrush, while thick in places, wasn't a bunch of palmettos. This made walking a hell of a lot easier. I was making pretty good time, knowing the rain would keep most two-legged critters away. By my watch, I had walked for about three hours through the woods. Lochloosa Lake was due east of me about ten miles, according to the map; it was a natural barrier and should be easy to find.

Every ten or twelve paces, I would check my compass to verify direction. I was holding a good easterly track and making good progress. It was during one of these little stops that I thought I heard something. I had the goggles lifted and was using the red LED of my headlamp to read the map. The bad thing about a red light is you can't see any red marks on what you're looking at. I flipped the light off and looked around, listening. There it was again; it was certainly a helo, but it wasn't a Blackhawk, from the sound of it. It was much faster sounding, not the heavy thuds of the big bird. This bird was to my west and sounded like it was orbiting somewhere, making a pretty wide loop.

Knowing there wasn't anything I could find out about it, good or bad, I dropped the goggles down and started walking. My biggest worry appeared before me, to my regret—a swamp, a huge damn swamp. I had to detour south to get around it. There was no way I was getting any wetter. My feet were already a little wet from the water running off the poncho; thank God for Merino wool socks. They were wet, but they were still warm. My southerly detour eventually brought me to a road that ran east-northeast. Standing in the brush on the side of the road, I listened for any sound of people.

Tired of walking through the woods for so long, I really wanted to walk on the road. There wasn't any sound or light, so I walked out onto the pavement and continued in a roughly east direction. This was so much nicer—easy, hard, and flat. Funny how your perception of things changes. I was happy to be walking on a paved road. A couple of weeks ago, I'd have been pissed that I was walking on anything!

Not long after starting out on the road, I found that my decision to take it was the right one. I crossed a bridge over a small river. If I had tried to walk through that swamp, I would have had to swim, and that just wasn't going to happen. Being on the road, I was making great time. After another couple of hours, the road I was on dead-ended into another. The sign said SE CR 325. Stepping off the road into a small clump of trees, I checked my map. Cross Creek was just south of me; it sat between two large lakes. The only way to turn south was to go through it. Otherwise, I would have to hump around the lakes. Both were big and would add miles to the walk. I decided to try to make it through town. It was late and still raining, so there shouldn't be anyone about, I hoped.

Cross Creek was a small town made famous by Marjorie Kinnan Rawlings's book *The Yearling.* It wasn't much of a town, and I hoped to get through it without any trouble. It was about a three-and-a-half mile walk down 325 to town. For about a third of the way, it was desolate country, no houses. I stayed on the shoulder of the road, walking in the open. It was almost one in the morning by the time I reached the outskirts. The only sign of life was the smoke coming from a few of the houses with chimneys, and there weren't many of them. It was cold, real cold. The front had moved through, and the rain had slacked. I stopped in a spot between houses and slipped off into a small patch of trees to take off the poncho. I had been walking with my hands in my pockets but used this break to put my gloves on.

I stood in the shadows for a couple of minutes, watching the road leading into town. There was no movement. More interestingly, there was no roadblock. I pulled the goggles down and turned them on, without the IR source, to scan the street for light, nothing. Satisfied there wasn't anyone around, I hefted the pack and stepped back out onto the road. Coming into this little village, there was a bridge over a small branch of the creek. The water was so low that it was actually just a series of puddles. Just after the bridge was the heart of this little place. There was a bar/diner/package store combination that sat on the edge of the main creek. It was as deserted as everything else. Continuing on through town, I never saw a soul.

It wasn't until I was almost through town that I saw the first sign of real activity. My goggles picked up the light as a glow over the trees. I was coming around a bend in the road, and the light was illuminating the low-hanging clouds. Whatever it was, it was damn bright. I paused in the road and lifted the goggles. Looking over the trees, I saw the orange color bouncing off the bottom of the gray blanket overhead. I took my time edging around the bend. The light was coming from a huge bonfire burning in the parking lot of a small Baptist church. At least two dozen people were there.

Stopping at the edge of the parking lot, using the trees to cover me, I watched them as they prayed and sang hymns. An old, bent-over preacher was leading them as they sang out into the night, asking the Lord to forgive man for his wickedness. Everyone deals with adversity in different ways. If this was how these folks were dealing with it, that was fine by me—more power to them. I went to the other side of the road, putting as much distance between me and them as I could. I didn't want to disturb them, and, frankly, I didn't want them to disturb me.

There was no real cover on this side; there were yards but no trees. I was walking in the grass on the shoulder to prevent my boots from scraping on the road. As I came abreast of their fire, the old preacher was consumed in prayer, with his arms outstretched and his face to the heavens. He was bringing fire and brimstone down on the sinners who had brought down the Lord's vengeance. There were shouts of "Amen!" and "Tell it, brother!" He lowered his arms and faced the crowd before him. He looked directly at me and called out, "Brother! Come join us and beg the Lord's forgiveness of your sinning ways! Armageddon is upon us! Repent your sins and save your soul!"

For an old, bent-over man, he had a hell of voice on him. The entire assemblage turned as one toward me. They stood there for a moment, facing me, the light of the fire dancing on their faces. Then the calls started from the crowd, "Come, brother, join us! Come repent! Join us!" I turned to keep heading down the road.

The old preacher called out, "Brothers and sisters, we have a nonbeliever among us! Let's show him the light! Bring him into the fold!"

Shouting "Amen!" and "Praise the Lord!" some in the crowd started to move out toward me. I unslung the carbine, holding it at the ready. As the crowd drew near, they called out, "Fear not, brother, we only want to save your soul!"

"Children of the Corn," that's what this feels like, "Children of the Corn," standing here with this group in a semicircle around me. All their faces were dark, as they had walked out to the road where I was, and the light from the flames was behind them. These folks were doing their best to get me to join them in their prayer circle. The group began to part from the rear, and then the old preacher appeared in front of me. He didn't really look like what you would expect. He was wearing a blue gingham shirt with blue work pants; his shoes were the type of black work shoes you would expect to see on a fifties-era warehouse worker. In his youth, he would have been a tall man; his long arms belied his short stature.

The light from the fire behind him lit the silver crown of his head in an almost pink light. Standing in front of me, he went into his pitch, "Son, the hour is upon us. Repent your sins and save your eternal soul!"

This was followed by a chorus of "Hallelujah!" and "Amen!"

"I appreciate that, mister, but I'm just trying to get home," I replied.

The old man wasn't swayed from his goal. "The Lord has judged man and found him wanting!"

"Yeah, and left him wanting even more," I replied. Apparently that little statement had an effect on the old sooth. He just stood there looking at me. His eyes were nothing more than black sunken pits in his face, from where I stood. After a brief moment in his creepy gaze, I simply turned and began to walk away, down the road. I didn't fear these folks. I never heard them leave the road, never heard another word spoken. The road out of Cross Creek curves gently as you leave town; when I finally did look back, I couldn't see the church, only the orange glow cast by the flames around the bend and on the low clouds.

Walking along in the dark for a bit, I started to think about those folks back there. Did they really expect some sort of miracle or salvation to be delivered unto them? Or were they simply so overwhelmed, so impotent to do anything about their current situation that this was the only thing they could do in the face of it? It didn't really matter to me; they were no threat to me and, therefore, no concern. I dismissed the thought with a shake of my head.

Trudging along, I flipped the goggles down to check out the road—nothing ahead. Turning them off, I flipped them back up and started thinking of home and how I didn't call today. I hoped that they weren't worried and that they were all okay. This, in turn, made me start to think about the last call to Sarge and his cryptic message, the reason I didn't call home. Why in the hell was he leaving his place? What would cause that? I guess the possibilities for that scenario were unlimited at the moment. I guess I would find out a little more later today, and I would call home today no matter what.

Passing a small road, the sign on the corner indicated I was on CR 325. A small house was on the corner. It was dark, but I moved to the far side of the road, just in case. Getting past the house by a hundred yards or so, I stopped to check my map. Dropping the pack, I stretched my back and dug the map out of my cargo pocket, using the red LED on the headlamp to find my location. This small road intersected with 301 just east of here. Highway 301 was a major road that I didn't particularly want to travel on. This section of it ran almost due north from there; ideally I needed to head south-southeast. There were no roads leading that direction, so it would be overland.

Coming to the intersection of 301, I checked my watch through the goggles, 3:47 a.m. Within the next two hours, I needed to find a hide for the day. One of those little green DOT signs read Island Grove—didn't look like much. Turning south on 301 and moving as stealthily as I could, I got back into an uninhabited area. Seeing no houses, I checked the compass and turned off the road to my planned overland route. Almost immediately,

I crossed a small paved road. Damn, thought this would get me out into the woods. Pushing past the road, it wasn't a hundred yards before I crossed another larger paved road. Damn! Past this, I entered the bush again, thankfully.

Walking on, the trees started to thin dramatically. Before long, I found myself on a prairie. Looking through the goggles, I couldn't see the other side. There was no cover on this thing. It was really early; there shouldn't be anyone around, so I started out across the plain. Being out in the open like this made me feel naked, completely exposed. That's an odd feeling for the modern world, being afraid to be seen.

Shortly after entering the prairie, I had to cross a fence. Starting to cut it with my Leatherman, I paused and decided to climb it. There could be cattle out here, and I didn't want to let some poor rancher's cows out. Climbing fences with this pack was a pain in the ass. I had to take it off, put it over first, climb my big ass over, and then shoulder the pack again. I hated climbing fences.

The front that passed through yesterday was carried in on some pretty stiff winds. Now that the front was south of me, the winds were gone. Shouldering my pack, I thought I heard voices out in the dark. I froze, my pack half on, and listened—nothing. After struggling back into the pack, I grabbed up the carbine and took a look around the prairie, green gloom, nothing but green gloom. Moving as I was was taking me away from Island Grove, leaving the little hamlet over my left shoulder. It was over my left shoulder that the field suddenly lit up, the green view of the goggles blazing.

Dropping where I stood and pulling off the goggles, I rolled out of the pack, struggling with its weight on the ground, I felt like a damn turtle on its back. Finally freed from the pack, I rolled around to the direction the light came from; the field was dark again. Lying prone with the carbine across the pack, I continued to scan the pitch blackness. It didn't take long for the light to cut across the field again; this time I locked on the location of the source.

The light, bright-ass light, swept back and forth across the field. Was someone looking for me? I chuckled to myself, remembering the words of a good friend of mine: "It isn't always about you." Asshole, I muttered under my breath. The light stopped its sweep; it was locked onto something in the field off to my right. Looking out there, I saw two does, maybe seventy-five yards from me.

Whoever took the shot made a damn good one. She dropped right where she was, without taking a step. The other one bounded off into the darkness. The light stayed locked onto her but began to jiggle around, drawing near. Shit, someone's coming. A couple of minutes later, two figures appeared by the doe. One figure was tall, and the other was short. From the sound of the voices I could tell it was a kid—a girl—and a man. The girl held the light as the man knelt to work on the deer.

Being so close, I heard them talking. The little girl was excited about the prospect of food, something that had been in short supply, apparently. She was chastised by the man, from the tone he was clearly her father, a couple of times for shining the light around the field, putting the blade in his hands in the dark. It seemed that Amy was afraid of the dark. I felt a tug at my heart as I listened to him talk to her. He spoke softly and gently to the little girl, explaining to her that this was what was needed if they wanted to eat; she was a trooper and took the grisly scene before her in stride. It so reminded me of my little one, always ready to go fishing and help clean the fish. "Help" usually consisted of touching the fish's eyes and washing the fillets with the hose on the cleaning station behind the shop.

He finished his field dressing quickly, an experienced hand, I would guess, and they were headed back the way they came. He dragged the doe by one of the ears, his rifle in the other hand. The light blinked out shortly after they started moving. I lay there listening to them go, the sound of the deer scuffing across the ground and the little girl's voice fading. When I felt they were far enough away I jumped up and quickly shouldered the pack. I wanted out of this damn field.

I went toward the gut pile, curious more than anything else. I was very surprised to find that he left the heart and liver. With food in short supply, I couldn't imagine leaving any cut behind. Steam still rose off the pile of offal; this mixed with the smell of the rain-soaked prairie. It created such an intense natural aroma—one that was nearly impossible to describe. Fog was already starting to rise off the rain-soaked grass. Not being a fan of deer liver, I picked up the heart; taking a quick minute to find a Ziploc bag in the pack, I dropped it in. I was having some fresh meat for breakfast or dinner or the next time I ate.

I finally came off the prairie through the Orange

Creek Restoration Area, only having to climb two more fences. Taking the driveway out of the restoration area, I was at another road. On the other side was a small forestry sign indicating the boundary of a conservation area, meaning no houses, perfect. Crossing the road, I checked my watch again. It was almost five—time to find a camp.

A small dirt lane led out into the bush, heading off in the southeasterly direction I needed to go. Knowing that roads increased risk, I took it anyway. The benefit of moving farther, faster, and easier was worth it. The roadbed didn't show any sign of travel, no tire tracks or footprints other than those of deer, coons, and other critters. There was no sign of people anywhere, so I started to look for a place to camp near the road, making it easier to start off in the evening.

A straight horizontal line in the trees caught my eye through the green haze of the goggles. It was unnatural and didn't fit with everything else. I moved a little closer to see what it was and discovered a small metal shed. It was off the road a little and covered in old grapevines. Winter-killed stems of dog fennel and beauty berry plaited the sides and door. Stopping a couple of yards from it, I stood and listened for any sounds of people. Satisfied it was empty, I pulled the door open, stepping on the fennel stalks to swing the door out. Inside was a dirt floor, covered in litter in the form of cigarette packs and butts, empty beer cans, and condom wrappers. Fortunately, I didn't see any condoms.

Going in, I dropped my pack in one corner and used my boot to sweep all the litter to one side. This little shed was about eight-by-eight and made a nice little hide for the night. From the look of the outside, no one had been around it in a long while. Satisfied that there wasn't anyone's DNA lying around in a latex sock, I laid out the sleeping mat and sat down on it. From the pack, I pulled my stove and fuel bottle, mess kit, and deer heart. Inside the top flap of the pack I keep a small cutting board; it's one of those really thin ones and is only about ten by twelve inches. A board or something flat would be nice to lay it on. Looking around the little shed, I didn't see anything, so I went out to walk around and see if there was something out there.

Behind the shed was a trash pile—full of old cans, pieces of junk, old hoses, and a bunch of little black plastic pots, the kind you use to start plants in a greenhouse. In the junk, I found a rather stiff metal sign that read, BEWARE OF DOG, in fading red letters. It would make a good base for the cutting board. Carrying it back inside, I set it down and pulled the Glo-Toob out and turned it on. There weren't any windows, so the likelihood of anyone seeing the light was slim. Setting the stove up, I dumped the contents of the pot out on the sleeping mat and poured a couple of inches of water in it. Digging through the pack, I found an accessory pack and took out the salt packet and poured it into the water and stirred it up.

With the cutting board on the sign and that on one end of the mat, I laid the heart out and made half-inch-thick cuts across it, starting at the bottom and working my way up. I cut the valves out and trimmed some of the meat from around them, placing each piece into the salted water. Once I had cut everything I could from it, I lit the stove with my fire steel and set the pot on to boil. I buried the left-over parts of the heart in the corner of the shed, using my little trowel.

Since I was going to have fresh meat, I decided to splurge a bit. Pulling a pack of cocoa from the pack, I set a canteen cup of water on the Esbit stove and lit the tab with a BIC. Rooting around some more, I found a pouch of Mexican rice and stuffed it in an MRE heater with a little water. The water in the pot began to boil, so I turned the heat down a bit to maintain a low boil and put the lid on. I pulled the sleeping bag out and used it as a big pillow to rest an elbow on while my dinner heated up. The tab in the Esbit stove burned out. The water wasn't boiling, but it was steaming, so I dumped the cocoa in and stirred it up. Checking the heart, it was already turning a dark brown—good enough.

Taking the pot from the stove with the lifter, I went outside and around to the junk pile, where I poured out the water, and then I came back inside. In my mess kit, I keep a small bottle of olive oil. I poured enough in to coat the bottom of the pan by rolling it around. Then I shook one of the small bottles of Tabasco into the pot and set it back on the stove, using the little folding spatula to stir the cut-up heart and sauté it in the oil. It smelled great and was making me seriously hungry.

Checking the pouch of rice, the heater was hot and swollen. Taking it out of the heater, I cut open the pouch and dumped the rice into the pot and mixed it with the heart. I sat there and ate, savoring every bite. It was so good—hot, fresh meat, and the sweet cocoa washing it all down. The meat was a little tough; it's better to soak it in the salty water for a while. Nonetheless, this was the most satisfying meal I'd had in a long time.

With a full belly, I packed the stove up and poured a little more water into the pot. Using the little bottle of dish soap and scrubber, I cleaned the pot and used the soapy water to wash the cutting board, then rinsed them with a little more fresh water from the Platypus bag and dried them with a clean bandana. After putting everything back into the pot, I strapped the top back on and stowed it in the pack and put the cutting board back in the flap pocket. I cleaned my knife with the scrubber and dried it with the same bandana and then sheathed it on my belt.

Leaning back on the sleeping bag, I finished my cocoa and just relaxed. After a good meal and a long night of walking, I was drowsy. Then I remembered the can of Cope. I fished around in the Devildog and found the can. To my surprise, it was still pretty moist. I took a pinch and sat there enjoying the little buzz it gave me. I didn't keep it long, though. I was tired, so after ten or fifteen minutes, I spit it out in a corner and started getting ready to go to sleep.

I rolled the bag out, took off my boots and coat, and climbed into the bag. The carbine was leaned against the wall by my head; the .45 came in the bag with me. The goggles were lying close by my head; staring at them with no real thought in my head, I remembered I had batteries that needed charging.

Climbing out of the bag, I slipped my boots back

on and dug out the Goal Zero panel and charger. I found the dead batteries in the Devildog and put four of them in the charger then went outside to set it up. Not wanting to leave it where it could be discovered, I placed it on the roof on the reverse slope from the road I walked in on, propped at a slight angle facing south. The vines on the roof weren't very thick, and I used some of them as the prop. The clearing behind the shed where the junk pile was should provide enough sun to charge them.

Returning to the shed, I climbed back in the bag and turned off the little light. Lying back, I started to think of home again. It had been better than two weeks now, and I could only lie here in this shitty little shed wondering what was going on at home. All I could do was hope that everything was okay and that they were all well, safe, warm, and not hungry. As thoughts of home faded, thoughts of all the others came into my mind—Thad, Sarge and the Three Muskee Queers, and Jess. I kind of bailed on her, and now I felt bad, even for Jim. There could have been more there, but there was so much going on. Thad trying to drive to Tampa, on I-75 of all places, gave me little hope for his success. I hoped he made it, but I didn't hear him on the radio yesterday—not good. But then I had missed calling home, so hopefully it was nothing.

Thad drove out of the little hammock toward the overpass. It was still dark, so he had the headlights on. It would be light soon, and he just wanted to get on the interstate and make as many miles as possible.

Approaching the overpass, he pulled off the road. This was just an overpass, no ramps onto I-75. Pulling down the embankment, he found someone had already cut the fence, saving him from having to do it. Maneuvering the truck through the open section of fence, he hit the pavement of the northbound lane and stomped on the pedal, pushing the old truck hard, heading south in the northbound lane. Most folks had pulled their cars off the road when they died, but some real window lickers left their cars in the lane right where they died. What kind of idiot does that? Fortunately for him, there weren't too many window lickers.

The problem with being on this side of the road was that he couldn't see the signs. As soon as there was a break in the guardrail, Thad steered the old truck across the center median to the southbound side. At least over here he could use the mile markers and signs to keep track of his progress. Thad didn't live in Tampa proper. He lived in the Land O' Lakes area; he used Exit 285 off 75. He figured he was at least a hundred miles from his exit off the interstate.

Not two miles from where he got on the interstate was an exit for Micanopy. There was the usual assortment of sad little gas stations there, the type that were just on the edge of profitability. They had a major oil company name on the sign but smelled like curry and spice and sold the oddest assortment of merchandise on the planet, everything from seashell bric-a-brac to "Lucky 7" dice and ski masks. Ski masks, in Florida? The other real oddity at this exit was the strip club. It was "World Famous" and catered to truckers.

Approaching the exit, Thad tried to push the old truck a little harder. He wanted as much speed as he could muster. The interstate passing over the surface road below would be a natural choke point, and Sarge's crew had warned him about these as possible ambush sites. The eastern sky was starting to lighten as the old truck roared across the overpass, the frame bottoming out with a thunk as the old worn-out shocks couldn't take the weight of the truck as it crested the rise.

Other than the bouncy ride, he made it across without incident. Looking down on the road below from the top of the overpass, it was obvious that people were down there, still hanging around the little stores. Even from this distance, he could tell one of them had been looted; all sorts of crap littered the parking lot. About five minutes after the overpass, he approached his next obstacle. It was an overpass over I-75, like the one leading to Bill's house.

The "Three Muskee Queers," as Morgan called them, had covered this sort of obstacle in their training. Thad scanned the overpass for anyone on top, as well as where the embankments met with the upper road. Seeing no one there, he focused on the other side. Thad eased the truck all the way over to the left until he was actually on the shoulder; then as he went under the leading edge, he started to move to the opposite shoulder as he passed under the bridge; again he made it by without incident.

Thad executed the same maneuver at the next overpasses without incident. The miles were flying by. All he could think about was home—Anita and little Anthony and, of course, Momma. A couple of years ago, she got to the point she couldn't live on her own anymore, so he moved her in with them. Anita didn't work, so there was always someone home with her. Thad made enough driving his truck that his wife didn't need to work. It made him feel good to provide for his family, sufficient that they lived comfortably and wanted for little.

Rolling along, he was thinking of Anthony with his Erector Sets and Legos and other building toys. He was obsessed with them and built some of the most amazing things, especially for his age. At seven years old, he was damn smart. A big green sign told Thad that Irvine was ahead. It wasn't so much a town as it was a place; there was a truck stop off the interstate there that he knew well. Thinking of it, he remembered there was a Wendy's there. "Damn, I'd love a big hot 'n' sweaty burger," he said out loud to himself. The pass over the surface road came into view; even from this distance, he could tell someone was standing on it, at the peak. The eastern sky was getting brighter, bathing the road ahead in a soft light.

The figure was too far away to really see, but there was definitely a person standing near the inside guardrail. Thad eased the truck over; the small figure rapidly increasing in size as he hurtled toward it. The figure was leaned against the concrete barricade; Thad saw him stand up and step out into the lane. Thad moved over into the emergency lane, trying to put some space between them. The man, who was now close enough to see, started waving his arms and stepped out into the right lane. Thad couldn't move over any farther.

Pressing the accelerator down, he white-knuckled the steering wheel, gritted his teeth, and started to move back out into the right lane. The man on the overpass flinched when the Chevy emblem on the hood lined up with his chest. He stopped waving and started to half run, half skip toward the left lane while still waving his arms. Thad blew past him and looked in the rear side mirror to see the guy kick the gravel and debris on the side of the road and then throw his hat on the ground with exaggerated force. Thad watched him standing there with his hands on his hips as he slowly disappeared in the mirror, watching the back of the truck as he sped away.

Three miles later, about three minutes after passing the guy on the bridge, another overpass loomed. Checking it for any sign of people, he didn't see anyone but still executed the standard maneuver for passing under one. This time, he went to the far right, on the shoulder. As he was passing under, he made his change to the left. What he hadn't seen were the three men on the bridge. They were staying down below the tops of the concrete barricades, looking through the joints where they connected. There was a gap about an inch wide that allowed them to look down at the road. The other thing he didn't notice was the CB antenna, connected to a CB sitting on the overpass. They had hauled a car battery up there to operate the radio and had received a call from the boys down at Irvine that a truck had just passed.

They had hauled material up to the top of the overpass with a wheelbarrow—cinder blocks, bricks, and a logging chain. While they couldn't be certain where the truck would come out, they compensated for it by dropping their deadly missiles in both lanes. Thad was just to the left of center of the left lane as he was coming out; he saw the block for an instant before it crashed through the windshield.

That little shed ended up being a good choice to sleep in. With no windows it was fairly dark, and I slept like a rock. When I woke up, I looked at my watch through sleepy eyes. It was 1:45. I lay there in the bag, warm and comfy and not wanting to get out. I'd like to have just stayed there, but I needed to get home. I finally rolled out of the bag and slipped on my boots, laced them up and put on my light coat. I decided to take advantage of the little spot and cook some breakfast. Using the canteen cup, I made the last of my oatmeal with some powdered milk and sugar. After cleaning it up, there wasn't much water left. The Platypus bag was empty, along with the two-quart canteen. There was a little water in the one quart, and the stainless steel bottle was full, but that didn't leave much. I needed to find more.

With the change in our comm schedule I was to contact Sarge around three, so I had a little time. I packed up all my gear and decided to use the shed for one more thing. I dug a cat hole in one of the corners, just in case someone found their way in here, and left a very satisfying dump. I went out and took the panel off the roof, stowed it, and then hefted the pack; feeling good, I headed out looking for a tree to string the antenna in.

Finding a nice tall pine, I dropped the pack, took out the slick line and antenna, and set the plastic-wrapped radio out. Ha, I got the line up to the top of the tree on the first throw and hoisted the antenna up. After unwrapping the radio and connecting the antenna, I checked the time, five minutes till three. I checked the notebook, tuned the radio and waited another couple of minutes. About five minutes later, I keyed the mic and made the call.

"Walker to Foxtrot Sierra Mike."

Immediately there was a reply, "Foxtrot Sierra Mike, I have you five by five."

"Authenticate x-ray," I replied.

There was a pause. "Orange," came the reply. The delayed response was a little unsettling.

"Roger that, SITREP, en route to Hotel, SNAFU," I replied.

"Roger that. We're mobile now. Will relay destination later. What's your distance to Hotel?" he asked.

"About forty miles. What's your situation?" I asked.

"TARFU. Foxtrot Sierra Mike out."

"Walker out," I replied.

I sat there thinking about those guys. I hoped they were all right. What in the hell would make them leave the house? I began to hear a helicopter again. It sounded like it was north of me. I quickly pulled the antenna down and packed up the radio. I didn't know what the helo was up to, but it seemed to show up whenever I used the radio, and it didn't take a rocket scientist to add those two up.

It was still a couple of hours before it got dark,

but I headed out anyway. I needed to find some water. Leaving the relative safety of the trees, I stepped back onto the little dirt trail. Standing there, I did a pretty quick survey to see if there were any tracks—same as before, just deer and other critters. Following the trail, it came out on an open field, and I turned to the left to follow it. Out in the field was a low spot and what looked like the top of a dock. Dock means water, but from where I was standing, I couldn't tell.

I decided to watch the field and surrounding area for a little while. Stepping off into the trees, I dropped my pack and took out the binos. Glassing the field and tree line behind it, there wasn't a sign of anyone, but I had time. Making myself comfortable against a big pine, I figured I'd wait until almost dark before moving out into the open. The sun cut through the cover where I was sitting, and what little there was felt good on my face. I still heard the helo working an area behind me but sounding like it was making some wide orbits, and they were getting closer with each one.

The binos were up to my face when it thundered directly overhead, going straight out into the field in front of me. It was a Kiowa Little Bird. When the pilot made a hard bank, I saw him. There were no doors on the ship, and he and his observer were looking down. I sat there still as stone, with my head turned down slightly so the bill of my hat would cover my face from their altitude. The helo made a wide loop and turned back the way it came, the sound slowly dying off. It felt like my heart was going to pound its way out of my chest, I heard my pulse in my ears. I was scared shitless; I didn't know if they're looking for me, but I sure didn't want to find out.

Sitting there trying to relax, letting my heart rate drop, there was a tickle on my neck. Reaching up with my left hand instinctively—fuck!—I slapped at my neck and saw something fall to the ground. I jumped up, knocked my hat off, tripped over the carbine that was at my feet, and landed on my back. My hand was on fire; there was a small red dot in the fleshy part of my palm just below my index finger. Looking on the ground where I saw it fall, I found a damn scorpion almost three inches long. Florida has a lot of scorpions; most of them are small, but this one was huge. "You little bastard, if I was 'Bear' Grylls, I'd eat your ass," I said out loud. I settled for grinding him into the dirt and pine needles with the toe of my boot.

Fortunately, the sting of the small scorpions in Florida feels worse than it actually is. Some people can have swelling in the affected area, but other than that, the sting isn't too bad—hurts like hell, but that's about it. I squeezed the little red spot. I don't know why, but what else could I do?

The sun was starting to go down, and I really needed water. Shouldering the pack, I headed out across the field to what looked like a dock. Just as I hoped, there was a small pond in the field with a dock on one side. Cautiously approaching the pond, I dropped the pack and took the filter and empty containers to the water's edge. The pond sat in a small depression, so I wasn't visible out here. However, I couldn't see around the area either. The water in this little pond looked kind of strange. It was sort of a milky green color. Scooping a handful up, it looked clear in my hand, so it must have been the bottom. It was either lime rock or an old phosphate pit. At the moment, I didn't care. I needed some water.

It didn't take long to get all the containers filled and everything stowed back in my pack. I was moving again about twenty minutes after stopping. Checking the compass, I headed out on the southeasterly track. The area was all scrub, broken up by the occasional swamp or bay head. Going around these to keep from walking through them took me on a route that resembled a drunken snake. I constantly had to verify my direction with the compass. Fortunately, there was zero sign of people out here, save the occasional dirt road, none of which ran the direction I wanted to go.

Chapter 8

After Morgan and his crew left, Mike and the guys sat down to brief Linus on what they knew. Their mission was to make contact with the sheriffs of Levy, Dixie, Columbia, Gilchrist, Lafayette, Taylor, and Marion counties. They were to do this without being detected by the locals. If they were compromised, they were to eliminate any witness to their presence. Once contact was made with the sheriffs, they were to determine their willingness to work with the federal authority, assess their needs, find a suitable location for advance bases of operation, and get them to relinquish their local autonomy to the incoming federal presence.

Any sheriff that refused was to be noted and relayed back to the operations folks, where contingencies were being developed for dealing with them. They had been inserted close to shore in Levy County, in a very rural, sparsely inhabited area. After the briefing on their mission, before they even left for their insertion, the guys had decided they wanted no part of this. The talk of "contingencies" to deal with any sheriff that didn't go along with the plan bothered them. Most folks do not realize the power the sheriff wielded. He or she was the supreme elected leader in the county. The sheriff's money might come from the commission, but he or she was the Big Yamma Yamma.

Once inserted, the guys proceeded with their mission as planned, with the exception that they laid out the feds' plan to the sheriffs. Most of them had some colorful words for what the feds had planned. The only ones that were eager for the intervention of the feds were the sheriffs of Alachua and Marion. These two contiguous counties had rather liberal sheriffs. They were particularly excited about the prospect of disarming the citizenry of their respective counties and implementing the new "Aid Distribution Assistance Monitoring" plan, referred to as ADAM. The stated goal of the plan was to provide aid in the form of food, water, and clothing to those in need. The real intention was to remove any means of self-support from as many people as possible and make them completely dependent on federal aid to survive.

This plan had been under way for many years, in various parts of the country, with varying degrees of success. This opportunity presented the perfect chance to catapult the plan downfield toward the ultimate goal. By a perceived fortuitous set of circumstances, an event of a magnitude the administration could only dream of fell in their lap, and they would be able to paint a certain segment of the society as the culprits. When the news of who did this reached the cold, hungry, scared people, their reaction should turn them right into the open waiting arms of the federal government. The only problem was the guns. The American people possessed enough guns to arm half the armies of the world, and those were just the ones the .gov crowd could account for. But there was a plan for that too.

After the guys had made contact with the various sheriffs and knew who stood where, they decided to go rogue and help the other side. By informing the sheriffs that had their heads screwed on right, they won the support of them. By letting them know where some of their counterparts stood, they were able to help draw up a defensive plan for them. They had purposefully saved Dixie County for their last stop, knowing Sarge was there, and they could depend on him, so long as their reason was sound. If not, he would be the first to turn them in. After they laid everything out for him, Linus was pissed. He always suspected the shithead 'n chief would try something like this if given half a chance; well, now he had it.

It was shortly after Morgan and his crew left that Ted spotted an observation post on the far side of the river from Sarge's house. It was upriver near the bend on a high bank on the inside of the curve. They watched it for two days and, using their radio and encryption codes, were able to determine that they were under surveillance. They had identified their hide and had a count of three men. The situation became a point of contention as to what they needed to do about it. Sarge wanted to go out and kill the occupants; Mike and his guys weren't on board. After all, they might know these guys, and they might not even know who they were watching.

The plan that they developed was for Mike and

Ted to go out and around them on this side of the river. They would cross the river upstream of the observation post and come at them from the rear. Ronnie and Sarge would keep their attention by having a barbecue on the deck, complete with plenty of beers to make 'em thirsty. The mission would be carried out at night to minimize any chance of accidental encounters with civilians.

The plan was to find out who was there. If they were guys that Mike and Ted knew, they would try to persuade them to break off their mission and come with them. If they weren't so inclined or were openly hostile, they would be neutralized. Ronnie had Sarge's scoped M1A in the shed on the back of the property. The window in the rear of it faced the river and had been transformed into a sniper hide. When the guys were in position, they would key the mic on the handheld ham they had with them. Ronnie would go to the hide and offer cover for them.

Mike and Ted each had a Taser in addition to their weapons. They carried these with them on their mission from the start as a way to deal with civilians if they were discovered. These would be used first if it came to it; live fire was the last resort. Using a game cart, they transported Linus's canoe to a landing upstream and crossed over. After crossing the river, they approached the hide from the rear at an oblique angle. Once they were within sight, they observed the three men for a while. They didn't recognize any of them. Their identity was revealed when they made a radio call to give a SITREP. The call sign they gave was for the DHS unit operating out of the same base they deployed from, Junkyard.

None of the guys in their unit liked having the feds there. They completely segregated themselves from the troops, going so far as to have strung barbed wire and posted armed guards. None of the troops were allowed anywhere near them. It was a very uncomfortable situation; the tension of having two groups of highly trained and armed men in such close proximity to one another was dangerous.

Once they determined these guys were from the wrong side of the tracks, they came up with a plan. One of the three was in a sleeping bag, another was preparing food for himself, and the third man was on watch. They would get within range of the Tasers and hit the one on watch and the support man. The one in the bag would be dealt with in whatever manner the situation required.

Mike keyed the mic twice on the handheld. The radio in the OP squawked twice, drawing the attention of the support man and the one on watch. They looked at one another, and then the support man went to the radio. Just then a rapid series of pops started coming from downriver. The one on watch pulled down his NVGs and started looking toward Sarge's house. The second man had a headset on and was actively looking for the source of the transmission. "Firecrackers. They're lighting firecrackers," the one on watch said over his shoulder.

With these two distracted, Ted and Mike moved the last couple of yards, a Taser in one hand and a suppressed 1911 in the other. They fired the Tasers almost in unison, both finding their mark. The two men went rigid, the support man falling over on the one in the bag. The sudden impact caused the one inside to cuss and try to fight his way out of the bag. When his head popped out, he was looking into the suppressor of Mike's pistol. The five seconds timed out, and the Tasers released their victims. Both of them released the triggers and pressed them again, sending the stricken men on another five-second lightning ride.

Thad instinctively jerked the wheel hard to the left. The block struck the top of the windshield at the roof line. Half of it crashed through the glass and landed on the bench seat, tearing a huge hole in it. The other half bounced over the roof into the bed. Thad slammed on the brakes in response to the impact. The windshield was spider-cracked across its full length. The truck went into a skid, the rear coming around on the left. Being a truck driver, Thad knew how to counter it; letting off the brake, he steered into the skid. This straightened the truck, and he floored the pedal again. The driver's window was open; he stuck his big arm out, giving whoever dropped the block the international peace sign. They responded by taking a couple of shots at him.

Ocala was just ahead. There was no way Thad wanted to drive through it during the day. Ocala was a major population center, the only one he had to go through to get home. If there was going to be any trouble, it would be there. This stretch of the interstate was bordered by pastures for the most part. Ocala is well known for the horse ranches that are all over the area. Driving along, he kept his eyes open for some trees. If he could find a good hiding place, he could lay up for the rest of the day—moving again after dark to try to get through town.

A few miles past his little incident, Thad found what he was looking for on the northbound side. He crossed over under another overpass and drove off the shoulder of the northbound lane. There was a fence along the interstate. Pulling up to it, he stopped the truck and got out—his shotty in one hand and his Gerber multitool in the other. Standing in the open driver's door, he took a minute to do a look 'n' listen. Satisfied there wasn't anyone in the immediate area; he went up to the fence, cut the field wire at one of the posts and pulled it back out of the way. Climbing back in, he drove the truck through and parked it under the trees.

After shutting the truck off, Thad climbed out; digging around in the bed of the truck, he found a piece of baling wire and took it out to the fence, where he used it to secure the fence so anyone taking a casual look wouldn't notice it was cut. Back at the truck, Thad walked around the area under the trees to make sure no surprises were waiting. Finding nothing, he went back to the truck and looked at the windshield. It was shattered, and there was a dent where the glass met the roof. He stood there looking at it, shaking his head. Going to the rear of the truck, he dropped the tailgate and sat down, grabbing his pack to find something to eat and drink some water.

Rummaging around, he pulled out an MRE and one of his water bottles. Sitting there, he ate the

MRE cold and washed it down with water. Picking up his pack, Thad moved over to a clump of brush to rest. He didn't want to be right at the truck in case someone came by to take a look. With the key in his pocket, he wasn't worried about anyone stealing it. Thad pulled his poncho out and spread it on the ground and laid down on it, cradling the shotgun in his arms. Lying there with his eyes closed, he started to think of home and how much farther he had to go.

Once the three guys were secured with flex cuffs, Mike and Ted began their interrogation; they were not very forthcoming. Mike sat down on the ground in front of them as Ted went through their gear, looking for intelligence. All three were wearing MultiCam uniforms like the one he wore. Two of them were younger, late twenties, and looked like gamer types. The third was a little older and had a military bearing about him; he was the one Mike started to question.

"You guys looking for us?" Mike asked.

"You didn't think we would just forget about you guys, did you?" he answered with a grin.

"Why are they so worried about us?" Mike asked.

"Oh, we're not worried about you guys. We figure there will be plenty of your boys that won't go with the program. That's why we're here, to keep the riffraff in line." Again with that stupid grin.

"Well, you seem awful sure of yourself for someone in cuffs. You guys were so easy to take down that a kindergarten class could have done it." Now

Mike had a grin. Ted laughed over his shoulder. Mr. Confidence looked over at his compatriots. He obviously wasn't pleased to be in this situation.

"We're not all this easy. If I had my way, you assholes would've been dead by now," he answered with a sneer.

"That wouldn't have been as easy as you think there, sport," Ted replied over his shoulder.

The other two guys were just sitting there. One of them was a light-skinned black guy; the other was Hispanic of some variety. "Getting a little real for you boys, huh?" Ted said to them. They just sat there, not saying anything. "What was the point of this little sneak 'n' peek?" Ted asked, elbowing one of them in the shoulder as he said it.

"They aren't going to tell you fuckers anything. They know better," Mr. Confidence said.

"You may not tell us, but I know someone you will talk to." Mike stood up and pulled his Surefire Aviator from the pocket on his sleeve and stepped out to the edge of the river. Pointing it toward the house, he flashed it once, paused, and then three times in rapid succession. Two flashes came back to him, and, a few minutes later, he heard the old outboard on Sarge's boat sputter to life and start to move toward them.

Ted stood up after going through all the packs. "Oh, you guys are in a world of shit now," he said. Going over to his pack, he pulled out three croaker sacks. "Let's get you boys dressed for the party." He quickly pulled a bag over the heads of the two gamer kids. "Smells like shit, huh?" he said as he moved over to put one on Mr. Confidence.

"You ain't putting that fucking thing on my

head!" he shouted. He had his chin stuck out in a futile attempt at indignation.

Ted drew his 1911 and rapped him in the side of the head. "Play nice, or I'll hurt ya." The blow dazed him enough that Ted pulled the bag over without any trouble.

"You fuckers are dead!" Mr. C shouted through the bag.

"Better than you have tried and failed, friend. Better'n you," Mike said.

"These our dates?" Sarge said as he climbed up the bank from the river.

"Yeah. Aren't they purdy?" Ted said, laying on a thick southern drawl.

That was more than the young black guy could take; he started to scream through the bag, "What the fuck? What the fuck are you going to do to us? We were just sent here to look for you guys. We didn't do anything to you!"

"Shut the fuck up! They aren't going to do anything to you," Mr. Confidence shouted through his sack.

Linus knelt down to get on their level. "Son, you are wrong about that. I have a bunch of things planned for you boys. I learned a bunch of real interesting shit in places like Vietnam, the Big Sand Box, and a few less tropical hellholes. You better believe I will do things to you. What I do is completely up to you, though."

The prisoners were loaded up and taken back to the house along with all their gear. The area was sterilized, ensuring nothing was left behind. Getting them in and out of the boat was a little difficult. The hide was above the river about four feet. Mr. Confidence didn't want to cooperate with going down to the river, so Sarge just pushed him down the hill; he tumbled asshole over teacup, landing in the shallow water at the river's edge. He was cussing for all he was worth. Linus was laughing at him. "Shut up; I'll only say it once."

"When our people get here, I'm going to kill you, and I'm going to make it hurt," he sneered through the bag. Sarge reached into the big johnboat and picked up the club he kept there for braining gar. Sarge hit him just above his left ear, not real hard but just enough to make it smart real bad. He let out a cry.

Sarge replied with, "Told you I would only say it once."

The other two managed to find their way into the boat without too much trouble. At the dock behind the house, everyone managed to get out of the boat without incident. Ted and Sarge led them to the garage, while Mike and Ronnie took all their gear into the comm cave for a thorough search. The garage was already prepped for their arrival; three pieces of rope hung from the joists overhead. Their hands were secured in the front, so it was easy to raise them above their head and put them through the loops. This was done one at a time, so that they had to stand on their tiptoes to support their body weight.

During all this, Mr. Confidence cursed and threatened them. Once, he tried a forward kick at Ted, who blocked it and, raising the leg, struck him in the crotch with an open hand, using the web of his hand to drive his captive's nuts into his chest. He got real docile after that, letting out a groan, while hanging from the rope secured over his head. The other two babbled a mile a minute; they were obviously terrified.

Sarge stepped back and looked at them. "Well, are you boys comfy? Can I get you anything?"

The two young guys started running their mouths. "What do you want? We don't know anything. What are you going to do to us?" were a few things that came out between sobs.

"They look too comfortable to me," Ted said. He stepped toward them and unbuckled the Spanish kid's pants and pulled them and his skivvies down to the top of his boots.

"What the fuck? What the fuck are you doing!" he screamed.

Ted went down the line doing the same to the other two. When he got to Mr. Confidence, he laughed. "I didn't think the water was that cold."

"You are one sick man," Sarge said, shaking his head. "But I like it. Now don't you boys go anywhere. I'll be back."

They went back into the house to help Mike and Ronnie go through the gear for anything that could help. Sarge was laughing as they walked in, and Mike looked up and said, "What?" Sarge told them what Ted had done. Mike and Ronnie both started laughing.

"Yeah, we learned that from some Israelis we did some interrogations with once. It always seems to have a profound effect. Only they would have some poor bastard tied to a chair and just unzip him and pull his pecker out. Scares the shit out of 'em." He was shaking his head and laughing.

Studying my map for a minute, I realized there was a huge obstacle in front of me. The Ocklawaha River was only ten or twelve miles away, and I should easily hit it tonight. There was only one way across it that I knew of, and that was the bridge at Highway 40 to my south. This posed a serious dilemma. If I continued forward, I had uninterrupted forest. Detour south to hit the bridge, and I would be in a more populated area, not to mention the fact that I had no idea what the situation was like at the bridge. It would be a natural choke point to keep people in the Ocala area from entering the forest. The locals in the forest considered it their private little camp; tens of thousands used the land, but they looked upon those perceived intruders with quite a bit of umbrage.

Knowing what the river was like, I knew I wouldn't be able to cross it without a boat. It wasn't too wide, but it was fairly deep and was bordered on both sides by a substantial swamp; that alone would be tough to get through. Letting my eye wander around the map, another option jumped out at me. The bridge on 316 at Fort McCoy crossed the river farther north, closer to me. It wasn't a main artery like 40, which runs all the way to Ormond Beach, and might be easier to cross. That was the way I'd head. Maybe I could get over that one, plus it was closer to being in my line of travel.

With the decision made, I folded the map back

up into its bag and stuck it in my pocket. Setting out again without much to do but think, my mind started wandering again, drifting from Thad and how he was doing, to Sarge and the guys and what prompted them to bug out, to home and my girls. Home—Lord, how I wanted to be home. The throbbing in my hand caught my attention. Checking it, I saw and felt the swelling that was starting. It wasn't much, but my fingers felt tight. I took a quick break to get out some Benadryl; maybe it would help to counteract the sting. After taking the pills, I started out again for Fort McCoy.

Thad snoozed in his little hide, waiting for the sun to drop. He didn't really sleep; it was more of an in-between state, not fully conscious but not out. This was a thing he did often when driving his truck. If he started to feel particularly sleepy, he would pull over, set the alarm on his phone for twenty minutes, and snooze. The boost this gave him was great; sometimes it felt like he slept for hours. Sitting up, he looked around. No one was in sight. The truck was right where he left it. Packing his gear, he tossed the pack into the passenger seat, took a leak by the driver's door, and walked out to the fence he had cut. Undoing the piece of baling wire, he pulled it back out of the way and rolled the piece of wire up and went back to the truck.

Sitting in the cab, he dug around in the pack and pulled out a packet of MRE crackers and a pouch of peanut butter. He sat there as the sun dropped, eating his snack and drinking some water from the bottle. He wanted it to be completely dark before leaving. Ideally, he would wait until late at night, but he wanted to get home, and Ocala was in his way. He would have to cross three major intersections, Highways 27, 40, and then 200. These were all major roads with a lot of businesses at the exits. Being on the west side of Ocala, it was also where the trouble would be. If he could just clear those, he would be all right.

Knowing he had to do something, or he would leave, Thad decided to set up the radio. Pulling the antenna out, he tossed it up over the tallest oak he could find and connected it to the radio. Pulling out the notebook, he flipped through the pages until he came to today's codes. Sitting there, going through the book, he remembered the last transmission and what Morgan had said, no transmissions for twenty-four hours. Thad had tossed his watch shortly after the event since it didn't work. He should have been on the radio around three. Looking up, he knew it was more like six thirty or seven; he'd missed it.

Since the radio was set up, he started to flip through the frequencies. His antenna set was less than ideal. Running at a long slope, it was better for catching local talk. Being more horizontal, it would pick up transmissions that bounced straight down. Turning the knob, he found someone transmitting. It sounded like he was in Beirut; there was constant gunfire in the background. The operator was shouting into the radio to what Thad guessed was others in his party. They were trying to maneuver on some people that were attacking their location; he didn't know if these were the good guys or the bad guys.

Listening to the radio chatter, he finally realized the transmissions were coming from Ybor City, in Tampa. Just as he figured things would be in that old city, it sounded like hell. Any town that has an intersection called Malfunction Junction has to be on the edge of crazy, and it finally got the nudge it needed to fall off that edge. Thad sat there listening to the radio; his heart was heavy. Thad's wife, son, and mother were nowhere near the chaos he heard on the radio, but it was too close for him; he couldn't take any more. Shutting off the radio, he disconnected the antenna and pulled it down. After tossing it back onto the floorboard, he went to the bed and pulled the two five-gallon gas cans out and started pouring them into the tank of the truck.

Sarge was laying all the documents they found on the three goons on one of the tables in the shack. Mike and Ted were going over them, piecing what they could together. Sarge walked out of the room toward the garage. Inside he found them still hanging there. The two young guys were just standing there, chins on their chests. Mr. Confidence was working on the rope. Just as Linus came through the door, Mr. Confidence landed on the deck; he had jumped up in an attempt to loosen the rope. It didn't work. All three of them looked up as he came through the door.

"You still full of piss 'n' vinegar?" Sarge said as he closed the door. "Let's see if we can take some of that out of you boys." He clapped his hands together and rubbed them, blowing into his cupped hands.

"Getting cold in here. From the looks of you boys, you're a little chilly." Sarge went out the side door of the garage and returned with a hose.

"What the hell are you doing?" the young black kid asked. "You haven't asked us anything. What do you want?" The only sound they heard was Sarge's boots and the hose sliding across the concrete slab of the garage.

"We'll get to that soon enough. I just want to make sure you boys are motivated to answer them when I ask 'em," Sarge replied. He pointed the hose at them and started to spray them down with cold water. All of them tried to turn to avoid getting hit in the face with the water. This only presented Sarge with a dry spot to hose down. All three of them shouted and shrieked when the cold water hit. When he was satisfied they were soaked, he released the lever on the nozzle and stood there looking at them. "Y'all look like a bunch of damn drowned rats."

From the level of bitching, Sarge was pretty sure the prisoners were miserable. Going back into the house, he found the guys in the cave going over the captured intel. The men they caught were DHS goons sent to find them. Shortly after they ceased radio contact, these three were sent to look for them. The documents contained maps of the area, clearly showing their infiltration and exfiltration routes along with alternatives. Sarge's house was prominently marked on the map, so that meant that others knew the location.

A quick discussion resulted in the unanimous decision to bug out. Staying there was a guaranteed way to get caught. Not knowing when the crew they had was scheduled to call in, caution dictated that they leave as soon as possible. Sarge instructed the guys in what to start packing; the radio gear was the highest priority, then weapons, food, and additional survival gear. As they started moving gear out to the living room, Sarge headed for the garage. "Let me go see what they have to say. Two of them seem eager to talk."

The temp outside was in the upper fifties, comfortable. But inside the block walls of the garage, it was much colder. The concrete floor and poured block walls held the cold inside, acting like a meat locker. All three were still hanging there, shivering violently; hypothermia was starting its course. Linus walked in and stood in front of them. "Now, I'm going to ask you boys some questions. If you answer them, I'll take you down and get you warmed up, and no harm will come to you. If you want to be dumbasses and try to be tough guys, you will suffer." He reached down and picked up the hose. This caused the two younger members of the team to start to whine and mutter through chattering teeth. Starting with the young Spanish kid on the end, pulling the sack off, he began his questions.

"What was the intention of your surveillance here?" The kid lifted his eyes; his jaw was clenched tight.

"Dd . . . d-don't . . . ss . . . say anything," Mr. Confidence on the end managed to get out. Without looking up, Linus sprayed him in the face with the hose, never letting his eyes drift from the young man trussed up before him. The freshly wetted victim let out a howl and struggled weakly against his bonds. The young kid stared back at Sarge who raised the hose up to his chest.

Before he could squeeze the lever on the nozzle, the kid started to stutter. "W . . . we were t . . . to watch an' ss . . . s-see what they w . . . w-were doin' an' w . . . who they were w-with."

"Now that wasn't so hard, was it? And I'm a man of my word." Linus laid the hose down and walked over to a set of shelves on the side of the garage. He picked up a wool army blanket and a clothespin. Returning to the young man, he draped the blanket over his shoulders and pinned the top together under his chin. The kid rolled his shoulders against the coarse wool.

"Go on, what was the intention?" Sarge asked.

"If i-it was det . . . termined they were colluding w-with hostiles, a . . . a strike tt . . . team would be inserted to e-eliminate them. If a strike team couldn't get in, th-th . . . then a UAV strike would be used." The kid lowered his eyes.

"Which UAV?" Sarge asked.

"Reaper," the young black kid answered.

Sarge looked over at him. "Well, I'm glad you smartened up." He wrapped him in a blanket and pulled the sack off his head, and then he looked over at the third man. "Well, Mr. C, would you like to warm up?" Linus asked as he snatched the sack off his head.

Mr. C attempted to glare back at him; however, he was shivering so hard he had little muscle control. "F . . . ff-fuck you," he managed.

"Well, you are one tough bastard. I'll give you that."

Looking back to his cooperative captives, he asked, "Is the Reaper on station now?"

"I-it wasn . . . n. . . . n't when w-we last called. I . . . it's a con . . . t . . . tingency," the young black kid said.

"Where did you guys deploy from?" Sarge asked.

"Eglin. We moved t . . . to Camp Rudder," the Spanish kid replied.

That made sense; it wasn't far and was in a very uninhabited area. Aircraft could launch from there and head out over the gulf and not be detected by civilians.

"All right boys, I'm going to ask one more very important question." He made eye contact with both of them. "And you better answer this question very carefully. If you lie to me, I'll have to hurt you, and I don't want to hurt you, but I will." To emphasize his point Sarge went over to the workbench and picked up a can of barbecue lighter fluid. Walking back over to them, he pulled his 101st Zippo out of his pocket. The two that had been answering his questions were struck with terror; their eyes got huge, and their mouths hung open.

"Anything, I'll tell you anything!!" the young black kid screamed with surprising clarity.

"When are you to call in next? I want your call sign and the frequency to be used." Sarge lifted the top on the lighter fluid and flipped the Zippo open. Before the Zippo even clinked open, the kid was spitting the words out.

"Dogtown, call sign is Dogtown. We are supposed to call in at oh two hundred!"

"Codes," Sarge said flatly.

"In the binder, it's all in the binder," the Spanish kid replied.

Sarge flipped the Zippo closed and put the fluid back on the workbench. "Very good. I'll be back to get you guys down in a minute." He looked over at Mr. C. He was not doing well, only semiconscious. Sarge headed back to the cave to get the guys.

After topping off the tank with the ten gallons and tossing the cans back into the bed, Thad was ready to go. He just couldn't wait any longer. Climbing into the truck, he started it up and headed for the interstate. It was dark, but the new moon provided enough light to see the road, so he drove blacked out. The group of men standing around a burn barrel at the top of the overpass didn't hear the old truck until Thad was already heading down the exit ramp on 27. They jumped and began to shout and run to the edge of the overpass, looking down as the truck sped down the ramp. Others came running out from under the overpass as the truck careened through the intersection, heading west. Thad heard a couple of pops and one thunk as he pressed the old truck harder.

He had changed his mind at the last moment, taking the ramp on a whim. The thought of going down the long straight interstate scared him. It was a gamble either way, really. Trying to get over to 200 and then to 41 would put him in a fairly populated area; more people meant more chances of trouble. He would have to go through or around several small towns but decided this old bypass to get home would be the best choice in the current situation.

Speeding down 27, Thad passed a few people out on the side of the road. All of them jumped off the road and looked on in a kind of awe as the truck raced by them. Only a couple of minutes after turning off the interstate, he came to the intersection of W CO 225. This would take him to 200. Thad had many little sneak-arounds like this for times when I-75 was backed up, as it was all too often. Anything on the side of the road would cause people to slow down and gawk. God forbid there be an accident in the travel lanes; you would be stuck for hours.

Turning onto the county road, Thad gunned the engine again. The road soon turned into a four-lane divided highway, with a large grassy median. It was bordered on the left by cookie cutter residential neighborhoods. Passing them, he noticed many fires, and folks cooking in the backyards; he assumed they were cooking over grills. The glimpses of the streets he caught between the houses showed there were many people out; that struck him as odd, figuring most people would be inside after dark. His luck ran out at the intersection with Highway 40. Approaching the intersection that had convenience stores on two corners, he found it had a crude barricade in the form of disabled cars and trucks that had been pushed or pulled out into the road. All four sides of the intersection were thusly blocked, forming a box of cars.

Slowing a bit to find a way around all of it, he saw what he needed. On the northwest corner was a vacant lot with a lime rock drive running through it, and it wasn't blocked. Thad gunned the engine as people started to come out from the gas station across the street from the lot. Just as he entered the lot, kicking up a cloud of white dust, a four-wheel ATV came screaming out of the station's parking lot. Looking over his left shoulder, he saw it had two figures on it. Suddenly memories of what happened the last time a four-wheeler gave chase came flooding into his mind. The sight of that poor kid lying there on the road and his life slipping away from him filled his head.

More people came out from the station on the other side of 40. They were running out into the road, and then another ATV appeared, heading for him. Thad hit the asphalt on the other side of the lot and dropped the hammer on the old truck. The ATVs were gaining on him, and he rocked back and forth in his seat, willing the truck to go faster. "Damn, they fast," he muttered, watching the rear-view mirror as the two narrow sets of headlights gained on him. Realizing they would catch up to him before he could outpace them, he decided to take the offensive. He hadn't done anything to them and took heart in that fact.

As the two ATVs got within ten feet or so, Thad slammed on the brakes, locking the tires up. The closer of the two slammed square into the bed of the truck with a loud "wham." The other tried to steer around the truck, the left front wheel connecting with the bumper and catapulting the two riders over the handlebars. Thad immediately floored the truck; this time he never even looked back.

If I had my current position right, Fort McCoy would be just south of due east from my current location. Using the compass, I oriented myself to an almost due east track and started off. This was the ideal terrain to walk through—many open pasture areas, planted pine with no underbrush, and the occasional bay head. There were zero houses out here, so the walking was almost carefree. Not seeing anyone or anything that hinted of people, I let my guard down and was whistling, though softly. The area was crisscrossed with roads, most of them going north-south; never did find one going east.

After walking for a couple of hours, the batteries in the goggles started to go out. I dropped the pack and dug fresh ones out of the little bag on my waist. Since I was stopped, I decided to have a bite to eat and dug an MRE out. I ended up with Southwest beef and black beans, a pouch of tortillas, and some Mexican rice. Retrieving a heater and adding water to the pouch, I set it aside to warm up. A cup of coffee would be good right now, so I pulled the Esbit stove out and a tab. With a cup of water on over the tab, I sat back and listened to the night sounds. Crickets for sure, but somewhere off in the distance was the call of an owl. Everyone says an owl goes whoo, whoo, whoo, but that isn't it; it's a deeper call carried across the night like a bass drum beating in the jungle. Once, for a moment, I heard a whip-poor-will, but it didn't last long.

The tab burned out, so I added the coffee pack, creamer, and two sugar packs. It's funny how fast your opinion of what's good can degrade; this elixir was wonderful, almost magical. Sitting out here in a stand of planted pine, the biting aroma of the pine wrapping around me, the light smell of the coffee mixing with it, brought back memories of a Christmas spent in Maggie Valley. We rented a little cabin on the side of a creek. I will never forget trying to sneak presents into that little place without the kids seeing. Mountain air, tonight it almost smells like mountain air.

With the heater done, I pulled the entrée and rice out and opened the tortillas. I spooned rice and beef 'n' beans into them, eating them folded over taco style. It was actually pretty good. Well, after getting the bottle of hot sauce it was. With dinner done, I licked my spoon clean, rinsed out the canteen cup, and stowed everything. The pile of empty pouches was lying on the ground, and I looked at them. I have always been a conscientious camper—never leave trash and usually carry out more than I carried in. However, at the moment, things were a little different. It's not like the trash man was coming around on Wednesday. I couldn't just leave the pouches where they were, so I carried them off into the pines, kicked away some of the needles and covered them. With my trash somewhat concealed, I shouldered the pack and set off east.

The first houses of Fort McCoy came into view about ten after two in the morning. Not wanting to go through town, I skirted the edge of the houses, staying just out of the line of sight. This track eventually brought me to the Ocklawaha, or, I should say, the swamp. Edging my way around the border of it was slow-going, trying to stay on high ground. I never saw anyone, save the occasional candle or lantern coming from a window. Continuing to move slowly, it took another couple of hours to make my way to the bridge. Now I had to decide if I was going to cross that bridge or stay on this side for the day.

Seeing the bridge made the decision for me; I actually heard it before I saw it. All the bridges over the river are elevated; they rise probably fifty feet above the river. The top of the bridge was lit up like a Christmas tree. Two diesel-powered light towers were set up on top of the bridge, and several armed, uniformed men were manning it. Staying back in the swamp, I surveyed the situation. Observing the bridge from end to end, sitting in the middle of the road at the end of the bridge was a rubber-tired fighting vehicle, a Stryker, and I bet there had to be one at the other end.

On this end was a barbed-wire barricade and sandbag emplacements with crew-served weapons. This was a no-shit for-real military blockade. If they were blocking this little bridge, then they were certainly blocking the others on the river. Seeing the extent of the operation here, I was suddenly struck with fear. There could be, certainly would be, roving patrols. There could be seismic sensors out here. I had no idea how extensive this blockade was. Turning around, I walked back out, trying to stay in the exact tracks I walked in on. I was still a couple of hundred yards from the bridge, and I damn sure didn't want to get any closer.

Finally getting out of sight and sound of the bridge, I stopped in a thick place on the edge of the swamp. *Shit! I have got to get across this damn river. If*

I can make it across this, I'll be in the forest and shouldn't have too much more trouble. After all, my place backs up to it. A shot rang out in the distance; there were muffled shouts, followed immediately by automatic weapons fire. From the sounds of it, everyone on the bridge was firing at what was probably some redneck in the woods with a .30-30. At least their attention was focused elsewhere for the moment.

Just upriver from the bridge was a power-line crossing; a little dead-end road led up to it. But that was still too close; I could see the bridge from the edge of the river, so I continued upstream. Rounding a small curve in the river, the bank opened up. There was a boat ramp and a dock with an open parking area. Staying in the bush, I watched the parking lot for a while; after all, I had the time. It wasn't fifteen minutes before an up-armored Humvee drove slowly through the parking area, blacked out. I dropped flat in the bush and didn't move. The truck made a loop through the parking lot and headed back out. The urgency to cross this damn thing just got worse. As soon as the truck was out of sight, I opened my bag and pulled out the last two drum liners I had. I put the pack in one, and stripped down to my skivvies, stuffing my clothes and the small bag into the other. The only thing I kept out was the carbine. I tied both of the bags off with tie wraps and headed for the river. It was cold out, but I really didn't notice. Well, my nuts did, but the rest of me was too hyped up to care.

Going down the boat ramp, I hit the water and started across it as quietly as possible, trying not to even ripple the water. With everything in the big bags, they floated; the one with the pack was low in the water, but it didn't sink. A sandbar ran out into the river here; it made me need to move more in a diagonal upstream to get across the river. I reckoned the route I took ended up being almost two hundred feet. It really didn't take long, but it felt like hours in the water.

Climbing out on the far side, there was an area of low, sparse brush. None of it was more than four feet high, but I had to get some clothes on. I was freezing in the cold air. I tore the bags open and got everything out. From the pack, I pulled the spare T-shirt and used it as a towel to sort of dry off. After getting dressed, I stuffed the empty bags and wet shirt back into the bag and put my feet in the boots. Shouldering the pack, I headed off without even tying my boots.

Mike and the guys were busy moving gear. All the radio equipment was stacked in the living room, along with weapons and ammo. Mike was setting down a couple of cases of MREs as Sarge came back in. "Hey, come out here and help me cut these guys down."

"What are you going to do with them?" Mike asked.

"I figure we'll leave 'em tied up in the shed. Their boys ought to be along soon enough to get 'em. We need Ronnie too. One of 'em is in bad shape," Sarge replied.

"Hey, Doc! Get your bag of tricks an' come out to the garage!" Mike called out.

"On my way," came a reply from somewhere in the back of the house.

Sarge and Mike walked out to the garage. Mr. C was out. Walking up to him, Sarge pulled the Benchmade Griptilian from his pocket and flipped it open. "Grab him around the waist," he said to Mike. Mike wrapped his arms around the limp man's waist and took some of the weight off the rope. Sarge reached up and cut the rope. As Mike was laying him down, Ronnie came through the door.

"Ooo, he doesn't look good," Ronnie said. Kneeling down beside him, he took a temporal scan thermometer out and ran it across his forehead. "Not good, 96.3. He's got cyanosis on his face and hands." Looking up at Sarge, he said, "We need to get him warmed up quick."

"What do we need to do with him?" Sarge asked. He was placing flex cuffs on one of the other two after cutting him down.

"Put him in a bed, wrap him in blankets, and put hot water bottles in with him would be best," Ronnie relayed as he was cutting the man's clothes off.

"We ain't got time to waste for that shit. Mike, get him down, and take them into the spare bedroom. Ronnie and I'll bring him in." Mike let the other two pull their pants up, their hands being secured in front of them, and pointed to the house.

Ronnie and Sarge came into the room carrying the limp body of Mr. C. "All right, you two, strip to your skivvies," Sarge ordered.

The two stood there, looking at one another and then back at Sarge, not sure what the hell he had in mind now. Sarge looked over at them after depositing his load in the bed, "Either you do it, or I'll do it for you. You won't like it if I do it," he said.

"You better listen to him. Believe me, you don't want him to strip you down," Ted said.

After their hands were freed, the two men reluctantly started to undress. "What the hell are you going to do now?" the black kid asked.

"You two are going to get in the bed with him, one on either side. Then I'm gonna cuff you two together to make a dipshit sandwich. Your body heat will warm him up. Now get in there," Sarge replied.

With the two men now stripped to their skivvies, he ordered them into the bed. "Nut to butt, boys, nut to butt. It's the best thing I can do for now." With one on either side, Sarge cuffed their hands together, left to left, right to right. They were both facing the same direction, so they were cuffed front to back with their unconscious partner in the middle.

With their captives now secured, all four of them went out to the living room. Mike crossed his arms and looked at Sarge. "Well, now what?"

"We need to get the hell out of here, and fast. The easiest way is the river. We'll use my boats and go toward the gulf. There is a little slough down there about twenty-five miles from here. I have a little huntin' camp back in there that we'll use for now. If we pack 'em right, we should be able to get everything in one trip," Sarge replied.

"Let's get to it then," Ted said.

They all started hauling stuff out to the boats. Sarge had two aluminum flat-bottomed boats—

great for a river that was full of old snags and submerged logs. It took another couple of hours to get everything loaded, but they even had enough room to bring some of the batteries and a couple of solar panels for power.

Every firearm Sarge had was loaded in, along with every round of ammo. They even took all the captured gear from the trio spooning in the back bedroom. There was still a lot of gear that Sarge wanted; he knew he would never be coming back to his house.

"Let's go next door and see if the neighbors are there," Sarge said. Picking up his M4, he headed out the door with Mike in tow.

Cutting through the woods to his neighbor's, he knocked on the door. "Phil! It's Linus. You home?" With no answer, he pounded on the door. After no response, they walked around the house, shining their weapons' lights into the windows. "He ain't here. Must be up in Tennessee with his daughter," he said. Turning, he headed for the river, with Mike covering the rear. Just like at Sarge's, Phil had a dock on the river with an aluminum boat in a manual hoist.

"Let's lower this thing and take it over to the house," Sarge said as he started to crank the handle on the hoist, lowering the boat into the water. It took a few minutes to get the outboard started after sitting for so long, but they finally got it to fire, and the two of them headed back up the river to his house.

Pulling up to his dock where the other two boats were, Ted called out, "Nice, I thought that's what you were doing. We already carried the rest of the gear down here."

With all four of them at the dock, it didn't take long to get the third boat loaded. When everything was on board, Sarge headed back to the house while the guys went over the boats, ensuring everything was ready for the ride upriver. Back in the house, he headed for the bedroom and found the trio right where he left them. Mr. C was coming around but not enough to be mouthy.

"All righty, boys, we're out of here. I assume your folks will be here soon enough. You guys need to think about which side of this fight you really want to be on. It isn't too late for you. If we ever meet again, I'll kill you on the spot." Sarge turned and walked out of the room. He walked slowly through his house, taking it all in for one last time. Stopping by the fridge, he pulled out the case of Sam Adams he had put in earlier and headed for the boats.

All three boats were idling at the dock. Sarge handed out the beers and climbed into his boat with Mike. "Well, boys, y'all ready?"

He was answered by the sound of outboard engines dropping in gear. Everyone pulled down their NVGs, moving the boats out into the center of the river, and headed toward the gulf.

There were so many cars on the road, on the shoulder and sitting across the lanes, that Thad had to turn the headlights on. Crashing into a car at forty-five or fifty miles an hour in the dark just wasn't an option. Taking Highway 40 hadn't been his intention, but here he was. It was probably ten miles or better to the intersection with Highway 41; ten miles through a relatively populated area.

The sight of headlights coming down the road brought some people out to the side of the road just to watch the truck pass by. He passed a group of three boys on the shoulder; they were pumping their fists up and down like kids do to get truckers to blow the air horn. It brought a smile to Thad's face as he passed. He did not, however, deliver the horn toot they wanted.

The road rolled by, and things almost seemed normal; if it wasn't for having to weave around stalled cars, it would've been. The farther west he went, the fewer cars were on the road; he was able to speed up and relax a little. He covered the fifteen miles to the intersection with 41 in about twenty minutes.

"Homestretch," he quietly said, making the left at the intersection. His reverie was short-lived. Almost as soon as he made the corner, there were people all over the road. It was probably ten at night, but there were a lot of people out. Letting the truck idle up to the group, he saw that they were coming and going from a large church. Some were carrying plastic bags away, and others had paper plates.

A man in a yellow reflective vest and a flashlight stepped out into the road and waved him forward. Thad eased up. As the man approached the truck, he laid the shotgun on his lap.

"Hi, there," the man said, shining the light at the driver's door, keeping it out of Thad's eyes.

"Hi," Thad replied with a nod.

"Looks like you got lucky," the man said, looking at the old truck.

"Yeah, it's still runnin'." Thad was looking in the side mirrors and past the man at some of the people starting to gather around.

"Do you need anything? We have hot food and drinks," he offered with a smile. The last thing Thad wanted to do was get caught up owing anyone again. The last time that happened, he didn't want to think about it.

"No, sir, I've got everything I need. I just want to get home. It's taken a long time to get here, and I have a long way to go yet," Thad answered.

"Okay, then, where you headed? Maybe you can give some of the folks we have stranded here a ride. I'm Roger, by the way." He stepped forward to offer his hand to Thad. As he got close enough to see into the truck, Thad raised the shotgun so he could see it. Startled, Roger jumped back with his hands up.

"I ain't going to hurt you. Put your hands down. And I ain't taking anyone with me either. I'm sorry, but I'll be on my way now." Thad laid the shotgun down on his lap.

"Sorry, didn't mean no harm. We're just trying to help people and thought you might be able to help," Roger said.

"I don't mean no harm, but trying to help people has caused me a lot of grief. Good luck to you." Thad let the truck start to ease forward. No one tried to stop him or even said anything. He got glares from some of them, but he passed through without incident.

A couple of miles past the church, he passed the burned-out shell of a Winn-Dixie store. The parking lot was littered with trash and the remains of burned-out cars. Thad tightened his grip on the steering wheel and pressed on into Dunnellon. Seeing the destruction, he was nervous. It was the first time he had seen anything like it, and it didn't bode well for the kind of folks that lived there. A little farther on, he passed a Walmart. It sat too far off the road to see clearly, and he wasn't about to go in for a look. Passing through the business district, he saw several people out, hanging around some of the stores, drawing many leering looks.

What looked like an old Ford Fairlane passed Thad going the opposite way as he came into the heart of the little downtown area. He couldn't see into the car, but it did a slow roll as they passed one another. Thad watched the car in the side mirror; it slowed to a stop and then started a U-turn. Thad immediately floored the truck. The tires on the old Fairlane squealed as it accelerated in the turn.

Passing over the Rainbow River, he saw the Fairlane's headlights gaining on him. The pedal was to the floor; all he could do was hope. The two vehicles raced down the road, the Fairlane slowly gaining on the truck. Thad had his eyes glued to the mirror and had to swerve a couple of times to avoid colliding with stalled cars.

As the car caught up to him, it moved over to the left like it was going to pass. Thad cut it off; it jinked to the right, trying to come up on the passenger side. Thad closed the door again. The next time the car tried to come up on the left, Thad slammed on the brakes and the Fairlane flew past him, sliding as its brakes locked up.

Thad made a quick right onto a dirt road. Hell,

it wasn't even a road; it was a power line right-of-way. The truck bogged down in the soft sand a couple of times, but he was moving fast enough that he didn't get stuck. There was no way that car could follow him down this damn thing.

In the mirror, Thad saw the Ford back up and stop where the right-of-way crossed the road. He continued to bounce down the sugar-sand path. The Ford sat there for a minute and then squealed its tires as it accelerated down the road. The path Thad was on made him slow down; the soft dirt prevented him from going too fast, not to mention banging his head on the top of the cab as he rumbled over the bumps and humps.

Thad crossed two paved roads but stayed on the right-of-way. He was passing behind some houses but never saw anyone. As he was crossing the third paved road, the headlights of a car caught him broadside in the center of the road. He stomped the pedal again and kept going down the dirt path.

Looking over his right shoulder, Thad saw the Ford making another U-turn, the tires screeching in complaint as the car was forced around. A few minutes later, he saw the car was keeping pace with him, about a block away, on a road that ran parallel to the right-of-way on his left.

"Shit!" Thad shouted, banging the steering wheel. The Ford suddenly stopped. Thad kept on down the track. He crossed two more paved roads but stuck to the dirt. That damn car couldn't follow him on it. "What the hell do y'all want?" Thad muttered as he rounded a small bend on the right-of-way. Up ahead was a four-lane road he had to cross.

The Ford came flying up the road and stopped in the center of the crossing. Four men climbed out of the car and started to spread out in front of him.

Coming out of the brush on the side of the river, I realized real quick I picked a bad, really fucking bad, spot to cross the river. What I couldn't see from the other side was the series of long, low buildings sitting behind a small berm. Several Hummers and other military vehicles sat around the buildings; even worse, there were sentries.

I stayed behind the berm and skirted the river, moving to the north. South was the bridge, and I already had seen what was there. Slipping down the bank, the ground started to get mucky. I stepped out of my left boot and had to stop to get it back on—laced them both up and tied 'em tight. Kneeling in the muck, I looked down the bank and saw nothing ahead of me but swamp. It looked like the little strip of land I was on was quickly running out.

"Shit, fuck, shit!" I cursed under my breath. "What the hell am I going to do now?" It was about five thirty and the sun would be rising soon; there was no way I could get caught out in the open here. With limited options, I opened the pack and pulled one of the drum liners out and took a tie wrap from the little bag. Pulling the sleeping mat out from under the straps, I put the pack in the bag along with the little bag, after putting the XD in my waistband. I took off the Carhartt and stuffed it in the bag as well. Lastly, I dropped the NVG case in and tied the bag closed.

Belly crawling to the river, I was covered in stinking, slimy muck. Dragging the bag behind me with one hand and the carbine in the other, I was trying to get to the river. Stripping down this time was out of the question. I could just imagine getting myself shot 'cause the moon glared off my bare white ass as I swam across.

Finally sliding into the water, I used the rolled-up mat to keep afloat, by lying across it, and holding on to the bag—all while trying to dunk the carbine to get some of the stinking-ass muck out of it. Naturally, the current wanted to carry me toward the bridge, so I also had to try to swim; staying near the edge of the river, I could kind of walk and grope my way along the water plants.

The river looked like it intersected with another. Off to the right was actually a man-made canal. This whole structure I had stumbled into was an abandoned lock system that was never finished. Continuing to go upstream, I finally came to a sandbar and was able to drag myself out of the river.

Now that I was out of the water, I was cold. I needed to warm up, but first I had to get the hell away from the river and fast. The eastern sky was already starting to change from the inky black of predawn to the cobalt blue of early morning. Soon the sun's rays would pull back the veil, and I needed to find a hidey-hole before the curtain went up.

Pulling my pack and coat out of the plastic bag, and being in a hurry to get moving, I stuffed the liner in a cargo pocket. Checking the compass, I oriented myself in a southeasterly direction. After putting on my coat, I stumbled and splashed through the swamp for what seemed like an eternity. The cold was taking its toll on me. I was starting to feel a little delirious. Just when I thought I couldn't go any farther, I found a high dry spot with palms and palmettos on it.

Dragging my ass out of the cold water and up the high ground, I collapsed. I had to force myself to get back up. Opening the pack, I pulled the waterproof bag with my clothes in it out. Stripping down till I was naked, I pulled on a clean set of skivvies and pulled the sleeping bag out. Using the light coat, I sort of dried off and then climbed into the bag.

Once I was in the bag, I managed to pull the woobie out and drag it into the bag with me and roll up inside it. Making sure the carbine was beside me and the XD was in the bag with me, I was out like a light.

A very low-flying helo jolted me awake. Opening my eyes, I just sat there not moving. I felt punch-drunk, and my eyes didn't want to focus. Listening to the ship—the canopy was too thick to see through—I could tell it was close. After a couple of minutes, it sounded as if the ship moved off. After listening for a minute and not hearing anything close, I crawled out of the bag and dressed in some dry clothes. Squatting under a cabbage palm, cradling the carbine, I started to figure a way out of here. East was my only option. Due east should keep me away from the road and anyone on it. Knowing which way I was going, I started to get ready to head out; but, damn, I was tired.

I had a pile of wet clothes to deal with. Stuffing them into the drum liner, I rolled it up and stuffed it in the pack. From my clothes bag, I pulled out a pair of dry socks and put them on; then I stuck my feet in the cold, wet boots. Ah, that sucked! The helo came back around. It flew almost overhead, but I still couldn't see it. If they had a FLIR on board, I was seriously hosed. Each time the bird came around, I would sit still and not move, hoping they wouldn't find me.

The bird moved off again, and I started to think about what I may have done that could have turned them onto me. Then it hit me—the sliding down through the muck to get to the river. I was sure that left a hell of a trail. Maybe they would just think it's a gator slide, and then that little voice popped into my head. "It ain't always about you." There's a lot of truth in that. Why in the hell would they be looking for me? I'm nobody. Certainly they had bigger fish to fry.

After packing the sleeping bag and the rest of my gear, I pulled an MRE oatmeal raisin cookie out for breakfast. Shouldering the pack, I started to pick my way very slowly through the swamp. I didn't want to get soaked again, so I was going slow; plus, I was eating a cookie and was damn hungry. The helo eventually moved off; I hoped that was good news. I crossed several small creeks; some of them I was able to step over, and some I crossed on downed cypress trees.

After about an hour of slow stumbling, I reached the edge of the swamp. I came out into a nice area mixed with oaks, pines, juniper, and palmetto. Peering into the woods, it appeared that it opened up a little ways ahead. This was less than ideal; I wanted to break out into the scrub and quickly put some distance between me and Uncle Sugar's finest. The other side of the little hammock I was in butted up to a chop where the timber had been taken a year or two ago.

Some scrub was out there, but it was short. No way in hell I was going to try to cross this patch in the daylight. Instead I looked for a place to bed down till dark; I was tired as hell anyway. Finding a nice juniper tree, I crawled under it and laid the sleep mat out and pulled the woobie out too. Taking the wet clothes from the bag, I hung them in the branches of the tree to let them dry as much as possible. Using the pack as a pillow, it was time to snooze for a while.

Dale and Phil had been lifelong friends. They grew up in Dixie County, and neither one of them had ever been more than a hundred miles from it. When things went to shit, they naturally got together to take care of each other and their families. The problem with these two was that they always lived life just outside of the law.

Numerous arrests, none major, and the constant threat of jail kept them from turning into hard-core felons. Still, they were two of the most notorious poachers in Dixie County. Both of the FWC officers knew them by sight, boot track, and for one officer, smell. Dale never did let Phil live down getting caught and fined for turkey hunting on private land, when the game warden smelled his way to him and his can of sardines in hot sauce.

Dale was the brains of the operation, and Phil was his faithful understudy. Between the two of them, they poached more gators, deer, and turkeys, and snuck more submerged one-hundred-year-old cypress logs out of the Suwannee River valley than any other fifty men combined. They did it to feed their families and provide a little cash money to boot.

With the threat of the law now a mere memory, they decided to up their game. Spending so much time on the river, they knew it like the backs of their hands. In the days following the event, in the course of their regular work of poaching the river, they started to notice the boat traffic picking up. It was Dale's idea to set up on the river and "tax" folks. They never cleaned anyone out, but Dale was the one who decided when sufficient tax had been paid.

Being as notorious as they were, most folks they stopped on the river handed over what they were told to. The fact that these folks also knew that Dale's boy, Tim, was on the bank covering them with a rifle, not to mention the AK that Dale held on them, guaranteed no one would put up a fight.

The folks around the area were smart though and soon figured out that these two would-be pirates only operated during the day. So most everybody switched to night travel on the river. Dale was pretty sharp too and picked up on the change. So tonight they were sitting on the river, just around a bend downriver from Fanning Springs. Phil had his pontoon boat anchored on one side of the river, and Dale was in his skiff, tied to the side of it.

They sat there drinking shine from pint mason

jars, another one of their "cash money" sources. The standard procedure was to sit in the boats, getting slowly pickled, until they heard a boat coming; then Dale and his boy would take their boat out into the center of the river to stop whoever was coming, leaving Phil to cover them. Both of the boats had Q-Beams, and they used these to blind and intimidate the other boats.

Sarge sat on a cooler in front of the center console of his boat; Mike was driving. They all had on full battle rattle, body armor, sidearms, and enough mags for the M4s to break contact with almost any size force. Not to mention the FN Minimi SPW they captured from the DHS goons. The appearance of this particular weapon really bothered all of them. What in the hell were those guys doing with something like that? Basically a shortened M249 with a telescoping stock, Sarge fell in love immediately. Add in the eight hundred rounds those morons packed in and the guys almost saw Sarge's O face.

Sarge twisted the top on one of the Sam Adams and turned it up, taking a long pull on the bottle.

"Hey, give me one of those," Mike yelled above the outboard.

Sarge cocked his head to one side and yelled back, "You're driving, dickhead; no." Then he turned the bottle up, draining it. Tossing the bottle over his shoulder, Mike had to knock it out of the air to keep from getting hit by it. He saw Sarge's shoulders bouncing up and down and knew he was laughing.

"Mean ole prick," he said out loud.

Sarge cocked his head to one side. "What?"

"Nothing." Mike shook his head. *How in the hell did he hear that?* "How far we going?"

"Just drive, Junior. And don't start the 'are we there yet' shit." Sarge opened himself another beer. Mike just shook his head.

They continued down the river—the three boats in single file, blacked out, no running lights. Twenty-five miles was a long way on the water, and they soon settled down for the ride. Since all the guys had NVGs, they didn't need to use any lights, but no one else on the river had them. They picked up on the first boat they encountered long before they got to it. Their spotlight shining around alerted the guys to their location.

As they approached a bend, Mike slowed the boat. The other two came up on either side of them. "We'll go around the bend. If it's clear, I'll shine my laser up in the air. If it ain't, you'll know," Sarge said. The guys all nodded, and the lead boat pulled away. Sarge stood up and stepped to the bow of the boat, the SPW at the ready.

As they came around the corner, they spotted the boat immediately but were not detected by it. Mike was cruising rather slowly up the river; it looked like the other boat was engaged in froggin' or looking for gators. Sarge watched the boat for a minute through the NVG; a small family was on the boat—man, woman, and a child. The cough of a small voice drifted across the river.

"I don't think they're anything to be worried about," Mike said.

"Probably not, but let's say hi," Sarge replied. Flipping the NVG up and putting a hand to his mouth, he called out, "Hello, the boat!" The spotlight swung around, shining across the river and settling on their boat. Sarge waved at the boat as Mike steered toward it. The other boat turned out toward the river, stopping rather far away. Mike reached down and hit the switch for the IR laser on his M4; it was tucked into a handrail on the side of the console, muzzle up.

As Mike motored closer to the other boat, a man's voice called out, "That's far enough." He still had the spotlight on, pointing it into the river, and they clearly saw him pick up his shotgun. The woman and child were sitting on the bow of the boat.

Sarge raised his hands. "We don't mean no harm there, friend. Just wanted to see how things were on the river."

With Sarge's hands in plain view. The man came a little closer. "Just out trying to scrounge some dinner," he offered.

"Why so late or early?—depending on how you look at it," Sarge asked.

"I don't like to come out during the day, wanted to get the boy out of the house for a bit. Plus he's a good frogger," he said, nodding and smiling at the little boy, whose face lit up with his father's praise.

"Any trouble out here?" Sarge asked.

"No, not really. But then we stay close to home," the man replied.

"Probably a good idea," Sarge said.

The boats were drifting closer, and the guy seemed to relax a bit. When he heard the other boats coming, he stiffened and looked at Sarge with fright on his face and then at his family. Sarge raised his hands again. "Don't worry; they're with us." The little boy coughed a raspy cough.

"Is the little man sick?" Sarge asked.

"It's just a little cold," the woman answered.

The other two boats came alongside Sarge's boat. "Hey, Doc, you got anything to give to a little frogger with a cough?"

"I think I can find him something," Ronnie answered and started to dig around his bag. Putting the boat in gear, he eased up to the other boat. The man caught the gunwale and held onto it. Ronnie handed over some cough drops and a small bottle of Vick's. "Give him one of these and rub this on his chest at night to help break that stuff up," Ronnie said, handing them to the woman. She took them.

"Thank you so much. We don't have anything for him," she said.

"You guys in the army?" the man asked.

"Not anymore," Sarge answered. "And if you see any of them, I suggest you stay away. Ronnie, give 'em a case of MREs." Ronnie handed the case over to the man.

"Hey, thanks a lot. We sure can use this. Fish is getting old," he said, smiling to his wife, who smiled back.

"You guys be safe," Sarge said with a nod.

"You too. Thanks a lot," the man said with a wave.

Sarge nodded to Mike, who put the boat in gear, dropped his NVGs, and headed down the river. The other boats fell in line. Sarge plopped back down on the cooler. Cruising down the river, they encountered a couple more boats, using the same procedure to approach them. All the folks were in roughly the same situation, hungry and afraid. Sarge doled out a little more charity, and Ronnie applied a clean dressing to the arm of a guy who was bit by the four-foot gator he had wrestled into his boat. He needed antibiotics, but they had precious few of them and didn't offer any.

Rounding another bend in the river, they were met by the twin beams of spotlights from either side of the river. The lights instantly shut the NVGs down, and the guys had to flip them up. Thinking it was an ambush, all the three boats were pushed to full throttle. A shot from the boat that moved to the center of the river was answered by a long burst from the SPW in Sarge's hands. Ronnie and Ted were both firing at it with one hand and steering with the other. Ted was firing at the boat on the side of the river.

The spotlight in the center of the river fell into the water. The guys let up as they came abreast of the boat, since there was no return fire. The spotlight off to the side was shining straight up. Ted broke off and went toward it. Coming up to the pontoon boat, he saw a man lying on the deck in a fetal position. "Show me your fuckin' hands!" Ted screamed. The man rolled onto his back with hands out; he had pissed his pants and looked terrified.

As Sarge's boat approached the other one, he and Mike were both at the ready. The white fiberglass interior of the boat was full of blood; it was splattered all over it. A body lay on its side on the deck. Another figure was lying on the opposite side, with his hands over his head. "Show me your hands, asshole, or I'll fuckin' smoke your ass!" Sarge yelled out. A boy about sixteen rolled over. Blood was splattered across his face.

Thad slowed the truck to a stop; there was still a hundred yards between them. An asphalt driveway ran down the right-of-way to where he brought the truck to a stop. The four men were spread out across his path. There was plenty of room to go through them but not without taking fire. Thad put the truck in park and stepped out. The four men spread out on the road just stood there.

"What'da ya want!" Thad called out.

The one leaning on the hood of the old Ford answered, "Yo truck."

That just pissed him off. They already had a car that ran, and now they wanted his. This was what things had come to, the iron rule. Those with the iron and the will to use it, make the rules. Checking them out, Thad saw that one of them had what looked like an AK. The other three didn't appear to have any long guns. Thad started to develop a plan. "I'm comin' over," he called out to the supposed leader of this little tribe.

"You bes' be real slow about it," came the reply.

Thad put the truck in gear and started to ease forward. He was still trying to put his plan together; it really all depended on where the men were when he stopped. As he got closer, they started to gather around the car. As they did, Thad could now tell that none of them had a long gun. He didn't even see a handgun on any of them. If they had them, they were under their coats. That would certainly help. Thad slipped the shotty into his lap, holding it with his right hand, the muzzle pointed at the door. As he got closer, the one that had spoken stepped toward the truck. "That's right, keep coming," Thad muttered. He was just barely creeping along.

The man coming forward was proud of himself. He was talking it up to the guys with him. Thad couldn't hear what he was saying, but they appeared to be eating it up. They were all laughing and really carrying on, excited about getting another ride for their group. The other three fell in behind the one with the AK. As Thad brought the truck to a stop about ten feet from them, the one with the AK started to walk up to the window by himself. As he stepped up, he had a huge grin on his face, full of himself.

"Good fa you. Now get yo ass out of my truck," the man said.

The other three were still eating it up. "Yeah, get yo ass outta our truck."

Thad raised the shotty a bit; as the man stepped forward, Thad pulled the trigger on the shotgun. The blast caught him high in the chest, knocking him over backward. The other three dove for the ground. Thad jumped out of the truck, drawing the Glock as he went, before the others could react. One of the three rolled onto his back and went to draw a pistol from his waistband. Thad planted one of his size thirteen boots on the kid's neck; he had the shotty pointed at the second one of them and the Glock at the third.

"I'll be keeping my truck. What the hell makes

you damn people think you can just take what you want from others?" Thad said; he was incredulous and wanted to kill them all. "You two, on your belly. Put your hands out to your side. If you try anything, I'll kill you."

The other two were looking up at the big man. The fear on their faces was real. It was something they weren't used to; they were used to being the ones feared, not the ones in fear. They had run their game around Dunnellon with little opposition. They knew who they could go after and who to stay away from; this was their first mistake, and it was huge.

"Come on, man, all we wanted was the truck. We wasn't goin' to do anythin' to ya," the one with the shotty trained on him said.

"It's my truck!" Thad screamed at them. "See what you caused here!" He nodded to the nearly decapitated body lying beside him. The sound of the man under his boot gagging got his attention, and he looked down. The madder he got, the more pressure he had unintentionally applied to the man's neck. He had both his hands wrapped around Thad's ankle. "You still think you a badass now?"

The kid's eyes were huge, and he was gasping for breath. "I told you two to roll over. Do it now!" Thad shouted. The two immediately rolled over. One of them started to blubber about not wanting to be killed. With the other two on their bellies, Thad looked down at the one under his boot. "I'm gonna take my foot off your neck. When I do, you better roll over. Try anything, and I'll unload this buck in your face, understand?" Thad lowered the shotgun so it was pointed at his nose. The kid tried to nod, Thad lifted his boot, and he rolled over.

Thad tucked the Glock into his belt and knelt beside him, watching the other two as he did. Reaching under the kid, he pulled the pistol out of his pants. Lowering his head, he whispered into the kid's ear, "You so much as sneeze, and you're a dead man." Thad quickly searched the other two, finding one more pistol. He took the two pistols and threw them into the cab of the truck and picked up the rifle, which turned out to be an SKS with a thirty-round mag. Keeping an eye on the men on the ground, he pulled a hank of 550 cord from his pack and went about tying the hands of each of them.

"What're you gonna do to us?" one of them whined.

"You worried about yourself; ain't none of you so much as looked at your buddy over here." Thad pointed to the body. "All you worried about is yourself. You're pathetic."

Thad walked over to the car to see what they had in it. Lying in the front seat, he found two boxes of ammo for the SKS. The floor was littered with beer cans and liquor bottles. Opening the trunk, he found more liquor; he was hoping for food. Sitting in the driver's seat, he turned the key on to check the gas level, quarter of a tank. Oh well, if it had more gas, he was thinking of taking it. The old truck was starting to suffer a bit. He pulled the keys from the ignition and put them in his pocket. Taking the ammo and a bottle of vodka from the trunk, he went back to the truck and tossed those into the cab and turned to the three men tied up on the ground.

Then he had a second thought and returned to the trunk of the car and pulled out the remainder of the case of vodka. Thad opened all but one of the bottles and poured them in the car, making sure to coat the seats and floorboards front and back. Taking the last bottle out of the case, he reached into the backseat and pulled out a T-shirt, and, ripping a piece off, he soaked it in vodka and stuffed it into the neck of the bottle. Then he took a lighter from his pocket and lit the rag. Looking back at the three men on the ground, he flung the bottle at the dash with all his might; it exploded into flames, and the fire immediately engulfed the entire car.

"Let's see how bad y'all are now," Thad said as he climbed into the truck and started it.

"You just gonna leave us here! Tied up!" one of them shouted.

"What was your plan for me?" Thad asked as he put the truck in gear and drove away.

Knowing that 41 should be off to the east of him, Thad turned the truck out onto the paved road the bandits had come down. He was right and hit 41 in less than half a mile, where he made a right and headed south. There would be other little towns on his path home; he just hoped they would be easier to get through. Looking down at the dash, Thad noticed that his little run through Dunnellon had cost him some gas. He had less than half a tank now. Trying to find gas was now his primary concern. Having to walk the rest of the way home just wasn't an option he wanted to think about.

After about fifteen minutes on the road, he came into the small town of Hernando. This was where

200 and 41 merged, with 200 coming in from the left. There was a gas station that could be entered from either of the two roads. Thad let the truck coast into the station. He had been driving with the headlights on, since the area he was driving through was virtually uninhabited. Swinging into the station, the headlights illuminated a camp of sorts. A number of men were gathered around a burn barrel under the canopy for the fuel pumps. They stood up, reaching for rifles as they did. Knowing he was taking a chance, Thad wanted to see if he could get some fuel.

The men were all on their feet. There were five of them, looking at the truck. Thad stepped out with his hands where they could see them and called, "Y'all got any gas I could trade for?"

"Yeah, we got gas. What'cha tradin'?" came the reply.

"I got a few things; depends on how much I can get," Thad said.

"Pull the truck up here to this pump." One of them pointed to a pump.

Thad hopped back into the truck and pulled up to the pump. Most of the men went back to the barrel, keeping an eye on him and the truck. One of them walked around to Thad as he got out. "What'cha got fer trade?" Thad reached into the cab and picked up the bottle of Vodka off the seat.

"I got this." He held it out. The man's face lit up, and he let out a holler, drawing the attention of the others.

"That'll do jus' fine," he said. "Crank that generator!" he called out. A moment later, the hum of a generator could be heard from the back of the station. The man stuck the bottle of vodka in his coat pocket and picked up the pump handle. He opened the cap on the gas tank on the truck and stuck the nozzle in. With the gas flowing, the two of them started to chat about things a bit.

"Where you comin' from?" the man asked.

"I was up near Tallahassee when it happened. I'm trying to get over toward Tampa," Thad answered. He had his hands shoved into the pockets of his field coat, the Glock tightly gripped in his right hand.

"That's a hell of a trip. How was it? Any trouble?" the man asked.

"Yeah, it ain't been easy. There's been some crazy damn people. How about 'round here. You guys had any trouble?" Thad asked.

"Thur's been some. Couple of times, some have tried to hit this place. We keep men here around the clock, only store in town. Plus they's a kerosene pump here, and lots of folks need that right now. We offer protection, and the owner pays us with fuel and a little food, but that's starting to run out now." The handle on the pump shut off; the truck was full.

"Yeah, I've seen a few people who was working together, an' I've seen some straight-up craziness too. Seems a lot of folks think they are owed whatever they need or just want and just try taking it from folks," Thad said.

The man pulled the nozzle from the truck and put the cap back on. "Yeah, this truck looks like you've seen a little shit." He nodded to the windshield as he hung the handle back on the pump.

"Somebody dropped a block off an overpass on 75," Thad replied.

The man let out a low whistle. "Shit, yur lucky ta be alive."

"Well, I hope the owner is okay with that bottle for the gas," Thad said as he stuck his hand out.

"Oh, this one's off the books," the man replied as he took Thad's hand and shook it. They both let out a little laugh. "Good luck getting to Tampa. I wish more folks acted like this, makin' a fair trade for what they needed. We've seen our fair share of them what think just 'cause we got it an' they don't, we should give it to 'em."

They shook hands, and Thad climbed into the truck and started it. Pulling out from under the canopy, he waved out the window as the men began to pass the bottle around the fire.

Chapter 9

My nose tickled. In my half daze, I blew at it. It still tickled, so I reached up to wipe my face. Opening my eyes, I was greeted by a face covered in camo paint; a boonie hat sat on the head.

"Mornin', sunshine." A smile spread across the face, bright white teeth shining through the greens, brown, and black on the face. Instantly my heart was in my throat. Looking past the face, I saw the backs of two more men, facing away. Looking back at the one before me, I did a quick look-over of the figure before me. He was wearing woodland camo and cradling an AK in black furniture. Well, he wasn't a fed.

"Mornin'," I said as I started to sit up. The XD was still in my hand, under the blanket.

"Don't do anything silly now," the camo'd face said, nodding toward the blanket. "I know what you got under there, and that." He reached down and slid the carbine out from under the sleep mat.

"Well, I guess that all depends on you guys," I said. Not knowing what was about to happen, I was glad the pistol was still in my grip. I flipped the blanket down as I sat up and rubbed my face with my left hand.

"Aw, you ain't gotta worry about us. We caught on to you when you approached the bridge. We tried to catch up to you before you crossed the river, but you picked the worst place in the world to cross, and we weren't about to follow you. I'm surprised they haven't found your ass yet. You should have seen all the shit you stirred up when they found your tracks. Good idea getting back in the river and going upstream. They were looking downriver for you. Some poor bastard on the bridge got his ass chewed for letting you get by," he said.

Well, maybe this isn't going to be a bad thing after all. "Who are you guys, and what are you doing out here?"

"We're just a group of locals that don't like the way the feds have come to *help*. Where are you headed?" he asked.

"I'm just trying to get home down near Altoona. I was up near Tallahassee when the shit hit the fan," I replied.

"That's a hell of a trip. I wouldn't think most folks could even do it," he said, looking over at my pack.

"Yeah, well, I have always kept my pack in the car, just in case. I'm close now, so it shouldn't be too hard. All I have to do is make it through the forest." He let out a grin when I said that.

"You're heading to Altoona. You plan on going by the bombing range?" he asked.

"Maybe." I wasn't sure who the hell this was, or what they were up to yet, so I didn't want to give too much away. "You guys the ones they were shooting at from the bridge last night?"

"Hu-hu, no, that wasn't us. There are plenty of people around here that don't like what's going on. If we're getting shot at, then someone has really fucked up," he replied.

"So what's up? What are you guys here for?" I asked.

"We saw you sneaking around, and we're just curious what you were up to. Figured we would pay you a visit and see what's up," he said with a smile.

"So what now?" I asked.

"Whatever; we just wanted to check you out. As soon as we saw you, we knew you weren't a threat to us," he replied.

"Are you a threat to me?" I asked him. The XD was still in my hand. This was just a little weird. What the hell did these guys want, really?

"We aren't a threat to anyone trying to live as a free man," came the reply.

"So, then, who are you a threat to?" I asked with a sideways glance. I started to look around a little and saw, in addition to the two I already knew about, another guy. He caught my attention, as he had a long gun strapped to his pack and was holding an AK that looked a lot like the one this guy had.

He just smiled at me. "Anyone who stands in the way of it."

I stood up, and he did as well. I looked around a minute and then stuck my hand out. He reached out and took it. "I'm Morgan," I said as we shook hands.

"Name's Norman," he replied with a firm handshake. A quick round of introductions revealed the names of the others in his group. There were Roy and Frank, and then there was Daniel; he was the one with the bolt gun strapped to his pack.

As I was shaking his hand, I had to ask about the pack and rifle combo. "What pack is that?"

He gave me a grin. "Nice, isn't it?" He turned slightly so I could see it. "It's an Eberlestock Skycrane. Damn thing cost me a fortune, but with the way things are now, it was money well spent."

"What kind of shooter you got in there?" I asked him.

"It's a Remmy 700 SPS with Leupold glass on it," he answered.

"Damn, you spent a shitload of cash on that whole setup. The bag and rifle, that's some pricey goodies," I said.

"Yeah, but I'm single, and it's what I did in the Corps, so I wanted to keep my skills sharp. It isn't the rifle I would like to have, but it gets the job done," he replied.

Taking a look at my watch, about three, I had a while to go before I could leave, but I could try to get in touch with Sarge in a little bit.

"You guys have a group? Or is this all there is?" I asked.

Norman and his boys looked at one another, and then Norman said, "We have more folks but not too many."

"Not like we didn't try to get more folks on board, but most folks just didn't get it. They damn sure wish they had now, though," Frank said.

"Yeah, I can relate. I tried too. Most folks just didn't get it. It was maddening how anyone could look around and not want to be prepared," I said. These guys were all on alert. Someone was always looking back toward the river, and another was always looking out toward the chop. "Where are you guys headed, or are you just out here for a sneak 'n' peek?"

"We heard about the roadblock here at the bridge and came over for a look," Norman replied.

"Where are you guys out of?" I asked.

"We have a place out on the other side of Kerr's Lake," Norman answered.

"Well, sounds like we're headed different directions," I said.

"Not really; I asked about the range earlier because we were heading that way for a little look-see over there. Something's up over there, and we want to get an idea what it is," Norman said.

He went on to explain about the helicopters heard flying a path that sounded to be between NAS JAX or Camp Blanding and the range—at least they thought the range. Their group was curious to see what was up, so these guys were sent out to find out what was going on. Norman was probably in his forties, former army, and a lifelong woodsman. Daniel was a marine recon sniper, only out a couple of years now, and another dedicated hunter. He was the designated tracker, as Norman said he could track a bumblebee through a briar.

Frank was just a good ole redneck. Having spent his entire life growing up in the woods and wilds of Florida, he was more comfortable outside than inside and had no idea what the Internet was. Roy made up for Frank's ignorance on electronics. He was the youngest of the group, being in his late twenties, and had been a forward air controller in the air force. He spent three tours in Afghanistan and was a whiz with all things electronic.

The boy lay there in stark terror, looking at the two men standing over him; one had a machine gun pointed at him.

"Mike, check that one out," Sarge said. "Get on your feet, boy, real slow like."

The boy rolled to his side and stood up. Looking over, he screamed, "Daddy!"

Ronnie came up on the other side of the boat; he took a quick look at the body and then looked up at Sarge and shook his head. Mike had rolled the big man over on his back. He had taken two rounds from the SPW, one just under his jaw—it made a hell of a mess—and one through his clavicle. He was dead.

"You killed my daddy, you sons of bitches!" the boy screamed. He started to move forward; Sarge hit his sternum with the muzzle, pushing him back.

"Your daddy fired on us. We fired back, son. If you want to blame someone, blame him," Sarge replied. The boy started to cry, crossing over the back of the boat to where his father lay in a bloody mess. He knelt beside him, clutching one of his big hands, and wept.

"We wasn't going to hurt anyone. When he saw you guys an' all your guns, it scared him. He accidentally pulled the trigger. It was an accident," he said through tear-filled eyes. He was looking up at Mike, who was standing over him.

"What the hell were y'all doing out here to begin with?" Mike asked him.

"We're just trying to get by. That's all," he mumbled.

Ted motored across the river to where the other three boats were. He had Phil sitting on the deck at the bow of the boat. Slipping the boat out of gear as he came up, he caught the side of Sarge's boat. "They were lying up to ambush folks, collecting a *tax* from them," he said as he tied a line to a cleat on the stern of Sarge's skiff. Sarge looked over at the man sitting on the deck; he had his knees pulled up to his chest, his chin resting on them, and his arms wrapped around his legs.

"Pirates, huh?" Looking back at the boy, he said, "So your idea of getting by is to steal from folks on the river, is that it?"

The boy looked up. "We never hurt anyone. We only took a little."

"Well, then, your daddy got exactly what he deserved. Mike, take all the guns. Ted, did you get his?" Sarge was looking over at the other pathetic bastard.

"Yeah, I got 'em," Ted answered.

"You can't take our guns. We need 'em," Phil protested. He finally looked up when he realized they were taking all their firearms.

"Need 'em for what, Phil?" Mike asked.

"For protection an' hunting. How else we suppose to feed ourselves?" Phil protested.

Sarge pointed to the body lying in the boat. "See what having guns did for you! You fuckers don't need guns. Everyone around you does when you have 'em! You're plain ole thievin' white trash, and the world would be better off without you!" Sarge was furious.

Phil jumped to his feet. "Wait a damn minute!"

he shouted. He was met by a butt stroke from Ted's rifle and crumpled onto the deck with a groan.

"Ted, take that piece of shit back to his boat. Ronnie, go with him. Take any fuel he has and anything else we could use. Mike, pull the line on that tank and take it." Sarge pointed to the fuel tank in Dale's boat.

"How are we supposed to get back home?" the boy shouted.

"Not my problem, son. Next time, you better think about how you *try to get by*. And you better be damn happy I don't shoot your ass right here. I should," Sarge bellowed at him.

That terrified look came across the boy's face again. The thought of being shot out there on the river scared the shit out of him. Momma would never know what happened to him. Mike pulled the gas tank from the boat and set it into theirs. Ronnie tossed a line around a cleat on the front of the skiff and towed it across the river to the pontoon boat. Ted boarded the pontoon and took the gas tank and set it into his boat. He also took the half case of shine sitting on the deck. This elicited a "Hey!" from Phil. Ted answered him by drawing his pistol and pointing it at Phil's face. He promptly raised his hands and sat down on one of the pedestal seats and hung his head.

Ronnie tied the skiff off to the pontoon. Ted climbed back into his boat and shoved off. "If we ever see you again, I'll kill you," Ted said as he put the boat in gear and moved out into the river where Sarge and Mike were waiting. Once all the boats were back together, Sarge pointed downriver, and they headed out in a string, leaving the other two boats rocking in their wake. With their goggles back on now, they raced down the river. All of them were thinking about what had just happened. All of them, being military men, considered it with detached emotion; it was an ambush, and they came out on top. Sarge was the only one a little distraught over it, not because he killed a man, but for the boy who was brought up by a man who put him in that position.

The Suwannee River was a twisting, turning cut of black water. It was almost the color of coffee, and even in the daylight, you seldom saw the bottom. Rounding a bend, Sarge was knocked off his cooler, flying forward onto the deck. The outboard raced as the shear pin on the prop broke away when it dug into the sandbar. Mike immediately pulled the throttle back and killed the engine. The other two boats went wide out into the river and then slowly came over toward the stricken boat. Sarge was on the deck, cussing a storm.

He stood up and looked at Mike with rage on his face. Mike just shrugged his shoulders. "What?"

"You damn dipshit! You hit the fuckin' sandbar!" Sarge was trying to get his shit together.

The other two boats eased up. "What happened?" Ted called out.

"Dumbass, here, hit the sandbar. We're going to have to replace the shear pin and hope that's all that broke. You guys cover us while we sort this out," Sarge said.

"Roger that," Ronnie replied as he moved his boat out into the river, downstream from where they were. Ted took his boat and moved upstream.

Sarge looked up at Mike and pointed into the water at the stern of the boat. "Get in."

"Aw, come on, Sarge, can't this be done from in here?" He was looking into the cold, dark water.

"Nope, now get your ass in the water, dipshit," Sarge said as he pulled a small toolbox out from under the console. Mike put one foot on the stern, took his carbine off, and hopped into the water with a splash. Sarge hit the switch on the throttle to raise the outboard out of the water. Mike stood in the knee-deep water, looking up. Linus had an evil grin on his face.

"What the fuck, man?" Mike complained.

Sarge handed him a ratchet with a socket and a pair of pliers. "Get to work, shit bird." Then he sat down on the driver's seat and opened another Sam Adams.

Even without a watch, Thad knew that it was early in the morning and that with the coming of dawn, people would start to come out. He decided to go ahead and try to get through Inverness before dawn. South of there was more forest, and he could find a place to lay up for the day. It was only eight or ten miles—shouldn't be any real problem.

He was able to speed down the road. Most of the cars had been pushed to the side of the road. *Awfully considerate of 'em*, he thought. It wasn't until he got to the plaza where the Publix and Kmart were that he encountered people. From what he could see, they were lining up for food. There was every mode of conveyance known to man in the parking lot: horses, bikes, cars, trucks, and ATVs, even a wagon pulled by a couple of mules. He slowed as he came by, just looking at the scene below. There were enough other vehicles around that he really didn't draw any attention.

From the looks of things, they were either feeding right there or distributing food, maybe a combination of both. Not being interested in anything they had, he pressed on and made the south side of town without incident. Just south of Inverness was a park called Fort Cooper. The Withlacoochee State Trail runs parallel to the highway and fronts the park. Across the street was the Inverness Municipal Airport. As with all local airports, it's out of town a bit, so there would be fewer people around. Thad seriously doubted anyone would be having a picnic at the park right now.

Finding a place he could cross the trail and enter the park, Thad pulled the truck across the paved walkway and into the park. Thad had been here before, on a Sunday drive with his wife and son. Pulling into the park brought memories of little Tony climbing the old oaks. He started to drive back toward the campsites without even thinking about it. Realizing what he was doing, he pulled the truck off the path into the woods. Heading for the campground was not a good idea under the current circumstances.

Winding his way through the trees, he finally came to a small bay head. The area was thick with tall pines and large, spreading oaks. "This oughta do," he said as he shut the truck off. Climbing out, he stretched and walked around, taking a look at the area. He couldn't see or hear anyone, but he could smell a campfire, and that concerned him a bit. Going to the rear of the truck, he quietly lowered the tailgate, hanging the little loop of cord to hold it up. Taking a seat, he pulled the pack over and fished around until he found an MRE and pulled it out and then went back in after a heater. He wanted some hot food this morning.

Pouring a little water in the pouch and stuffing the beef stew in, he set it aside to warm up. A hot drink would be nice; he went into the pack and found the canteen cup stove and a pack of hexamine tabs. Using the canteen, he filled the cup and set the stove on the ground. Putting a tab under the stove, he lit it with a BIC lighter and then set the cup of water on it. Once the water was heating, he went back into the pack to find the pouch of cocoa he saw earlier.

With his breakfast warming, Thad went to the cab and pulled the captured weapons out. He looked the SKS over, getting a feel for how it operated. He never owned a rifle; this would be his first. Looking at the pistols, one was a Ruger P89 and the other was a Hi-Point C9. He didn't really like the Hi-Point but thought the Ruger was a pretty good piece. He mentally marked the C9 as a barter gun if it came to it. Thad sat on the tailgate of the truck and ate, enjoying the hot food. He let the water heat until the tab burned out and then dumped the cocoa in and stirred it up. While he was drinking his cocoa, he cleaned up the dinner, throwing the empty pouches in the bed of the truck.

Pulling out his sleeping bag, he laid it out on the front seat of the truck. He laid the pack on the floorboard and crawled into the bag. As he was getting settled into the bag, he thought about cracking the windows to prevent condensation. Looking up at the huge hole in the glass where the cab met the windshield and then back to the hole in the rear glass, he thought it was pointless. Thad tried to get comfortable on the bench seat; he had his shotgun lying on the bench in front of him and the Glock in his bag with him. He stuck the Ruger into the door handle by his head and tried to go to sleep.

A noise woke him up. He opened his eyes and gripped the shotgun. The noise was coming from the rear of the truck. There was definitely someone in the bed of the truck. He heard them going through the junk scattered there. He lay there cursing himself in his mind for sleeping. Here he was wrapped up in a damn bag and someone had snuck up on him.

He lay there for another minute, weighing his options. Certainly they knew he was there, but maybe they thought he was asleep. With his head against the passenger door, he partially saw out the driver's window and most of the windshield. Only, from this angle, Shaq could be standing in front of the truck, and he wouldn't be able to see him. Turning his head slightly, he looked up at the hole in the rear window. There were some cracks radiating from it. He settled on a plan; he would sit up as fast as he could and shove the barrel of the shotgun through the glass and fire at whoever was out there.

The noise grew louder, and Thad steeled his nerves and, with a guttural scream, bolted upright. He shoved the shotgun through the glass with such force that the knuckles on his left hand wrapped around the fore end went through the glass. The scream, combined with the sound of the shotgun tearing through the glass, caused the three raccoons in the bed of the truck to jump straight up. One of the poor critters was in line with the barrel when Thad pulled the trigger, turning it into a red mist of goo that flew over the tailgate. The other two made for the brush, making more noise than the Confederate army marching onto the Dade Battlefield.

I looked over at Roy. "You guys got any comms?"

He looked at me and replied, "We have some. Power is the biggest issue, especially with portable radios."

I took that to mean they either had CBs or hams. CB would be bad for long-range comms, but maybe they weren't worried about it. We were all standing around; I wasn't planning on leaving until after dark. I didn't know what these guys were planning.

"What are you guys gonna do?" I asked them as a group.

They all looked around at one another. Norm finally spoke up. "We're headed over to the range. Since you're headed that way, why don't you come with us?"

Here was the conundrum—I didn't know these guys, but there was safety in numbers. These guys looked pretty well equipped and hadn't done anything to threaten me; if they wanted to, they could have killed me. Just a couple more questions to make me feel better about it.

"What are you guys going to do when you get there?" I asked the group again.

Again, Norman answered me, "We're just going to look around. See what's going on over there—if anything is going on over there."

"You guys mentioned helicopters. Have you seen any?" I asked.

"No, we've heard them and been told by others, but we haven't seen any," Norman replied.

"What if you do see one?" This was what I was really curious about.

"Shoot it down," Frank replied.

Norman shot him a look. "He's kidding. We just want to have a look."

"Well, I'm not ready to take on the military yet. I have seen their helicopters and don't want any part of them," I replied.

This statement brought raised eyebrows from them. They looked around at one another again. I went on to explain about seeing the Kiowa. I didn't tell them about seeing it right after I used the radio. I still hadn't told them about having it yet. There was quite the conversation about why no one had seen any others, and why I saw a Kiowa and not an Apache or other gunship. These guys were full of theories. I just wanted to get home. Listening to enough of their banter, I finally asked when they planned to leave.

"We're ready anytime," Norman answered.

"You guys move during the day?" I asked. This surprised me.

"Yeah, like I said, we haven't seen any helicopters and have a pretty good idea where they are, so moving during the day isn't an issue to us," Norman replied.

I shouldered my pack, and we started out. Daniel was in the lead, then Norm, Roy, me, and Frank, who was bringing up the rear. We started out heading southeast, walking single file and as quietly as we could. We hit a paved road in less than half a mile. When the road came into view, Daniel held up a fist and slowly started to drop to one knee. The others all did likewise. Seeing the hand signal, I was reacting as well. Frank put a hand on my shoulder, applying a little pressure. That kind of bugged me. I turned my head slightly to one side.

"I know. You don't have to worry about me." Frank pulled his hand away without saying anything. Daniel approached the road, slowly, very cautiously. Slipping up to the road, he took a long look. We probably sat there for fifteen minutes.

Daniel finally started to rise. We all followed him. Moving up to where he was, everyone took up a position where we could provide over-watch. Daniel went first, in a rush. He provided cover for the rest of us, each taking a position of cover on the opposite side of the road. All this seemed a little ridiculous to me. We weren't in combat, after all. We had to execute the same procedure on another road. This one happened exactly like the previous, with the exception that Frank didn't grab my shoulder.

Late afternoon in the piney woods was nice. This area was nothing but pines. There was some underbrush, palmettos, and cleared chops. The palmetto flats were a little rough to try to push through. As we were bulling our way through one particularly rough patch, I suddenly had a horrible thought. Ticks. I could only imagine how many ticks I would have on me. I hadn't worried about bugs in some time—no skeeters and no bugs. But this place was without a doubt overrun with ticks. Note to self, strip down and do a body check.

As we walked along, I pulled the notebook out and consulted the codes for today. The way the code was written, it was a simple revolving system, with an offset. So each day I just went to the next page, simple and effective. The offset in time from our radio encounter put me calling about five o'clock. It was almost that time. I was nervous about letting these guys in on the fact that I had a radio, but I was going to call in to Sarge and hang out a bit and call home.

"Hey, guys, I need to hold up," I said in a low voice.

They all turned around and looked at me. "I need to do something." They still just stood there, looking sort of expectantly at me. Dropping my pack, I took out the antenna and the slick line and looked for a suitable tree; the choices were endless. Picking one out, I tossed the line up and pulled up the antenna. Roy looked over at me. "You got a radio?"

I was attaching the antenna when he asked. "Yeah, a little one," I replied.

Roy walked over, the others taking up a defensive perimeter. He looked down at the Yaesu. "Yeah, it's little, but that's one hell of a radio," he said with an edge to his voice. "Where did you get that?"

"From a friend of mine. Do you guys have hams?" I asked him without looking up.

"We have one that we use to listen with. You aren't going to transmit with that thing, are you?" His brow was furrowed; his eyes were kinda squinted.

"Maybe, I'm checking to see if someone is on the air," I replied. Finished hooking up the antenna, I looked up at him.

Roy looked over at Norman. "No wonder he's seen a Kiowa. They're tracking his signal."

Norman looked over at me. "When was the last time you transmitted? Where were you?"

"It's been a while, and I was far away from here. Long before I ever got to the bridge," I answered.

"We'd appreciate it if you didn't transmit right now, least not while we're here," Roy said.

"I know what you guys are worried about, but I don't think they—whoever they are—have the ability to triangulate. Each time I saw the birds, they were always searching around; only once did it ever fly right over me. Even then, it didn't see me," I said as I was plugging the headset in. I flipped the power switch and started to sift through the frequencies. I knew what freq Sarge would be on but didn't go straight to it. The radio traffic was picking up. Slowing on one freq, I caught a ham near DC. He said the city was absolute chaos. You couldn't go outside, and even if you stayed inside and someone noticed you were there, you ran the risk of being overrun. I never heard whom he was talking to. The guy must have breathed through his ears, as he never let up. What came next on the station shocked the shit out of us.

In a very clear transmission came, "Transmitting station, you are in violation of executive order

10995. Under the rules of martial law, you are ordered to cease all transmissions and disable your transmitter immediately. Any further transmissions will result in severe consequences."

The transmission was repeated. As it began to repeat, I motioned for Roy and Norman to come over. Each of them put one side of the headset to an ear and listened. Their eyes grew wide, both of them looking at me. I simply nodded my head. When the transmission was done, they handed the headset back. I cupped one earpiece to my head in time to hear the guy near DC come back over the air.

"What the fuck are you doing? We need help, and you're telling me to get off the radio! Send me fucking help before these animals kill us all!" he screeched into the radio.

I looked over at Norman. "This guy is screaming back at them."

"What are they saying to him?" Roy asked.

"Telling him to shut the fuck up, basically," I replied. I spun the dial on the radio to the freq I was expecting Sarge to come up on. I usually called him, but I hoped today he called me. The hisses, pops, and whines filled the earpiece as I tried to tune the radio. Suddenly, it all cleared as a signal came up in Sarge's gravelly voice. Two words came through the speaker. "Broke Dick."

"What the hell?" I said out loud, reaching for the notebook in my cargo pocket. Flipping it open, I went through page after page, looking for "Broke Dick." On the back of the last page, against the hardcover, I found a few rather colorful codes. This particular one coincided with what I just heard on the radio. Martial law had been declared, and radio transmissions were being DF'd. DF stood for direction finding. Well, no shit, Sarge. I just sat there. He had a printed reply that I was to make, just a couple of clicks of the PTT button. I decided my reply was better and just as short.

Keying the mic for a second, I replied, "No shit, Sherlock," and released the mic. I can only imagine the colors that old bastard's face turned when I did it.

"Hey, I thought you weren't going to transmit!" Roy shouted at me.

"I didn't say I wouldn't. You asked me not to, but I didn't commit either way. Did you catch the part about martial law?" I asked.

"Yeah, we heard it. Figured it would happen sooner or later," Norm said.

"You guys still heading for the range?" I asked.

"This doesn't really change anything for us," Norm replied.

After taking down the antenna and packing all the radio gear, we started back out toward the range. Our current position was just south of Kerr Lake. Norm's crew had a topo map of the area. After a quick check, it appeared we were about fifteen miles from the range. Fifteen miles of scrub between us and it. Man, this was going to suck. After a short discussion, we all agreed to go over to Kerr Lake before heading to the range. This crew had a place on the east side of the lake, and we all needed some water and rest.

They wanted to check in with their people too about what we just heard on the radio before heading to the range. Since this crew hadn't done anything to make me suspect any foul play, I agreed. After all, if they wanted anything I had, I would never have woken up from my nap.

We walked east toward the lake in the fading sun. The air was cool, and the evening was nice. The sounds of the insects in the piney woods filled the air, disturbed only by the soft crunch of our boots on the sand. We were walking down a dirt road. I personally thought this a little foolhardy but was assured that we were in no danger out here "in the sticks." The little road broke out into a clear-cut area right at dark. Leaving the relative comfort of the trees, we headed across the chop and came to a road called Moorhead Park, which led to a boat ramp on the lake. As we approached the lake, the temp seemed to drop; it felt cooler closer to the water.

We walked down to the water's edge. The view across the lake was beautiful. The western horizon was a lovely shade of rose. I actually felt kind of relaxed. The eastern sky in front of me was a deep blue, almost black. Roy came up to where I was on the dock. I had walked out onto it, one of those floating ones. "Hey, can you set up your radio?" he asked. He was standing beside me with his arms folded across his chest, looking across the lake.

"Oh, now you want to use it?" I half laughed.

"Well, I thought we'd call a cab, unless you want to swim." He nodded across the lake.

"Gonna call your folks on the other side?" I asked him without looking over.

"Yeah, they have the radio on. I know what freqs they monitor, so I'll call for a boat," he replied.

"Sure, I could use a boat ride," I said.

We walked back to where I had dropped my pack on the bank. No one had tried to get the radio themselves. That made me feel a little better about this whole detour. I set up the radio, throwing the antenna up through a rather short tree, but no farther than he was going to transmit, it should be fine. After getting it set up, Roy came over and knelt down.

"Hey, uh, you mind giving me some privacy here?" he asked.

That made me a little nervous. What didn't he want me to hear? "Well, that makes me a little nervous, ya know."

"I dig it. It's not like we're setting you up for anything. It's just that we don't know you. Just like you don't know us, we don't want you to know our call signs and freqs," he replied.

That actually made sense to me but still made me a little uncomfortable. I agreed, however, and walked off toward the lake again, my carbine slung over my shoulder. Roy made his call, and a few minutes later, he came up beside me on the dock. "Thanks, man; our ride's on its way." Far across the lake, the faint sound of an outboard motor could be heard, but it sounded far, far away.

Mike had the pin in the old Evinrude changed in no time. All the while, Sarge sat in the driver's seat with his boots up on the engine's cowl, drinking a beer. Mike finished up and climbed back in the boat. Sarge handed him a cold beer as his reward.

"Thanks, Sarge."

"You earned it; just don't wreck my damn boat again," he said with a sly grin.

"Deal," Mike said as he turned the bottle up and drained half of it in one long pull. "Damn, that's good. Of all the things in the world I'm going to miss, cold beer will be the worst." He turned the bottle up and drained it. "On a hot day, I'd almost suck a dick for a cold beer."

Sarge looked up at the young warrior. "Really, hmm."

Mike got a worried look on his face. "I didn't mean literally, dammit!"

"Who you tryin' to convince, me or yourself?" Sarge jabbed back. He used a paddle to push the boat off the sandbar and into the river and then sat down and lowered the outboard into the water and started it up. Putting it in gear, he headed back down the river. The other two boats fell in line. Mike stepped up to the bow and picked up the SPW and sat down on the cooler as Sarge flipped his goggles down.

The rest of the trip up the river to Turkey Island went uneventfully. They made it without seeing another boat. Passing the island, Sarge knew that after two more turns in the river, his little canal would be on the right. Slowing the boat, he began to scan the river's edge. It didn't take long to find it—the little cut that ran off to the north. He followed the river until it was nearly the width of the boat.

"Catch that tree ahead," Sarge told Mike.

Mike stood up, and Sarge brought the boat slowly up to a large old cypress tree. The other two boats came up from behind and shifted into neutral, letting the boats drift up and form a chain. Ted was looking around. "Now what?"

"Keep yer panties on, Maggie," Sarge said as he stepped up to the bow of the boat. Lying over the side, he reached down into the black water and groped around. "Dammit, where are ya? Come on, what the hell?"

"There ain't no oysters down there, ya know," Ted called out.

Through his goggles, Ted saw the old first sergeant turn to look at him. Even in the dark, it was enough for him to look away into the swamp like a kid would when mom or dad gave them "the look." Finally, Sarge called out, "Ah ha!" With a grunt, he pulled the end of a large old cypress board out of the water. Pulling the old board up, they saw that it must have been five feet long, three inches thick, and about twelve inches wide—not to mention cut from a cypress log that probably lay in the river for a hundred years. He held it out horizontally over the river.

After a couple of tries, Sarge let the board go. It appeared to be floating on the river. Fishing his hands in the water around the edge of the board closest to the boat, he made a couple of adjustments. Once he was satisfied with its location, Sarge stood up and stepped out onto the board, one hand on the old tree for support. He began to dip the toe of his right foot into the water, feeling around. Finally, he settled on what he was looking for and stepped forward, repeating the process with his left foot.

Mike was standing in the boat, watching this in amazement. "Oh, my god, the old fart can walk on water," he said out loud. Doc and Ted started to laugh.

Without even looking up, Sarge fired back, "Shut

up, asshole, or I won't give you a beer when you're done." Mike just shook his head.

After a couple more steps on the water, Sarge disappeared into the blackness of the swamp. It was as if he'd stepped out of this realm; he was just gone. If it wasn't for the sound of him moving around in the blackness just out of their sight, the guys could have thought he was eaten by the night. Mike flipped his goggles down just in time to see the end of a large cypress plank falling out of the night. He jumped back, stumbling over the cooler. "Shit!"

From the black came Sarge's reply, "He-he-he." After a couple more adjustments, the old man came out of the swamp and walked right up to the boat. "All right, boys, tie the boats together and follow me."

With the boats all tied together, Doc and Ted climbed from boat to boat to reach the plank bridge Sarge had laid out. Once they were in the boat with Mike, they all looked down at the bridge. "What the hell is this?" Doc asked.

"Just a little secret of mine. I drove some posts down into the water here; that first board I cut from an old cypress log I pulled from the river. It's water-logged and sinks, so I leave it between the posts. Once it's down, I can get back in here to the other one, stepping on the tops of the other posts. That takes me back to my boardwalk. Come on." Sarge turned and walked off into the black swamp. The three guys were standing in the boat. Mike looked over at the other two and shrugged his shoulders. As gingerly as he could, he stepped out onto the board. He looked like he was walking through a minefield the way he moved.

Following the boardwalk, they came to a little

cabin built on posts sunk into the swamp, using cypress trees in some places for additional support. The cabin was completely invisible in the dark. The only way they knew it was there was that Sarge had lit a hurricane lantern inside, lighting up a rectangular block in all the blackness. As Mike walked up, he had his arms out like he was balancing himself. The sense of vertigo in the darkness, no handrail on the boardwalk, worked to make him feel as if he was going to fall over.

Inside the cabin, Mike looked around. There were deer hides on the walls, a turkey tail in a fan, and two gator skins stretched out. Looking around, he said, "What the hell is this?"

Ted came up behind him and stuck his head in the doorway. "Looks like a poacher's shack to me."

Mike started to laugh out loud. "Holy shit, Sarge is a fuckin' poacher!" He doubled over with laughter. Sarge came up behind him and kicked his legs out from under him, causing Mike to fall back, banging his head on the plywood wall.

"I ain't no damn poacher!" he yelled out.

Seeing what his raiders had been, Thad fell back onto the bench seat with a bellowing laugh. As he did, the knuckles that went through the glass pulled out. The pain from that made him quickly bolt upright again, breathing in hard through clenched teeth. "Ooooo!" He was shaking the hand. Taking a look, it wasn't bad, just a bunch of small cuts, nothing serious. He kicked out of the bag and got out of the truck.

Walking to the back of the truck, he picked up

the coon by the half of its tail still there. He was holding it up at eye level, looking at what was left.

"Damn, mister, you ruined it," came a small voice from his right. Thad looked back over his shoulder and saw a boy of nine or ten standing there. He was holding a little Marlin .22. He startled Thad, but Thad just didn't feel threatened.

"Yeah, ain't much left, huh?" Thad replied.

"Watcha gonna do with it?" the kid asked.

"Nothin'. You want it?"

The boy's face brightened. "Yeah, sure. My mom'll make something out of it."

Thad held the carcass out to the boy, who came over and took it as if he was being handed a loaf of bread. He held it down to his side and looked at the truck. "You shore are lucky to have a truck that runs."

"Yeah, I got a long way to go, though. Where you from?" Thad asked him.

Pointing back through the woods, the kid said, "We're over at the campground. We was here camping, but now our car won't start, so we're just here."

"Who you here with?" Thad asked.

"My momma, daddy, and two sisters. Daddy's laid up drunk, so Momma told me to go find some dinner. The fish weren't biting in the lake, so I came out here to see if I could see something," the boy replied.

"How old are your sisters?" Thad asked. He had a soft spot for kids—just couldn't help it.

"They're three, twins," he said.

Thad went to the cab and pulled out his pack and fished around until he found an MRE pound cake and a pack of peanut butter. "Here, take these with you."

The boy took the two pouches from Thad; reading what they were, his face really lit up. "Hey, thanks a lot, mister! Really!" The boy turned and struck out for the camp. Thad stood there shaking his head, watching the boy run. It was a scene out of history, a rifle in one hand and a coon in the other.

Thad scratched his head, noting he needed a haircut. Since he was up, he figured he would take care of the call of nature. Fortunately, he still had about half a roll of ass wipe left. He grabbed the roll and his shotgun and headed for the brush. Even though no one was around, he needed some privacy. As big and intimidating as he was, Thad had some serious insecurities about taking a shit in front of anyone. That was the primary reason he didn't go into the military. The whole shit, shower, and shave in front of dozens of other men was just something he couldn't do.

Just as he was trying to finish his business, Thad saw the boy come walking back toward the truck. "Well, dammit," Thad muttered while trying to stealthily clean his backside. The boy was standing there looking around and then looked over his shoulder and shrugged. A man came into the little clearing. He was carrying the .22 rifle. "Whur's that big buck, boy?"

Now Thad was worried that little runt went and got his damn drunk daddy to come back for the truck. From his spot in the brush, Thad saw them between the fronds of a palmetto. Well, he could see the boy and the man from the waist down. The boy didn't look happy; he was clearly uncomfortable.

"Come on, Daddy, let's go. He gave me that stuff. He's a nice guy," the boy pleaded with his father, who responded by slapping him in the back of the head.

"Shut the fuck up, and do what yer told. Go see if the keys is in that truck." The boy plodded off toward the truck. Now that the boy was away from him, Thad took the opportunity to stand up; his pants were around his ankles though, so this couldn't turn into a running fight.

With the shotgun shouldered, Thad raised up out of the palmettos. "Right here." He was off to the man's right. It was obvious that he was half in the bag, but he had a rifle in his hand. The man looked over at Thad bleary-eyed. "What do you want?" Thad asked him.

"I need a ride to get my family out're here," he mumbled.

"I don't think you came here to ask for no ride. Now drop that rifle on the ground," Thad said.

The drunk got a smirk on his face. "He-he, ain't no nigger gonna tell me wut ta do." He started to shift the rifle in his hand; he was holding it by the receiver. Thad didn't wait to see what he intended to do. His words were enough.

The 00 buck caught him square in the chest and carried him onto his back. The rifle fell to the ground beside him. When the shot went off, the boy jumped. Thad looked over at him to see what he would do. To his surprise, the boy walked over to his daddy's body and looked down at it. The man wasn't dead yet, but it wouldn't be long. He turned his head toward the boy and tried to raise a hand. The boy was standing over him, looking down.

"You deserved that," the boy said and spit on his face and then kicked the dying man in the ribs, causing him to let out a barely audible groan.

Thad lowered the shotgun and pulled his pants up with one hand. Stepping out of the bush, he walked over to the boy, who was watching his father die. Without even looking up at Thad's approach, he said, "Sorry he called you that."

"Ain't no matter. I'm sorry he made me do it," Thad replied.

"I ain't; I've wanted to do it for a long time. He's an asshole—beats my momma up." And after a pause, he added, "An' me. We're better off without him." He reached down and picked up the rifle and then looked up at Thad. "Thanks for helping us."

Thad was a little perplexed. He just killed this kid's father, and he was thanking him for it. It just wasn't the kind of thing he expected. "Is there anything I can do for you and your momma?"

"Naw, we have the camper. It's as good as home. There's a lake here, woods, and even a water pump at the camp, the old kind you pump up 'n' down. I like it here," the boy replied. He stood there looking at the body for another minute and then looked up at Thad with a squint. "I'm gonna go tell Momma; at least now she won't have to be afraid no more." He knelt down beside the body. Thad thought he was going to say some kind of good-bye, but instead he went through the pockets and pulled out a pocketknife and Zippo lighter, stuffing them in a pocket of his own. With that, the boy turned and walked away.

Thad decided he had had enough of this place and wanted to get the hell away. Even though it was light out, he decided to leave right then. Getting the truck back out onto 41, he headed south. The shotgun was in his lap, and the SKS was on the seat beside him. Driving during the day made him nervous, but getting home was a compelling reason to do it. Thad kept his speed between fifty and fifty-five. The road had the occasional dead car on it, and, much to his surprise, he saw many people out and about.

Most of the folks he saw paid little attention to him; a few looked but no one made any sort of threatening moves. He was surprised at the ingenuity of some of them. Bikes seemed to be the primary mode of transportation. It wasn't like the videos he saw of China where hundreds of people were on bikes, but it was the predominant method of getting around. Some of the bikes were pulling trailers of various construction—some were pretty ingenious, and some were a Rube Goldberg affair.

There were also a number of horses, and one wagon was pulled by a team. A few miles after getting back on the road, he passed a place where there appeared to be a flea market of sorts. A bunch of booths were set up; it kind of reminded him of Barter Town. That thought gave Thad a chuckle. Since there wasn't anything he really needed, he just decided to pass it by. Another few miles down the road, and he was back into a more rural area, fewer houses and, as a result, fewer people.

Brooksville was the last obstacle Thad had to get past. If he could clear that without issue, then he'd be home free.

As the sun dipped below the western horizon, the sound of the boats coming across the lake grew louder. Looking toward the east, across the lake, it was almost black. I walked off the dock to my pack and pulled the NVGs out and strapped them on. Norm came up to me. "Is there anything you don't have in that pack?"

I just chuckled. "Plenty, brother, plenty."

"I wish we had some of those. We just never had the money to get them. You know, before all this, we worked so hard. There was just so much to get. Looking back on it now, I see every place we slipped up, what we did that we shouldn't have, and didn't do that we should have."

I stood there looking across the lake, looking for the source of the sound coming across it. "I can relate, man. I just hope what I did makes a difference, if I can just get home."

We stood there talking about things for a minute—food, water, power sources, how much gas was stored, and how much we wished we had stored. Norm was talking about the difference between ethanol gas and regular gas when the sound of the boats suddenly grew louder; that caused Norm to stop. "Huh, that's weird. Sounds like they just came around a corner or something." He strained his eyes to look out at the lake.

Even through the goggles, I still couldn't see the

boats. The new, louder sound wasn't coming from the boats. I started looking around, looking for the sound. It was still kind of low, very rhythmic. I cupped my hands behind my ears and swiveled my head back and forth. The sound was coming from the north, maybe another boat?

"It's coming from over there." I pointed to the north out on the lake.

"What is it, another boat?" Norm asked.

I was still looking out over the water when I caught movement; it looked like it was far out on the lake. "There it is, and it's damn fast." All I saw was something moving; it was below the horizon and looked like it was on the lake. The spotlight coming on and the helicopter flaring as it approached the boats left no doubt what it was.

"Oh, shit!" Norm shouted. We all scrambled for cover. I grabbed my pack and ran under some trees close to the ramp and dove on the ground behind a trunk. The bird had the boats in the light. They immediately separated, splitting off from one another. The ship stayed with one of them. To this point, the helicopter had done nothing more threatening than light them up with a spot. However, it was surely no coincidence that it arrived after the radio call; they were getting better at it, apparently.

Someone in one of the boats began to fire at the bird—rapid shots from a semiauto rifle. The helicopter banked hard away, killed the light, and, from the sound of it, made a wide loop over the lake. It finally revealed its location by the long stream of tracers pouring down from the sky. We clearly saw the muzzle blast from what could only be a belt-feed weapon. Tracers were hitting the water; some were skipping off and would make a slow, graceful arch out over the lake. We still saw muzzle flashes and heard the report from the weapon firing from the lake. It was soon silenced, however; the only indication of the boat's location was the appearance of a small flame out on the water that quickly grew in intensity.

Norm and his crew were freaking out. They were shouting back and forth at one another while all this went on. Frank was losing his damn mind. Roy was holding him back. He wanted to fire on the helicopter. Daniel and Norm were in a very animated discussion about what to do. I was still lying under the tree when the bird engaged the second boat.

The second boat was probably three hundred yards out in the lake when the bird made its first pass over it, the machine gun on board belching flame and tracers in a long line. This time they were so close I saw the gunner. There was a door gunner sitting in the back of the Kiowa. I didn't think they used a door gunner on those, but there he was. Being so close this time, Roy couldn't hold Frank back. Frank let out a scream and ran to the water's edge. He fired his AK from the shoulder in one long continuous burst until the magazine was empty.

Of all the things that were going on, the fact that these guys had modified their rifles to full auto surprised me more than anything. Frank was changing mags. The bird was still firing at the boat when a second helicopter screamed over our heads. Now the shit was deep. This was not the kind of fight

I wanted any part of. As the second bird came overhead, Roy and Norm both began to fire at it. I rose to my knees and pulled my pack on. I was getting the fuck outta here. There was no way I was about to take on gunships with a damn carbine. I watched the gunship bank hard to its right as it lined up on a run on our tree line. Norm, Frank, and Roy were all standing in the open, firing blind into the night at the sound of the ship.

As the helicopter started its run, I moved around to the back of the tree trunk to have some protection. I was off to the right of those three idiots standing out in the open, and hopefully out of the line of fire. Looking out at the ship, it was coming straight out of the lake, like a boat heading for the ramp. The guys were standing abreast of one another in the center of the ramp. They didn't stand a chance. I tried to scream at them to get them to take cover, but there was no way they could hear me over the sound of their rifles.

The helicopter was coming straight at them. He was about five hundred or so feet off the water. The pilot let the tail of the ship slip to its starboard, giving the gunner a clear line of sight on the boat ramp. The gunner opened up on the three men; tracers started slamming into the water in front of them. The gunner slowly walked the rounds into them. Norm dove for the ground. Roy and Frank just stood there firing. Frank's AK ran out of ammo again. He was fishing a mag out when he was stitched up the middle by the gunner. Roy looked over to his left where Frank fell. He too was immediately cut down.

As the ship passed overhead, Norm rolled onto his back and fired at the belly of the bird as it screamed by. Right after the ship cleared the trees, I saw Daniel jump up from the tree line on the other side of the ramp. He sprinted out toward Norm, who was picking himself up off the ground.

"Norm! Let's go! We gotta get the fuck outta here!" He was screaming as he ran.

An eerie silence filled the night. The ship that had been firing on the boats was nowhere to be seen. The one that just made the run on us was gone for the moment. Norm was standing there kinda shell-shocked. Daniel ran up to him and grabbed his shoulders. Norm just looked at him, holding his AK by the grip slackly at his side. Daniel was talking to him, shaking him, trying to bring him around. Seizing the moment while the birds were gone, I dumped my pack and ran over to where Frank and Roy lay.

Frank was way dead; he was missing the top of his head. A round had hit him just above the left eye. I checked Roy real quick. He was dead too. What looked like several rounds had hit his chest and right leg. I grabbed Frank's rifle; but after a quick check, I had to discard it. A round had blown the gas tube off the barrel. Picking up Roy's rifle, it looked serviceable, albeit covered in blood. Working frantically, I pulled mags out of their vests as fast as I could. Pulling one mag out of Roy's vest, the spring came out of the bottom and all the rounds fell out. I dropped that one; in all, I was able to get seven mags from between the two of them.

This seemed like it took forever. I felt like I was

out there for hours, but probably it was not more than a few minutes. Hearing the gunships again, I ran for the tree where my pack was. Daniel was still talking to Norm, who was still catatonic. Running past them, I slung the AK and held all the loose mags in one hand, cradling them against my chest, and grabbed Norm by one shoulder.

"Move. Here they come! Go, go, go!" I shouted. Daniel had him by the other shoulder. We ran off toward the trees, dragging Norm with us. We threw Norm under a stand of palmettos, and Daniel and I dove for different trees. We were both under large cedar trees with low, sprawling limbs. They provided pretty good concealment. One of the helos made a fast pass, blacked out. It continued out over the lake and then swung around and made another run. This time, it came in parallel to the shore, keeping from flying the same line each time. Whoever was flying that thing obviously had some stick time in a combat zone.

After the second pass, the other ship came in and began to orbit the boat ramp. The first one came back in real slow this time, its spotlight illuminating the ramp area. The bird came into a hover over the bodies of Frank and Roy. The gunner leaned out with one foot on the skid. From where we were, we clearly saw him. The light reflecting off the lake was more than enough to light him up. I was lying on the ground, under that cedar tree, thinking how easy it would be to shoot that guy off the skid and just how damn crazy you would have to be to do it.

That last thought barely finished in my mind when the sound of a full auto AK erupted from my left. In disbelief, I looked over to see Norm walking out of the trees, the AK at his shoulder, and spent casings spewing from the hot weapon. I looked back at the helo just in time to see the gunner fall off the skid, his weapon falling into the shallow water at the edge of the lake. The man hung from the safety strap secured to the center of his back by his harness. The pilot broke out of the hover immediately, pouring on the power. I could just see the pilot jerking the collective up to his armpit as he shoved the cyclic forward, looking for speed and altitude.

Norm kept up a steady stream of fire on the ship. He seemed to have some sort of control over himself. He was firing short bursts. Norm fired on the helo until the second one made a fast run on him. Rounds from the door gunner started hitting the pavement twenty yards from him. It gave the gunner an eternity to walk the rounds in. All he had to do was walk the rounds left or right, allowing the ship to bring the rounds right over Norm. We sat watching this unfold. From our position, it was clear what was going to happen, and there wasn't a damn thing we could do about it.

The image of a tracer round ripping through the man will be burned into my mind for eternity. Norm collapsed where he stood; his body simply went limp, and he fell back—his knees bent to the side and his left arm lying across his chest. No Hollywood theatrics, he simply fell where he stood. The helo continued to the south, over the tree line we were in. It came back out of the west, down the boat ramp. As it got closer to the spot, it came on again. With the bright light washing the area, I saw smoke coming from Norm's chest.

The pilot came over slow. The gunner opened up

on the corpse. He chopped him to pieces and then moved over to the other two and did the same. Obviously they were making a statement to anyone who would find them. The helo orbited the area a couple of times. Daniel and I both lay there with our faces in the duff from the cedar trees. I didn't even want to look up, like a child in his bed. If I couldn't see the monster, the monster couldn't see me. After the bird was gone, we continued to lie there. After all the recent noise, the silence was deafening. I looked over to Daniel, who was looking out at the bodies.

"What the fuck made them do that?" I asked quietly.

Daniel dropped his face into the forest floor again, shaking his head. Raising it, he said, "Frank's and Norm's sons were on those boats. They were coming over here to get us." He sighed.

That certainly explained why they reacted the way they did, but getting yourself killed in a lopsided fight with a couple of helicopters didn't avenge anyone's death.

"What are you going to do now?" I asked him.

"I guess that I need to go back and tell everyone what happened. I'm sure they saw the light show." He was shaking his head at the prospect of having to tell so many of the losses they had just suffered.

I rose to my knees and pulled the pack up. "Sorry, man, they should have just laid low. But I understand why they did it." I picked up the carbine and stuck it muzzle first down between the main pack and the outside pouch. Daniel slowly got to his feet. He looked as though he had the weight of the entire world on his shoulders. I asked him what frequencies on the radio they monitored, and he gave them to me, and I wrote them down in the book Sarge gave me. Without much of a good-bye, he turned and started off into the woods. It was a long walk around Kerr Lake.

On the top of my small bag, I had a Maxpedition Rollypoly bag clipped on. I took it off and opened it up and threaded it onto my belt on the left side and packed all the AK mags into it. After putting the little bag around my waist, I pulled the map out and took a look at it. From where I was, I needed to head southeast. After stowing the map, I shouldered the pack and started out.

"Damn, Sarge! That hurt." Mike stood up rubbing his head.

"Aw, poor baby, did he hurt his widdle head?" Sarge said, using an overly exaggerated sad face. "Welcome home, boys," he said with his arms outstretched.

The little cabin was a plywood and tar-paper shack about twelve by twelve. There were two windows in it and one door. Sarge explained to them how he built it as a place to go when he wanted to hunt and fish or just get away. He hauled all the materials in by himself in his boat and took about six months to build it. There was a little table and a couple of chairs, a "kitchen" with a counter, a propane stove, and a sink. The sink was supplied by a twelve-volt DC pump from a jug underneath the counter and drained into the swamp, feeding the catfish.

Leaning in a corner were several folding cots. On a shelf on the wall were a couple more lanterns and a cabinet with a mishmash of other camping supplies. Sarge laid out the immediate plan to get the boats unloaded and the gear stowed in the cabin. Then they were to string a camo net Sarge had in a bin outside across the creek they came up to hide the boats. That way, anyone who might venture into the creek wouldn't see the boats. Hopefully, they wouldn't even notice them and just turn around and leave.

This work took a couple of hours. Sarge clucked around his radio gear like a mother hen. All the batteries and panels were stored outside. All the food, electronics, and Pelican cases of God knows what went inside. It was late, and everyone was getting tired. Ted volunteered for first watch. The others went in and set up cots and were soon out.

Ted set up a folding camp chair on the boardwalk, put on his NVGs, and set his M4 across his lap. With the exception of Sarge's snoring, it was a quiet night. His thoughts started to wander: What were they going to do? How were they going to get around, or were they stuck in this little cabin? And most importantly, what could they do about what was about to happen?

Thad drove into the outskirts of Brooksville about eleven in the morning. This was not his first choice, driving through town in the daylight, but he was so close to home, so close. Up ahead was the split; Broad Street went to the left and through a small business district. It made a ninety-degree curve to head west into town. Howell Avenue went to the right and ran straight through. Howell was his first thought, but then he remembered it would bring him right past the courthouse and police department. He stayed to the left and went down Broad.

He was relieved when another car passed him going the opposite direction on Broad Street. The car passed him, and the occupants didn't even look over. Passing the elementary school, there was a long line of people. There was quite the crowd gathered; they were passing through a gauntlet of tables and people in Red Cross vests and others in fluorescent ones. It looked like they were handing out various kinds of aid supplies.

In a field between the school and the new courthouse, a little barter town was set up. This was the second one he saw today—looked like they were becoming more common. Making the curve to the west, he saw another line of folks in front of a small building. The sign over the building read SWILLEY'S TAVERN AND PACKAGE. In this line, unlike the one at the school, all these folks already had something in their hands. The items ranged from live chickens and goats to guns and gas cans. Thad looked at them and just shook his head, wasting valuable supplies for a drink.

He made a left, putting him back on 41. After a short drive, he came to East Early Street and made a right. This was a shortcut that would take him to South Main, where he made another left. This would take him to the west side of Brooksville but into a more populated area. A spur-of-the-moment decision made him jerk the truck onto the railroad easement. Thad knew Brooksville well, and he suddenly realized he could take the easement and get through town without seeing anyone if he went this way.

The easement was a good idea; he didn't encounter a soul and made it through town without incident. He wasn't going very fast, just steady. Soon he was in an area of forest. Stopping his truck for a minute, he pulled his map out to look at it. The map showed the tracks curving off to the west soon. He needed to get off the track, or he would be heading away from his house. He decided to start looking for a place to get off on the east side of the tracks.

It didn't take long to find a place where the trees were thin enough to get off the easement. He had to cross the tracks first though. The old truck complained when he started to climb the rock grade up to the track. It took several attempts, one ending with the front tires buried in the rock, forcing him to rock the truck back and forth to free it. On his final attempt, he hit the grade about twenty miles an hour. Climbing the rock quickly, he tried to get the wheels parallel to the tracks and ease over them.

That just didn't work; trying to go slow over the tracks wasn't going to work. Instead, he turned the wheels into the tracks and gunned the engine. Rocks were slamming into the bumper and flying off into the woods on the west side of the tracks. Finally, the truck lurched over the first track. He kept up the power and got the front wheels over the second track, the rear wheels bouncing over the first and then the second as he started down the grade on the east side of the track.

Finally on the other side of the tracks, he stopped the truck. Sweat was pouring down his face. It wasn't that hot out, kinda warm compared to recent days, but he was sweating like a lawyer standing before Saint Peter. He took a drink of water from one of his bottles and wiped his face with a rag he pulled from his coat pocket. Thad climbed out of the truck and stretched his back, flexing his arms out straight, angling them behind his back. After taking a leak beside the front tire, he climbed back into the truck and started looking for a way through the trees.

He found what he was looking for and was surprised to find a small dirt road, a very pleasant surprise. Following the road out, it dead-ended into another. He took a right and was once again headed south. The dirt road soon turned into a lime rock road that shortly turned into a paved road. Passing a sign, he saw he was on Culbreath Road. He had no idea where it went, but it was going south and, by his estimation, straight toward home.

Everything was going fine; the area was very rural, hardly any houses and, best of all, no people. A subdivision was coming up on the left. Thad was looking at the houses coming up. He didn't see anyone and was starting to speed up when his heart stopped. Thad was going about fifty-five. In the center of the road, crossing from the left side, was a little tot on a tricycle. She was right in front of him. Slamming the brake pedal to the floor, he watched in horror as the little bike and the blonde pigtails disappeared under the hood with a sickening thunk.

The sound of metal grinding against the pavement added to the squealing from the tires to create a torturous sound. The truck finally lurched to a stop after what seemed like a hundred miles. He threw the driver's door open and stepped out onto something soft that gave with his weight. His right foot was still in the truck when he looked down at the plastic doll leg under his boot. It took a moment for it to register what he was looking at and another moment for it to come together in his head what was happening.

The sound of several feet slapping the pavement brought him out of the cloud of confusion his mind was swimming in. He looked up in time to fall back into the truck as a golf club hit the rear post of the door, warping the club around it. Thad had ahold of the steering wheel with his right hand, holding himself from falling out onto the pavement. In the blink of an eye, he drew the big Bowie knife Morgan had given him. He had hung it on his belt, opposite the Glock, and never thought about it again. Still, he drew it in one fluid motion with his left hand.

Launching himself out of the cab with his right elbow, he buried the big blade into the man's middle. He could feel the man's sternum bump against the top knuckle of his thumb. The man collapsed forward, dropping the club and lying over Thad's arm with a half groan, half scream mixed with a choke. Standing behind him was another man. This one had an aluminum baseball bat cocked for a swing. Seeing his cohort dropping, he was looking at him and not at Thad. Thad shoved the crumpled man forward, the second stepping back, with the bat still cocked. As the gut-stuck man fell to the ground, Thad drew the Glock. As he leveled it off at the man with the bat, the guy looked at him. His eyes were huge; his mouth fell open, and Thad pulled the trigger.

The shot sent the batter flailing to the ground. That was when Thad saw the third man. He was unarmed and had been behind the second. His hands were half raised, his eyes massive, and his mouth open in a silent scream. Thad looked at him; he didn't look like someone you would need to be worried about. He was wearing Dockers and loafers with tassels. Tassels, for God's sake! The guy had pissed his pants and was shaking like a cat shitting razor blades.

Thad's eyes narrowed. "What kind of sick bastard does something like that?" he screamed, pointing to the doll leg lying under the driver's door. The man couldn't even try to speak; he just stood there shaking. Thad's fury was growing. "Well! Who's idea was this sick stunt?"

With his hands still raised, the man folded a finger over and pointed to golf club guy. Thad looked over at him, the Glock still trained on the piss stain. "You figured you'd just take my truck, huh?" He nodded his head. "Once you start down this path, robbin' folks, you can't come back. But I'm gonna give you a chance. If you die, it's your fault." The faintest look of relief washed over the guy's face. Thad lowered the pistol and shot him in the upper thigh. The piss stain let out a scream, grabbed his leg, and fell over.

Thad didn't even look at him. Walking back to the truck, he bent over at the doubled-up form by the door and used one of his village stomping boots to roll the body over. Without much thought about it, he reached down and grabbed the handle of the knife and quickly pulled it out. He took a moment to wipe most of the blood off on the button-down shirt the corpse wore. He sheathed the knife and climbed back into the truck and started it up. He backed the truck until the tricycle came out from under it. The doll was in pieces, and the bike was a hunk of scrap metal. Pulling around the bike, he took one last look out the window at the three bodies on the road. All three were still there. The one that still had a chance had done nothing to help himself yet. He still lay there clutching the leg. "Your choice," Thad said as he headed south.

Checking my watch, it was only about eight thirty. Early enough that I should be able to put some miles behind me tonight. Looking at the map earlier, it looked like I had a little less than thirty miles to go, and all of it in the forest. Only a few paved roads passed through the forest. The two major ones were Highway 40, which ran east and west, and Highway 19, which ran north and south. I should only have to cross each of them once, as my plan would take me cross-country. Fishing into the little bag, I pulled out the Silva compass and put the cord around my neck. If I did this right, I should be able to hit the Juniper Run and get some good, clean water. By the time I got there, I'd need it.

The terrain between Lake Kerr and Juniper was upland pine forest. Much of it was managed forest and logged out when the timber was mature. What this process left behind was a patchwork of clear-cuts with brush, knee high to eight feet. Then there was a second growth with taller trees and underbrush and the older growth. I passed through these in the dark in random order, always looking for lines of weakness through the underbrush. The underbrush consisted of palmettos, scrub oaks, small cedars, myrtles, and various bushes. At times, it could be impenetrable, and you really had to fight your way through.

In one of the thicker areas, I stopped for a water break and dropped the pack. I sat on the stub of a burned-out pine stump and took a long drink from one of the steel bottles. It was so cool and so good that I almost drank the entire thing. Sitting there, I was thinking of how I could speed this up a bit, and then I remembered the pruning shears in my pack. I groped around in the pack till I found them. Finishing off the water, I refilled it from the Platypus pouch and readied the pack. Shouldering the bag, I started back out, cutting some of the more troublesome limbs and branches in places to get by.

Using the shears, I made my way through the tougher areas, but I didn't cut anything near any of the numerous dirt roads I crossed. I would cross the dirt roads and then walk on the scrub or grass or whatever I could for a ways and then turn into the bush. This wouldn't fool an experienced tracker but would buy me some time if someone was after me. Again the thought popped into my head: *Why would anyone be after me? I haven't done anything wrong. All I'm doing is trying to get home.*

It took over seven hours to cover the roughly twelve miles to Juniper. Walking through the dark, the thick bush slowed me down. The change in terrain told me I was close. It went from the upland pine to a lowland and then to a swamp. I knew the run was close. I smelled it long before I was close enough to see it. The Ocala Forest was a favorite overwintering area for the Rainbow people. They are a group of hippies that descend on the forest every year. They claim to be about peace and love, but all they really did was squat on property, both public and private, and sit around and stink. And it was that stink I was smelling, although after this long without running water, it could be anyone really. It was a little early for them to be here; they usually didn't show up till February.

Stopping in the swamp, I tried to get a feel for where the campground was. I wasn't sure, but if I headed east I would certainly miss it and hit the run someplace. So that was what I did. I turned to the east a bit and continued through the swamp. After a little while, I came to the run and knelt down in the bush near the water's edge. I dropped the pack and slipped up to it. Using the stalk of a palm frond I checked the depth; it was about four feet. Water that deep meant I was pretty far from the spring, so I started looking for a place to set up camp.

It didn't take long to find a good spot. A huge old gum tree on the river's edge had been undermined by the current and had fallen over, away from the run. The crown of the tree was a tangled mess, with limbs and dead leaves in a thick ball. Once again dropping the pack, I worked my way into it. Using the shears and the saw on my Leatherman, I cut a few selective branches that would give a big enough area to camp in but provide good cover from the outside. There was a nice thick limb coming out of the trunk that had broken off about two feet out. It was probably three inches in diameter and made a brilliant seat.

I hung my poncho from the branches to provide some overhead cover and then laid the mat and bag out. Taking off the boots and socks, I let my feet air out—and damn, did it feel good! My feet were resting on the GORE-TEX bivy, and it felt like the softest thing I had ever stepped on. Since it wasn't terribly cold tonight, I decided to take my pants off and sleep in my T-shirt and drawers. Undoing my belt and pulling the pants off, I scratched at an itch on my waist. My fingernail hung on something, so I used the red LED on the headlamp to look at it. To my horror, it was a tick the size of a kernel of corn! Daammmiittt! I grabbed it by its engorged body and pulled steadily on it until it popped out. The bad thing was, if there's one, there's probably more.

Using the red LED, I did a quick check, pulling off five more of the little bastards. The worst part was that now that I knew they were there, I itched like fury all over. Taking out the FAK, I used a disinfecting wipe to clean all the spots I pulled them from and decided to do a thorough check in the light of day. By now the eastern sky was starting to turn gray, so I climbed into the bag with the XD. I propped the AK against my limb seat and stuck the carbine under the trunk, just in case.

Drums. The sound of drums woke me. Fucking drums? Unzipping the bag, I sat up and started to scratch. I knew those little shits were all over me.

Scraping my nails over my scalp, those damn drums started to get louder. I looked around for the source of the annoying sound. It sounded like it was coming from the campground. It was cool this morning, and my T-shirt wasn't cutting it. I wanted to get dressed, but first I had to finish looking for hitchhikers.

Using my signal mirror, I did as thorough an inspection as I could, finding three more in various uncomfortable places. The one thing that really stuck out was how shitty I looked. I needed to shave. Before I did anything like that, though, I needed to do a little recon around the area to make sure no one was going to walk right up on me. After dressing and putting on my coat, I picked up the AK and tucked the XD in my pants. In a swamp, sounds can be confusing; they can easily fool you. I took a few minutes to figure out where the sound was coming from.

Determining the direction the damned racket was coming from, I started out. I went to great pains to be quiet, using as much stealth as I could. But in the end, it was a waste of time. I could have driven up to them on a damn bulldozer, and they wouldn't have heard me. I came up from behind the old wheelhouse. There were probably thirty of them, all sitting around the edge of the swimming area. Several of them had drums and were steadily drumming away. They sat there swaying back and forth, some with their hands raised over their heads. From the looks of them, they weren't any threat to me and seemed to be thoroughly stoned or otherwise fucked up.

Back at my camp, I decided to risk getting cleaned up. I was filthy, felt filthy, and needed to get a little clean. I pulled the hygiene kit from the pack and one of my bandanas from the bag. I fished the last pair of clean drawers I had out of the pack too. I still had the clothes I had dried after swimming the river in the drum liner. Pulling them out, they had a slight mildew smell but seemed cleaner than what I had on. After my recent encounter with ticks, I decided I needed to do something about keeping them off me.

Before heading down to the run to wash up real quick, I pulled a small plastic OD green pouch out of the pack. It's a military clothing treatment system. I picked up a few of these at a surplus store; they seemed pretty handy. I should have used this thing long ago, but being in a hurry will make you forget things. In the little pouch, there were two big OD Ziploc bags, a couple of the thinnest plastic gloves in the world, two vials of Permethrin, and two pieces of green string. Taking one of the Ziplocs, I poured about half a canteen cup of water in it, per the instructions, and then poured in the Permethrin. I folded the pants long way and rolled them up and used a piece of the string to tie it off. After shaking the bag with the solution, I dropped the pants into the bag.

I used the second bag and repeated the process and dropped the other Columbia shirt and T-shirt in it and sealed the bag. I shook the bag real good to get the solution mixed around and set them aside to soak. The instructions said they had to soak for three hours, but I just didn't have that kind of time. Leaving them to soak, I picked up the AK and the hygiene kit and went to the run. After looking around to make sure no one was about, I slipped out of my clothes for a quick wash. The water was cold but bearable. The one thing I really wished I had was a damn towel. I had a pack towel. I knew right where it was. It was lying on the camping supplies shelf in my shop—lot of damn good it was doing me there. At least a small pack cloth was in the hygiene kit, and I was able to dry off some. I got dressed in the dirty clothes I had been wearing, but at least with some clean drawers!

Sitting on my limb seat, I put the Merrells on for a change. Grabbing the pot and dumping out the contents, I went back to the run and filled it with water. Back at the camp, I set up my stove and put the water on to warm. As the water heated, I dug the razor and soap out of the kit and set them aside and then found the mirror in the bag and laid it with them. A shave would make me feel like a new man. In between, I would shake the bags with the clothes in them. I was going to let them soak for an hour and a half.

Once the water was hot, I soaked one of the bandanas in it and wrapped it around my face. After repeating it another time, I used the bar soap to lather up and shaved. Not quite as good as having real cream but not bad. It took several passes to carve the beard off my face; but when I was done, my face felt so much better. Now that that was taken care of, the clothes had been soaking for right at ninety minutes. Using a pair of the nitrile gloves from the FAK, I pulled the clothes out and wrung out as much of the solution as I could and hung them to dry on the outer limbs of the dead tree. When the old tree came down, it knocked a hole in the canopy, and sunlight poured in. My laundry would dry pretty quick, I hoped.

Grabbing the pot, my filter, and all my water containers, I picked up the AK and went back to the run. After rinsing out the pot, I set up the filter and started filling containers. I was knelt down beside a big tree with a small palm growing at its base. Starting to hear voices, I quickly finished filtering water and gathered all my stuff. The voices were coming from up the run, so I quickly headed back to the tree. With the AK at the ready, I watched the run, still looking for the source of the voices. Eventually a canoe came into view; three of those hippies were in it, two men and a girl. They were working their way down the run. I saw the tips of fishing poles sticking above the side of the boat as they went by. The girl in the center of the boat was firing a glass pipe with a BIC. She let off the lighter and took a long drag before passing it to the guy in the rear.

I sat there shaking my head, watching these idiots smoke as they went down the river. I had done this run many times, and it was usually a one-way trip. A shuttle ran between the takeout and park. There wouldn't be any shuttle now, so they would have to try to paddle back up. A couple of years ago, a woman was killed by a gator while swimming in the run. There were real dangers on this little piece of water.

After they were out of sight, I decided to eat something. I heated some water in a canteen cup for some coffee and used a heater to warm an MRE. There was still a pack of crackers and a pouch of cheese, so I snacked on those while I waited for everything to heat. I guess it's the kid in me, but I love the cheese and crackers in an MRE; it's the best part. Once the water was heated, I made my coffee and sipped on that while I waited for the heater to finish.

Just as I was tearing the top off the MRE, I heard some shouts come from downriver. Sitting there with the pouch in my hand, half opened, I listened to the swamp. I heard the girl; she was pretty excited about something. Then a shot, a loud shot, and she screamed. Loud bangs from something hitting the aluminum canoe floated through the trees. I reached over and picked up the AK, checking the safety. From where I was, I couldn't see downriver. I was on the upriver side of the trunk, and the tangled ball of the tree's crown blocked my view.

Silence filled the swamp again; all the sounds died out. I chalked it up to them finding a gator or a snake and shooting it. With everything quiet again, I went back to my brunch. I had just stuffed the last bite of beef ravioli in my mouth when the bow of a canoe came into view. This one was a fiberglass boat painted in a camo pattern. The girl was in the center, crying, with a camo-clad man on either end. Both of them had a rifle in their lap, but from where I was, I couldn't tell what kind.

Following that canoe was another, with three men in it, all dressed like the first guys, in camo. A man sat in the center of this boat with a rifle sticking up between his knees. This boat was a Gheenoe with a trolling motor hanging off the stern. It was up out of the water, and they were paddling along.

I just didn't like the looks of this crowd, and I didn't see the other two guys that had been with the girl. They were obviously raiders of some sort.

Sitting in the dark with his thoughts, Ted heard the unmistakable sound of a helicopter. It was somewhere out there; he didn't know where, but he did know who was probably in it. Before they deployed, he never liked those assholes with DHS. They strutted around like they were a higher power. Since the implementation of martial law, the DHS secretary was now the de facto ruler of the United States of America. And while they never let him or the other guys from Fifth Group in on what was going on, they had a pretty good idea. He and the guys in his team had a new name for DHS, Dick Head Security.

Oh sure, they strutted around like they were King Shit on Turd Island; but the couple of times they actually got into it with them, they looked more like the Disabled Home Security. They were full of piss and vinegar; but when the metal hits the meat, they just can't compete with real training and experience. Ted knew of two of them that would never "enforce the law" again. It was time for his relief, so Ted went inside and woke Sarge up. The old man rolled out of his rack and had his boots on in one fluid motion. The old bastard never ceased to amaze him.

They walked out onto the deck together. Sarge was stretching and sorting his gear out. Ted stood there in silence while he got squared away but couldn't keep his mouth shut.

"You make more noise than a damn troop of Boy Scouts," Ted said.

Sarge never even looked up from the primping he was doing. "Shut up, fuck stick." Sarge finished and checked his weapon. Looking up at Ted, he said, "You still here?"

"What the hell are we going to do?" Ted asked.

"Well, you guys are going to have to decide which side of this fight you're going to be on," Sarge replied while staring out into the darkness.

"What do you mean? Which side?" Ted asked with a bit of confusion.

"If what you guys told me was true, I was in long enough to know what's about to go down. With the current administration in the White House, they are going to attempt a bit of *cleansing*." Sarge slowed and stretched out the last word.

Ted stood there for a minute, mulling that over. "You really think they're going to try that? I mean, what's the point?"

"The point, son, is that there are two kinds of people in this country. Those that think for themselves, take care of themselves, and know they have to work for what they want in this world. Then there are those that are happy to do what they are told as long as they are fed, clothed, and given a free cell phone and place to live. As long as those in control provide for their needs, even if they aren't to the level they want but are just enough to satisfy them, then they will paint their ass white, put their heads down, and graze with the rest of the antelope," Sarge stated matter-of-factly.

Ted stood there rocking on his heels. He raised

his M4 up, holding it by the fore grip with the Magpul stock resting in the crook of his elbow. He looked over at the old first sergeant, the finest example of a warrior he had ever seen. "There is a third kind; some of us are sheepdogs." With that he turned and started into the cabin.

"Good man, good man," Sarge replied, nodding his approval.

Ted went in and pulled his sleeping bag out, laying it on the cot. He kicked off his boots and climbed in. He lay there for a minute, thinking about what Sarge had just said before drifting off to sleep.

Mike was lying in his cot sound asleep. He was sleeping so deeply that he wasn't even dreaming. It had been a long time since he slept like this. But the current company he was with and the location they were in provided him enough comfort that he slept like the dead. That was until Sarge came in and waved a broken banana oil ampule under his nose. He immediately gagged and started to cough. Sarge moved quickly down the line of cots, placing the ampule under the noses of the other two. In short order, they were all gagging and coughing. They looked up through teary eyes to see the old man standing over them, laughing a belly laugh through his Promask gas mask.

Mike sat up trying to stifle a cough. "Damn you, old man!" he choked out.

"Rise an' shine, you candy asses!" came the muffled reply through the mask.

Sarge pulled the mask off as he went out the door onto the deck, laughing all the way. The other three rolled out of their racks and started getting ready for the day. Outside, Sarge had a coffeepot set up, a little single burner stove. The coffee was bubbling up into the percolator when he picked it up and poured his porcelain 101st Airborne mug full. He sat down in the camp chair and listened as the Three Stooges bumped and banged around inside; the sound of all the scraping and banging brought a smile to his face as he took a sip.

Mike was the first to come out on the deck. He had his GORE-TEX parka on against the cold, his hands were stuffed into the pockets, and his M4 was slung over his shoulder. "You . . . are . . . a rotten old fuck," he said.

Sarge was blowing on the cup and started to laugh. "Worked, didn't it?" he replied.

"Yeah, effective," Mike replied. "Got another cup?"

"On the shelf in the kitchen," Sarge replied as he took another sip.

"You call that a kitchen? I wouldn't feed my dog out of there." Mike fired off as he opened the door.

"Good thing you didn't bring him," Sarge responded.

Mike led the crew back out to the deck, each of them with a mug of his own. All of them had the Screamin' Eagle on it, and most of them were chipped or cracked. All of them looked like they had been used to drain motor oil from an old Peterbilt before the old coot turned them into coffee cups. As they came out, Sarge lifted the pot and started pouring the cups full.

Doc was looking into the bottom of his cup. "Have you *ever* washed these things?"

Sarge moved the pot over to his cup. "That which doesn't kill you only makes you stronger there, Doc," he said as he topped the cup off.

Mike held his cup out, and Sarge started to pour it full and then shifted a bit and poured hot coffee all over his knuckles. "Shit! That's hot!" Mike yelped as he set the cup down, shaking his hand in the cool air.

"That's for calling me a rotten old fuck earlier," Sarge said with a sly grin.

Chapter 10

Rolling down the road for a short piece, Thad passed a small store on the left. Several people were standing out front in a line. Again, it was another example of the emergence of a barter economy. The folks standing out front had the same assortment of commodities in their hands—a goat on a leash and more chickens—and a young boy had a stringer of bluegills. There were more bikes and trailers, and if he had been in a better mood, he would have laughed at the lawn tractors with the little trailers on them. As the truck rumbled by, many sets of eyes were on him; they undoubtedly heard the two shots.

Heads on swivels tracked the truck as he passed, but no one did any more than that. Seeing the sign for the store with a "Campers Welcome" sign hanging from it, Thad started to form a picture in his head about the men he just encountered. They had probably been down here in their campers and probably had a family with them. That thought made him pause. But then he thought again that he wasn't the cause of what happened; he just reacted. Thad decided right then that he wasn't going to give anyone the benefit of the doubt any longer. If you appeared to be a threat to him or his family, he was going to kill you.

Thad knew he was close; it wasn't far. He was being lulled by the view. Huge old oaks grew on either side of the road, broken occasionally by fields or houses. He thought back to Morgan and wondered where he was. The thought that maybe he should have taken him home popped into his head. But it was so far out of the way that it would have added a hundred miles to his trip. Besides, Morgan probably wouldn't have let him anyway.

Then he thought about Sarge and the guys. He had been talking to the old man for about a year on the radio, and they had met a couple of times. He was a hell of a good guy, and he hoped he was okay. Then Jess came to mind. He realized that he left so quickly that he never said a proper good-bye. Thinking on that for a minute, it saddened him. She was a pain in the ass and beyond naive, but she was funny, and he liked her.

The trees and fields rolled by in rapid succession and then another indication that he was getting closer to home—Culbreath Road turned into Bellamy Brothers Road. He didn't even notice the change at first, and when he did, it brought a smile to his face. Aside from the change in name, there was no difference in the road—same trees, same fields, and still no people to speak of. Approaching a small bridge, Thad's knuckles once again tightened around the wheel. There were two or three—he couldn't tell yet—people standing on it. As he got closer, he saw it was three kids, boys about twelve or thirteen.

They were fishing from the bridge and shooting what looked like a rifle into the trees along the bridge's edge.

Thad slowed the truck as he approached the span of concrete over the little creek. The boys, seeing the truck approach, focused on him. He saw them elbowing each other, pointing at him. He reached across the seat and pulled the shotgun into his lap. The three boys were sitting on the concrete barrier as he drove the truck onto the span. He slowed the truck to a stop as he came abreast of the trio, looking out the passenger's window at them.

"Catching anything?" he asked.

"We got two cats, nice ones," a redheaded kid with a face covered in freckles replied, squinting one eye against the sun. He had a Benjamin air rifle lying in his lap.

"Good deal. Wha'cha using for bait?"

"Night crawlers," the youngest of the three, or at least the smallest of the three, replied with a hillbilly drawl that was out of place in Florida.

"Good." Thad was nodding his big head. "Y'all seen any trouble?"

"Naw, ain't no trouble around here. No power or cars or anything, but everything's been okay," the freckle-faced kid replied.

"Well, good luck with the fish," Thad said as he waved at the boys and started off down the road again. The boys gave him a wave as he pulled away.

Thad drove on. He didn't encounter anyone until he got close to Highway 52. There, on the northwest corner, was a small building with several people standing in a line out front. The sign over the door read NO NAME PUB. More people trading away supplies they might actually need for a drink. As he came by the bar, more heads swiveled to look at him. No one made a move toward him, though.

Thad scanned the crowd, looking for any faces he might know. He was close to home and knew this little watering hole well. The truck was sitting at the intersection like it would have during normal times, waiting for the light to change. Most of the people in front of the bar were looking back at the truck. It was the same old assortment of stuff—some junk, some guns, and others with nothing in their hands. A couple of other cars were in the lot and an old pickup. Leaning against the bed of the truck was an old man in overalls; he had a Ford cap pulled down low over his eyes. Even without seeing his face, Thad knew who it was. Mr. Jackson lived just down the road from him.

Thad pulled the truck into the parking lot and up beside the old man. The old man didn't even move; he was still leaning against the bed when Thad eased the truck up beside him. He reached up and raised the bill of the cap, pushing it back on his head.

"Lookey, lookey what found its way home," Mr. Jackson said, pulling a toothpick out of the side of his mouth.

"Hey, Mr. Jackson, how you doin?" Thad replied.

"Oh, I'm fine. You know she's been worried about you. She knew you'd make it home, but she's been plenty worried," the old man said.

"I been worried about her too. What're you doing up here? You don't drink," Thad replied.

"Oh, I'm jus' lookin' over what folks is bringing up here fer trade," he said.

Mr. Jackson was a notorious countywide wheeler and dealer. He bought and sold, or bartered and traded, for anything and everything. He hadn't worked in years, many years, but he made enough money through his "dealings" to live comfortably in the house he owned outright.

"Whur'd ya git the truck Thad?" the old man asked.

Before Thad could answer, a shot rang out and then several shots. The people in front of the bar started to scatter, and then more shots. Thad looked over his shoulder as he raised the shotgun from his lap. Mr. Jackson didn't even move. "Don't worry about it, Thad; second time this week. Somebody prolly tried somethin' inside." Thad looked back at the old man, who was still leaning against the bed of the truck.

Shouting from the front of the bar brought his attention back around. Two men were carrying another out by his arms and legs. He had several obvious gunshot wounds and was bleeding heavily; he was limp and not responsive to the jostling. The two men carried him out into the parking lot and just dropped him. They were followed by another man with an AR-15. The man with the rifle looked around. The people who had been standing in front of the bar were peeking from around corners or from behind cars in the lot.

"Let this be a lesson to anyone who thinks they are going to steal from me!" he shouted. "I make fair trades with y'all, but if you try'n steal from me, I'll kill your ass!" With that he turned and went back inside.

Thad looked back at the old man. "Exciting times, huh?"

"Naw, things are just going back to the way they was meant to be. You steal from someone, they might kill ya. You offend a man, he might break yer jaw. Ain't no more panty-waisted lawyers to get in the way," the old man responded.

"Believe me, I know," Thad said. The old man just looked at him for a moment.

"You have trouble getting back?" he asked.

"Some more than I wanted. I'm gonna head on home. I want to see Anita and Tony," Thad said.

"You do that. I know they is waiting on you. I'll stop by later," Mr. Jackson said.

"Okay," Thad replied as he dropped the truck into gear.

He crossed over Highway 52 and continued down Bellamy Brothers Road. Up ahead, it would make a hard right-hand turn. After the turn, it was just over a mile to Swiftmud Road. Thad rounded the corner and floored the gas. Talking to Mr. Jackson, he knew his family was okay. He hadn't said any different, and he wanted to get home to them. Home, the odds had been against him that he would ever see it again, but now he was less than two miles away. He made it to Swiftmud in no time and rounded the corner.

One more mile, one more mile, and he'd be there. Thad pushed the old truck hard, slipping on the curves. He had to tell himself to slow down. It would be a shame to kill himself in a crash after all the shit that he'd been through. He eased up a bit but still slid into the driveway in a cloud of dust and gravel. The dust was still rising when he jumped out of the truck. He was rushing toward the house when a shot rang out; he dropped to the ground as a shrill voice screamed out, "Don't you move, or I'll kill you!"

Thad was on the ground with his face in the dirt. The dust was starting to settle, "Anita! Anita, it's me!"

"Thad? Is that you?" came a cautious reply.

He stood up and saw her on the porch, a pistol in her hands. "Yeah, baby, it's me. Now don't shoot me. I done had enough of people shooting at me." He stepped toward the house. Anita saw him and dropped the pistol on the porch with a yelp. She ran down the stairs and into the big man's open arms.

After they passed, I stepped out of the tree and checked on my clothes. They were drying nicely, so I flipped them over, trying not to touch any part that was still too wet—don't want that crap on your skin. Sitting back down, I started to think about home. I was so close now. One, maybe two more days and I would be there; that is, if there weren't any more problems. I pulled the map out and took a look at it. I would need to modify my route, more south-southeast; but even in the dark, there was no way I could get lost out here. Even if I lost my compass, I could still find my way home.

My biggest concern was those damn hippies up the river. I was sure there were more of them in the forest. Add to that the countless rednecks I could potentially run into; there was still plenty to be cautious about. I was orienting the map with my compass when a shot rang out upriver. Immediately my eyebrows went up. I was still hunched over the map. All of a sudden, it sounded like the streets of Fallujah. All hell broke loose.

I made myself a little flatter. Damn that gut keeping me away from the ground! I could tell it was several different caliber firearms—some shotguns, and certainly some handguns. Several people were shouting and screaming. It was definitely more than the five guys I saw come past a while ago. Then, to add to the mix of sound, I heard the unmistakable whining ring of a VW start up. The engine raced with its high, chirpy, whirling sound. I listened as it faded away; sounded like it was heading out toward Highway 40.

The shooting died down to the occasional pop. I was lying under the trunk of the old tree listening—a couple of more shots and then more yelling. The shooting picked back up again for a minute before dying out. Not knowing what in the hell was going on, I just lay there. I didn't have anywhere to go anyway. I rested my head on my arm and closed my eyes; no one could see me under here; besides, I had the AK in my free hand.

Splashing caused me to open my eyes. I just barely saw the heads of two men in a canoe paddling furiously down the river. One had on a boonie hat that I remembered from earlier. I got a bit of a chuckle thinking about these guys thinking they would go up and take on that bunch of hippies.

While most of them were just people disenfranchised with the modern world looking to live in a simpler way, their ranks were full of lowlifes. I was certain that the hippie crowd had some firepower. Now it was confirmed.

I wasn't thirty feet off the river and heard them as they came by. "Man, that was a bad idea. I told him that wasn't going to work," the one in the boonie hat said.

"Well, you damn sure ain't got to worry about him no more. They shot the shit out of him. Who would have thought them damn dirty hippies had that many guns?" the other one replied.

"No shit, right?"

The two men paddled on down the river out of my sight. At almost the same time, I started to hear the banging of the campground's metal canoes coming down the river. It would appear that the hippies were in hot pursuit of their attackers. They should have just cut their losses. They were making so much noise they would be easy to ambush. It wasn't long before they came into view. I propped myself up on an elbow to get a better look at them. They were in two canoes, three men in each one. They looked just like you would expect too, long hair and beards and dirty-ass clothes.

"I'm gonna kill those redneck bastards—they killed Moon Dog," one of them almost shouted.

"Don't worry, man; we'll get 'em. An' we still have one of them back there at camp. He can pay for all of 'em," another answered.

They continued on out of my sight, and I went back to dozing in the midday warmth. I pulled the poncho liner out of the bag and draped it over me; it was comfortable, and I felt like a nap. Lying there, I started to wonder what they would do if they knew I was there. I mean, I hadn't done anything to them; but if they saw me, I doubt they would be very welcoming. I lay there dozing for some time, not asleep but not fully awake, until the banging of the campground canoes started again. I sat up and watched them as they passed.

This time, they passed in silence, except for the banging of paddles and branches on the canoes. After they were gone, I decided to tend to a couple of things I had neglected for a while. I hadn't cleaned my pistol since all this started, so I pulled it and the Otis Tactical kit out of the Devildog bag. Laying a bandana down on the ground, I stripped the pistol and thoroughly cleaned it. Satisfied with it, I set my eyes on the AK. I knew it had been fired and not cleaned since, so I proceeded to strip it down and clean it.

My kit doesn't have a thirty cal brush, as I don't have any thirty cal weapons, but I pulled several patches down the bore, cleaning it as best I could. It was surprisingly clean, aside from the general crud of me pulling it through the bush. After that was done, I set about cleaning the carbine. It took me a minute to remember how to fieldstrip the thing. It had been many years since I had held one of these, let alone took it apart. Once all the weapons were clean and the kit was stowed back in the Devildog, I leaned back against the tree.

There was no way in hell I could go back to sleep. I was awake for the duration now. Instead I got the solar panel out and set it up and connected the battery. I should have done this earlier. After it was set up in a sunny spot with the tree between it and the river, I sat back down in the hide. I was still antsy; I needed something to do. I pulled the ESEE-4 out and my knife kit.

Looking it over, there was some discoloration starting on the blade and even some very light rust. My field kit for the knives was kept in a small Maxpedition pouch designed to hold a battery carrier, but it worked better for this for me. In it was a Rust Eraser, a medium and fine four-inch diamond hone, a DMT fine diamond card, and a fine ceramic tri sharp. With these tools, I can maintain my blades to shaving sharp in the field, so I set about dressing up the blade. Using the eraser, I cleaned all the discoloration off the leading edge of the blade and the laser etching and then used the card to dress up the edge on the blade.

I had finally killed all the time I could; there was nothing else to do, and I was starting to go stir-crazy. Time to go. Checking my clothes one last time, they appeared dry, so I took them down and changed into them. While doing so, I made another discovery. You know the good thing about ticks? You can see them and pull them off; but chiggers, on the other hand, you cannot. My legs were covered in little red spots, as well as my waistline. Just looking at them, I started to itch, but I didn't scratch yet. The first time you scratch one of them, you will claw your hide off; nothing feels better than to dig at them. I remember taking the little one to Lake Dorr when she was littler to swim. She lay in the sand and played, and the next day she was absolutely covered in chiggers. That was the first time I had ever seen anyone get chiggers from the sand.

After dressing and lacing up my boots, I started to pack everything back up. The weather had warmed up nicely, and I didn't need a coat; my long-sleeve shirt was plenty. However, I did make sure the light coat was easily accessible because as soon as the sun went down, it would cool off. Thankfully, it was cool; if not, there was no way in hell I could be in this swamp in the summer. The damn skeeters would carry me away. My activity drew the curiosity of a squirrel that came out onto the limb of a juniper tree not far from me.

The little rat wasn't sure what to make of me and sat there on his perch, flipping his tail. I looked up at him with a smile. I had raised several of the rats and always enjoyed watching them. "What are you looking at?" I said. His little tail stopped, and his body stiffened. Then he started to bark. He raised absolute mortal hell at me. Aggravating little shit.

Once everything was packed, and I had double-checked to make sure, I strapped the Devildog around my waist and hefted the pack onto my shoulders. After adjusting the waist belt, I picked up the AK and started to move upriver a bit, looking for a shallow place to cross it. I didn't have to go far to find a spot where the water was only about a foot deep, with a white sandy bottom. Having been on this river many times, I knew that pretty bottom looked nice and firm; however, it was anything but firm.

Before venturing in, I looked around for a large

stick to brace myself with. Finding what I needed, I made my way to the edge of the creek and started into it. It didn't take long for the stick to come in handy, as a step with my right foot sunk it halfway to my knee. Using the stick for support, I wrenched it out and continued on. The entire time I was in the water, I was listening for the telltale banging that would indicate someone was coming downriver from the campground but never heard anything. I guess the hippies don't like to go out after dark in the swamp.

The other thing I thought about was gators. Although with the cooler weather, they were not much of a concern. With things warming up, they would certainly start to move around a bit, looking for a sunny spot to warm up. This close to the campground, though, there weren't too many gators; farther down was an entirely different story. Juniper Creek ran into Lake George, which was connected to the St. Johns and was absolutely chockablock full of the big lizards.

The crossing went without incident, save one more foot extraction. On the other side, I hunkered down in the brush for a minute to get my bearings with the compass. From my work on the map earlier, I knew I had to take a heading of about 150 degrees and follow it pretty close. I wanted to hit a strip of land that ran through a chain of lakes, to the east of the bombing range. Norm's guys had mentioned that something was going on over there, and I didn't want to get too close to it.

Poor Norm; I started to think about him and his boys. I wondered how Daniel was doing. No time for that; checking the compass, I started out on my heading. It felt like squirrel hunting, the way I was slipping through the swamp, checking the ground for each step, using what I call the fox walk. This was something I read about a long time ago and started using while hunting. Instead of coming down on the heel of the foot, your foot comes down on the outside edge of the ball. Then you roll your foot into the step with the heel coming down last. If there was anything underfoot, you could usually feel it and either reposition it or move your foot. It was not as effective in these Bellevilles, but it still worked.

I was closer to the campground than I suspected. The smell of cooking fires was drifting through the woods, and I thought I heard something. It was clanking, like pots and pans or something, although I couldn't be sure with the tinnitus ringing in my ears. I sure wish I had used more hearing protection in my younger days. My head stayed on a swivel—take a step, listen, take a step, and listen. This made for very, very slow progress, but it was still light out, and I didn't want to stumble upon anyone. My clothes were earth tones and not camo, so if anyone looked my way, they would likely see me. Getting closer to the campground, the noise picked up. There was no doubt many people were here. If I remember right, I should be east of the Fern Hammock loop. It was one of the primitive loops and had some pretty nice campsites in it.

The closer I got, the louder the sounds of people became. Fortunately, it was by now getting on about six o'clock and the light was starting to fade, especially under the canopy I was walking through. Mixed with the smell of wood smoke was the scent of cooking food. I couldn't discern any one aroma in particular; it was several things mixed into a potpourri of smells. I caught brief glimpses of flames through the brush and the occasional voice, never much and always fleeting. Before I even realized, I was past the campground. The first indicator was the silence, other than the change of the critter shift. All the squirrels were gone now; some birds were calling from their nests, and the night shift was coming on.

As luck would have it, I had come down a finger of the swamp that came right to the edge of Highway 40. The light was almost gone now, so I dropped the pack and took a knee. Finding the NVGs, I pulled them out and strapped them to my head, turning them on. Giving the tube a minute to warm up, I sat in the dark listening to the sounds of the night shift. A sudden noise to my seven o'clock caused me to spin around and raise the AK, flipping it off safe. Something was moving out there, probably an animal, but better safe than sorry. I flipped the goggles down and looked out into the woods.

I couldn't see anything; there was nothing to see, but the sounds continued to increase. It sounded as if a pack of wild hogs was coming through the bush. I knew what was out there, but it didn't help my heart rate at the moment. As my heart pounded in my ears, the beast of the darkness came out into view. The first thing I saw was his fiery eyes in the glow of the goggles. He was low to the ground and was coming right at me. It sounded like he was dragging a mountain bike on its side behind him.

Then he came fully into view—his armored shell and long tail. A damn armadillo makes more noise than any other animal out there. In a dark and spooky place, they can scare the absolute shit out of you! I started to giggle to myself. These damn things had caused me increased heart rate while deer hunting, waiting in a stand in the quiet. One of them starts through the underbrush, and you can just see the ginormous fourteen-point buck; his rack looks like a rocking chair on his head.

With my attention back on the task at hand, I spent some time looking out at Highway 40. I couldn't see anything either way; there was nothing to cause any concern. Satisfied there wasn't anything out there, I eased up to the edge of the bush and made a rush across the road. I just knew someone had to have heard me. The pack jumping around, the weapons and mags, and other associated gear sounded as if I was dragging a tin trash can across the damn road with me.

"Well, what's the plan, Sarge?" Mike asked after taking a sip from his cup.

Sarge sat there with the cup in his lap, holding it with both hands. He was staring down into it and swirling the coffee around. "It all depends, really. We need some more info. Those kids they sent out to look for you isn't a good sign."

Doc was holding his cup up, looking at it suspiciously. "Yeah, seems a little heavy-handed," he said.

"It would appear they are playing for keeps," Sarge said, still looking into the cup.

"But for what? What the hell are they planning on doing? What's the point? They talked up that flare for a week before it went off. Everyone knew it was coming, just not that it would cause this much damage," Ted said.

Sarge stood up. "The flare didn't cause all this damage. No doubt it contributed to it, but not all this. There's more at work here. And as for why, the current administration has made no attempt to conceal their desire for a fundamental shift in this country. Remember, he said he was going to *transform this nation*. Well, what better chance? What if—and this is just a crazy, old retired vet talking here, you know, one of the guys on the DHS watch list—they either detonated or allowed to be detonated an EMP type device?"

"That's a bit of a stretch," Doc said, finally risking a sip from the cup he had been inspecting.

"Maybe, but what better cover? Hell, there may not even have been a flare. I don't know. We don't know enough yet, but we have to figure this out," Sarge replied.

The men stood there in silence, drinking their coffee and looking out into the swamp. The sounds of the swamp coming to life were all around them, and the swamp was filled with fog rising off the water. Finally, Sarge spoke up. "We need to get this place up and operational. The panels need to be installed to collect as much sunlight as possible while being somewhat concealed. We need to get the radios set up and the power supply—that's our first priority. Ted, I want you to get the radio you had and the one we got off those boys set up, and start monitoring them for any traffic. Just do not, under any circumstances, key the mic, understand?"

"Roger that." Ted went over and began to open some of the Pelican cases they brought, pulling out radios and carrying them inside.

"Mike, I need you and Doc to set up the panels. There should be enough cable to run it back into the cabin. I'll work on setting up my rigs. We also need to pull the battery from one of the boats and put it in mine. I'm going to rig one of the radios in it so that we can move away from here to transmit if we need to."

"Where do you want to put the panels?" Doc asked.

Sarge stepped out to the edge of the deck and pointed up into a large cypress tree. "See that bracket up there? That's where I hang a couple of them when I am out here hunting. Put them up there."

"Don't you mean poaching, when you're out here poaching?" Mike said with a snicker.

Sarge looked over at him. "Do you want to go swimming?" He turned and went into the cabin.

Doc stood there on the deck, looking at Mike. "How long have you guys known him?"

"Hell, seven, maybe eight years. Why?" Mike was looking up at the bracket in the tree.

"I know you guys all know each other, and I trust you guys, but this is all getting a little crazy, don't ya think?" Doc was staring out into the water.

"You got a better idea? We talked about some of this before we ever left. Those assholes with DHS have a real hard-on right now. They just can't wait for the chance to go out and kill a bunch of people. You remember when they started talking about providing aid? Who was and wasn't on that list? Their plan to confiscate weapons, to find anyone who had stored anything—food, water, fuel, and, certainly weapons—and take it all? How it was *unfair* that some of those *extremists* had hoarded all that stuff. I think the old man is right, and the shit is really about to hit the fan." Mike was looking right at him when he replied.

"You're right, I just never thought the army I know and love would ever go for something like this," he said with a hint of sorrow in his voice.

"It's not. That's why they sent the amateur hour out to look for us. You didn't see anyone from the teams around, did you? You on board with this?" he asked.

"Yeah, not like there is any choice. If what Sarge said is true, then I am damn sure on board," Doc replied, setting his cup down. "He makes the worst coffee I've ever tasted. Let's get to work." Mike slapped him on the back, and the two set about finding all the equipment they needed to set up the power system.

Back in the cabin, Ted was setting up the crypto gear, and Sarge was setting up his system. "We need some more table space, Sarge," Ted called out as he set the second radio on the little table.

"Yeah, we're going to have to make a run into town tonight and hit the hardware store for some lumber. We'll build some here and some shelves. I have a little bit left over from building this place.

Out back is one of them plastic garden storage things. There's tools and shit in there. Let me set this up, and we'll see what we got," he said as he set the big radio on the kitchen counter.

Ted and Sarge walked outside. Mike called over to Sarge as soon as they came out. "Hey, old man, how in the hell do you expect us to get up there?" he said, pointing up the big tree.

"What, you can't climb a tree?" he fired back.

"How in the hell do you expect me to climb that? There isn't a limb for thirty freaking feet," Mike said.

"Come on, Junior, follow me." Sarge headed around behind the cabin. He went over to the big cabinet and opened it up. Inside was an assortment of stuff—tools, hardware, and other junk. He reached down into the bottom and pulled up a small cloth bag and handed it to Mike. "Use these."

Mike took the bag and opened it. Inside was a bunch of the screw-in tree steps. Mike held one up, looking at it. "Nice. I like 'em."

"Kind of hard to keep a ladder around here," Sarge replied.

Mike and Doc took the steps and went back out front. Looking at the tree, Mike found the existing holes from where Sarge had screwed these things in many times before. After screwing in the ones he could from ground level, he took a length of rope and a carabiner from his pack. Looping the rope around the tree, he clipped it to the D-ring of his rigger's belt with the carabiner. Climbing up those first steps, he hitched the rope up the tree with his free hand. Once he was high enough to put the next steps in, he leaned back against the rope. Repeating this process, Mike was up high enough to hang the panels.

The bracket already had the bolts and hardware to secure the panels in the holes. Doc threw him a hank of 550 cord, and he used it as a tag line to haul them up one at a time. Using his Leatherman MUT EOD, he tightened all the bolts as he set the panels in place. With the panels in place, Doc tied the end of the cable on, and Mike pulled it up and connected it to the cables coming off the panels.

"Hey, Doc, see if he has a hammer or something and something to secure the wire to the tree with," Mike called out.

Doc went out back and found a hammer and some Romex cable nail-in straps and brought them out. He dumped the straps into the bag the steps were in and tied it and the hammer to the cord. Mike pulled it up and secured the cable as he came down. This time, though, he had trouble getting his safety rope around the step. "What a pain in the ass!" he complained as he was trying to free the rope from a step.

Doc fed the cable from the panels into the cabin through a hole that Sarge had made just for the purpose. He and Mike went about setting up the batteries, charge controller, and inverter on one side of the cabin. The location of the panels was not exactly ideal, but Sarge had trimmed away branches in the past to give a decent southerly exposure and enough light to keep the batteries up if they conserved their power consumption. Sarge looked up and realized that all four men were inside the cabin. They had all been so busy with their assigned tasks that no one even realized that there wasn't a watch posted.

"Hey, you bunch of dickheads! What's wrong with this picture?" he shouted out. Everyone stopped what they were doing and looked around at one another. Doc was the first one to catch on. "I'll go out and keep an eye on things, Sarge." He went over to the door and picked his rifle up from where it was leaning against the wall and went out.

"At least one of you has some damn sense," Sarge replied. "We have to keep someone on watch at all times. I know it's going to be a pain in the ass with only four of us, but we have to do it. Mike, you sit down now and write up a duty schedule, put watch rotation and mess duty on it," the old man said.

"Roger that, Sarge," he replied as he sat down at the table, putting on a set of headphones to listen to the radio while he worked on the schedule.

"You guys hungry?" Sarge asked. Ted nodded to him; even Mike looked up and nodded his head.

Then from outside came a "Yyeesss!" from Doc.

"All right, I'll rustle some grub up for us," Sarge said.

Sarge went over to his kitchen and set out his Coleman Dual Fuel stove on what was left of the counter space. Going outside, he rooted around in the cooler he loaded from the kitchen of the house and carried in a bag of taters and onions. After lighting the stove, he set a big cast-iron skillet out on it, black as coal, and dropped a big spoon of Crisco in it. Grabbing the little bottle of dish soap on the sink, he washed his hands. He had a cutting board that fit over the sink. Setting it out, he started to cut the spuds. When the spuds were chopped, he dumped them in the skillet and started chopping the onions. After adding them to the taters, he put a lid from the Dutch oven over it and cleaned his cutting board.

Going back out to the cooler, he came back with a dozen eggs. From under the counter, he pulled out three cans of salmon and opened them. Emptying them into a bowl, he cracked in a couple of eggs and added some onions he saved when he chopped them up. Reaching back under the counter, he found a half can of Italian bread crumbs and poured those in till it felt right. With everything in the bowl, he mixed it all together with his hands and formed the mix into cakes.

He lit the other burner on the stove and set another skillet out and dropped in another spoon of shortening. While it melted, he stirred the taters around, making sure nothing was sticking. With the grease melted, he added four of the cakes to the skillet and got down to some serious cooking. The little cabin filled with the aroma of cooking onions; add to that the smell of the salmon, and it was enough to drive you mad. It brought all work inside the cabin to a standstill as the guys looked over his shoulder. Sarge pulled the ever-present dish towel off his shoulder and swatted at them. "You got shit to do; git!" Ted and Mike both went about looking busy while they waited for the food.

Once everything was ready, he served plates heaped with taters and onions and a couple of salmon patties each and handed two of them out to Mike and Ted. Walking over to the door, he picked up his rifle and stepped out. "Doc, go on in there and eat."

"Hey, thanks. That smells damn good," he replied.

"Just hurry up; I ain't eat yet either," Sarge fired off in reply.

Doc went in and ate with the other two, while Sarge sat in his camp chair on the deck.

Chapter 11

"Daddy!" a little voice called out. Thad looked up from his wife and saw his son coming down the stairs of the house. His mother was standing in the open door.

Little Tony ran up to him; Thad knelt down to catch him. The little boy wrapped his arms around his father's neck. "Where have you been, Daddy? You were supposed to come home a long time ago."

"I was working on it, buddy; I was working on it," Thad replied with tears in his eyes.

He stood up, picking the boy up with him. Anita came up and took his hand, her little hand disappearing into his. As they walked up the stairs, Thad's mother was leaning on her cane in the doorway. "'Bout time you gots yoself home," she said. Leaning the cane against the doorframe, she reached out with both hands for his face. He had to stoop down for her to grab it. Tilting his head, she kissed his forehead. "You sho' need a haircut." She chuckled.

Thad reached up and rubbed the quarter inch of hair on his head. "Yeah, getting a lil shaggy." He gave out a little laugh.

They walked into the house, and he fell into his

easy chair. He hadn't even thought of it the whole time he was gone, but now that he was home and sitting in it, it was the most comfortable thing he had ever sat in. Anita left the room as little Tony jumped into his lap; Thad reclined the chair all the way back, and Tony lay down on his chest. Anita came out of the kitchen with a plate, a sandwich on it, along with some okra and rice. Thad's mother put up her hand. "Let him be, sweetie, look at him. He plumb wore out. Let him be. He home now an' that's all that matters."

Farles Lake was about a four-and-a-half-mile walk as the crow flies from my current location, so it would probably take a little bit longer than that, as I could not simply walk a perfectly straight line out here. Once I hit the other side of the road, I stopped and listened for anyone who may have been around. There wasn't a sound. It's funny how paranoid you can get.

Just as I was about to take off again, looking out into the scrub I had to hike through reminded me of the ticks 'n' chiggers. My clothes were treated, and that should help, but I was going to increase the odds. Dropping the pack, I tucked my shirt in and buttoned the sleeves at the wrists. I bloused my pants inside my boots, buttoned the shirt all the way up, and even dug around in the Devildog until I found my buff and pulled it over my head, tucking the opening under my chin, and put my hat back on. After stuffing the loose end of the buff into my shirt, I was as armored against the damn bugs as I could get.

After hefting the pack and picking up the AK, I started back out on my trek. My plan was to hike to Farles Lake; I could refill my water from a pitcher pump there and then continue on. I figured three, maybe three and a half, hours and I should be there. The hiking wasn't too bad, a little rough in spots but not difficult. Doing my usual "take a couple of steps and listen" routine demanded a slower pace. No matter, though; it was rather comfortable out tonight, even without a coat, and I was making decent time toward home.

It was about eleven thirty when I hit the northern end of Farles Lake. The picnic area was on the south end. There wasn't a camping area on the lake, just a "day use" area, as the forestry service likes to call it, but it did have that pump. Now I should have known that there isn't a camping area there in normal times, but these aren't normal times. It was about ten minutes till midnight when I reached the south end of the lake.

My trip through the scrub to this point had been completely uneventful, aside from the usual assortment of limb whips to the face and stumbles over deadfalls. After scrambling over the ridge, I was relieved to make it to the lake. The Ocala National Forest is a vast hunk of land, acres and acres of acres and acres. Water, however, was the commodity. So, as was the case all over the world, when you found water, you found life. Tonight on the south side of Farles Lake, I found life in the form of more Rainbow people.

How I didn't smell the bonfire, or see the light from the fire, is a mystery. It wasn't a big fire, but I surely should have seen it. The half-moon out tonight was bright enough that I had raised the goggles and was walking the trail in ambient light. Being so close to home and on very familiar ground, I was daydreaming of my girls. I was thinking of the girls working the handle of that pump and squealing with pure youthful joy as the water would issue forth from the head. It was with this thought in my mind that I came out into the clearing on the lake side. And here was where I came out into the light of the fire, and the eyes of at least a dozen hippies fell on me.

They were seated around their fire—on the ground, in camp chairs, and on logs dragged up to the fire. There were women, men, and children. They were all quiet and peaceful-looking as I appeared before them. Of course, all that changed when they saw me. Here I stood before them with a large pack on, rifle butt sticking out of it, an AK across my chest, the NVGs on my head, and the bloused boots and the buff covering most of my face. As my presence was registered by them, one at a time, they began to react. The children naturally started to cry; one woman screamed, which brought others to the fire—armed others.

Everyone was coming to their feet; the women and children were receding from the fire, and mostly me; many armed men were gathering around it. No one had spoken a word yet—they or me. We were all standing there, waiting for someone to make the first move. I certainly didn't want trouble with them; sure they're a bunch of stinking hippies, but they hadn't wronged me yet. A sudden thought popped into my mind; it almost made me laugh out loud at the thought of it. It was so damn ridiculous that it might just work with this crowd.

I rummaged around in the Devildog slung on my waist with my left hand as the grip on the AK was in my right. Finding what I was looking for, I clutched them into my fist.

"Hey, you guys, seen any of those asshole forestry cops?" I called out.

"Naw, man," came a reserved reply from somewhere on the other side of the fire.

Pulling the two baggies out of the small pack, I said, "Cool. You guys got any papers?" If anything would break the ice with this crowd, this was it.

"No papers, man, but I got a pipe!" came a quick reply from a figure walking around the pit toward me. The guy came around to me and produced his pipe with a flourish of a smile. "Come on over to the fire and take a load off, man."

Rusty, the kid with the pipe was named Rusty. He had *kind* hair, the kind you find on a mangy dog that hasn't ever seen a comb. He had a crooked smile with an underbite; it made him look a little comical. He flopped down on a log, and I handed over one of the bags. "Hey, thanks, man, we haven't had any decent weed in like forever." A small crowd was starting to gather, so I passed the other bag off to a blonde chick wearing a white linen shirt. That caused the crowd to split up and give me some thinking room. I wanted a little quick info and then to get the fuck outta here.

"How long have you guys been here?" I asked to no one in particular.

A voice that I couldn't match to a face replied, "A few days."

"Have you guys seen any feds around here or anywhere?" I asked again.

"Yeah, they go on patrols in Hummers. They're using the bombing range. Sometimes there are helicopters flying in and out," Rusty answered, and then he fired the pipe and took a long drag, holding it in, his face turning darker even by the firelight. He offered the pipe to me; I took it and passed it to the first waiting hand.

"You've seen all this in a few days? Have they ever said anything to you?" I asked.

"Yeah, they drop off food and bring around a doc. They searched for weapons, telling us they are now illegal, but we hid them. Other than that, they leave us alone. I think they found some people who didn't go along with their program, though; we've heard some hellacious shootouts. We watched a helicopter just kick the shit out of someone once—lots of gunfire," a man in a leather hat answered.

"What's the program?" I asked. The pipe was starting to make the rounds, though, and I wasn't sure what kind of information I'd get out of them.

"Their program, Department of Homeland Security. Do what they tell ya an' they won't fuck with ya. Try'n argue with 'em, and they'll bring the boot down on ya, hard," an older man replied; he was wearing a woodland BDU top with the sleeves cut off and a boonie hat.

One of the pipes made its way back to me, I had no intention of hitting it, and I needed a way to get the hell out of here. I had a little info—about all I was going to get out of this rabble anyway. Passing the pipe off again, I stood and said, "I gotta piss. Is the shitter across the road still in operation?"

"Yeah, man, go drain yer lizard," came the reply.

I stood up and started to walk away from the fire. "Hey, man, leave your pack an' gear here. Take a load off."

"I'm good, old habits and all. Gotta keep my gear with me, ya know," I answered back.

I was heading for the road; the shitter was on the other side, the south side, and there was what appeared to be a camp past it near the tree line. Not sure who in the hell would want to have a tent near the foul-ass shithouse, though. There didn't appear to be anyone over here. The fire across the road seemed like it drew all the hippies like moths to a flame, or in this case, hippies to a pipe. Pausing by the shitter for a minute to make sure no one was around, I headed out past the camp and into the tree line again, back into the damn scrub, and without the freaking water I came here for to begin with.

I should have had enough water to get home if it really came down to it, but there are a couple of options out here if you know where to look. Not long after hitting the bush again, I hit the Florida Trail. There was no way I was going to walk the trail. Not only does it not go straight in any freaking direction but mainly because trails were for folks that want to get ambushed. So instead of trying to pick my way around the trails, I went off trail and picked my way through the scrub. I was taking an approximate heading of 170 degrees from Farles Lake to get home.

Less than a mile after starting out, I came to an east-west-running road. I took a knee by the side of the road to watch it for a minute. To the west was the range. To the east was Buck Lake. Pulling one of the stainless bottles out for a drink, I thought of walking down to the lake to refill everything. But I was still a little close to the range for my taste. While I hadn't seen or heard anything that would give me pause, I was not taking any chances. I had just stuffed the water bottle back into the Devildog when I saw the headlights. They were to my west and moving to the east. If they continued, they'd pass right in front of me.

I simply sat still and watched them. They were probably two miles off; I could have crossed the road and never been seen. But if they were wearing any NVG gear or had a FLIR on board, then they could see me, so I waited. About a kilometer from my position, the two vehicles turned to the north. That road was the outer perimeter of the range, probably their roving patrol, I noted.

With them out of the way, I crossed the road and found my rhythm again. Plodding along in the green glow of the goggles, I started to envision my arrival home. Walking up the driveway in the pale light of morning, the dogs run up and bark at me and then, realizing it's me, jump up. Then everyone inside realizes I'm out there, and they all run out and have a big group family hug in the driveway. It brought a smile to my face just thinking about it.

Then I started to laugh a little as the real version popped into my head. It went something along the lines of me lying in the yard with the dogs all over me and Mel firing *warning* shots into my legs. I started to laugh; it was funny because it could damn well happen. That made me start to think about how to make that first approach of the house. Then I remembered that Danny said they had the road blocked, something else to think about.

Grabbing an empty water bottle out of the bag brought me back to my current situation. I stowed the empty and pulled the other half-full one from the other side. Blue Sink was below me somewhere. It wasn't far, but I would need to veer back to the west a bit to hit it; it's an old sinkhole full of nice clean water. I could only hope there wasn't anyone around; it used to be a popular place on the weekends, but under the current circumstances there shouldn't be anyone around.

So I modified my route back to the west until I saw a road off to the right and paralleled it. The sink would be in line with my route now. It didn't take long to strike a small trail that led to the hole. It was fairly wide with clean white sand. As I started down it, I was more interested in the bottom of the trail than anything else—watching for footprints, tire tracks, or any sign of people. There wasn't anything; the trail was old and windswept. Aside from the tracks of deer, coon, bear, and other assorted critters, it was clean. The number of bear tracks was a little disconcerting. I have a thing for finding bears in the woods, usually when I don't want to.

As I got closer to the hole and could start to make it out in my goggles, I went off trail again and found a place where I could monitor the entire sink. I just wanted to take a few minutes to make sure no one was around. Sitting there in the dark, scanning the water's edge and surrounding trees brought another thought to my mind—of the change, the massive change this had brought upon us. You couldn't simply walk up to the water hole anymore like you could a couple of weeks ago. Now you had to look at it like a gazelle in Africa would. Was there a predator around the banks? Was there a predator in the water? Was it safe enough for me to try it?

How weird was that? What a fundamental change in the way we lived our lives. But I sat there and watched, looking for any sign of a lion or a crocodile. After fifteen or so minutes, I was satisfied I wouldn't be eaten, so I slipped down a little closer to the water, where I dropped the pack and took out all the containers and the filter. After pausing for another brief check, I eased down to the water and lay on my stomach. The AK was beside me in the grass. I put the filter to work quickly and got everything filled with clean water. I could probably have drunk this water straight, but I had a filter, so why chance it?

I was closing the drawstring on the bag for the filter when I heard a siren start up north of me. It started out low and rose into a high pitch where it worked back and forth. The sound of small-arms fire soon followed it. Making my way back to the pack, I quickly stowed everything, then looked back up the little trail I had come down on. The sky was brighter back toward the range. There surely was something going on over there, and it didn't sound good.

Not long after the crackle of the small arms

started, a helo rose up into the sky. It was blacked out, flying without anticollision lights. But a gunner was on board, and he was lighting up the sky. I stood there in the trail; I was a couple of miles away and caught glimpses of the bird as the pilot banked and dove the ship. They were after someone, for sure. Who in the hell would try to hit that place? And more importantly to me, who was in there? I'd seen a few helicopters, what looked like Kiowas to me, but not a true gunship. No Apaches or Cobras. If the military was out there, why didn't they have the big guns out? But then, why would they? Shouldn't they be trying to help people out? It was more than I could figure out right now, and I was close to home. I just wanted to get home.

Shouldering the pack again, I picked up the AK and started down the trail away from the sink, taking a minute as I did to drink the cool water I had just filtered. Thoughts of Mel and the girls were on my mind again as I walked along. I knew I shouldn't be on trails, but this one wasn't big enough for a car, so I felt safe in doing so. Nonetheless, they were on my mind as I watched the sand pass by. It was times like this, when the task at hand required no more thought than breathing, that I would think of home; it didn't last long, though. A sudden thrashing of the brush brought me around real fast.

I stopped where I was and flipped the safety off the AK and held it at the ready. Damn, I wish this thing had a laser; I didn't know how in the hell I'd make an aimed shot with these goggles on. The sound was at my eleven o'clock. Something was in the scrub and not being particularly quiet about it.

There was the faintest of a breeze on my face, so the wind was coming right at me. Cautiously, I took a few steps forward and then turned on the IR source on the goggles to get a better look into the scrub. What I saw was the front end of a large black bear sticking out of the bush on the left side of the trail. He was looking right at me from less than thirty feet.

So why did I walk toward the damn noise? What the hell was I thinking? With the wind in my face, he was trying without success to wind me. In the goggles, his eyes glowed and gave him a supernatural look. Raising his head, he would sniff the air, trying to get an idea of what was out there. I stood without moving, hoping he would just pass by or turn and go back into the woods, but it seemed like it was taking forever for him to make up his mind what he was going to do. So instead, I figured I would try to ease away from him, just take a step back; that's what I thought.

As soon as I lifted my boot, he heard it; the ears went up, and the head went down. Now it knew I was there, just not sure where or what. The bear stepped out into the trail, facing me, his head still down, and he started to chomp his jaws. That was a sure sign in bear language that the shit was about to hit the fan. All the books and experts say never to run from a bear. And there I was holding an AK that I could easily shoot the damn thing with, and what did I do? I went into what I call a blind lateral panic. I turned and ran—I mean ran like a fat kid from the neighborhood bully.

I don't know what the bear did; I never stopped

to see where he went. I made it back to the sink before I finally stopped, out of breath, and felt like I was about to die. I dropped the pack and fell on the ground beside it, trying to catch my breath. I never saw the bear again; I'm sure he did the same thing I did. As I sat there in the sand, catching my breath and sipping on some water, the sound of the helo came back out of the night. Sitting there, I listened to it for a while. It was still up north of me; however, there wasn't any more gunfire. After a bit, it sounded like the bird landed; the sound died out, and the night went quiet again.

Checking my watch, it was now about three thirty, a few more hours of dark before the sun came up, so I needed to get my ass in gear. Getting up, I shouldered the pack and this time went off trail on my southerly route. It is hard to describe how difficult it is to walk through the scrub. The pack hangs up, and the weapon sling and the stock from that damn carbine that I was really starting to hate hang up. You trip over snags, your boot laces get untied, and then you stop to retie them and tuck them into the boots to prevent that from happening again. Finding a line of weakness through the scrub is all you can hope for. It is truly tough going.

The next couple of hours went without incident, aside from the previously mentioned issues with merely moving through the damn woods. Sometime shortly before six in the morning, I came across a small lake. It was one I had been to before, so the sight of it brought me some confidence. I was close to home now. Baptist Lake was a typical forest pond. Nothing special about it. People go to it to go mudding in their 4x4s. The sky was starting to lighten up, and I was coming out of the tree line on the north side of the lake.

Stopping just inside the tree line, I checked the area for a minute. Something was on the south side of the pond. Staying in the tree line, I followed the shore around to the south. Three things were lying out there, but between the fog and the dim light, I couldn't make them out. Having not seen anything to cause concern, I stepped out toward them. As I got closer, it became obvious what it was.

Three bodies were out there. Staying off to the side to look things over, a picture started to form. There were multiple sets of tire tracks, all from the same vehicle, it appeared. One of the bodies was a young girl, nude with long blonde hair. She was the last one to be dumped, it looked like. She couldn't have been there more than a day. The other two had been there longer, one of them a lot longer. Not wanting to but knowing I needed to, I stepped toward the bodies.

The one that had been there the longest was unrecognizable. She had been really worked over by the buzzards. The next one was in a little better shape, but I didn't recognize her. The last one, with the blonde hair, looked familiar. Her lips were swollen, and the eyes were gone, but she looked familiar. There were marks around the wrists and ankles where I assume she had been bound and a rope was around her neck that I assume was used to kill her. Beer cans were everywhere and the remnants of fires, fires that had been burning while the bodies were here. Rags of clothes were scattered around and a single shoe. This place had a horrible feel to it, not like it used to when all you were looking for was some mud to sling.

This was truly disturbing; this close to home, and someone was killing and dumping girls in the woods. God only knows what was done to them before they found their way here. My desire to get home just got more intense. Turning my back to them, I started to walk out of the area. The trees on the southeast side of the pond were full of buzzards, just waiting for the sun to come up so they could go back to the buffet.

With the sun slowly coming up, the goggles were no longer needed, so I took them off and stopped for a minute to stow them in the pack. Digging in the outside pouch of the pack, I found an MRE pound cake and unwrapped it, shouldered the pack, and ate it while I walked. I couldn't shake the image of those bodies from my mind as I walked. I kept seeing one of my girls lying there, and that filled me with terror.

To get to the house, I would be coming into a more populated area. Not wanting to get shot by some dude taking a piss off his back porch in the early morning, I made sure to keep inside the tree line, working my way southeast. Eventually I would hit Highway 19, and I decided to walk the last piece on the road in the daylight. I was close to home and would hopefully know some of the people if I came across any.

I hit the road in Pittman, just up from the house. Taking a minute to check the road both ways, I didn't see anyone, so I stepped out and started to walk down the shoulder of the road. It felt weird underfoot, the pavement, after walking through the scrub for so long. It was surreal to step out of the woods into Pittman. I had driven this road thousands of times and knew it well. Now I was walking down the road instead of driving, but I could actually see my street up ahead on the left. I never encountered anyone, not a soul, never even saw anything that would indicate anyone was around.

Approaching my road, my gut was in my throat. I was excited and scared at the same time. Stepping off the paved road onto our dirt road, I immediately saw the roadblock. At the sight of me stepping onto the road, the two men standing around the burn barrel immediately left its warmth and shouldered their rifles. The barricade was made from pine logs and was substantial; a truck would have a hell of a time getting through it. I let the AK drop and raised my hands as I approached. I saw them and recognized them both. I just hoped they recognized me.

"Morgan?"

"Yeah, Lance, it's me."

"Holy shit, man, you actually made it. We were told to watch out for you, but it's been so long since anyone heard from you, we got worried," Lance replied.

I approached the barricade. Lance stuck out his hand, and I took it. He had a big smile on his face. He needed a shave, but he looked good. "Welcome home, man; welcome home."

Sarge sat on the deck, sipping a cup of coffee while the boys ate. He had been out for a while, but he would still take care of his boys first. And that was just how he thought of them, his boys. Inside he heard them talking, heard the boots scuffing the floor, while outside it was quiet, and he could think. Now that they were here, he wasn't sure what in the hell to do exactly. They bugged out because of the surveillance team that was inserted in his house. They had to bail from that, no choice. But now what?

The guys finished eating, and Doc came out and relieved Sarge on the porch. He went back inside and sat down to a plate of his own. Mike and Ted went about cleaning up the dishes. Sarge sat down at the table and put a headset on to listen to the radios. He was making a list on a notepad while he ate and listened. There were some things he wanted to get from the hardware store in Suwannee. It was while he was writing down how many two-by-fours he wanted to get that he found a transmission on the radio.

It was a recorded loop telling everyone there would be a radio address by the secretary of Homeland Security. The address would lay out the rules of martial law that the country was now under. Sarge stuffed another bite of patty into his mouth with a grunt. The recording said the broadcast would be at eighteen hundred hours today, so they had some time before it to get some stuff done. Sarge sat there and flipped through the frequencies a little longer; he was thinking of Morgan and Thad. They had not been in communication since the last time they were interrupted while talking. He wondered if they ever made it home; he knew deep down inside they would, but he sure would like some confirmation.

With breakfast out of the way, Sarge decided it was time to get on with the day. He had made his list of what he wanted to get from the hardware store, so he went and opened one of the Pelican cases and took out a few gold and silver one-ounce rounds. He fully intended to pay for what he wanted.

"Hey, you guys come outside," Sarge said as he went out the door.

Outside, Doc was leaning against a corner of the cabin. Sarge laid out his plan to run down to the gulf and to visit the little town of Suwannee. The hardware store there was owned by an old man named Don and was where Sarge had bought all the material for his cabin. He wanted to get on the river while it was early so they could get back. They were taking two boats; one of them would have to stay behind to provide security for the cabin.

"You think it's a good idea to travel in the daylight, Sarge?" Ted asked.

"It's a risk, but I want Don at the hardware store to see me coming and not get all jumpy because we come up in the dark. Plus it will give us a chance to take a look around," Sarge answered. "So who's staying here?"

"Aw, come on, paw, we all wanna go ta town," Mike said in a thick hick voice.

"Just for that, you're staying here, dipshit."

Mike and the others just laughed, and Sarge went back inside to get his gear. Ted and Doc started to prep the boats for the trip downriver. Mike went out behind the cabin and came back with a fishing pole from the little storage locker. He was going to get a little fishing in while they were gone.

Sarge came out with the SPW and put it in the bow of his boat, along with his carbine and a small cooler. "Mike, keep the door open. The radio is set on the forty-meter band. We'll be on there in case anything happens."

"Roger that, Sarge. You guys be careful," he replied.

Doc stepped into Sarge's boat, and Ted got in one of the others. It took a few minutes of maneuvering to get them headed out toward the main river, but they finally managed with only a moderate amount of cussing from Sarge. The two boats eased up the little creek and stopped just short of the main channel. They sat there for a minute, checking out the river; not seeing anything, they moved out into the main river with Sarge in the lead, sitting on the cooler in front of his console. He held the SPW by the barrel with the butt on the deck. Doc and Ted opened the throttles, and the boats zipped down the river.

Suwannee was about ten miles downriver from Turkey Creek; the ride would take about fifteen minutes. The morning was clear and only slightly cool. The fog rising off the river was light, and they were able to push the boats. This early morning, they passed a couple of boats out on the water. No one appeared to be any sort of threat; they mostly just waved a hand or a rod tip as they passed by. From the looks of things, it was just normal folks out trying to catch something to stink up a skillet.

The two boats made it to town without incident. As they got closer, the boat traffic picked up considerably. Almost all of Suwannee was accessible from the water; it was a series of natural and man-made canals. The hardware store, more of a combination of hardware and marine hardware, was located just off the main channel of the river. Coming out of the main channel, Sarge was surprised to see so much activity. A number of boats were in the canals. He guided Doc with hand signals to the dock for the hardware store and reached out and caught a cleat and tied the boat off and then stepped out onto the dock. A few people were out there, and they drew some strange looks, the three of them all in Multi-Cam BDUs with weapons hanging off them. The SPW lying on the deck of his boat was a sure source of curious looks.

Sarge found old Don behind the counter in his store. Don was the kind of old man that looked like he was born onto the stool he always sat on behind the old cypress counter. The store had been there for as long as anyone could remember—that included Don on his stool. He was an old cracker that didn't suffer fools well. He and Sarge got on like two peas in a pod. Sarge went in with the M4 slung across his chest to find Don behind the counter. He had his arms folded across his chest and the stub of an ever-present Backwoods cigar in his mouth. Over the course of the day, that cigar would slowly disappear, but it was never lit.

"Ha, the fucking marines are here!" Don called out as Sarge and Ted walked into the old store.

"Typical civilian, can't tell the difference between a real soldier and a fucking jarhead," Sarge snapped back. He walked up to the counter and put a boot on the old brass rail and an elbow on the counter. "How ya doin', Don?"

"Fair ta middlin'. How 'bout you, Linus?" Don replied.

"Just another day in pair of dice," Sarge answered.

"Huh, if this is yer idea of paradise, I'd hate to see yer idea of a bad time," Don said.

"Clean the hair outta your ears, old man. I said *pair of dice*. The way things are going it's a crapshoot."

Don let out a laugh with that one. "Pretty good. What kin I do for ya?"

Sarge laid his list on the counter, sliding it over to him. Don took the glasses from his head where they perpetually resided and put them on the end of his nose. Holding the note out at arm's length, he looked it over. "Well, I got all that. But what'er ya gonna pay with?"

Sarge reached into his blouse pocket and pulled out a half dozen silver rounds and dropped them on the counter. Don reached over and took one, inspecting it closely by looking over the top of the glasses. He looked past the coin to Sarge. "This'll cover it. You need some help loadin' it?" Don nodded to the two young guys that were sitting on a wire reel in the open door of the warehouse. They were typical Florida redneck kids, Wrangler jeans, T-shirts, and Realtree camo hats. Ted was standing not far from them with his carbine across his chest; Doc was out on the dock by the boats.

"Sure, can they round it up and carry it out there, and we'll sort it out between the boats?" Sarge answered.

"Billy!" Don called out, waving him over. "You an' Tommy get all this out there on the dock an' help the A-Team here load it up."

The boy took the slip of paper from Don and looked at it. "Sure thing, Mr. Don." With that, the two boys disappeared into the bowels of the warehouse to start pulling the lumber.

"You seen anything of the government, Don?" Sarge asked, turning to look out the big open door to the river.

"We've seen some, DHS guys mostly. They come in town and *requisition* a lot of stuff. They aren't doing nuthin' to help anyone, so far as I've seen," Don said with a hint of disdain in his voice.

"Seen any trouble around here?"

Don rocked back on his stool. "Shit, ever'one here know ever'one else, so ain't no one gonna try 'n' steal anything. How 'bout you, any trouble up yer way?"

"We've seen a little. Had to leave the house when some unwanted visitors showed up. Had a run-in on the river with some would-be pirates. But that's it," Sarge answered.

"Must'a been some bad hombres to run you an' these boys off'n yer place," Don said with a raised eyebrow.

"They thought they were, but we knew they'd have friends coming to look for them, so we skedaddled," Sarge said.

Billy and Tommy came out of the warehouse

pulling a lumber cart with them and headed toward the big door. As they went out, Ted started telling them where to put the stuff in the boats. Sarge stayed inside chatting with Don, and Doc kept his position as lookout. The boats were almost loaded when Ted and Doc both came inside the doors. "Sarge, we got some company," Doc said as they stepped in behind the big sliding door.

"Who is it?" Sarge asked.

"Light boat, three men, long guns and uniforms," Ted answered.

Sarge stood up so he could look out at the dock. The boat was coming up in front of theirs and tying off to the dock. He quickly gave orders for Doc to go upstairs to the loft and find a place to cover the door. Ted went back into the warehouse and took up a position behind a pallet of Quikrete. Sarge was trying to figure out where to go when Don called to him.

"In here, Linus," Don called and jutted a thumb toward a little office door behind the counter. Sarge started to go behind the counter and stopped. He looked up at Doc. "Where's that fuckin' Minimi?"

"In the boat, Sarge," he answered, looking out the big door. He could already see the boots of the first guy approaching the door.

"Shit!" Sarge said through gritted teeth as he went into the office door and quickly closed it.

Billy and Tommy were out on the dock going about their business as the three DHS agents approached. When they first approached, Billy stepped onto the boat and laid a sheet of plywood over the SPW. As the agents approached, one of them stopped to look into the boat. He didn't see the weapon, but he saw the radio mounted to the console. He looked at one of the other agents and nodded to it; the other saw it and gave a nod in return. The two of them walked through the big door to find Don on his stool.

"Ya here to steal some more from me?" Don said by way of greeting to them as they came in.

The agent casually walked up to the counter and laid his M4 on it. "Whose boats out there?"

"Just some boys that came in for some supplies," Don replied.

While Don and the agent were talking, a man outside on the dock came up to the agent standing in the door and started to talk to him. Doc saw the man pointing to the boats and gesturing through the big door. It was obvious what was going on to him—some sorry bastard trying to garner favor with the DHS thugs at their expense. The agent spoke with the man for a minute before coming inside. He went up to the counter where the first agent and Don were still engaged in a lively back-and-forth. The two of them stepped off to the side for a moment and spoke and then the agent returned to talk to Don.

The agent from the door caught the attention of the other and jerked his head in a "follow me" kind of motion. They started to move out toward the warehouse. The first agent walked back up to the counter and looked at Don. "Where are they? They have an illegal radio in that boat and, from what we were told, weapons. You know damn well all weapons were to be turned in."

"How in the hell are people supposed to know that? There ain't no fuckin' TV or radio," Don spat back at the agent. "You assholes ain't helping anyone."

"We put a radio in town. I think you're well aware of that. Now I'm not here for a damn debate. Where are they?" the agent asked again, this time with an edge to his voice.

"I told you I don't know. They went into town, I guess. They dropped off a list of what they wanted and left." Don rocked back on his stool and folded his arms across his chest.

The agent looked down on the counter and picked up one of the silver rounds. "An' they paid in sterling? That doesn't strike you as a little odd? Not to mention you can't have this either. I'll be confiscating these." The agent picked up the other coins and dropped them into his pocket.

Don launched himself off his stool. "Wait a damn minute! You ain't taken that; that's mine!"

The agent hit Don in the chest with an open palm, knocking him down. He stepped around the counter and drew his sidearm; he stepped over Don, who was sprawled on the floor. Pointing the weapon at his face, he said, "I can do whatever the fuck I want. I'll kill your stupid ass if I'm so inclined. You are at the very least guilty of harboring armed fugitives, and for that alone, I could kill you!"

Don raised his hands over his face, trying to shield it from the blast he just knew was coming. The agent continued, "And there isn't a damn thing you can do about it!"

Sarge was in the little office listening to the exchange just outside the door. He was getting pissed; the old man hadn't done anything wrong, and he felt responsible for the knuckle dragger that was fucking with him.

"For the last time, where are they!" the agent shouted as he kicked Don in the leg.

From behind the door of the office came a voice, "In here." The agent looked up quickly and then looked back at the other two who were already moving toward the little room. He stepped over Don toward the office, positioning himself in front of the door. Inside Sarge listened to the boots scuffing on the floor. When he was confident the agent was in front of the door, he took a step back and grabbed a file cabinet to brace himself. The agent reached for the knob with his free hand just as Sarge kicked the door out. The door slammed into his hand, instantly breaking his index finger and thumb; the force of the blow knocked him onto his ass.

Before the other two could react, Doc fired one round that hit one agent in his right ear. He was dead before he hit the ground. Ted took out the second one with a double tap to the back of his head. He too was dead before he hit the ground. Sarge was out and on top of the asshole that was in front of the door. The agent was lying on his back, holding his hand; his pistol was on the ground beside him.

"You can do what you want, huh? You can kill him if you want, huh? What the hell has he done wrong?" Sarge's voice rose in octaves as he spoke.

Ted and Doc quickly secured the bodies of the other two and began to strip their weapons. The agent was lying on his back glaring back up at Sarge through gritted teeth. "You're a fucking dead man. You have no idea who you're fucking with."

"Oh I know exactly who I'm fucking with. You're the same kind of asshole I had strung up in my garage," Sarge said to him.

The agent's eyes got wider; he looked up at the old warrior standing over him. "You, you're the one! Ha-ha-ha-ha, you just wait till we get ahold of you. People like you need to learn your place in the world, and we are certainly going to teach you," he snarled back. Spittle was coming out of his mouth; he was so mad.

"Sarge, we gotta go, man," Ted called out.

"On your feet, asshole." Sarge reached down and grabbed the man by his shirt and jerked him onto his feet.

He still had that sneer on his face when he looked over at the bodies of his two compatriots. Then he looked at Ted and Doc. "You must be two of the fucking traitors we're going to skin alive. The gloves are off, boys. When we catch you, you'll beg to die."

"What's the plan, Sarge?" Doc asked.

Don was back on his feet, although a little shaky. The agent looked at him. "You too, you fat fuck; you're a dead man." Don's face showed the terror he felt; he believed what the man in the black BDUs said to him. He looked at Sarge with fear in his eyes.

"Shut up, dumbass, you're in no position to make any threats," Sarge said. He reached out and grabbed the man's broken fingers and twisted them. He let out a howl of pain. But he wasn't going down without a fight. With his good hand, he grabbed

Sarge's wrist and rolled it back and away, while he lowered his shoulder and charged into him. The two men fell to the ground behind the counter.

Ted and Doc both ran toward the counter as they heard a yelp of pain. As they rounded the counter they saw Sarge standing over the man with a fistful of the man's testicles. He was lying there in some serious pain. Sarge gave him one more good squeeze before he stood up. Doc and Ted stood there for a minute looking at him as Sarge straightened up.

"There is only one way to deal with people like you," Sarge said as he drew his pistol. The sound of the shot filled the empty warehouse. "Get their bodies into their boat and let's get out of here." Sarge knelt back down beside the body and pulled the rounds out of his pocket. He stood up and handed them to Don. "I think these are yours. I wouldn't stick around here if I was you."

They dragged the bodies of the three agents out to their boat. A small crowd was gathered outside on the dock. The man that had been talking to the agent earlier was there in the front of the crowd. He was wearing a dirty red flannel, the kind that's lined with insulation. Everyone looked on while the bodies were piled into their boat. As they dropped the last agent into the boat, he stepped forward.

"What do you think you're doing? They're with the government. You can't just go around killing them," the man in the flannel said.

Sarge looked over to him. "And what have they done for you? They came in there and threatened that man's life for no reason other than selling some lumber. You ready to roll over and let them tell you what you can and can't do?"

"If they will provide for us, I am. We need some help. Where the hell is it supposed to come from if not them?"

"Well, you may be ready to roll over on your back and spread your legs, but I ain't," Sarge replied.

With that they hopped into the boats. Sarge got into the agents' boat. "Follow me." He started the boat and cast off the lines; Ted and Doc did likewise. Sarge headed out to the river and turned toward the west, heading to the gulf. They ran the boats out into the open water of the gulf for about a mile before Sarge kicked the motor out of gear. He stepped back to the fuel tank and pulled the line out of the red plastic tank. Opening the cap he dumped the fuel on the bodies and all over the back half of the boat. From under the console, he pulled an orange Olin flare kit out. Waving Ted over, he stepped back onto his boat and took a handheld flare out and struck it. Tossing the flare into the boat, he waved them back toward the river. As they headed back up the Suwannee, the boat became a ball of flame, thick black smoke billowing up from the slick surface of the gulf.

"What was that about?" Ted asked.

"Sending a message," Sarge answered over his shoulder.

"I think they'll get it," Ted replied.

The trio made it back to the cabin without incident, although all of them kept their eyes on the sky. Once back, Sarge filled Mike in on what went down and made a point to make sure that everyone knew they had just killed three federal agents of the DHS. After that, Sarge laid out the plan on what he wanted built, and the guys all got to work on it.

Thad slept all night in his chair. He never stirred. He woke in the morning to the smells and sounds of breakfast cooking. He clearly smelled eggs and bacon and heard the grease in the skillet popping. But how in the hell did they have bacon? He rose stiff out of the chair and walked into the kitchen. Anita looked up from her work at the stove as he came in. His mother was sitting at the table, nursing a cup of coffee. She looked up and smiled at him. "Mornin', son," she said with a big smile.

"Mornin', Momma," Thad said.

He sat down at the table and turned over a cup for himself. Taking up the percolator, he poured a cup of coffee. Anita called for little Tony to come in for breakfast; the little boy came in at a run and sat beside his father, as if it was just another day. Anita dished out some scrambled eggs for the boy and then looked at Thad.

"You hungry?" she asked.

"I'm alive, ain't I?" he answered.

She smiled at him and returned to the stove. In short order, she was setting a plate down in front of him with eggs over medium, bacon, sliced tomatoes, and a thick slice of bread and butter. Thad looked down at the plate, amazed at what was set before him.

"How did you get all this?" he asked while looking at the plate.

Anita sat down at the table with a cup in her hand. "Ole man Jackson is making salt-cured bacon. I have some tomato plants growing out back in a little greenhouse we made out of some plastic. And your mother made the bread. We don't have too much flour left, so enjoy it," she answered.

"Well, God bless, Mr. Jackson," Thad said as he picked up a thick slice of the bacon.

The rest of breakfast was spent on light small talk, a lot of it with little Tony. Now that he was home, Thad realized just how much he had missed the little guy and his wife and mother. It was the warmest feeling he had ever experienced sitting at the little kitchen table with his family.

Anita asked about the truck—where he got it and how the trip home was. He told her of Morgan and Sarge and the guys that showed up there. He didn't tell her about much of the trip; he didn't want to think about it himself. And he knew she couldn't handle some of what he had done—no, he would just keep that to himself. After breakfast, he would go through the truck, but, for now, he just wanted to enjoy this a little longer.

Over the last cup of coffee, Thad asked how things had been around home while he was gone. Anita told him of the hardships of no power, no news, and not knowing where he was. Even with all that, they lived far enough out that they hadn't seen any sort of trouble. The few neighbors in the area worked together to help each other out. She traded some of what they had extra of for things they didn't have. With what they had stored in the pantry, they hadn't gone hungry, although dinners of rice and beans got old at times. Overall, though, things weren't as bad as they could be.

Thad stood up from the table and looked at little Tony. "You wanna come help me clean out the truck?"

The little boy jumped up from the table, causing it to slide a bit. He ran for the door ahead of Thad; Anita called out for him to put on his jacket as they went out. Thad went to the truck and pulled the pack from the bed and then went to the cab and pulled all the guns out. He laid the rifle and shotgun on the hood. Then he took out the pistols and laid them out as well. Climbing in the cab, he was about to remove the radio to set up in the house when he remembered what Sarge said about not transmitting from the house, or the same place twice. He decided to leave it in the truck for now. Later today, he would go out and try to radio Sarge; maybe he could even find Morgan on the radio.

While he was getting the last of his stuff out of the truck, Anita came outside. She came up to the truck and looked at the guns. She stood there for a minute and looked the truck over—the smashed windshield and the bullet holes. Thad saw her looking at where the block had hit. She looked up at him. "Was it that bad?"

"Yes, it was. I hope to never have to do anything like that again," he said flatly.

She was quiet for a minute. "Thad, did you have to kill anyone?"

She was looking up at him, her arms wrapped around her waist, holding the sweater closed. He looked into her eyes. "Yeah, baby, I did. I did what

I had to to get home to you and Tony. Nothing was going to keep me away. And I'm sorry, but I'm not going to talk about it again."

She wrapped her arms around him, laying her face on his chest. "I'm just so glad you're home."

"Me too, baby, me too."

Chapter 12

Robert was the other guy at the barricade. He stuck out his hand, and I shook it. He was one of those neighbors that lived in the area. We would wave to each other on the road but didn't really know each other. I hadn't ever spoken to him until the Fourth of July. I had to go out looking for the dogs after they ran off when the fireworks scared them. He told me to take his four-wheeler and go to the house with it. I thanked him for that; it was a weird thought to be riding on something instead of walking. I walked over to the ATV and took off the pack and set it on the rear rack. They followed me over as I was taking off the rest of the gear.

"How was it out there, man?" Lance asked.

"It's bad in places. There were a few places that weren't too bad. But there are some crazy-ass people out there. I saw some truly horrible shit," I answered as I stepped up onto the ATV.

"Well, what you did was crazy. I couldn't imagine doing it. Were you alone the whole time?" Robert asked.

"No, I traveled with a couple of people—a girl at first, then a big dude named Thad. He was great. I wouldn't be here if it wasn't for him." I took off my hat and turned my head so they could see the scar.

"Holy shit, what the hell happened?" Lance asked.

"The girl we had with us shot me in the head on accident. We were being hunted by a group of people and were hiding in the bush. Last I remember was one of them seeing a footprint on the ground and turning toward us. Thad opened up on them, and it scared her. Thad told me she went to cover her head, and the pistol she had went off and hit me. He got me out."

They both stood there just looking at me in silence. They looked at one another and then back at me. Lance started to slowly shake his head. "Damn, man. You are one lucky SOB."

"Yeah, it wasn't easy. I'll tell everyone about it later. I want to go home right now," I said.

"Yeah, man, go. There's some girls that are going to be very happy to see you," Robert said.

I turned the key on and hit the starter on the ATV. It immediately purred to life. I sat there for a minute; a little grin came across my face, and I shook my head a little. It was a strange sensation. I looked at them one last time and put it in gear and headed down the road. I didn't go fast; I was actually enjoying the ride, kind of taking my time. As I approached my driveway, I stopped for a minute to hop off and open the gate. The dogs started to bark and ran toward me from the house. They stopped short, still accustomed to the inground fence that no longer worked.

I got back on the ATV and started up the driveway; the dogs were still going nuts. Meathead's hackles were up, and he looked fierce. As I got close to him, I called out his name. He paused for a minute and looked at me. Then little Sounder ran up and jumped onto my leg, licking my hands. The big idiot came running up, and I climbed off. I knelt down and hugged the dogs, Sounder licking my face and Meathead chewing on my hand. That was his thing; he wouldn't bite hard, but he liked to have my hand in his mouth. I sat there for a minute, petting them, hugging them, and then I heard the front door open.

My drive was circular, so you couldn't see the house from the road or even the front of the driveway. There was a thick screen of oak trees, and in front of the house were some enormous old azaleas. They were probably ten feet tall, and in the spring are just full of blooms. I loved them when they were flowering. Climbing back on the ATV, I started toward the house. As I came around the center island of trees, I saw the front of the house through the azaleas, but it was still obscured.

Pulling up in front of them, I stepped off. There, standing on the front porch, was Mel. She had my AR in her hands. She was looking at me, but she either didn't recognize me or it wasn't sinking in yet. I looked at her for a minute. "Well, you gonna shoot me or not?"

Her face changed; she set the rifle on the top of the rail and ran down the steps. I headed for her, and she threw her arms around my neck and tried to squeeze my head off my shoulders. I wrapped my arms around her and picked her up in a big hug. She was crying, and, honestly, I had tears in my eyes too. We stood there in the embrace for a while; I heard her sobbing. She let go enough that I could look at her. Her eyes were red and puffy; then I gave her a long kiss.

During all this, of course, the dogs were still all over us, jumping up, tails wagging. Mel pulled my hat off my head and ran her hand through my hair. She immediately felt the wound on my head. "What happened?"

"It's a long story. We'll get to it in time. How are the girls? How have you been?"

"They're good, still asleep. We've been okay. Things are getting harder lately, though," she said.

I took her hand and walked up onto the porch. We sat down on the bench. I gave her another hug and another kiss.

"I was so worried about you guys. All I wanted to do was get home."

She started to tear up again. "We were worried too, especially Taylor; you know how she is. But I knew you'd make it back. When you called on the radio, it really helped just to know you were okay. Why didn't you ever call back?"

"It seems there may be part of the government that doesn't want people to use radios. They would come on the radio every time we used it. Helicopters would show up," I said.

"We who?" she asked. I looked at her with a quizzical look. "You said we would use the radios, who was *we*?"

"I met up with some people that helped me a lot. If it wasn't for them, I wouldn't be here. Getting here was harder than you can imagine," I said.

She reached out and rubbed the scar on my head again. "This?"

"Among other things, I walked with this girl and another guy for a while. We tried to help some people one night, and things got ugly. The girl accidentally shot me when it hit the fan. If it wasn't for Thad, the guy, I wouldn't be here. He got me out and took me to the house of a friend of his. They patched me up. That's where I got the radio," I told her.

She leaned over and hugged me again. We sat there for a long while, on my porch, my house. She finally leaned back and asked if I wanted to go wake up the girls. I said, of course, but I wanted to do it a particular way.

"Is there any of that pancake mix left?"

"Yeah, we have tried to conserve. At first, I didn't do so good, but we changed that," she answered.

"Are you using the kerosene stove?"

"You remember how I said I hated that thing?" I nodded. "Well, I still hate that thing! I just can't get the hang of it," she said as she put her face in her hands.

"That's okay. You know I like it, and I'll do the cooking. How about that?"

"Fine by me!" she said as she stood up. Taking my hand, we walked in the house together. I paused at the door for a minute. She looked at me.

"I just want to savor this," I told her. I reached out and turned the knob and opened the door. It looked just like I remembered.

We went into the house; it felt surreal. I thought I might never see it again. In the kitchen, there was a light on, an electric light. I looked at it and back to her. "Is the solar still working?"

"Yeah, it's been on the whole time. You just don't know what a difference it's made. It's caused some trouble too, though," she said.

"Trouble how?"

"There are a couple of people around here that think this should be a community resource. Danny had to come down one day and make some of them leave. They wanted to take it," she said.

"Over my dead fucking body," I said.

"Well, now that you're here, you can deal with them," she said.

"Who was it?"

"Guess," she said.

I knew who it was. I guess every neighborhood has a person like that, the busybody that gets in everyone's business, the town gossip. Our particular version was a woman in her late fifties; her name was Pat, and she and I hated one another. I had not thought of her while I was gone. I actually never thought she would be like this. I sort of figured she would be the one that would stand up against this sort of thing.

"Food is the other issue. People are starting to run out. We had to move the chickens to the back porch. Someone was trying to get in the coop one night, and Meathead started barking. They ran off when I came outside. So Danny came down, and we moved them to the porch," she said.

"Yeah, it always amazes me how quickly people turn into good little socialists when they run out of their stuff. As long as they have something, it's theirs.

Let them run out, and you need to share. Don't worry, no one is taking anything from us," I said.

I went into the kitchen and opened the fridge. The light came on, and it was cold inside. I stood there shaking my head. It actually worked. I didn't have a big system, but it was more than enough for our little house. There was a bowl of eggs on the shelf. I took one out and, to my surprise, a jug of milk. "What's this?" I asked Mel.

"Powdered milk—the kids hate it, but they are getting used to it," she said.

In no time, I had the batter ready for the cakes. Taking a box of matches from above the stove, I lit the Butterfly. It was set up on the center island. I was already thinking about taking out the old electric stove and building a shelf in its place for the Butterfly. In the cabinet, I found one of my cast-iron skillets and set it on the stove. After pouring in some oil, I let it heat for a minute and then poured in the batter for the first cake. The smell started to fill the kitchen; it wouldn't be long before it would bring 'em out.

I didn't really think this out completely. Lee Ann was the first one to come out. When she did and saw a man standing in the kitchen, she screamed. "Mom!"

I turned around; she scared the shit out of me. "Hey, kiddo. Want some pancakes?"

She stood there for a minute, and then it finally sank in. "Daddy!" She ran over to me and hugged me. Her scream woke up the other two, who came out. Little Ash was rubbing her eyes. I looked over at her. "Hey, Little Bit."

She looked up at me and blinked and then rushed over, wrapping her arms around my waist. By the time Taylor came out of her room, she came straight over and gave me a hug. They were all talking and crying at the same time. Little Ash was jumping up and down, and I thought she would vibrate through the floor. It was hard cooking the rest of their breakfast with all of them attached to me, but I didn't complain. They all took turns flipping the cakes or pouring the batter.

When things got close to being done, Taylor went and set the table. I had lit another burner and had a pot of water from the Berkey boiling. Lee Ann got out the French press and put some coffee in it. I poured in the water when it was ready, and she took it to the table. Mel got a glass of V8 for me—oh, man, I love that stuff. I had forgotten all about it. With everything ready, we went and sat down at the table. There was quite the argument over who got to sit beside me, but it was sorted out pretty quickly. The girls were all full of questions, but I avoided anything unpleasant. They told me about the adventures of the dogs and the chickens.

With breakfast out of the way, the girls started to clear the table. I went around and gave them all another hug and kissed each of them on the forehead. I suddenly felt tired—not like "I've had a long day and I'm sleepy" tired but like "I could sleep for eternity" tired, just exhausted, completely spent. I told Mel I was going to go lie down. I went into our bedroom and lay down on the bed in my clothes. It felt so good, that Tempur-Pedic mattress. Mel came in with me and lay down beside me. She laid her head on my chest and each of the girls came in to give me another hug. I assured them I would be here later and just needed to get a little sleep. Little Bit climbed up in the bed between us and snuggled up beside me.

As soon as Sarge and the guys left the warehouse, Don jumped into his skiff and went home. Darrell, the guy in the red flannel, glared at him as he hopped into his boat. Don just ignored him; Darrell always had been a bit of an ass. He was certain that DHS would be sending someone around to look for their people, and he didn't want to be there when they showed up. Don lived off Mullet Road, and as with most houses in this small town, he had both water and road access. He more often than not took his skiff to work—just didn't have to fool with traffic laws that way.

Back at home, he grabbed a Natty Lite from the cooler on the kitchen floor; it was full of coolish water, the ice long since melted. Walking into the living room, he flopped down into his recliner and rocked it back and looked out the window at the river view. The property his house was on had been in his family for a long time. It was worth a lot; all the neighboring houses were far more opulent than his. Actually he was despised by some of them. His little "shack," as they would call it, really pissed some of them off. But it was his, and he owned it outright. He had never been married and lived there alone. Don's life revolved around the hardware store, fishing, Natty Lite, and his shows—*Jeopardy* and *Wheel of Fortune* in the evenings.

Just as Don suspected, DHS did send someone

looking for their people, and from the response, they must have found something of the boat. It was later in the afternoon when several boats raced into the canals of Suwannee. DHS had set up a staging area at Cedar Key as they leapfrogged down the coast from Eglin AFB, and Suwannee was just a few miles by boat north of that. One of their primary goals was to get to the Crystal River Nuclear Power Plant.

The DHS agents went through the harbor area of town, rounding people up. Anyone they saw was grabbed. Darrell wasted no time in volunteering what he knew. He took them inside the warehouse where they found puddles of blood and drag marks, and then they went back out to the pier. He was telling them how their agents were loaded onto their boat, and it was taken away by three men in camo uniforms—how they were armed and that they seemed to look to an older man for direction and called him Sarge. While Darrell was laying all of this out for them, a young man with a neat beard was fishing from the pier. He was questioned by the agents when they first arrived but was quickly dismissed because he seemed like a dimwit who wanted to talk about fishing. He was within earshot of where Darrell was spinning his yarn for the agents.

The agent that seemed to be in charge of the show asked Darrell who was in the warehouse, and he gladly told them it was Don Tuttle and where his house was. The bearded guy reeled up his line and collected his tackle box and started walking down the pier as the agent in charge began giving orders for his men to go find him. Darrell said he would be happy to take them to Don's house. A small explosion at the end of the warehouse caused them all to jump and the agents to take cover. A fire quickly started as a result, and this got everyone's attention.

Don was sitting in his chair working on his sixth beer when a boat came up to his house. He stood up and saw men in camo uniforms jump out and head toward his house. His beer hit the floor and began to run out into the carpet. He stood there slack-jawed for a moment before he turned and headed to the kitchen. Jerking open the backdoor, he was met by another camo'd figure. "Don't kill me!" he shouted before the man hit him in the chest with a Taser.

Darrell led the agents to Don's house; they deployed agents to the bank before they got there and gave them time to get in position around it before they came up from the river. In a coordinated assault, they hit the house. The rear security found the backdoor of the kitchen open and cautiously entered. The house was searched, and when Don wasn't found, they brought Darrell up.

"Where else would he go?" the agent in charge asked.

"I don't know. I assumed he came home. He doesn't do anything else. He hasn't got anywhere else to go," Darrell replied, looking around the empty house.

"If you're lying to me or trying to help him, you're going to be in as much trouble as he is. We're under martial law now. The rules are different," the agent said.

Darrell got a look of fear on his face. "What? No, I'm not trying to help him! I told those men what they did was wrong, that we needed help from the government. I'm trying to help you," Darrell pleaded.

"We'll see." Turning to one of the other agents, he ordered, "Cuff his ass up and bring him with us. Tear this place apart. I want anything you can find on this guy," the lead agent said as he walked out of the house toward his boat tied up to Don's dock.

As he went out, another agent cuffed a protesting Darrell and started for the door with him. Other agents began to search the house. An agent in the kitchen went through the cabinets, checked the fridge, and was pulling the drawers out and dumping their contents on the table. Finding nothing, he looked around and saw the cooler. Walking over, he kicked the lid open with his foot. The four one-pound blocks of C4 inside detonated with a thunderous explosion. It was overkill, blowing the walls out and dropping the roof of the front half of the house back onto what was left of the floor.

Darrell and the agent that was leading him away were blown into the river. The lead agent was just stepping onto his boat when the detonation occurred, and he was blown into the river as well. But as he was down at the water, he was left relatively unhurt. The other two men thrown into the river, however, were not so fortunate. The agent clamored up the dock, spitting out the brackish water of the canal. "God dammit!"

Don was lying in the bottom of a boat; there was a sack or something over his head. He couldn't see. All he heard was the sound of the outboard and felt the boat as it maneuvered. He was terrified, not knowing who had him or where they were taking him. He felt the boat slow down, the outboard lowering in RPM until it was at idle. Then he heard the hull grind into the sand. Someone grabbed him and pulled him to his feet. The sack was pulled off his head; he squinted against the bright afternoon sun, and everything was a little out of focus.

"Sorry, we had to do it like this, Mr. Tuttle, but we didn't have time to explain," a bearded man in a camo uniform said to him.

"What do you want? Are you going to kill me?" Don asked.

"No, we're not going to kill you. But those DHS guys might have, and we didn't want you talking to them," the bearded man replied.

Don looked around; another boat was there as well, and there were four other men, all in camo and all armed to the teeth, from the looks of them. He looked around at each of them. "Then what do you want with me?"

"Those guys are after some friends of ours, and we need to find them. You know where they are?" one of the others asked. He was wearing a pair of sunglasses, the kind that wrap around your head and make you look like a bug.

"You mean Linus?" he asked.

"Is that the one they called Sarge?" the bearded man asked.

"Yeah, them other two called him that."

"Do you know the names of the other two?" the bug asked.

Don thought about that for a minute. "I think he called one of them Doc or something."

The other men shared a look, and then the bearded man said, "Yeah, that's them. Do you know where they are? It's really important that we talk to them as soon as possible," the bearded man replied.

Don sat there for a minute thinking about that. He had an idea where Linus's camp was. They had talked often when Linus came down to buy supplies for it. He just wasn't sure if these guys were on the up and up or not. "How do I know you're friends of theirs?"

"You don't; you just have to trust us. We aren't going to hurt you. If we were, we'd be asking these questions in an entirely different way," the bug said.

"Gotta map?" Don quipped.

I slept until about four in the afternoon; it was the best sleep I ever had. Just being home, in my bed, the feeling was indescribable. When I woke up, I was alone. Mel and Little Bit were gone. I went out to the kitchen to find Danny and Bobbie there with Mel. They looked up as I came in. "Dude, took you long enough to get home," Danny said.

"You have no idea," I said as I shook his hand.

"Glad you made it back," Bobbie said.

"Me too. I can't describe the relief," I said.

Mel came over and put her arm around my waist and laid her head on my shoulder. "Me too," she said.

We stood around the kitchen and chatted for a while about how things were going. They caught me up on some of the local news—who was getting by, and who was starting to get a little weird. While we were talking, Mel went over to the fridge and came back with a glass of tea for me. "Oh, bless you, woman." I took the mason pint jar from her and drank it down in one long gulp. "Damn, that's good." She took the jar, refilled it, and handed it back to me. This time, I drank it a little slower.

"Damn, man, you act like you haven't had that in a while," Danny said with a laugh.

"Dude, I have drunk more water in the last couple of weeks than I did my entire life leading up to it," I said as I took another long drink.

"Hey, Howard told me there is supposed to be a radio address at six today. Do you have a radio?" Danny asked.

"Yeah, I have my little one. We'll have to find it. Hey, Mel, where's my pack?"

"It's on the porch. Robert came by and got his four-wheeler earlier and put all your stuff on the porch," she replied.

I went out and got my pack and brought it in. Opening it up, I dug around until I found the little pouch with the radio. While I was in there, I pulled the Yaesu out and set it and the antenna aside. Danny came over and picked it up. "This what you were talking on?" he asked.

"Yeah, that's it," I said.

"Where did you get it?" he asked, looking the radio over.

"Long story, but later, after the radio address, I'll try and contact him," I replied.

While we were waiting for the radio address, I decided I wanted a shower. If the solar system was working as it appeared to be, then the pump should be working. I looked over at Mel. "Does the shower work?"

"Yeah, but it's cold water," she said.

"Right now, I don't care," I replied as I headed back to the bedroom.

"Yeah, go; you need a shower. You stink to high heaven," she said as I closed the bedroom door.

She was right; the water was cold. But I didn't care; I took my time to wash my hair and lather up a rag and thoroughly wash my nasty ass from head to toe. Then the best part, I took out some clean clothes—pants, T-shirt, and socks. It felt so damn good to be in clean clothes; they felt good, smelled good, and looked good. The one thing I noticed was that they were all a little loose fitting. All that walking was good for me, although I can think of better diet and exercise programs.

Heading back into the kitchen, I was greeted with a catcall from Mel, "Oh, you look so much better," she said and then walked up to me and smelled my chest. "And smell sooo much better," she said with a smile. It was getting close to six, so I took the little radio out to the front porch and took the little wire antenna reel out. Unrolling the antenna, I threw it up into a wild plum tree and strung it back to the porch. I clipped it onto the extendable antenna on the radio and switched it on.

"What frequency is it supposed to be on?" I asked Danny.

"I don't know. We'll just have to go through it till we find it," he replied.

At about six, I started to scan the FM bands, looking for a signal, but didn't find anything.

Switching to the AM, I started to go through them. It didn't take long to find it. It took a few minutes of tweaking to get the signal dialed in. The broadcast was already under way by the time I got it tuned.

> Under martial law. We must take these extreme measures because of the dire situation the country is in. Ignorance of the provisions of martial law will be no excuse for violating any of its provisions. It is the duty of all citizens hearing this broadcast to inform their fellow citizens. We understand there are not that many functioning radios out there right now. Efforts were made to put radios into population centers. However, we know the efforts were not as successful as we would have liked. Again, that is why it is important to pass this info along to anyone you meet.
>
> Under martial law the government has the right to seize certain commodities. As a result, any form of functioning transportation, including cars, trucks, boats, aircraft, and trains, will be confiscated. We know this will not be popular; but under the circumstances, it is necessary. If you are approached by any law enforcement entity, you must surrender your vehicle to them.
>
> Additionally, we understand that there are many people in this country that stored food, water, fuel, and other items. Martial law now makes it illegal to hoard anything. If you have more than three days of food in your posses-

sion, you must surrender it to the appropriate authority. Any fuel must be surrendered. As any functioning vehicles must also be surrendered, no one will have the need for fuel. That fuel will be needed by those agencies tasked with providing aid.

Anyone caught hoarding will be dealt with severely. I again repeat, you must surrender anything more than three days' worth. If you cannot find either a DHS or FEMA representative to turn your commodities over to, you may distribute them to those in your community. The last item that is now outlawed under the act of martial law is firearms. All firearms must now be surrendered to DHS and FEMA agencies. No one will be allowed to be armed. This is being done because of the level of violence in some of our cities and rural areas. Anyone caught with a firearm will be imprisoned. I urge you to keep in mind that while we are under martial law, constitutional protections do not apply.

If you are caught with any of the above-mentioned contraband, you will be imprisoned. Considering the situation we are now under, imprisonment takes on a new definition. The days of going to jail and sitting around waiting for a court date or going to prison to serve out a sentence are over. If you are arrested, you will be placed into a work camp where you will earn your keep. There is no such thing as a free ride. The rest of the country is going to have to work their way out of this situation, and so will anyone who is arrested.

Anyone who refuses to surrender their firearms, shoots at, or kills a federal agent will be executed. No long trials, no appeals. There simply doesn't exist the means to do these things now. That is why it is of the utmost importance to follow the direction given to you by the authorities.

Aid will begin to be distributed as soon as possible. We will focus first on population centers where the resources can reach the most affected people with the limited resources we have. We will reach out to rural areas as more resources become available, but you must be patient. This will take time, but help is coming. If we all work together, we can overcome this, but we must set aside our differences to do so.

There is no more right or left, Democrat or Republican. We are Americans, all of us. And to get through this, we must work together. In the spirit of working together, please turn in all the aforementioned contraband. Whenever you do, you will be given relief supplies. We hope this makes it easier to turn in these items. If you know of anyone who is refusing to turn in contraband, simply notify the authorities, and upon the successful recovery of the contraband you will be rewarded with additional supplies.

Again, we must set aside our differences and work together to get through this. As

> Americans, we have come together in the past, and we must do so now. If everyone does their part, we will come out of this stronger than ever before. Thank you for your time. And please, follow these instructions.

After this part of the broadcast, another voice came on to give locations of FEMA shelters and aid locations. All of the places listed were major cities. From the sound of things, they were far more worried about the large urban centers than they were the rural country. Was it because they were worried about losing control of those areas, or because they knew those areas were going to go along with the program? *Folks in rural areas are not going to be nearly as open to surrendering what they have, especially now considering the situation we're in.*

"You have got to be kidding me. Surrender your food and guns? They are out of their fucking minds," Danny said.

"You know, I heard from someone who has a little inside info that they wanted to fundamentally change the country. I guess this is their play. Did you notice there was no 'God bless us' in there anywhere?" I replied.

"Yes, I did. What are we going to do? We can't give away our food. They didn't list a place we could get to for more. We could go to Orlando, but they would take the Suburban," Mel said.

Mel looked at Bobbie, wide-eyed. "We aren't giving anything up," Bobbie said.

"We don't have much now. How do they expect us to survive?" Danny said.

"They don't. I think it's part of the plan—to eliminate those of us that are prepared," I said.

We sat and talked for a little longer, tossing around different ideas and different scenarios. Then I told them I needed to go make a call. I wanted to see if I could reach Sarge and the guys.

"Can't you just do it here?" Mel asked.

"No, it's too dangerous. If we transmit from here, then our location can be identified, and that's a bad thing," I said.

"Where are you going?" Danny asked.

"Out into the forest, at least five miles from here. I'll take the Suburban to make this a quick trip," I replied.

"I don't want you to leave. Things are getting a little scary. There are more and more strangers around lately," Mel said.

"I know, babe, but I have to do this. I'll be all right. Believe me, after what I went through to get home, this is a cakewalk," I told her.

"I'll go with you," Danny said. That caused Bobbie to look over at him wide-eyed.

"What?"

"I'm not going to let him go out alone. No one leaves here alone anymore, remember?" Danny said.

Her mouth curled into a frown, and she shook her head but didn't say anything else. I went inside and got my AR and then out to the shop for my vest and some more ammo. It felt so good to open those ammo cans and see all that ammo. I spent a few minutes loading some and stuffing them into the vest. The vest already had everything else on it. Back in the house, I tucked the XD into its holster and put two spare mags in their pouches. I pulled the NVGs out and put them in a day pack, along with some water and an FAK. I carried all this out to the truck and then went back and got the radio and its batteries.

Danny had his AR with him and his Glock. We climbed into the truck and headed out. We paused at the roadblock for a minute; two different guys were there now. We stopped for a minute to talk; I told them that we were leaving and that we would be back shortly. I turned out onto 19 and headed north.

"Where we going?" Danny asked.

"I figure out off 445, near the parking area for the motorcycle trail," I replied.

"Cool."

Danny sat back with his AR on his lap, keeping an eye on his side of the road. The sun was starting to go down, the light fading. The air was mild out, not cold but far from warm; it was a nice ride. As we passed through Shockley Heights, there were a few people out. One of the properties right on the side of the road had a group gathered there around a bonfire. We drew looks from all of them as we went by, heads craning over shoulders to look at us.

"Watch 'em. If any of them try to follow us, let me know," I said to Danny.

"Already on it," he said as he shifted in his seat to look back over his shoulder.

We made it to the parking area without incident. I pulled in and over toward the restroom. That was the only place with any trees. After stopping, we got out and took a minute to check the area to make sure there wasn't anyone around. The place was empty, so I took out the antenna and slick line and, after a couple of attempts, got it up into a tall pine. After connecting the wire to the radio, I turned it on and pulled the notebook out of my pocket. It took a few minutes to figure out what frequency to be on. After figuring it out, I tuned the radio.

There was a voice I instantly recognized. After a moment, there was a break, so I keyed the mic.

"Driver, is that you? This is Walker."

Danny looked over at me. "Walker?"

"I'll explain later," I said.

"Hey, Morg, I mean Walker. Good to hear from you. Where are you?" Thad asked.

"I made it. How about you?"

"I made it too. Been worried about you," Thad replied.

"If you girls are done, let's get down to business," Sarge's voice came over the radio.

"Nice to hear you too, old man," I said into the mic.

"Took you long enough to get there. We have to keep this brief. You guys go through the notebooks we gave you. There are some additional instructions in there. Walker, do you have a PC?" Sarge said.

"I'll have to check. There is one in the shop that may work," I said.

"Check it out and see. If it does, there is a thumb drive in your pack; find it. There is a text file in there. Read it and follow the instructions. Did you hear the broadcast?" Sarge asked.

"Yeah, we heard it here," I said.

"Then you guys know what's up. Driver didn't

hear it, but we already filled him in. Go back to the top of the radio schedule; we will be monitoring the radios from now on. If you need to, you can contact us at any time. Good luck, guys, and we'll be in touch. Foxtrot Sierra Mike out." With that, Sarge was done.

"Be careful. Driver out," Thad signed off.

"You guys stay safe," I signed off as well.

"Who all was that?" Danny asked.

"Friends I met on the way. They really helped me out," I said.

I was taking down the antenna, and Danny was standing watch. As I was putting the radio in the truck, Danny called out, "We got company."

I looked up and saw three men coming into the parking area; they were walking. Two of them were carrying rifles; one was a scoped bolt gun, and the other was a lever gun with iron sights. I didn't see a weapon on the third one. As they approached, Danny and I took cover on the far side of the truck and raised our weapons.

"What do you want?" I called out.

They stopped and looked at one another. "No need to be hostile, friend. We just came to see what you guys were doing. You know a running truck is kinda strange these days," the one with the lever rifle said.

"We aren't doing anything, and we're about to leave," Danny said.

"Fair enough. Can you give us a ride back up the road?" one of them asked.

"Sorry, but no," I replied.

"Come on, man, it's a long walk," the one with the bolt gun said.

"Not our problem. You walked over here, so you can walk back. I didn't ask you to come here," I said.

"Look, you just give us a lift, and everything will be okay," the one with no rifle said.

I am getting about sick of people doing this shit. They have a damn gun and think they can intimidate people. I can't for the life of me figure out what they are thinking. They can clearly see our rifles, and what they are carrying doesn't come close. It was too dark for that scope to be worth a damn. Fed up, I snapped my rifle up and fired two quick rounds into the ground off to the left of them. It scared the shit out of them; they jumped and covered their heads.

Before they could react, I started to yell at them, "Lay down your guns! Now! Lay them down and step away from them, or I will kill you all!"

They quickly dropped their guns and put their hands up. I ordered them to back up and turn around. They complied, and Danny and I approached them with our weapons at the ready. As we got closer, the three started to bitch.

"Dammit, man, we didn't mean you no harm!" one of them yelled out and started to look over his shoulder.

"Turn around! If any of you so much as sneeze, you're fucking dead!" I yelled out.

He quickly straightened up but kept up the complaints. "What are you going to do? We just came to see what you guys were doing, is all."

"With guns, you came out here armed to see what we were doing? Danny, grab the guns," I said.

Danny carefully approached them and collected the two rifles and then started to back up toward me.

"You can't take our guns!" one of them protested.

"We'll leave 'em on the side of the road for you. But I ain't leaving them here for you. I think you guys are full of shit and didn't just come here to see what we were doing. You're lucky to be alive. I think we should kill your asses," I said. That seemed to stop all the complaints.

We got back to the truck and climbed in, and I started it up. Danny kept them covered the whole time. As we drove out of the parking area, I went around the opposite side from where they were just to keep some distance between us and them. Danny was looking at them through the rear window when they dropped their hands and gave us the finger. They started hollering and raising hell. Danny cleared their weapons; and as we approached Shockley Heights, I stopped the truck, and he stepped out long enough to lean them against a tree on the side of the road. I told them we would leave them on the side of the road for them.

We made it back to the house without any further problems. As we pulled onto the road, the two guys at the roadblock came out from the barricade. We talked for a little, telling them about the radio broadcast and what it said. They were incredulous at the thought of having to give up anything, be it guns or food. The discussion revolved around the fact they were going to bring aid into the cities and not out to the rural areas, but they still wanted those in the country to surrender all our food.

Rick was one of the guys at the roadblock; he was a deputy sheriff and was a good guy to have around. He was into guns and hunting and liked to fish. He was extremely pissed. "I ain't giving them shit. It's crazy to force people to do that. And I'll tell you another thing, our sheriff isn't going to go along with that shit either!"

"Yeah, I think they are trying to make more people dependent on the government. Have you been to work since all this started?" I asked.

"Maybe so, but people are going to start getting crazy. It's already starting around here. Some folks in the neighborhood are starting to run out of food. I suspect some of them will try and turn in those that still have some. It's going to get ugly around here, I'm afraid.

"As for work, I haven't been in. Some of the brass came around and basically told us to stay around home and see to things, to watch the areas we live in.

"Hey, Morgan, can I bring a battery by and charge it? It's the deep cycle out of my boat. I have a small inverter that I use for a few things," Rick said.

"Yeah, man, absolutely; bring it by, and I gather, then, from what you said, you are the law around here," I said.

"Yeah, I guess so. Not that there has been anything to worry about yet."

With that, we left and headed for the house. The whole time we were there talking, Pat sat there on her bike, listening to everything that was said. Pulling up to the house, the girls came out, all of them. They met us on the porch, where we talked about what was going on. We left out the part about the guys at the parking area. Mel and Bobbie suggested we fix dinner and eat together. Having the solar system, small as it was, was a godsend. It kept the fridge going and ran the well; one was a necessity, and the other was a luxury.

Mel went to the freezer and pulled out the last pack of steaks. There were four sirloins in the package. We also pulled out a pack of hot dogs for the kids; they're weird and don't like steak. Who doesn't like steak? Out in the yard, Danny and I picked up a bunch of wood, stuff that fell out of the oaks, and started a fire in the Weber. In short order, we had steaks grilling.

It was a kind of celebratory cookout, me finally making it home; and the fact that they were here, we decided to splurge a bit. If you didn't know better, you wouldn't be able to tell any difference in things, except for the fact that instead of an apron, I was wearing an AR. The girls whipped up some garlic mashed potatoes and canned veggies. That, along with some sweet tea, made for a pretty damn good dinner. There was enough for everyone, and we all had all we could eat.

We sat around after dinner, just chatting. I was sitting there, looking around the room. Mel, my girls, and Danny and Bobbie—these were the people that I was close to. If only my mom and dad were here, then things would be ideal. I'd have to figure out what to do about them. But sitting here, this was as close to perfect as I could imagine right now. The girls were playing a board game and begging to watch a movie, but we said no. We all just wanted to sit and talk. They gave up on the movie and joined in on the talk; it was a truly pleasant evening. Danny said he had to be on the roadblock at four in the morning, and they were going to take off.

We walked them out, and they climbed onto the four-wheeler and headed home. Mel and I sat down on the porch; it was nice out, a little cool but not cold enough to need a fire in the fireplace inside. So we sat on the porch, not even talking, just sitting there and holding hands. I was thinking back over everything that had happened. How long had it been? I needed to look at a calendar to see. But for now, I was happy. After so long, I felt safe to be sitting at home. Sure there was a lot we would have to deal with, but for now, all I could think about was the woman beside me and the three girls inside. I put my arm around Mel; she looked over and I told her I loved her.

"I love you too. You okay?" she replied.

I looked over to her and smiled. "I couldn't possibly be any better."

Glossary

CME: Coronal mass ejection. This phenomenon refers to an ejection of plasma from the sun that sends varying degrees of highly charged particles into space directly toward Earth. Depending on the position of the event in relation to Earth, the effects can vary and can mimic an EMP in many ways.

COM: Center of mass. Used when referring to combat shooting, aiming for the center of the largest portion of the visible target.

EDC bag: Everyday carry bag. Sometimes people refer to this as a man purse. It holds items such as handguns, lights, knives, and other assorted small gear.

EMP: Electromagnetic pulse. There is a lot of information out there on this phenomenon, but it boils down to a pulse wave emitted by the detonation of a nuclear device.

ENO: Eagles Nest Outfitters. A manufacturer of quality hammocks, bug nets, and tarps.

Esbit stove: This is a small folding stove made from stamped steel. The better models are made from stainless steel and have welded connections. They use the compressed fuel tabs sold in many forms.

ESEE knives: ESEE is part of Randall's Adventure & Training and has been designing knives since 1997. They come with a lifetime "no questions asked" warranty.

fire steel: Fire steel is an alloy of various metals. It issues a mass of very hot sparks when struck with a piece of steel. A new fire steel has a layer of oxidation on it that must be removed prior to use; otherwise, the results will be very unsatisfactory.

GP-L4 radio: This is a compact ten-band radio with AM, FM, and shortwave bands. In addition, it has a small LED light. The radio is distributed by CountyComm.com.

Grilliput: Grilliput is a compact stainless-steel grill designed to disassemble and store in two long tubes used for the supports of the grilling area. This is a great little grill, with a price. It weighs just under one and a quarter pounds. Its compact size makes it perfect for field cooking, with a pot on it or by direct grilling.

IWB: In the waistband. This refers to holsters that fit inside the waistband of your pants and clip to the outside. These holsters are designed for concealed carry, and most manufacturers make them for specific models.

Leatherman Surge: The Surge is one of the two largest tools in the Leatherman line; it contains twenty-one tools.

Maxpedition Devildog: Maxpedition was established in 1988 and is a manufacturer of military-grade nylon gear. Their equipment is constructed with top-quality materials, 1000 Denier nylon, YKK zippers, and Duraflex buckles. They manufacture a full line of packs, pouches, and sheaths.

MRE: Meal, Ready-to-Eat. These are military rations that come in a variety of menus. The latest version of these contains a water-activated heater allowing the meal to be heated without external heat sources.

MOLLE: This is an acronym for Modular Lightweight Load-carrying Equipment. It is the system used to attach pouches, packs, holsters, and the like to vests, packs, and other military-grade hardware.

Platypus water bladder: These are BPA-free collapsible water bottles perfect for compact carry in packs.

POS: Point of sale. I threw this in there so that it's not to be confused with piece of shit.

PSK: Personal survival kit. This is a small kit kept on your person. It is the last line of defense in survival. It contains items to start a fire, catch food, and store water, and it has a small blade and a few first-aid items. The beauty of this is that you can make your own and customize it to the environment you're in.

ranger beads: This is a set of beads divided into two sections. With each strike of the left foot, a count is made (this varies according to the user). At ten, one of the lower beads is pulled down. Once all the lower beads are down, one of the upper beads is pulled down, and the lower bead is raised again. This makes one kilometer. (This is very dependent on the length of the user's stride; it is also something that requires one to maintain focus on those steps. It is hard for a single person to both keep an eye out for security and keep track of paces unless he or she is moving slowly.)

SOS survival kit: The kit mentioned is the SOL Scout. It contains numerous handy items, including a fifty-inch roll of duct tape, liquid-filled compass, fire striker, small vial of fishing gear, Heatsheet survival blanket, mini rescue mirror, Rescue Howler Whistle (very loud), and a few pieces of tinder. This is a handy kit to keep on one's person.

Springfield XD: The XD is manufactured by Springfield Armory. It is a fourteen-round polymer-frame semiautomatic pistol.

SweetWater filter: This filter is manufactured by MSR. It utilizes a 4:1 mechanical advantage to filter 1.25 liters per minute. Unlike many other ceramic filters, the filter element of the SweetWater is encased in plastic and is not subject to damage.

Tek-Lok: This is a support system for knives but can be used on numerous pieces of gear. It consists of a clip that mounts to the piece via two or four screws.

trioxane tabs: These are military-grade compressed fuel tabs used with an Esbit or canteen-cup stove. Primarily these are used for heating water;

however, they make a superb fire starter and will burn even if wet.

trucker bomb: This little roadside gem is created by truckers (and other drivers) who urinate into empty plastic bottles and then hurl them out the window. So think about this the next time you are walking down the side of a road and see a tempting full water bottle.

U-Dig-It: Manufacturer of a small, stainless-steel folding trowel. It is perfect to add to a kit for many uses, the least of which being to dig a cat hole for nature's call.

woobie: This is a term used by folks in the military for the famous poncho liner. The liner is a quilted nylon blanket with ties that allow it to be secured into the poncho, turning it into a sleeping bag.

Read on for an excerpt from A. American's novel *Surviving Home*, also available from Plume.

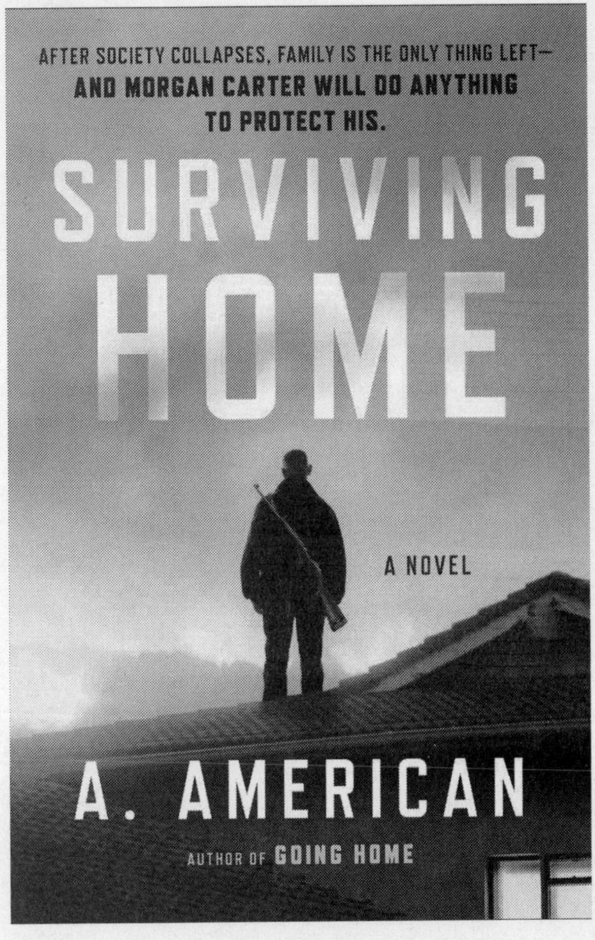

978-0-14-218128-7

A member of Penguin Group USA
www.penguin.com

Prologue

When it all went wrong, I was two hundred miles from home. I traveled a lot for my job, and I always had my get-home bag in my car. It wasn't that I expected things to fall apart, by nature I'm an optimist. But it always seemed to be the worst kind of irresponsibility to not be prepared. And it was that Boy Scout philosophy that saved my life.

The car quit, my phone was dead, and pretty soon I knew it wasn't just me. Everyone on the road was stuck and looking for a way home. I had known for a long time that if things ever went to shit, the average person was screwed: no power, no water, no food, no way to communicate with the government that was supposed to be running the show. And I knew that in that situation, my fellow citizens would quickly become the biggest danger. What wouldn't you do if you couldn't feed your family?

But what I wasn't prepared for was how quickly things would get bad. And in the weeks it took me to hoof it home, things got very bad indeed. The average person without food or water or hope would rob you for a meal. The average person in the same situation, but with kids to feed, might kill you.

I had thought about it a lot before the event, and I had tried to prepare. I didn't worry too much about my wife and three girls. My house was off the grid; we had food stored, solar power, and an independent water system. More important, I had good friends and neighbors. I knew people like my buddy Danny would look out for Mel and the girls. All I had to do was get home to them and everything would be fine. That's what I thought, at least.

Getting there wasn't easy. I got real lucky: I hooked up with Thad and Jess, and we looked out for each other. When I got shot, they saved my life and we were luckier still: we met Linus Mitchell—Sarge—a retired soldier, and some of his army buddies. They got me back on my feet and made it possible for Jess, Thad, and I to make it home to our families.

Coming home was the single best moment of my life. Things in my neighborhood were under control, and despite that the world had gone to hell, for a little while, it seemed like it was all going to be okay. We had a cookout the night I came home, and it wasn't very different from other gatherings like we had had a hundred times before: family, friends, and hope.

I know myself pretty well, and sometimes I can be kind of harsh about how people are adjusting to the world we live in now. It's a new world with new rules, and everybody has to make do for themselves. You have to make sure your family gets fed and make sure they're safe. There are too many people waiting for Uncle Sugar to fix things, people who thought at the beginning that if they just waited, things would go back to normal. But if I'm honest, the first night I got home, I wasn't too different. I thought the hard part was behind me, and I had no idea how bad things were going to get. I figured if I took care of my own, the rest would sort itself out. But I was wrong.

Chapter 1

We went to bed early after the cookout. It was nice to sleep in my own bed with my wife beside me. Ashley—mostly we called her Little Bit—wanted to sleep with us and really put up a fight, but we wanted some time to ourselves; it had been a while since we'd been together, and we were going to make up for it. Afterward, Mel was asleep and I was lying there, staring at the ceiling. In the past I would have gotten up and gone online, but those days were over. No more Internet, no more laptop, no more of a lot of things. I got up and walked out to the living room and sat down in my chair. The room was dark and silent. There was no AC running, no fan, no nothing.

Light washed over the window, and I heard an ATV heading toward the roadblock. I stood and looked out the front window as it passed by, and then the darkness and the silence returned. I sat down again in my leather chair, but soon I was up again and returned to my bed, and Mel.

Morning came and I was up before the sun. Mel was still asleep, as were the girls. I put on a pot of water to boil. I stood there for a moment taking the scene in, looking around at the kitchen, the fluorescent light glowing against the ceiling, and looking forward to coffee. The three-burner Butterfly kerosene stove is a truly wonderful piece of equipment to have. Once the burner is lit and the catalytic converter heats up, it produces no smoke and can be used indoors.

While the water was heating, I went out to the shop to look at the food stores. I was surprised at what I saw. Mel said she hadn't been very careful in the beginning, but that she had soon changed her ways and had started to conserve. It looked like the kids had put a real dent in the canned fruit. The soups and stews were hit rather hard, but there was still a lot there, and if we were careful, we could stretch it out for some time. It felt good standing there in front of those shelves, knowing it wasn't all a waste of time and money.

I grabbed a can of SPAM and headed back inside. The water was boiling and I added it to the press. I let the coffee brew for a minute, set a skillet on the burner and poured myself a cup with sugar and some powdered creamer. While the skillet heated, I added a little olive oil and sliced the SPAM. From the fridge I grabbed a few eggs and set them aside while the meat in the pan heated.

Mel came into the kitchen and said, "I smell coffee and SPAM."

"Morning, Sunshine," I said.

She went to the cabinet and returned with a cup and poured it full of coffee. She doctored her cup while I was flipping the SPAM.

"When do the girls usually get up?" I asked as I took the meat from the pan and cracked an egg into it.

"They usually sleep late, no school and all. They couldn't be happier," she said, taking a sip from the cup.

"Well, can't blame 'em. I would if I could," I said.

We sat down at the table in the kitchen and ate breakfast together. The sun was starting to come up and it looked like it would be a nice day. After another cup of coffee, I got up and headed for the bedroom.

"Really? After last night I can't believe you have the energy," she said with a smirk on her face.

I paused at the door, "I have more energy than you can imagine." I put on my Carhartt pants and my Ariat boots, something other than those damn Bellevilles I had walked two hundred miles home in. I pulled my tac vest on and draped the sling of my assault rifle over my shoulders.

Mel looked up from the cup in her hands. "Where are you going?"

"I'm going to walk up to the end of the road and talk to Danny. I just want to see how things are around here."

After strapping on the XD I headed for the door and walked down the drive toward the gate in the early dawn. The dogs, Meathead and Little Girl, came running up and jumping all over me. I knew I wouldn't be able to keep them in the yard, so I just let them follow me. We went out onto the road and turned toward the roadblock. It wasn't long before the dogs went nuts, barking and raising hell. I looked back and saw what they were barking at.

Coming down the road on her bike, like she

usually did in the mornings, was Pat. "Shit," I said as I turned around and kept on toward the roadblock. I could hear her bike closing on me, and it wasn't long before she came alongside.

"Hi, Morgan, I heard you were back," she said with a forced smile.

"Yeah, finally."

"How was it? Was it hard?" she asked.

I looked over at her. "More than you can imagine."

"I bet. We haven't been anywhere since all this happened. Neither of our cars work, so we haven't gone out," Pat said as she pedaled her bike.

We were almost to the roadblock. I just wanted her to go the hell away. "How's your family? Are your girls getting enough to eat?" she asked.

I saw what she was after. Pat was always a busybody, and now she was snooping around to figure out who had food. I just looked over at her and smiled. We reached the roadblock and I waved at Danny, who was walking toward me. He gave me a wave back and we shook hands.

"Hey, man," Danny said.

Pat rolled off to the side of the road and pretended to fiddle with the chain on her bike, just close enough to get an earful.

Reggie was at the roadblock with Danny this morning. He looked over and gave me a nod, and Pat waved at him too. He waved back without a smile. Our little neighborhood had two basic groups. There was Pat and her group, mostly old biddies and the ones where the woman of the house pretty much ran things, plus a few others that had that holier-than-thou attitude. The second was the rest of us, the ones who minded their own business but were always ready to lend a hand.

"Nah, haven't seen a soul, just like most days," Reggie said.

"Yeah, early on there were several people heading for the forest. Loaded with packs, some old trucks, some bikes and carts and shit. Then it pretty much dried up, not too many people anymore," Danny said.

"Then why keep this up?" I asked.

"Because there are still some shifty-ass folks that come through here, plus some other shit," Reggie said.

"Like what?"

Danny and Reggie shared a glance, then Danny spoke. "There have been a few girls come up missing. They disappear from their homes or when out walking around. No one knows what's happening to them, they just disappear."

I looked down. I had forgotten about the bodies—I mean, it was in my head, I just hadn't said anything about it. What with coming home and seeing everyone and the cookout we had the night before, it had slipped my mind.

"I was going to talk to you about it. I just didn't want to last night with the girls there. The last thing in the world I can imagine is one of them disappearing," Danny said.

"It's not that. I mean, it is definitely that, but on my way back, not far from here, I found the bodies of three people. One of them looked familiar, but I couldn't place the face, or what was left of it." I looked up at Danny and Reggie.

"Where?" Reggie asked, an edge to his voice.

"Sorry, Reggie. Morg, Reggie's niece has been missing for about a week. She lived over in Altoona near the Kangaroo store, and just disappeared," Danny said.

"Reggie, man, I'm sorry. I didn't know. I found them out at Baptist Lake. Two of them had been there awhile. There wasn't much left, and it was hard to tell whether they were male or female," I said.

Reggie looked me in the eye. "You stay here with Danny. I'm going to get Rick and Mark and some ATVs. Then we're going to go look for her."

"Bring someone back to man the barricade, I'm going too. Morg can ride with me," Danny said.

Reggie nodded at Danny then looked back to me. "What color was the hair, Morgan?"

I looked at Danny and he looked back with no expression. "Blonde, long, past the shoulders," I said.

Reggie's jaw tightened and he nodded his head. He went over and climbed on his ATV and took off like his ass was on fire. Pat managed to "fix" her bike a moment after and headed down the road as fast as her pudgy legs would carry her. Danny looked over at me. I shrugged my shoulders. "I didn't know," I said.

"I know, but this has had people scared. The thought that with everything else that is going on, some sick fuck is going around snatching girls has really had an effect," Danny said.

I leaned over the barricade and Danny came up beside me and rested his elbows on it. We just stood there as the sun climbed higher. He asked about my trip home and I gave him some of the details. I told him about Sarge and the guys, about Thad and Jess and what we had gone through. I told him the story of our ambush in detail, all that I remembered, anyway. I told him about Sarge's place and my trip through the forest. He laughed when I told him about the hippies.

"Man, I wish we were on the Run today, just paddling down without a care in the world," he said, staring off across the road.

"Me too, man, me too," I replied.

It wasn't too long before we heard the ATVs coming up the road. We both looked back and saw two four-wheelers and one Kawasaki Mule coming down the road. Mark was in the Mule. He and Rick, another guy from the neighborhood, had their uniforms on, Mark's sheriff's star clearly visible even at this distance. Behind them, her legs pumping up and down, was Pat. The guys came up and stopped. Reggie asked me to tell Mark and Rick what I had told him. As I relayed the story, Pat rolled up. I stopped talking as everyone turned to look at her.

Breathlessly she climbed off her bike and put the kickstand down. Mark had his son Jeremy in the Mule with him, and Lance was on the back of Rick's ATV. Jeremy and Lance would man the barricade while we were gone. Pat looked at Jeremy and told him to watch her bike while she was gone. We all looked around at one another, wondering where she was going. Without saying a word to anyone, Pat walked over and climbed into the Mule. Mark looked over at her and said, "What are you doing, Pat?"

"I'm going with you. This is serious, and we need to find out what's going on," she said as she pulled on a pair of knit gloves.

"You're right, it is, but you aren't going anywhere. Now please get out of there," Mark said.

"I most certainly will not. I have as much right here as any of you do," she said.

"I am still a deputy sheriff, and this is police business. I asked you once to leave. Now I'm telling you," Mark said.

Pat shot him a look, then one to me and Danny. "If those two are going, I can. They aren't deputies."

Rick looked over to Danny and me and said, "You two want to be deputies?"

We looked at one another and shrugged. "Sure."

"You're deputized," Rick said.

"You're not the sheriff. You can't deputize anyone," she fired back.

"Pat, I've been nice," Mark said as he and Rick moved toward her.

Sensing what was coming, Pat leaned forward and wrapped her arms around the roll bar of the Mule. Rick and Mark pried her arms off as graciously as they could. Pat was screaming like she was being eaten by a gator.

"Stop the damn screeching, Pat! You're being fucking ridiculous," Mark said.

They finally got her out of the Mule and walked her over to her bike, and Rick handcuffed her right hand to the handlebar.

"What are you doing?" Pat yelled.

Rick walked over and handed a cuff key to Lance. "When we're gone, take 'em off her. Take it off the bike first, then her wrist. I want those back." Lance nodded and pocketed the key. Pat shot him a look.

With Pat finally out of the way, Mark looked at all of us and asked, "You guys ready?"

Everyone nodded and moved toward their machines. I was headed toward Danny's Polaris when Mark called out to me, "Ride with me, Morgan, I don't know where we're going."

Mark pulled a bag from the bed of the Mule and handed everyone a radio. There were also three body bags lying there. "Where did you get these?" I asked him.

"The sheriff's office had some stuff that still worked." After he handed them out, we did a quick radio check. I climbed into the Mule and we pulled though the barricade.

I said, "Head up toward the Pittman Center and take that trail just past it, to the left. Baptist Lake is back there." He was focused on the road ahead and seemed a little tense. I asked, "Has old Pat been that big a pain in the ass the whole time? I mean, she's always been a pain, but that seemed a little over-the-top."

"Yeah, she's been trying to *coordinate* everyone to work together. She tells everyone what to do. She wants us all to throw everything in a big pile to share," he said.

"She must be about out of food, then."

Mark looked over at me and said, "That's what I think too."

I pointed out the trail shortly after we passed the visitor center in Pittman. We all turned off the road onto the trail. It didn't take long to get back to the lake. Winters were rather dry around there, and there weren't any real wet places to negotiate. We came at the lake from the north side, and the bodies I had seen were on the south side. I told Mark about where they were and pointed in the general direction. He stopped the Mule and waved the others forward. Reggie, Rick, and Danny all came up alongside.

"Rick, you and Danny go around that side. Reggie, you follow us around this side. Keep an eye out, and when you get down there, no one go running off toward the area. Let's see if we can find anything that might tell us who's doing this. We don't have a forensic team, but let's see if there's anything that might help us."

Everyone nodded and we all headed off. Reggie was trailing behind us and Mark wasn't going very fast. I glanced over my shoulder at Reggie and he just looked pissed. Looking over at Mark, I said, "Good idea having him follow behind you; he looks like he's ready to kill someone right now."

"That's why he's back there. I wanted him to go slow, otherwise he would have hauled ass down there, and if there was anything that might help he'd probably fuck it up. I sure hope this isn't his niece," Mark said.

It didn't take long to make our way around the little lake. The water was low and a large part of the bottom was exposed. As we neared the area where I'd found the bodies, I told Mark, and he stopped the Mule as Reggie came up beside us. "Why are we stopping?" Reggie asked.

"They were right over there," I answered him, pointing off toward the near side of the lake where three or four buzzards were taking to the air.

Reggie squinted his eyes and looked out over the dry lake bed. Rick and Danny had come out of the tree line a couple hundred yards to our left and stopped. We all dismounted and walked toward the bottom end of the little lake. There wasn't anything that said *Body over here!* and I couldn't really remember exactly where they were, but it wasn't a large area to search. Just a minute later, Rick found a femur. It was lying in the dirt alone, no other bones around it. Out of habit more than anything else probably, Rick took a business card from his pocket, folded it in half and set the little paper tent on the ground beside the bone.

From where we were standing, two lumps were clearly visible.

A few moments later we were standing over what was left of two of the bodies I had found just a couple days back. The one that had looked the worse for wear that day was now nothing more than bones held together by connective tissue. The one that had appeared to be freshly dumped was in pretty bad shape now; the various critters that feed on carrion had been hard at work. We stood in a semicircle around the bodies. Mark and Rick looked at the ground and the surrounding area for any sort of clue as to who had dumped them.

Reggie just stood there staring at the body with the matted blonde hair. Finally he looked over at Mark and said, "I want to check her and see if it's Christine."

Mark looked over at him and frowned. "From the condition of the body, how are you going to tell?"

"Looks like most of the back side is still there. She has a tattoo on her lower back, kind of a tribal thing with a butterfly in the middle. I want to know, now," Reggie said with a finality that Mark couldn't argue with.

Mark and Rick pulled black nitrile gloves from their pockets and put them on. Kneeling down, they turned the body over. While the animals hadn't been able to get at the back side of the body, the insects certainly had, but there was still enough of a tattoo visible to make it out. Reggie reached into his shirt pocket and pulled out a photo. It was of a blonde girl, probably eighteen or nineteen, with her shirt pulled up over her fresh tattoo. She was looking back over her shoulder at whoever took the picture with a huge smile on her face, her perfectly white teeth shining in the flash of the camera.

Reggie looked at the picture, then at the body, then at the photo. He handed the picture to Mark. "It's her. I have to take her home to her momma."

Mark took the photo and looked at it. He shook his head, looking at the once-beautiful young girl in the picture. Standing up, he handed it back to Reggie and walked over to the Mule and grabbed the body bags. "I don't see much here that would help us. We'll take the bindings and I'll make a sketch of these tire tracks; maybe they'll be handy later."

We spent about an hour collecting all the bodies.

One of them was pretty scattered, and we tried to make sure we found all the bones, though I know we didn't. When we were done we loaded two bags into the Mule. Reggie insisted on taking the one with Christine in it on his four-wheeler. He laid the bag across the rear rack and strapped it with a couple of bungee cords. With the bodies loaded, we all climbed back on the various machines and headed back toward home.

When we came to our road, the four of us pulled off, but Reggie kept going toward Altoona. He didn't say anything as he passed. We pulled up to the barricade, where Lance and Jeremy were sitting. Rick went up to Lance and put his hand out. Lance dropped the cuffs into it. Rick put them on his belt then looked back at Lance. "The key too." Lance gave a sly little smile and reached into his pocket and pulled out the key, handing it over as well.

"Did she give you any trouble?" Mark asked.

"She was pissed. She cussed you for all you're worth, but no, she didn't give me any trouble. She told me I would regret it and that you had no right to lock her up like a dog," Lance said.

I stepped out of the Mule and went over to Danny's Polaris and climbed on. "Drop me off at the house," I said as my ass landed on the seat.

Danny pulled up to the front of the house. After I climbed off, he asked if I could come down to his place later and see if I could come up with some ideas to get some power going. We shook and I went up to the porch where Mel was sitting with a cup of coffee. She waved at Danny as he pulled away.

"Where'd you go? I saw all the four-wheelers go by—what's up?" she asked.

I told her about the bodies. It upset her, the thought of some sick bastard running around doing something like that, at a time like this. She also worried for our girls, and I assured her that they weren't going anywhere without us, except down to Danny and Bobbie's house. There was only one way onto our street and we had decent security, so I wasn't worried about them walking down the road.

Mel asked if I wanted a cup of coffee, and I said I would love one. She went inside and came back with another cup and hers refilled. We sat on the bench drinking our coffee when the door opened and Little Bit came out. She was dragging a giant tawny-colored teddy bear, Peanut Butter. She looked so cute in her little footie PJs. Rubbing her eyes, she came over and climbed up in my lap and laid her head on the bear. It was wonderful beyond words to have that little girl in my lap, just to be sitting here with Mel and knowing all my girls were safe. After a moment she raised her little head and looked over the edge of my cup. "Can I have some coffee, Daddy? Can you move this?"

She was pointing at the AR lying on my lap. I pulled the sling over my head and set the rifle aside. "Sure, baby," I said as she took the cup with her little hands.

She took a sip and hummed with pleasure. She looked up with a big smile. "It's good. Can I have the rest of it?"

This was the eternal question from her: can I

have more? It didn't matter what it was, anything she had some of, she wanted the rest of. Maybe it came from having two older sisters, being the smallest: get what you can get, when you can get it. "Of course, drink it up. When you're done, go get dressed."

"Okay," she said and raised the cup again.

We sat on the porch and Little Bit finished her coffee. I tousled her long blonde hair, making her giggle. She finally finished her coffee and climbed off my lap and headed back into the house, the bear trailing behind her. Mel looked over at me and said, "You let her drink that, she's *your* problem for the rest of the day."

"No sweat. I have a lot to do today; she can follow along," I said and stood up. "I'm going to go out to the shop and check out the solar system and go through a few things."

"All right, I'm going to clean up the kitchen."

I headed out to the shop and was checking out the batteries, looking for any corrosion on the terminals, when I heard a high-pitched voice call, "Daddy?"

"In here."

Little Bit came through the door. "What'cha doin'?"

"Just checking a few things," I told her.

She helped me as I went over the batteries, cables, and inverter. Then I went through the food stored there. It still looked like a lot of food, but when you thought of the fact that there was no way to run to the store, it wasn't. I was standing there looking over the stores when Little Bit asked, "What's wrong, Daddy?"

"Nothing, just looking at all the food we have." I chose the words carefully so as not to let her think I was worried; this wasn't her problem and her little mind didn't need to be troubled with it.

"Yeah, we have a lot, don't we?" she said.

"We have some." I looked down at her, she turned to look up at me. "But don't tell anyone about it, okay?" I said as I patted her head.

She leaned her head against my side, turning her face into me. "I won't. Someone might try and steal it. If anyone tries to steal it, I'll shoot them with my BB gun," she said.

"Don't go trying to shoot anyone. If you see anyone, you tell me," I told her.

"Okay, can I go get my BB gun?" she asked.

"Sure, just be careful with it." She was on her way before I even finished saying it.

After she was gone I pulled the twenty-millimeter ammo cans out from under the shelves and did a quick inventory of the ammo. I had about forty-seven hundred rounds for the AR and 1,250 for the .45s. There were also close to a thousand rounds of .22, 110 30-30 rounds, and fifty twelve-gauge shells mixed between 00 buck and slugs, both high brass. I felt pretty good about the count. It wasn't an unlimited supply, but it was a substantial stockpile.

About then Little Bit came through the door with her Red Ryder in one hand, a length of 550 cord in the other. She said, "Daddy, can you put this rope on my gun so I can wear it like you do yours?"

I smiled at her and took a moment to fashion a sling for her little rifle. She stood there with a smile on her face, then put the sling over her shoulder when I was done and ran out of the shop. Going back inside, I found Taylor and Lee Ann awake. Lee Ann was standing in the kitchen looking in the fridge. "I'm hungry," she announced. "I want some eggs."

She took the bowl that had the fresh eggs in it from the fridge. "Dad, can you light the stove for me? I can't do it."

"Sure," I replied. I lit the stove and adjusted the knob for a low flame. She took a ten-inch skillet down and set it on the stove. I told her that was too big and I replaced it with an eight-inch. I showed her how to pour a little oil in the pan and keep the eggs moving so they wouldn't stick. Like any teenager, she told me, "I know," so I left her to her breakfast, telling her to clean up after herself and making sure she knew how to shut the stove off.

In short order there was a small argument over what she and her sister thought they should make. I was in the bathroom when I heard the sliding glass door open and close. As I was coming back out of my room, Taylor came through the door again with a can of Red Feather cheddar cheese in her hand.

"What are you doing with that?" I asked her.

"I'm going to make a cheese omelet," she replied as she reached for a can opener.

I took the can from the counter. "You do not just go get what you want out of the shop. You have to ask before you get anything. We have to be careful with what we have. We only have twelve cans of this; you can't just use it for yourself. Do you two understand?"

Taylor looked dejected. "Yes, I just wanted something different."

Lee Ann was nodding her head. "I didn't want the cheese anyway," she said.

I put the can back on a shelf in the kitchen and went to find Mel. We needed to talk about the food situation.

THE SURVIVALIST SERIES
From A. American

978-0-14-218127-0

978-0-14-218128-7

978-0-14-218129-4

978-0-14-218130-0

978-0-14-751532-2

PLUME
A member of Penguin Group USA
www.penguin.com